Cara Colter shares her life in beautiful British Columbia, Canada, with her husband, nine horses and one small ... She loves to hear from ... about her and contact he...

Michelle Major grew up in Ohio but dreamed of living in the mountains. Soon after graduating with a degree in journalism, she pointed her car west and settled in Colorado. Her life and house are filled with one great husband, two beautiful kids, a few furry pets and several well-behaved reptiles. She's grateful to have found her passion writing stories with happy endings. Michelle loves to hear from her readers at michellemajor.com

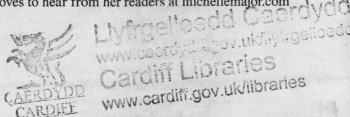

Discover more at millsandboon.co.uk

MATCHMAKER AND THE MANHATTAN MILLIONAIRE

CARA COLTER

HIS SECRET STARLIGHT BABY

MICHELLE MAJOR

MILLS & BOON

First Published in Great Britain 2021
by Mills & Boon, an imprint of HarperCollins*Publishers* Ltd,
1 London Bridge Street, London, SE1 9GF

www.harpercollins.co.uk

HarperCollins*Publishers*
1st Floor, Watermarque Building,
Ringsend Road, Dublin 4, Ireland

Matchmaker and the Manhattan Millionaire © 2021 Cara Colter
His Secret Starlight Baby © 2021 Michelle Major

ISBN: 978-0-263-29921-2

0221

MIX
Paper from
responsible sources
FSC™ C007454

FSC
www.fsc.org

This book is produced from independently certified FSC™ paper to ensure responsible forest management.

For more information visit: www.harpercollins.co.uk/green

Printed and bound in Spain
by CPI, Barcelona

MATCHMAKER AND THE MANHATTAN MILLIONAIRE

CARA COLTER

CHAPTER ONE

THIS WAS WHY, thought Krissy Clark, she had been avoiding Match Made in Heaven. It felt as if there was a possibility her aunt Jane could walk into the cluttered, tiny Queens office at any second. Krissy looked down at the file on the desk in front of her. It had been left open, as if her aunt expected to get right back to it. No doubt she *had* expected to get right back to it.

Make the first call, Krissy ordered herself.

She looked down at the file. It had a picture of a man stapled to an application form. He was on the better side of sixty, bald and bespectacled. His timid smile was so darn hopeful. All she wanted was a name and a phone number, but instead her eyes grazed the first heading.

What do you do for fun? Nothing naughty, please.

Krissy snapped the file closed. She did not want to know what—she looked at the name in bold, black Sharpie on the front—what Alexandro Helinski did for fun. This was why she could not take over her aunt's business. She didn't have the people skills. The instincts. That almost magical intuition Aunt Jane had possessed.

It had been three weeks since her sixty-six-year-old

aunt had died, killed instantly, struck by a car, just down the street from here.

Things had to be dealt with, and yet Krissy couldn't even make a decision about what to do with the ashes.

Spread them in the place I love most. That was what Aunt Jane's will had said. But all that came to Krissy was Macy's!

On a more practical level, the clients needed to be called just in case they had missed the obituary. There might be refunds owed. The office needed to be cleared, or another month's rent would come out of the small bank account Krissy found herself in charge of.

Her aunt had done it for love. If the bank account was any indication, there was no money in the match-making business.

And there it was. The real reason Krissy could not take over this business—aside from the fact she was deliriously happy with her own life—was simple.

She did not believe in love. Or at least not the happily-ever-after variety her aunt sold.

Come to think of it, Krissy had not really believed in much that Aunt Jane had believed in: horoscopes, cards, premonitions, reincarnation, life after death. Aunt Jane had claimed she still spoke regularly to Uncle Elias, who had died the year before Krissy was born, which was twenty-three years ago.

And yet, despite not sharing a belief system, she had loved her aunt madly: admired her ability to be genu-inely herself in the world, even when that self was a little left of crazy. Compared to the rest of her family, Jane seemed downright sane.

Krissy looked at the flashing red lights on the an-swering machine. Forty-two messages? She, herself, was not sure she got forty-two messages in a year. Still, listening to the messages might be a better place to start than with the files. She had managed to procrastinate so long it was now too late in the evening to be phoning people, anyway.

Her hand hovered over the play button, then dropped away. She rested her chin on it.

"Auntie," she said out loud, "if you can hear me, I need a sign."

Of what? That her aunt was, somehow, okay. That death, as her aunt had always believed, was just a transition, not an ending. That the aunt Krissy had always counted on to make her feel safe and loved in the world was still there, in some way, supporting her and guiding her.

Krissy immediately felt ridiculous. She was a university graduate. Her major had been in science. She loved systems—unlike the one she had grown up in—that had rules and predictable outcomes. Now she was in her second year of teaching. It was kindergarten, a daily hotbed of chaos and emotion, and yet she was proud of how she used her pragmatic nature to be the port of calm in that sea of tiny challenges.

She was an expert at detaching from emotion and all its foibles. It made her an excellent teacher; it had allowed her to build a perfect life. A few months ago she had bought her own tiny house, and now she had added a dog to the picture she was building.

Okay, the dog, a rescue, was maybe not quite as imagined, but—

Rap. Rap. Rap.

Krissy let out a little squeak of surprise at the firm sound and then laughed at herself, and at how hard her heart was beating.

For a moment, had she really believed her beloved aunt was knocking?

"No," she said out loud.

Yes, a voice inside her whispered.

The sound came again, more insistent. Not from heaven, after all, but from the direction of the front door. She squinted in that direction. It was dark out, nearly 10:00 p.m. A shiver ran up and down her spine, and not because a wind, too chilly for the first week in June, chose that moment to rattle the door.

There was a man standing out there, his knee-length black coat unbuttoned to reveal long legs in knife-pressed dark slacks, an expensive belt, a tailored shirt, a bold tie. He had dark leather gloves that he was slapping with faint impatience against his wrist, as if he expected her to jump up and open the door, despite the Closed sign, despite the fact it was an unusual hour, despite the fact she was in here alone.

Krissy regarded him for a moment. She did not go for blond men. Actually, there was quite a long list of the kind of man she did not go for, which explained why she was single.

And blissfully so.

Still, she could almost hear Aunt Jane's voice.

"Darling, I know I could make you the perfect match if you would just give me the chance."

And Jane was nothing if not tenacious. Just before she had died, she had called, breathless with excitement.

"I found him. I found the one for you."

There is no *one* for me, Krissy had told her aunt, not for the first time. Her aunt, of all people, should understand Krissy's allergy to relationships.

But the fact that Krissy had decided against entanglements of the permanent variety didn't mean she didn't enjoy the odd outing, a date, a *peek*. If Krissy was watching a movie, or studying cologne ads on the train, her ideal man was not blond. He was the quint-essential tall, dark and handsome.

The man at the door was tall, and he was handsome. He was broad at the shoulder, narrow at his hips, long in his legs. His face was *GQ* gorgeous—a wide, intelligent brow; high cheekbones; dark whisker-shadowed jaw; perfect nose; firm lips.

Under the outside light, his eyes appeared midnight black. The dark whiskers and eyebrows, the dark eyes, made the blond hair a bit of a shock. In fact, he radiated successful—very successful—businessman, but his hair was wheat and platinum, something sun-kissed and surfer-off-the-waves about it that was in sharp and intriguing contrast to the rest of his image.

He cocked his head at her, and Krissy gave herself a mental shake. She pointed at the Closed sign that hung in the door, and then at her watch.

Charades: too late to be calling on a closed business. She pretended to dismiss him, by looking down at Alexandro Helinski's file. She opened it officiously, being careful not to look at that question.

What do you do for fun?

That man outside the door looked like he might know a thing or two about having fun... Not that she cared!

The second question on Match Made in Heaven's application form.

What would you describe as your life philosophy?

Alexandro had answered, in a firm hand,

Take the high road.

Something sighed within Krissy.

Rap. Rap. Rap.

She deliberately looked at the next question, instead of looking up.

What do you consider the most important attribute in another human being?

Alexandro had answered Honor.

Krissy thought *this* was a man she would be interested in meeting. If he wasn't sixty-eight!

Her visitor at the door was not getting the message. He rapped at the door again. She glanced up, irritated. She was not opening the door to a complete stranger. It was practically the middle of the night.

When he saw he had her attention, he held something against the door, a small white card. His business card? Why would she open the door for a business card? Any ax murderer could have a card printed!

Still, from the look on his face, he wasn't going anywhere, one of those extraordinarily good-looking men far too used to getting his own way. Making it very evident that she was annoyed, Krissy got up from the desk and stomped over to the door.

She looked at the card being held to the glass.

It wasn't a business card, after all. It was an appointment card, for Match Made in Heaven, the blanks filled out in her aunt's own distinctive handwriting.

Jonas Boyden had an appointment here. And the date on it was for today. At 10:00 p.m. What was her aunt thinking, conducting business at that time of night in this quiet Queens street?

Now what? Krissy couldn't even make phone calls to tell people her aunt had died. It felt even worse to try and shout that horrible announcement through the thick glass of the doorway.

Besides, one of her aunt's many strengths had been her tremendous ability to vet people before they ever got through the door. Jane had taken to the internet like the proverbial duck to water. She was proud of announcing that she could find out anything about anyone. She had loved playing online detective. Krissy sometimes felt Jane enjoyed rejecting clients as much as she had enjoyed accepting them.

Jane claimed her high reject ratio made people want her services even more, had made them feel special to be chosen by her, part of an elite group. Having now seen Match Made in Heaven's bank numbers, Krissy wondered if Jane might have carried that philosophy a touch too far.

I always had everything I needed. Open the door.

Now she was going to talk to the dead? Obviously Krissy should not have come here tonight, even if it had felt pressing. It was too soon. The wound was too fresh. Krissy was not her normal self.

"Can we speak for a moment?"

His voice was muffled by the door. Even so, it had a sensual rasp to it. He gave her a small smile, no doubt contrived to make him look harmless, but the smile, revealing beautiful, even, brilliantly white teeth, made him more dangerous than ever.

Not in the stranger-danger way, but in the way that showed he had extreme confidence in his own ability to charm, and no doubt that confidence was well earned.

Jonas Boyden was exactly the kind of man who was extremely dangerous to a woman who was deliriously satisfied with her choice of a solitary existence.

What he definitely was not? Alexandro Helinski.

He was not the kind of man who would have needed the kind of services her aunt offered. Ever. He was the kind of man women flung themselves at, and he carried himself with that aggravating self-assurance of a man accustomed to that.

So who was he? A lawyer? Someone here about bills? A business associate of her aunt's? Why at this time of night? But if he wasn't a client, that might mean that he had not been vetted thoroughly. Still, that was her aunt's handwriting on the card.

Krissy wished she had the nerve to tell him to come back tomorrow, but wasn't that what she was doing with all her aunt's affairs? Trying to put them off until tomorrow? It would just take a few seconds to find out what he wanted, break the bad news to him and send him on his way. It might even be just the impetus she needed to get started on all the things that had to be dealt with.

She clicked the dead bolt and pushed the door open a miserly crack.

An alarm began to shriek. It was loud enough to wake the dead, which given her aunt's current status—and her request to hear from her—was terrifying.

The sound paralyzed Krissy, her feet felt pinned to the floor by it. She wanted to just cover her ears and shrink away from the appalling noise. Instead, she jumped away from the door and scanned the wall. Sure enough, there was a keypad, flashing the message *Enter Code Now.*

Code? She didn't have a code. She had come through the back door. She hadn't even been aware there was an alarm system.

"May I?" Without waiting for her answer, the man opened the door fully and stepped through it. A blast of wind came through with him and lifted some papers off her aunt's desk and tossed them onto the floor. Really, it was like meeting the hero in a gothic novel!

He closed the door quickly against the wind, barely spared her a glance, but even so she noted his eyes were dark: not black at all, but a rather astonishing shade of blue—navy, like the deepest part of the ocean.

His presence, the broadness of his shoulders under that exquisite jacket, made the cramped office seem even smaller. Between an overflowing bookshelf and a file cabinet with open drawers, it felt as if there was no place to go.

She squeezed back against the wall as he studied the control panel. Even so, his shoulder brushed hers, and a lovely scent wafted off him. It transported Krissy. The wailing of the alarm took a back seat. It was as if the solid strength, the timelessness, of a pine forest had come through the door with him.

He was that kind of man who made a woman, even one as deliriously independent as her, feel that if they did rely on someone other than themselves every now and then, it wouldn't be a weakness.

It would be utterly delicious.

CHAPTER TWO

JONAS FELT AS though his eardrums were being ripped out of his head. The woman, obviously wary of strangers, as she should be, was gazing at the control panel with consternation.

Madame Cosmos—his secret name for Jane Clark—was nowhere to be seen. Was this the woman that she had come up with for him?

She was definitely not his type. Not a speck of makeup, almost owllike with those huge dark eyes behind large glasses. Masses of luxurious dark hair were pulled into a sloppy bun. She was not very tall and she was not exactly plump, but gave the impression of hiding generous curves under an unflattering outfit.

Then again, given the task he had given Madame Cosmos, *not his type* might be exactly what was called for.

But yoga pants and a mustard-colored, too-large sweater? Sneakers? No one met their match like that. Plus, it was more than evident she had been surprised by his arrival.

No, she was obviously an office assistant, working late, or maybe she was even the cleaning staff. Madame Cosmos had obviously forgotten him. Was that so surprising, given what had appeared to him to be flakiness at their initial interview? She had asked him, with grave interest, his zodiac sign.

"What's the code?" he called over the din.

The woman covered her ears and glared at him. It was really no time to notice her ears were tiny and sported prim little pearls. Her withering look indicated it was more than obvious she did not have the code. Her eyes sparkled with warning not to mistake her for an idiot.

He could step back into the night and let her deal with it. But he had important business with her boss— *satisfaction guaranteed, indeed*—that could not wait. It was June already. The long weekend in July was looming large.

He stepped up to the box and lifted the panel on it. No code, and surprise, surprise, no off button. Beside the alarm panel was the electrical box for the office. It might be a better bet. He opened it, found the main power switch.

He glanced at her, and she nodded. He flicked the switch.

They were plunged into instant darkness, but the silence was blessed.

He took a step back and gazed at her in the faint glow of a streetlight coming in the window. He could see the rich shine of her thick chestnut hair, piled up carelessly on top of her head.

He had a shocking sense of wanting to slip those glasses from her face, a shocking desire to know what her hair would feel like beneath his fingers if he freed it to cascade around her shoulders.

Where had that thought come from? Jonas frowned. He was not a man given to that kind of wayward thought, nor was she the kind of woman who inspired them.

In fact, her look leaned toward a comfy Saturday-at-home-with-the-cat.

Still, there was a certain voluptuousness to her, a plumpness to a full bottom lip, a spark in those eyes that hinted at passion for a man patient enough to coax it to the surface.

What she wasn't, was any kind of a—

"Bimbo," Madame Cosmos had told him with a sigh, after having just met him, scanning him with shrewd eyes that had felt as if they stripped him to his soul. *"You have a long history of dating exactly the wrong kind of woman."*

Despite the fact Jane had come so highly recommended, Jonas should have cut and run right then. It was a measure of his desperation—or maybe his obsession with winning—that he had not.

What the young woman in front of him wasn't, Jonas reminded himself sternly in an effort to stay on track, was Jane Clark. In fact, she was the antithesis of the highly recommended matchmaker who had the flair and panache of a carnival fortune-teller.

He had a sudden, exceedingly uncomfortable thought. What if he was meeting his match? Right now? What if this was who Madame Cosmos had picked for him? Not just the antithesis of herself, but the antithesis of the kind of women he normally dated?

It seemed like the kind of stunt the old gal might pull. *Just throw them together, surprise them with each other and see what happens. See if they sink, or see if they swim.*

It made him look at the woman in front of him in a different light. An exceedingly uncomfortable one. She was definitely not the kind he had ever gone for. Something bookish and girl-next-door about her.

"I have an appointment," he said, "with Madame…
er… I mean, Mrs. Clark."

"Canceled," she said abruptly. "You'll be called." She
nodded toward the door, dismissing him.

Jonas absorbed the shock of being addressed like
that, but had to admit he was reluctantly intrigued.
There was that spunkiness again, that warning not to
mistake her for an idiot.

Jonas took a deep breath. *Let's find out*, he told himself. "I'm Jonas Boyden."

"I saw that on the card. What's your business with
Jane?"

"I'm a client."

He braced himself for her to arrive at the same realization he just had, to say, shocked, *But I am, too.*

Instead, she said, "A matchmaking client?" She
looked very skeptical.

"Indeed."

"You are not."

There it was again. A feistiness that belied the more
muted bookworm look. She was actually calling him
a liar, which should have been insulting. Instead, he
was intrigued.

Jonas cocked his head at her. "Excuse me?"

"You're no Alexandro Helinski."

"Who?"

"Never mind. What would a man like you need a
woman like my aunt for?"

Her aunt. Not his match, then. He was instantly relieved. And maybe, ever so slightly, disappointed.

"A man like me?"

"Don't women flounder at your feet?"

"Maybe I don't need that kind of woman." *Bimbos.*

"The floundering kind. I hired your aunt to find me a match."

"What kind of a match?" she asked, reluctantly curious, suddenly round-eyed, behind her glasses.

"A match made in heaven," he said dryly.

"You were going to let my aunt pick a wife for *you*?"

"Isn't that what she does?"

Krissy felt she probably looked like a fish gasping for air. She snapped her mouth, gaping open with astonishment, closed. A man like this would be using her aunt's services? There was no sense being curious. Her aunt's services were no longer available.

But curious she was. "You can't find your own wife?"

"I'm not exactly looking for a wife."

Of course he wasn't!

"The circumstances are unusual," he continued. "Your aunt wouldn't normally take my kind of request, but I needed a partner—temporarily—and she took pity on me."

A temporary partner? He was darned right that was the kind of request Jane would not have entertained! But she obviously had, though it was hard to imagine anyone taking pity on this self-possessed man.

"I need a fiancée," he said, "and I just don't have the time to sort through profiles, to research backgrounds, to assess suitability, to gauge compatibility. Your aunt promised to do all those things for me. She guaranteed satisfaction."

"A temporary fiancée." It sounded perfectly appalling. What had auntie been thinking?

"It's complicated. I won't bore you with the details."

Krissy was pretty sure she wouldn't be bored.

"But I do need to see your aunt. Urgently."

"I'm sorry, Mr. Boyden, my aunt won't be helping you." Krissy struggled to tell him that her aunt had died, but somehow saying the words made it seem all too real all over again. She took a deep breath, needing to get the words out without crying. Why couldn't he just leave, as she had asked him, and she could call him when she was more composed?

His brow lowered as Krissy's silence lengthened. Mr. Boyden was not used to people not helping him!

"I have a contract," he said. "Not to mention having made a small fortune of a down payment."

"Can you just leave me a business card?" Krissy said, suddenly weary. She was not going to be vulnerable in front of this man, announce to him bluntly her aunt was now deceased. "I'll call you next week and we'll arrange a refund."

"Next week?" he said dangerously. "Next week is too late. I don't need a refund. I need to be engaged!"

"That's ridiculous. And impossible."

"She hasn't done it, has she? She hasn't made me a match."

"No, I don't believe she has. I can't—"

He regarded her stormily for long enough that it felt as if she was going to stop breathing.

"What about you?"

"Excuse me?"

He stepped toward her. He didn't reach out and he didn't touch her, and yet Krissy felt as if he had taken her glasses off and was planning on running his hands through her hair.

"Yes, you'll do," he decided, a touch too clinically. "There's a little of that librarian look to you. Wholesome. The girl next door. Yes, you'll do."

Krissy's heart was beating madly, as if he *had* removed her glasses.

"I am not going to be your temporary toy!" she said. She wanted to sound firm, but her voice had an unfortunate squeak to it. *Librarian, indeed.*

He cocked his head charmingly at her, as if he was not being completely ludicrous.

"Toy," he said, his tone mulling. "No, no, I don't think so."

Why on earth would she feel vaguely insulted by his dismissal?

"That could lead to complications," he explained gravely. "That's in part why I turned to your aunt. No complications. Still, we would need to get to know each other first, before we made it official. It's important to know each other."

"You think?" she asked. He seemed to miss her sarcasm.

"It's for a family reunion in the Catskills, the long weekend in July. My sister would know instantly if you didn't know what my favorite color was. Restaurant. Movie. That kind of thing."

What kind of weakness was it that Krissy suddenly wanted to know what his favorite color was? Restaurant? Movie? Plus, the long weekend in July. She had always spent it with Aunt Jane, who knew, as her own parents had not, that occasions—birthdays, Christmas, Easter, the Fourth of July—were important to families.

His invitation felt like a reprieve from the looming weekend alone, but more, it felt as if she was being invited to step into the pages of a story, a very interesting story with all kinds of twists and turns and characters she knew nothing about.

Krissy did not like temptations. She did not appreciate her sudden awareness that the nice, safe, predictable life she had so carefully constructed for herself might be slightly… Well, boring.

That was her aunt's word, after Krissy had brushed off her enthusiasm about having found the perfect man for her.

You're too young to be so set in your ways, so allergic to adventure. Life is not meant to be such a bore, my dear.

"Come on," he said persuasively. "It will be fun."

Fun. So no matter what he said, there was an element of her being his toy in there. Temporarily.

What do you do for fun?

Krissy considered what she would put on that application form. She walked her dog. She planned lessons for her class. She took in the odd Broadway show. She read.

She resented Jonas Boyden for holding out this to her, like a carrot in front of a donkey reluctant to take even one step. And she detested herself for *wanting* something.

But what?

Something just a tiny bit unexpected in her routines, she admitted slowly. For life to surprise her.

As if it hadn't done quite enough of that! And what she needed to remember from her past, from growing up caught between a battling mother and father, was that the surprises were rarely ever of the pleasant variety, and that there were few things in life more dangerous than hoping it would be better. Her aunt's sudden death was a case in point about the nastiness of surprises.

"No," she said firmly.

He frowned, just like the kind of brooding hero who blew in on a dark night, just like the kind of man who rarely heard the word *no* from anyone, let alone a member of the opposite sex, just like a man who could turn a woman's world upside down without half trying.

He considered her thoughtfully, then lifted an elegant shoulder. "All right," he said, giving up with surprising ease, as if suddenly having a fiancée, or a toy, or whatever, didn't matter to him a whit.

Was she annoyed by that? No, she told herself firmly. She was relieved. That was all.

CHAPTER THREE

KRISSY'S RELIEF AT having the issue of being Jonas's temporary toy settled was short-lived. Over the broadness of his shoulder, she watched a police car slide silently up to the curb. Two officers got out, settled their hats on their heads and turned narrowed eyes toward her aunt's office.

"Oh, no! They must be responding to the alarm. I'd better go tell them that—"

Jonas stayed her with a hand on her shoulder, then turned and looked over his own shoulder. "I don't think you want to go racing out there when they could well think a robbery is in progress."

His hand on her shoulder did not feel in any way domineering. His voice was deep, quiet and reassuring. She felt protected. Again, Krissy allowed herself a sense of it being okay, every now and then, to rely on someone else. As long as it didn't become a habit! When his hand slid away from her shoulder, she realized how easily leaning on someone else could become a habit. Even an addiction!

The policemen were eyeing the building warily. It occurred to Krissy that she and Jonas were just two shadowy figures standing in a darkened building that an alarm—that had not been turned off properly—had gone off in.

"What should we do?" she whispered uneasily.

"Just wait. Let them come to us. Don't make any fast moves once they come through that door."

She gulped and scanned Jonas's face. He looked perfectly calm. In fact, irritatingly, he looked as if he might actually be delighting in this.

He glanced at her, his smile seeming to confirm he might be enjoying this just a tiny bit too much—a man who embraced the kind of adventures she was utterly allergic to!

"You can prove you should be here, right? On your aunt's premises?"

Her mouth opened. Then closed. He was obviously trying to rattle her. On the other hand it was a *burglar* alarm. It seemed there was a fairly good chance that she and Jonas were going to be presumed to be burglars!

"What kind of proof would they want?" she asked him, trying not to let on she felt quite nervous.

"I don't know. A note from your aunt? Evidence that you work here? Don't worry, though. They'll get it all sorted out. Probably at the station."

A flashlight shone through the window, bouncing off her aunt's cluttered bookshelves and file cabinet, but it just missed catching Krissy and Jonas in its beam.

"The police station? Am I going to get arrested?" she squeaked.

"It seems doubtful, but not impossible. If you do—"

"Yes?"

He leaned toward her and smiled a rather wickedly satisfied smile. "I can give you a get-out-of-jail-for-free card."

She scanned his face. She knew he was kidding, and was not kidding at the same time. He oozed the con-

fidence of that kind of man, the kind with the money
and the connections and the innate sophistication that
made people respect him and bend over backward to
solve his difficulties.

"Why in the Monopoly game of life do I always end
up in jail?" she wondered out loud. "Instead of owning
the hotel chain?"

Jonas threw back his head and laughed when she
said that. His laughter was like that get-out-of-jail-for-
free card he had just offered. It seemed almost enough
to erase the predicament they were in.

Unfortunately, both policemen froze outside, alerted
by the sound that someone was in the building. They
looked so *ready* to handle whatever jumped out at them.
Krissy had a new appreciation for the difficulties of the
job they were doing.

"Okay," she said, "I'll take that get-out-of-jail-for-
free card."

"Well, nothing is actually *free*," he said easily, his
tone playful, as if he hadn't even noticed guns. "We'd
have to negotiate terms."

She could not help but appreciate how his lightness
was distracting her from the very real intensity of what
was going on—policemen advancing toward them as-
suming there were criminals in the building.

"If I go to jail, I'm sure you'll be going to jail, too!"

He showed her the appointment card in his hand.
"No, I don't think so. This appointment card will show
I had legitimate business here."

"Well, then, you can vouch for me."

"Or I could say I interrupted a burglary in progress,
depending how willing you are to negotiate terms."

Jonas was teasing her. He was doing it on purpose,
proving that Krissy was not hiding her nervousness

as well as she might have hoped. The policemen had
moved out of her range of vision.

"It's not funny," she told him. "What are they doing
out there?"

"Calling the SWAT team."

She gasped.

"I was kidding. I think they are looking for signs of
a break-in. Broken glass. A kicked in door. If you do
go to jail—

"You don't really have a get-out-of-jail-for-free card,"
she said irritably. He obviously did not get the serious-
ness of this situation.

"No, but I have the next best thing. A team of lawyers on call. I'll lend them to you."

She groaned.

"For that cost we have yet to negotiate," he said silkily.

"What kind of man has a team of lawyers on call?"

"One who handles a lot of real estate."

"You ended up with the chain of hotels!"

"Very true."

She refused to be impressed. "That isn't the right
kind of lawyer!"

"It would probably do in a pinch."

"What's the cost?" she asked Jonas. He was so calm
and so confident that it eased a bit of her panic. He was
actually *playing*. Unfortunately, he was just the kind of
man you would want in your corner if you were about
to be arrested.

And, she warned herself, that you could get addicted
to playing with!

"Fiancée for a weekend."

The door flew open. The flashlight blinded her.

"It's a false alarm," Krissy cried. "I have a right to
be here! I'm the owner's niece."

She glanced at Jonas. He didn't look terrified at all, but faintly amused, as if this was going to be a great story to tell at the office. She was pretty sure he winked at her.

To be honest, if you had to find yourself in a situation like this, somehow it was a man like this one you would want at your side.

How could she possibly know *that*?

Jonas shot his companion in crime a look, but she obviously was not seeing the humor in any of this, especially now.

"We just have to ask a few questions and then we'll be on our way," one of the policemen said.

"Perfectly understandable," Jonas replied.

She shot him a look that said she was relying on him to get her out of this, to be her prince, riding in on a white charger to save her. He hadn't had anybody look at him like that since his mother and father had died.

And then his sister had cast him as her hero. According to her, he had lived up to her expectations.

But he had paid a price for shouldering all that responsibility very young. Ever since then, he'd avoided having people rely on him. According to his sister, Theresa, who liked to offer her opinion even when it hadn't been asked for—especially when it hadn't been asked for—it was her fault he had become the quintessential bachelor, so allergic to commitment he couldn't even have a houseplant in his apartment.

And now Theresa and his brother-in-law, Mike, were gleefully getting ready to cash in on a bet he'd made a long time ago, when he was young—and possibly full of tequila.

Be committed by thirty or—

"You obviously don't look like our typical burglars, but due to the circumstances if you could tell us your business here at this time of night, it would be appreciated."

"I have an appointment with Jane Clark," Jonas said.

"See, that's the problem," the policeman said. "She died last week, and there are actually people scummy enough to read the obituaries and target her premises."

Jonas felt a shiver of shock go through his system. He glanced at the woman, and could see she was fighting back tears.

"He's not a scumbag," the quavering voice beside him offered.

Given that he had held her over a barrel with his offer to help her for a price—even though he had been kidding—Jonas thought that was very generous.

"It's my fault. I should have been phoning people and letting them know about Aunt Jane. Just in case they hadn't done what, apparently, scumbags do and read the obituaries. I'm supposed to be looking after things."

She was so genuine that both the policeman relaxed noticeably. "Your aunt was a much-loved fixture in this community," one of them offered. "She'll be missed by all of us."

She hiccuped. And then a tiny little noise escaped her, like the mew of a hurt kitten.

All three men in the room reacted in the same way—silence, stiffening body postures, an exchange of panicky looks.

A crime in progress was one thing. Largely manageable, a defined response called for and given, an event with a high possibility of a defined and satisfactory ending.

Tears falling—female tears—was quite another.

Within minutes the explanations had been given and accepted, the men in blue had reset the alarm and left with what appeared to Jonas to be uncommon haste.

He could see why. With those huge dark eyes misted with tears, and that full bottom lip trembling with emotion, she had become the kind of woman any man feared most.

Totally vulnerable. Soft. Needy. One who could use a strong shoulder to cry on. He could, unfortunately, picture her clinging like a limpet, sobbing against him, him patting her back...

Stop it, Jonas ordered himself. He slid a longing look at the door that the other men had just exited, took a deep breath and decided to finish this business as quickly as possible.

"Your aunt died?" Jonas said. "Why didn't you say something instead of letting me act like a complete jerk?"

"Maybe not a complete jerk," she said with a little sniffle. "Fifty percent. You did offer me a get-out-of-jail-for-free card."

"Only not for free," he reminded her. "Why didn't you tell me? Right away?"

"I couldn't bring myself to shout it through the door. I've been having trouble letting people know. I think it helps me keep the reality of it from setting in. I know lots of people thought she was eccentric—

Madame Cosmos, he thought guiltily.

"But she was the most loving person I ever knew. She was the only person in my family I could count on. She was—"

And then she was crying. Big sobs that shook her whole body, exactly the kind of sobs he and the policemen had been trying to head off at the pass since the clouds of that particular storm had first gathered in her eyes.

"I thought I could just send you a letter. And the refund, so that th-this didn't happen."

What was a man to do? Jonas looked longingly at the door one more time.

"Hey," he said, trying for his most empathetic tone, "it's okay."

"It's not okay!" she cried. "I loved her. I loved her more than anyone in the whole world!"

Empathetic tones were probably not his strong suit. Her distress required a response from him, whether he wanted to give one or not.

Like a man going to the gallows—a man with not one single option left—he went to her.

"It's going to be okay," he said softly. The reassurance had not worked the first time, and it did not work now. The tears were streaming down her face. It was a good thing she didn't have on any mascara! A wail of pure despair came from her.

With no options left, he folded his arms around her.

His last hope was that she would be sensible—she looked like the sensible type—and that she would push him away.

But she did not. And oddly, he did not feel as if he had just climbed the stairs to the gallows. As she nestled into him, a lovely warmth enveloped him. He could feel her tears puddling on his shirt, and after hesitating for just a second, his hand found her hair and he stroked the wild, springy silk of it.

"I'm so sorry," he whispered over and over, his tone as soothing as he knew how to make it. Touching her hair seemed to be releasing a scent that reminded him of the bouquet of fresh spring flowers he had given his sister for Mother's Day. The aroma was fresh and light and ever so faintly spicy.

"Th-thank y-you." She didn't attempt to pull away. "I'm not usually so emotional."

"Ah."

"Really."

The really was followed by a hiccup. Adorable.

He acted fast. "I withdraw the proposal. The fiancée for a weekend, the whole fake mate thing."

She gave him a watery smile at the *fake mate* reference, then tilted her head and looked up at him, gauging something. Apparently, she reached the wrong conclusion, that he was a decent guy.

"These might be the dumbest words I ever said," she said softly, "but why don't you tell me why you have a sudden, urgent need for an engagement? My aunt must have thought your reasons were compelling. I might consider your offer, after all."

Now that he had actually felt her soft curves pressed against him, now that his shirt was wet from her tears, now that the enchanting scent of her hair was burned into his brain, probably forever, now that he had found her hiccup adorable, that didn't seem like it was a very good idea.

He stepped back from her rapidly and looked at her, took in those huge eyes, tears studded in the lashes and strands of luscious hair just beginning to pull free from the clasp that held them, the plump lip, that looked freshly licked, somehow, quivering.

Jonas was pretty sure he needed someone *not complicated* and he was pretty sure this woman in front of him would not fit that criteria. At all.

Her name, provided to the police, came to his lips. "Kristen—"

"Krissy," she corrected him.

"Krissy, it's okay. I'll figure out something else."

"But now I'm curious."

He suddenly did not want her to be curious about any part of his life. It felt extremely dangerous. There was an expression: curiosity killed the cat.

Only in this circumstance, the cat could be him!

CHAPTER FOUR

"I'M VERY SORRY about your aunt," Jonas said with formality, backing away from Krissy slowly, like a man backing away from extreme danger. He felt the door behind him. He put his hand on it. *Have a nice life*, he wished her silently.

"Wait! They reset the alarm! We will have to go out the back."

There was no *we*. Or at least after he escaped out that back door there would be no *we*.

"Look, I'm going to leave, too," she said, her composure returning and her tone soothing, as if she was talking to a flighty animal that was about to bolt. "We can go together. If it's not too much trouble, perhaps you could walk with me? I have to get to Penn Station to get my train home. You could fill me in on the details as to why you need a fiancée."

"Uh—"

"Fake mate," she said with way too much enjoyment. "You don't mind, do you?"

Actually, he did mind. He suddenly didn't want her knowing any of the details of his quest for a temporary arrangement of the fiancée kind. On the other hand, he did not want her going out the back door by herself, or walking by herself, either. And Penn Station at this time of night?

"Where's home?" he asked reluctantly.

"Sunshine Cove. It's a little hamlet in the Hudson Valley—

"I know where it is." A memory tickled. "Is Moo-Moo's still there?"

She smiled. Now there was a dangerous thing, far more dangerous than the tears that still wetted the front of his shirt. That smile—along with the fresh memory of her hair, wild and springy under his touch—confirmed his thought that lurking under that deliberately frumpy librarian look was something else entirely.

"Still there," she said. "The best strawberry milkshake in the world."

Jonas formed an unfortunate picture of those lush lips closing over a straw.

"A strawberry shake?" he scoffed, partly to erase the visual. "You don't waste a trip to Moo-Moo's and have a strawberry shake. You have the Triple Chocolate Volcano Sundae."

She frowned at him. "You needn't say that like a strawberry shake is boring."

"Well…"

"They use real strawberries!"

This, right here, was why he needed to cut his losses. She was prepared to defend a strawberry milkshake, as if he had somehow called *her* boring, and not the milkshake. And for some reason, instead of cutting his losses, he was prepared to goad her on.

"Caramel Cream Banana Bliss, Gooey Gluey Fudge Cake, Thunder Mountain Raspberry Dazzle or, wait for it, Strawberry Shake."

"Yes," she said stubbornly.

"Every time?"

"Sometimes I have a vanilla cone," she said, as if

this was an act of defiance that she was prepared to defend to the death.

"Now you're just trying to bug me."

She was silent.

"I suppose they use real vanilla?" Jonas asked.

"They do. You can see the pieces of ground bean in the ice cream."

"Well, that's exciting."

"We all have different ideas of what's exciting."

That made him look right at her hair. And then her lips. And then, hastily, away. He stuffed his hands in his pockets and rocked back on his heels.

He wondered, a renegade thought that he completely failed to head off at the pass, if they weren't talking about ice cream, what she would find exciting.

"You're very familiar with the menu," she said, her tone a little stiff, as if he had managed to hurt her feelings. Which he probably had. He wasn't good with the sensitive type of woman. She had claimed she usually wasn't emotional, but he was seeing no sign of that.

"I did try to work my way through the entire menu," Jonas admitted proudly. "Back in the day, Moo-Moo's was a big outing for my family."

It was the kind of memory that he, allergic to sensitivity, avoided. Still, it pushed in, the four of them piling into a station wagon for a rare day away from the failing family resort. The day would be laughter filled, love filled. That thing called family, feeling so steady, so safe, so strong, despite the cloud of financial insecurity they had lived under. How wrong a man—a boy at the time—could be in his sense that things could last forever.

Still, Sunshine Cove was exactly the kind of place he would picture Krissy living: one of those satellite enclaves served by commuter trains, the quintessential

Hudson Valley town with mature trees and old manor houses tucked back on big grassy lots, and a sleepy main street that felt like a homecoming.

"I think I had better—" *cut his losses* came to mind. And yet that was not the direction he was moving in. He knew what he was going to do. Felt weirdly as if he *had* to do.

Jonas heard a sound. What was it? A heating system with a squealing belt turning on? A cat fighting in the alley? For some reason, it shivered along his spine. "Did you hear that?"

"No, what?"

"It sounded almost like the alarm going off again, only way more quiet."

Krissy tilted her head at him.

Jonas could not tell her the full truth. It sounded like someone in the distance laughing. He was not sure he had ever heard Madame Cosmos laugh, but he was pretty sure if she did it would have the alarm-like stridency of a cackle of pure delight.

It made him reconsider what he was just about to offer to do. After all, what was the point of Krissy thinking he was the kind of perfect gentleman a strawberry shake woman like her would require him to be? And what was the point of leaving himself open to her curiosity when he had decided Krissy as his fake mate would be way too complicated?

"I don't hear anything," she said decidedly after a moment. "You think you had better what?"

What, indeed? he asked himself.

"I think I had better drive you home," Jonas said.

Krissy could hear the reluctance in his voice. Well, who could blame him? It was a long drive, and the round trip would take him deep into the night. Plus, she had cried all over him, and he had decided, on the basis of milkshake choice, that she was boring.

She suspected his motive was pity. Who wanted to be pitied by such an excruciatingly attractive man?

Still, it was so tempting! A car instead of the train, an opportunity to bring some of these boxes home. Plus, it would be so quick. And her dog had now been home alone for way too long.

Crusher. Was she actually dreading going home to the new resident?

Of course not! In fact, for the dog's sake alone, she should accept the ride. But underneath all those very good reasons to accept Jonas's offer, Krissy was aware of something else. Despite the disagreement over what was exciting in ice cream products—or maybe because of it—she *wanted* to spend more time with him. She was intrigued. She wanted to unravel the mystery of why Jonas, a man brimming with such confidence, such a sense of himself, was searching for a fiancée.

All the more reason to say no, as if a pro and con sheet was being built in her head. Despite his association with her aunt, he was a complete stranger.

On the other hand, she always said no. It was her default answer for nearly everything, including trying other items on the menu at Moo-Moo's. Why not say yes for once? Why not be open to life being surprising?

It occurred to her that maybe she just didn't want to be alone.

"That would be very kind," she shocked them both by saying.

Moments later, weighed down with boxes, they emerged from the alley behind Match Made in Heaven. Jonas led her down the street and stopped at a sleek-looking car that was not like anything she had ever seen before.

"What is this?" she asked, annoyed that her voice had a reverent whisper to it. Obviously, the kind of car a man like him—a Triple Chocolate Volcano Sundae guy— drove. Or a James Bond type. Or a business tycoon.

Her own car suddenly seemed as boring as her ice cream choices, an economical subcompact that was good on gas and was a less than exciting shade of white. In fact, her car was about the same shade as a vanilla cone.

This car was vintage, very sporty and low-slung. Without knowing a single thing about cars, Krissy knew it was powerful. It glinted a deep and glossy muted pewter under the streetlight.

"It's the cause of all my problems," Jonas said with rough affection. He opened the passenger-side door and leaned in, stowing the box he was carrying in the back. She ordered herself not to look at the way his jacket rode up and his slacks stretched tight, but part of her mutinied against the order.

Jonas was a beautifully made man!

She was blushing by the time he turned back to her, but thankfully it was dark enough out that he seemed not to notice. He held open the door for her, and she slid into the seat. She was immediately embraced by the scent of rich leather, mingled with another scent that she recognized from when he had held her. Tangy. Clean. Male. The end result was one of being immersed in the man's subtle sensuality.

A moment later he got in the driver's side, turned the ignition and the car growled to life.

"It's a Jaguar," he said.

He pronounced it *Jag-guare*, which for some reason was nearly as swoonworthy as him leaning over to stow those boxes.

"Nineteen sixty-four," he said proudly.

"And how is it the cause of all your problems?" Krissy ventured, after he had pulled smoothly into traffic. She had to admire the way he drove, handling the powerful car with the casual inborn confidence one might associate with riding high-strung horses.

"It was the first major purchase I ever made. Way back in the day. It was kind of like my *I have arrived* statement. I love this car madly."

She slid him a look. In the glow of the dashboard panel, it was evident all of that was true. He had definitely arrived. And he was in love with his car. She wondered how many women were jealous of his passion for the car, and Krissy vowed not to be one of them.

"And how is it the source of all your problems?"

"I acquired it the same week my best friend, Mike, asked my sister, Theresa, to marry him. We started our business together. That's how he celebrated his arrival. I bought a car. He proposed marriage."

Jonas's voice was rough with wry affection as he continued. "I thought they were both way too young to be making that kind of commitment. I told him I, personally, would be waiting until I was thirty. He scoffed at that, not seeing me as the commitment type, ever.

"Somehow, way too many celebratory shots of tequila later, I was betting the car—this car—that I would be as committed as he was by the time I reached the age of thirty. That is a date that is rapidly approaching and that my now brother-in-law is gleefully ticking off on his calendar."

"That's silly. He won't hold you to it."

"Oh, he will, and with delight, I might add."

"It's not like it's a legally binding contract, for heaven's sake."

"I shook hands on it. That's binding to me."

What do you consider the most important attribute in another human being?

She remembered how she had loved Alexandro's answer. Honor.

"That's a very twisted kind of honor," Krissy decided, for both Jonas's benefit and her own. "You're willing to *pretend* you have made a commitment to win a bet you shook hands on while clearly inebriated."

"Exactly," he said, and glanced over at her. He grinned with utterly enchanting mischievousness. "I guess you have to take into account the basic competitiveness of my relationship with Mike. If he won this bet, he would lord his ownership of this car over me for the rest of my life."

"That is a long time to have something lorded over you," she admitted. She felt like she was learning quite a bit about Jonas. He was fun loving. This *problem*—how to keep his car—was a game to him.

It was all quite charming. But buried in there was a larger message, the reason for the bet in the first place, the reason it had become a problem at all. The man was commitment phobic.

It would be best to accept this ride home from him and call it a day. Tangling with him in any way—particularly in a phony engagement way, fraught with the potential for complication and emotional catastrophe—was inviting peril into a life she had made deliberately safe.

Too safe, she chided herself. Strawberry milkshake safe.

"Are you close to your family?" she asked.

There was a long pause. She glanced over at him. She could see a sudden tension in his shoulders and around his mouth.

"What's left of them," he said quietly. "My parents were killed in a car accident when my sister and I were in our late teens. I think it made Theresa and me closer. And now that family includes Mike. And two monster nephews."

His voice was ragged with both pain and affection.

In the muted light of the dashboard, Krissy saw the utter torment of a man who had loved completely—and lost—cross his handsome features. It was far from the playboy image that she generally would associate with commitment phobia, and somehow it made him so much more compelling.

"I'm so sorry," she whispered.

"It was a long time ago," he said brusquely. "I'm not sure why it came up at all. I guess thinking about the excursions to the ice cream parlor brought it to mind."

In a moment of madness, egged on by the purr of the car engine and deep leather seats, heady scents, and most of all, by his unexpected vulnerability, Krissy took a deep breath.

Her aunt had always told her life could be an adventure, and here she was. Despite all her efforts to avoid it, the unexpected had found her. This morning the closest Krissy had come to excitement for a long, long time was stepping in dog doo.

But now, she was in a gorgeous car with an even more gorgeous man, and life for the first time in a long, long time seemed like it held the potential for... What? Almost anything.

"I'll do it!" she blurted out before she could change her mind.

She tilted her head to look at him, waiting for him to smile. Or laugh. She thought the twinkle would return to those deep sea blue eyes, and that he'd turn to her with gratitude and say something cool and approving like, *Thatta girl, say yes to the adventure.*

Instead, humiliation flared to life and then deepened as the silence stretched out between them, and he looked straight ahead. There was a faint frown around his mouth.

Jonas obviously had decided she wasn't suitable!

Krissy debated, briefly, leaping from the moving car. It was barely moving, because they had just stopped at a traffic light. But she couldn't even order a Triple Chocolate Volcano Sundae, let alone jump from a car to save her wounded pride.

Besides, there was no point letting him know how wounded her vanity was. And on a practical side there were the boxes stowed in the back to think about. She couldn't just abandon Aunt Jane's things over a point of pride.

So instead of making the dramatic escape she longed for, Krissy sank back in her seat and followed his example by looking straight ahead. She tried not to gasp when he changed lanes, and the car shot forward as he passed a truck.

See? The hard beating of her heart told her the sad truth. It was too late. She had gotten herself into a strawberry milkshake kind of rut, and you couldn't just decide to get out of it. You couldn't change who you basically were—and nor should you want to on the basis of how damnably attractive a man was.

She just wasn't a take chances kind of person.

CHAPTER FIVE

JONAS SLID KRISSY a look. She had her hands folded primly on her lap, and was looking straight ahead. Still, exactly because of her schooled lack of expression, he knew how deeply he had hurt her feelings.

Which was precisely why she would not work as a fake mate!

He couldn't have a woman whose feelings were easily hurt. Or a woman who made him blurt out his secrets, either. Why had he told her about his parents? He rarely mentioned the family tragedy to anyone. His pain was intense, and it was *private*.

But it also made him the man who most understood the desolation of loss, and he wanted her to know she was not alone with all those feelings. Jonas also found he could not be the kind of man to be responsible for hurting her more deeply than she already was. He had to break the silence that was causing her so much pain.

"I think you're just too close to your aunt's death," Jonas said carefully. "Obviously, it's too much to ask of you right now."

"All right, I understand," she said, clearly unconvinced of his sincerity, clearly determined to take his rejection of her as fake mate personally and as an insult.

"Good," he said, knowing he could only make this worse if he kept trying to convince her.

Then she said quietly, "Though I have to say, the last hour has been the most respite I've had from that awful swarm of feelings since I got the news my aunt had died. Her death feels like a nightmare I just don't wake up from."

Jonas remembered oh, so well the intensity of that awful swarm of feelings, that sense of having entered into a nightmare that wouldn't go away.

Don't do it, he ordered himself. But human decency required more of him. He'd known she was the kind of woman who would require more from him.

"Well, if you think it might be a distraction from your grief..." His voice drifted away.

"I was trying to do you a favor," Krissy said, her voice low, faintly wounded, but faintly angry, too. "Not have you take pity on me and feel like you're doing me the favor. Besides, I think based on my milkshake choices, you have found me lacking in some way, so I withdraw my offer."

He slid her another look. She turned her head quickly to look out the window, as if something really interesting was happening out there, when in fact they had just left New York and were now flying along in near total blackness.

How had this happened? He now felt like he should be *begging* her to do what he least wanted her to do, which was accept his original poorly conceived proposition.

"I haven't found you lacking," he said.

"Oh, please." She did not turn to look at him.

"No, really. It's not that at all."

"Uh-huh."

"Krissy, to be honest you just seem like the kind of woman things could get really complicated with."

"So, it wasn't all about giving me room to grieve!" she said, triumphant at having caught him in the little white lie. Told for her own good, but no brownie points there.

And thinking of her own good, Krissy was a little too smart for it. And definitely too smart for *his* own good, as well.

"In what way am I complicated?" she said dangerously.

In this way, right here, he thought, but wisely refrained from saying it. There would be no way to answer that question correctly, so he said nothing.

"Like I might not understand it was a game? Like I might forget it was all fake? Like my grief might make me needy and clingy? Like I might find you irresistible and cross the line? Like I'm just some pathetic homely girl who would be so far out of her league—"

"Stop it! You are neither pathetic nor homely. This is exactly the problem—you're complicated."

"And you like uncomplicated." She said it as a statement, not a question.

"Yes," he said, relieved that she got it. "That's what I asked your aunt for. Uncomplicated. Someone who would understand the clearly defined parameters of our arrangement from the beginning."

"I can't believe my aunt went for that."

"Well, she did. Not only did she go for it, but she took a big deposit and she guaranteed my satisfaction."

"Well, I offered to fulfill the contract, and you said no, so—"

"I didn't exactly say no."

"Your unenthused silence spoke volumes."

"I was thinking!"

"Yes, about how to get out of your ridiculous offer and my misguided acceptance of that offer. Which I accepted to help you. But you thought it would be too complicated, so now you have gotten out of it. Your contract with my aunt is null and void. And I'm not giving you a refund, either!"

"That's fine," he said tightly. "No refund is required."

What was required was that this awful journey with her be over. He was not cut out for rescuing damsels in distress. He was not a man accustomed to second-guessing himself, but he wished he had not offered her a ride home.

He was so glad when they pulled up into the tiny hamlet of Sunshine Cove. He put the address she gave him into the GPS he'd added to the car and avoided its instructions to take Main Street, which would bring them right past Moo-Moo's. Instead, he took the alternate route.

He pulled up in front of a cottage. Once it must have been the carriage house for the manor house that shared the lot. Now, its postage-stamp-size yard had been separated from the larger house with its sweeping lawns, by a thick hedge of lilacs, heavy with wilted blooms. The carriage house itself was tiny and looked like something out of a fairy tale—paned windows and pansy-filled window boxes, Tudor timbers exposed under the curving A of the roofline.

Krissy scrambled out of the car as if she was trying to escape something that smelled bad. He would have been quite happy to roar away, but unfortunately he had to help her with her boxes.

"Just put them there," she ordered outside her front door, not looking at him, fishing for her key. The scent of finished lilacs was heavy in the air.

A dog that sounded huge howled on the other side of the door. He decided he might be wise to make his exit before the beast was unleashed.

"Well," he said with relief, "it's been nice meeting you. Again, I'm sorry about your aunt."

"Likewise," she said. "Sorry for your losses. Nice meeting you. Have a nice life."

That was supposed to have been his line!

Before he could make good his escape, she said, "And just for your information, I would have been the safest bet ever for a fake mate, because I am *never* getting married. Ever. There was absolutely no possibility of a phony engagement to me becoming complicated."

Jonas highly doubted that. It was already complicated, because he wanted to ask her what had made her so vehement on the topic. Instead, he turned quickly and went back to his car.

Escape was within reach. Once he got to that car, he never had to see her again. Fake mate, indeed. Not complicated? From their very short acquaintance it was more than evident to him that Krissy was too sensitive, too smart and way too sensual in that understated way of hers.

Even glancing back at her, seeing her standing under the glow of her porch light, he had a renegade thought what it might be like if he had delivered her home after a date, what it would be like to be standing there debating whether or not to kiss her good-night.

You couldn't have thoughts like that with a fake mate!

He was sliding into his car when she got her key in the door.

The dog that erupted out that door was every bit as big as it had sounded like it would be: a monster of a dog, a creature of near-mythical proportions, its gray head the color and size of a rotted pumpkin.

It leaped at her with joyous enthusiasm that might have been adorable in a Pomeranian but was frightening in such a large dog. Its immense paws found her shoulders, and a huge tongue lolled out. Partly laughing, and partly outmatched, she turned her face away, but the dog was not to be deprived of its kisses.

She lost her balance in her twisting effort to avoid the worst of the slobbering affection and went to her knees. The dog shoved her the rest of the way over, and she was completely pinned as the giant dog jumped on top of her and swiped at her face with a tongue about the size of a paint roller.

Jonas suddenly understood the lack of makeup and the casual outfit. His escape thwarted, he got back out of the car and strode up the walk. Before he reached them, the dog froze, cocked his head and took off running.

Jonas arrived at Krissy and offered his hand. Her laughter had dried up the second the dog took off, but she still had that "just kissed" flush on her face.

He was so irritated—with himself for being so aware of her or with her easy acceptance of the dog's unacceptable behavior he wasn't sure—that he might have used a little more force than was absolutely necessary to yank her to feet.

She fell against him, and her hair finally pulled completely free from the clasp that had held it so sloppily in place. It cascaded around her shoulders in a rich wave of color, scent and curl.

For the second time tonight he found the lusciousness of her curves pressed full-length against him. How much could a man take?

* * *

Krissy could feel the hard line of Jonas's body and she tilted her chin and looked up into his face. The sudden downturn of his mouth—not happy to be rescuing her *again*—did nothing to detract from how handsome he was. In fact, it brought his every feature into sharp focus: the intensity of his eyes, the height of faintly whisker-shadowed cheekbones, the fullness of his lower lip, the faint cleft in his chin. His eyes trailed to her hair and then to her lips, before they came to rest, darkened, on her own eyes.

She knew he was every bit as aware of her as she was of him. Something unexpected sizzled between them.

She had opened herself up to being surprised by life and here it was.

She wanted to taste him. She wanted to kiss this man who was a virtual stranger. Was this the *complication* he had spotted so readily? Was this the danger?

Of course it was. She looked at the sensuous firm line of his lower lip. She should pull away, and yet she felt herself pull in closer, drawn to him helplessly, like a magnet to steel.

The bark of her dog in the distance jolted her out of her foolishness. She pulled away from Jonas and scanned the direction the dog had gone.

There he was, at the base of a tree, barking at the neighbor's cat that was glaring at him from a low branch.

"Crusher!" she called.

"Crusher?" Jonas said with a groan. "Seriously?"

The dog spared her a glance. The cat took its opportunity and leaped from the tree. The dog bolted after it.

She took off after Crusher, and with a sigh of pure resignation, Jonas took off with her. When the dog and cat went over a fence into a neighbor's backyard, Jonas put one hand on the fence and vaulted over it. She heard the distinct sound of his pants ripping as she scrambled after him.

She was fairly certain, as they dashed through darkened backyards, they were going to have their second encounter of the evening with the police.

Half an hour later, they finally cornered the dog and avoided arrest.

Jonas took off his belt to use as a temporary leash. There was a large tear in his slacks; the zipper had pulled clean away.

She started to laugh.

He glanced down at himself, and then back at her, sheepish.

"You're blushing," she crowed.

"I'm not," he denied firmly.

"And you're wearing tighty-whities!"

"I'm not!" he said.

"Well, what are they then?"

His blush intensified. He glared at her. "You said you wouldn't be complicated, but here we are in the middle of the night discussing my underwear."

But then a grin tickled the edges of his mouth, and then a snort of laughter escaped him. In a second, they were both laughing, doubled over with it, the dog bouncing between them, taking turns leaping on them and swiping their faces with his huge tongue.

At last, Jonas handed her the belt leash and pulled off his jacket, and tied it around his waist. He took the makeshift lead back from her when Crusher nearly yanked her arm off.

"Stop it," he told the dog. Or maybe he was telling

her to stop it, because she was still giggling, the moment effervescent with surprising delight.

The dog did stop. He quit pulling and walked quietly at Jonas's side, which was a good thing, because Jonas literally had his hands full. Krissy laughed most of the way home as he tried to keep his dignity while he juggled the dog, his beltless pants and his coat cover-up.

It was as if there had been way too much sadness of late, and the laughter had been waiting. Once uncorked, it wasn't going to be shoved back in.

Finally, they were back at the cottage.

He handed her the leash.

"Thank you," she said

They stood there in awkward silence for a moment. He looked at her in a way that made her uncharacteristic giddiness dry up and her heart stop.

"I have to go," he growled.

"Yes, you do," she said. Even though it was insanely late, and she had to teach in the morning, she had been thinking of asking him in for a drink.

He hesitated. "I was just thinking, that maybe we could make it work."

"Make what work?"

"You know. Fake mate."

So he didn't want whatever had sprung up between them to end, either. Which made the potential for complications seem extremely high.

And at the moment, Krissy, bathed in moonlight and laughter and dog kisses, found she just didn't care.

CHAPTER SIX

"I THINK MY sister and Mike would find you believable. A girl with a dog."

Oh. It was about Mike. And his sister. And the dog. In a roundabout way, the car. It was about everything except what had just leaped in the air, sizzling, between them.

There was no reason to be insulted by that! It reduced the possibility of complications, didn't it?

"Plus, it's evident to me," Jonas said, "you need some help with the dog. There is nothing funny about such a big dog being so poorly behaved. You could have been badly hurt when he knocked you down. What if you'd smacked your head on the pavers? What if that had been a child he leaped on like that?"

These were, of course, valid points, but Krissy's feeling of being insulted grew.

"Crusher is a rescue," she said defensively. "I haven't really had him long enough to work on his, er, issues."

"Well, start with the name. Because a dog will always live up to whatever name you give it."

"He came with that name."

"You can change it."

"I thought that was bad luck."

"For boats!"

"What would you suggest? Pansy?"

"Better," he said, deliberately missing her sarcasm.

He moved away from her and over to Pansy-Crusher, who was wriggling in anticipation of attention. Jonas studied the dog, touching that one ear torn off in a long-ago battle and taking in that the face was badly scarred.

Jonas turned back to her. "You know it's a possibility this dog is too much for you, don't you?"

That very thought had been niggling at the back of her mind almost since Crush—Pansy's—arrival. But she *hated* that he saw it.

"I'm prepared to do what it takes," Krissy said firmly.

Jonas studied her, then lifted a shoulder. "I guess we'll see," he said. "It would be a trade. I could show you a few things about handling the dog, and if it looks like we're compatible, you could be my fiancée at the reunion. It happens to coincide with my thirtieth birthday."

Krissy had never been to a family reunion. Neither her mother or father had enjoyed good relations with their extended families. Their family of three had lived on a desert island, but not the idyllic kind. Aunt Jane had been the only respite, the only rescue.

So this casual reference to happy family events made Krissy feel an uneasy sense of longing.

He cocked his head at her. "It's at our family resort in the Catskills. My sister and Mike run it now. It's always a fun time."

That uneasy longing grew in the pit of her stomach.

"Family and fun going together," she said, before she could stop herself. "There's a novel concept."

"Your family wasn't fun?" he asked, as if it was shocking news to him that families weren't fun.

Shut up, she ordered herself. "Just Aunt Jane. The rest of it was pretty much a war zone."

His gaze was deep and stripping, loaded with unwanted sympathy. Krissy tilted her chin proudly at him. "Your family doesn't fight?"

"Of course they fight. My sister is downright mean with a water balloon."

That kind of fight seemed so innocent. Krissy felt a longing she had suppressed push against the lid she had put on top of it.

"I'm not sure about the reunion," she said.

"We'll take it one step at a time," he said, his surprisingly gentle tone making another longing leap up deep inside of her.

"Homework," Jonas said, as if it were all settled, "Find a new name for the dog. I'll drop by Saturday. Early afternoon. One-ish, okay?"

He didn't wait for her answer. "If things go well, we'll take a walk downtown with him for ice cream at Moo-Moo's. Who knows? Maybe you'll order something exciting."

He said that as if there was hope for both her and the dog.

Say no, Krissy ordered herself. If she didn't, Jonas would take over her whole life before she even knew what had happened. She'd be renaming her dog and breathlessly anticipating going for ice cream with him and even thinking about ordering something different. She'd be looking forward to a family reunion, to that tantalizing glimpse of what normal was.

She didn't say no.

Instead, she watched in silence as he turned away from her, stopped at his car door to remove the jacket tied at his waist, then slipped inside and drove away.

"I feel as if I've just survived a hurricane," Krissy confided in Crusher.

And that, she told herself, explained the euphoria. Completely.

A few days later, on Saturday, getting ready for Jonas's arrival, Krissy told herself firmly it was not a date.

So how did she explain the pile of clothes on her bed, tried on, reviewed, discarded? The dog was now nestled in the middle of them.

"Get off the bed, Hans," she said to Crusher, trying out yet another name. The dog did not respond, and she shook her head. "Maybe better for a German shepherd," she decided.

The explanation for the number of clothes discarded was actually quite easy.

"It's like a job interview," Krissy told herself. "If you're going to be a fake mate to a man like Jonas Boyden, you have to look the part."

Of course, it was complicated, just as he had somehow known all along it would be. Because it was very difficult to find an outfit that was absolutely beguiling while looking like it was not trying to be, and that was also appropriate for a session of dog training.

And added to all that, it had to be appropriate for eating ice cream afterward, the outfit of a girl who was not afraid to be bold in her choices.

Krissy finally settled on a pair of wildly flower-patterned end-at-the-calf leggings and an oversize white T-shirt. She put on a pair of hot pink running shoes that matched one of the flowers in the leggings. She added a chunky, colorful necklace and earrings.

Then she took a curling iron to her hair, hated how it looked—trying way too hard—and scooped it back into a ponytail. Disliking herself for it, she added just a touch of makeup, a bit of mascara, a dusting of blush and hint of lip gloss.

She regarded herself in the mirror and thought she had hit just the right note: spontaneous, sporty, fun, someone not at all concerned about the complications of a fake match.

"What are you doing to me?" she told the urn of her aunt's ashes as she passed the mantel in her small living room.

Jonas arrived promptly, and she peeked out her front window as he came down the walk. The spring sunlight glinted off the wheat gold of his hair. He carried himself with the supreme confidence of a person who would never give a second thought to outfit choice.

And of course, he had that just right, casual in a short-sleeved navy blue button-down shirt, chinos and canvas loafers. The sunglasses gave him a bit of a film star aura.

She was aware, as she opened the door, she felt extremely nervous.

However, all the effort she had put into making a great first impression on their second meeting was for naught, because the dog bounded out the door.

"Louie," she cried, as the dog leaped up and placed its paws on Jonas's substantial shoulders, "stop it."

Neither the dog nor Jonas even glanced at her.

"Off," he said sternly. "Now."

The dog, shocked and confused by this rejection of his enthusiasm, lowered himself to all fours and then gazed at Jonas with some consternation.

"Sit," Jonas commanded.

The dog sat in three stages: his huge hind end swayed, then inched down, hovering, and then, finally, plopped all the way onto the ground.

"Is Louie what you've decided on?"

She frowned. All that work on the perfect look and not even a *Hello, Krissy, how are you? Looking lovely today, I must say.*

"Not really. I'm just trying it."

"Hmm. It sounds like a name for a dog that would trip over his ears, like a basset hound."

"Well, it won't do for him, then." They both looked at the dog's ears, the one in tatters.

The dog looked like it was considering getting up, and Jonas snapped a finger at him. He nestled back down.

Jonas cast her a glance, finally. "What did they tell you about him at the rescue center?"

He was being so all business. She longed for the laughter they had shared the other night. Should she remind him of his ripped pants?

No! She should keep it all business, too. Even the fiancée part, when they got to that? Especially the fiancée part, when they got to that! But how could you pretend to be someone's fiancée with this business-like attitude?

She thought of her parents. Civil, but distant, would be an improvement in some relationships!

"I didn't exactly get him directly from the rescue center," she admitted. "One of the other teachers at school had taken him, and it wasn't working out."

He looked exasperated by that. Where was the man who had made her laugh so hard? For both their safety, wasn't this coolness so much better?

"He wasn't working out for someone else, and so you took him?"

"Artie Calhoun, the fifth-grade teacher, brought him to the staff room one Monday morning. His wife had told him not to come home after work if the dog was still with him."

"The dog was being bad enough it was breaking up a marriage. That would compel you to step in, why?"

A question she had asked herself several hundred times!

"Look at that face."

They both looked at the dog. Hans-Louie, the pansy crusher, lolled out his tongue in a silly grin and did that thing with his eyes where he looked up at them with a certain forlorn hope.

"How could you not fall in love with it?" Krissy asked.

Jonas made a low sound partway between a sigh and a groan. She looked at him. True enough, Jonas did not look like he was a falling-in-love kind of guy. In fact, he did not look like a man who would give his heart easily. To anyone. Or anything.

Not that that was any of her business. Not that she wanted to even think about Jonas falling in love!

That would make their arrangement impossibly complex.

"Anyway," Krissy said, "I couldn't resist him, and he's here and I'm committed now."

Jonas winced at the very word and looked at her warily, as if he had discovered she was the superhero of lost causes.

The dog tried again to get his legs under himself.

"No," Jonas said with the authority of a drill sergeant. Crusher plopped back down, ducked his head and looked contrite as he sneaked looks at Jonas's face.

Jonas sighed again. "I didn't think a rescue center would match him with you. Don't look insulted! It's not personal. The dog may have been a fighting dog, which means he has aggression built into him. It's not a good thing for an inexperienced owner."

"He's not aggressive," she said firmly. "If he was a fighting dog, I think he probably washed out of fight class. He just hasn't had enough love."

Jonas actually groaned. "He doesn't need love. He needs discipline. Do you see how I'm greeting him? I'm not feeding his excitement. When you come home, don't even greet him. Don't even look at him."

"Really?" she asked, appalled.

"When you get home, get a leash and take him for a walk. Don't even go in the door until you've done that. Every single time. Because he's got way too much energy and it's a bad idea to reward that by letting him jump all over you. The affection should always be initiated by you, after he's earned it. And it should *never* involve him jumping on you."

Krissy could feel her back going up. He hadn't even noticed her outfit! Was Jonas always so bossy? Of course he was! He had that look of a man quite accustomed to being in authority.

Still, she bit back her irritation. She'd agreed to this trade. And really, she was being offered what she most needed right now. Which was not a fiancée, fake or otherwise. It was a well-behaved dog.

The kind of companion she could walk into her old age with.

"You seem to know quite a bit about dogs," she conceded.

"We bred, raised and trained hunting dogs when I was growing up. It was our off-season business."

"Oh, dear," she said. It was time to remind him of the other part of their deal. "I don't know how this is going to be a fair trade when you know quite a bit about dogs. I, on the other hand, know nothing about being a fiancée. Your fiancée."

"What's to know?" he said. "I'll put a ring on your finger. We'll gaze at each other adoringly."

A ring? She hadn't even considered that. And the gazing adoringly part seemed very dangerous, indeed.

"I think the family reunion would be too much," Krissy said carefully, "A whole weekend? It just gives too many opportunities to expose the fact we don't know each other."

"But by then, we will."

"We will?"

"Sure. We'll do a few dog training excursions, I'll take you out for dinner a couple of times. We'll know everything there is to know about each other."

That sounded scary!

"Then we'll go to the reunion, we'll cream all the competition in the water fight, eat too many hot dogs, sing by the campfire, show off your ring."

The picture he painted called to a little girl inside her who had craved exactly that kind of family and that kind of gathering. She had seen such things in movies and read about it in books. Kids at school talked about lives that made her aware that her life—her parents' battles followed by periods of crushing silence—was not normal.

Aunt Jane had known how wrong it all was. She had taken Krissy out of that situation as often as possible. Overnight sleepovers at her great little NYC apartment, trips, excursions, outings. And she had always assured Krissy, whenever they were alone together, that the home situation was not her fault. And yet how could it not be?

How could it not be, when Krissy had been the

reason—the accidental pregnancy—that had brought her parents together?

"Besides," he continued, oblivious to Krissy embroiling herself in distressing thoughts, "we'll bring the dog. You'd be amazed how a dog becomes the center of attention. My sister won't notice much else."

Krissy was not convinced the reunion could be a good idea. "I think maybe just dinner to introduce me to Mike and Theresa," she said. "Show them the ring. You can claim I had a previous engagement for the reunion dates."

"Let's just see how it plays out," he said. "Go get that leash and we'll start."

It was all wrong. Everything about this whole encounter was wrong. He was taking charge completely. He was triggering forbidden longings in her. She had thought it would be fun, but she felt tense. It was supposed to be the prelude to their engagement, but it felt businesslike and calculated. She had dressed up for it!

What was troubling her was it felt as if Jonas Boyden was here out of some unfathomable sense of responsibility for her.

He had been 100 percent correct in his assessment of their situation when he had refused her initial offer to be his fake mate.

It could get complicated between them. Fast.

CHAPTER SEVEN

KRISSY WONDERED IF MOO-MOO's was still on the table? It was such a small thing. It already felt way too large. If it was still on the table, she planned to be shocking. She planned to order the most exciting thing on the menu. She seemed to recall, vaguely, there was an item called Earth Orgasm on the menu, a concoction of organic yogurt, nuts and bananas.

That was ridiculous. She was being ridiculous. Embarrassingly so. She didn't even like nuts! And she wasn't all that fond of yogurt, especially in an ice cream shop.

But it was just more evidence you could not keep things uncomplicated with a man like Jonas Boyden. Particularly if you let your mind wander to orgasms in any form. Krissy did not like being ridiculous.

She was already nervous about the family reunion and it was nearly a month away!

So the best thing to do would be to tell him the deal was off. She needed to put an end to this now. She didn't need him to help her with the dog. There were thousands of books out there. And videos. She could ask him to recommend a few.

She opened her mouth to say it.

"See?" Jonas said quietly. "This is what you want. Do you see how relaxed he is? That's what you reward."

He dropped down on his haunches in front of the dog and took the big mug between both his hands. He massaged with his palms and his thumbs, pressing deep circles into the scarred face of the dog. Crusher-Pansy-Hans-Louie's tongue fell out of his mouth and he closed his eyes. A moan of pure bliss escaped him.

A light seemed to be shining out of both of them, man and beast.

Krissy watched for a moment, utterly entranced.

She sighed. She would just have to put her own best interests on hold for the good of her dog, she told herself as she went and got the leash.

A rare thing had happened to Jonas when Krissy had opened her door.

He'd been caught off balance, and not entirely because of the dog trying to leap at him. He'd been expecting the woman from the other night, the one with the frumpy sweater and shoes and messy hair and makeup-free face. The one who had brought out a surprisingly protective side of him. And not just because of the dog, though it was more than evident she was in over her head with the mutt.

But his protective inclinations had surfaced more because of what she had said about family and fun being a novel concept. About her family being a war zone. He had thought about that over the last few days way more than he should have. Grief was hard enough to deal with. How did you deal with it alone?

It made him so aware of what a gift his family was. Theresa, Mike, the nephews, but also that brood of boisterous aunts and uncles and cousins who always had your back, who always made sure you knew you belonged to something larger than yourself.

It made Jonas, perhaps foolishly, commit to something: showing her how it could be. He wanted her to experience his family reunion, and somehow the motive of having her as his fiancée had become muddied.

But the woman who opened the door had replaced the librarian-in-need with a woman who didn't look as if she needed his help at all.

Krissy, in the hot pink shoes and those crazy cut-off tights that made her legs looks endless, looked fun and sexy. She had on a touch of makeup: just enough to make her eyes look huge and gorgeous and to make her bottom lip look full and glossy and tempting. Her hair was pulled back in a stern ponytail, but it showed off the bone structure in her face.

And made him want to send it cascading around her shoulders the way it had the other night.

See? Complicated. He, a person who prided himself on his razor-sharp ability to focus, was off-balance.

A man, Jonas reminded himself, focusing on the only safe thing in the vicinity, the dog, should always go with his first instinct!

He took shelter from the bombarding of his senses by hiding behind what he knew about dogs, which was, thankfully, quite a bit.

As soon as she brought the leash out, the dynamic changed. Jonas became instructor, and Krissy became student.

"Let's start by giving him a name." He snapped the leash on the dog's collar.

"Beauregard!"

"Something short would be better. Preferably one syllable. Beau?"

Krissy actually blushed, as if he had asked if he could be her beau!

"How about Chance?" she said. "I'm kind of taking a chance on him."

"And giving him a second chance. From the look of his face, he's had a hard life."

"Perfect, then!" she said, beaming.

Happiness became her. As he watched the light come on in her face, he felt awareness whisper to life within him. Not just of her, but of what a beautiful day it was. Spring in the air, the leaves and grass nearly exploding with shades of green, the scent of blossoms in warm air, the sky bright blue and cloudless. The whole drive here, he had been so focused on his muddled thoughts, he had totally missed that.

Despite the opportunities for potholes and pitfalls, it seemed as if maybe coming to Sunshine Cove this morning wasn't such a bad road to have chosen, after all. He felt something relax within him.

Jonas demonstrated how to walk the dog in front of her cottage, walking away from her.

"Super relaxed," he said. "No tension on the leash. Expecting him to pace himself to you. You stop, he stops. You pick up the pace, he picks up the pace."

When he turned back, there was something faintly guilty in her face, as if she hadn't just been watching the dog! Unless he missed his guess, she'd been checking him out!

"He's always nearly pulled my arm off," Krissy said, just as if she had not been checking him out. "If he sees something, well, you saw it the other night. A squirrel, another dog, someone who looks friendly, he's off. To be honest, it's made me reluctant to walk him." She seemed to realize she was chattering. She stopped abruptly. She looked anywhere but at Jonas.

It added the most interesting little sizzle to his heightened awareness of the day.

Stick to business, Jonas ordered himself. "This is a big dog. He needs to walk twice every single day. Once in the morning and once at night."

"I know. You said I can't even go inside the house after work until he's had his walk. I can't believe how wonderful he is for you!" she said. Her eyes skittered back to him. This time they didn't skitter away.

There was something intoxicating about being admired by a pretty woman on a spring day. They walked through the sleepy, lovely streets of Sunshine Cove. An old man was getting his garden ready, stringing rows. Children shrieked on a trampoline. A small dog raced up to a picket fence and barked hysterically at them.

It felt as if they were a couple, and it felt shockingly good and not just because it suddenly seemed like he had a very real chance of convincing his sister and Mike this was the real deal and keeping his car.

"I can't believe he didn't acknowledge that dog," Krissy said beside him after they had passed the yappy Pom-cross.

"He needs a leader. He wants one." They arrived at the wide arch that led to the park and pathway that ran along the Hudson. Jonas passed the leash to Krissy. "Now you're his leader."

She took the leash gingerly. She stepped out hesitantly. The dog sensed her lack of confidence and pulled eagerly at the leash when a bike went by.

Jonas stepped in and covered her hand with his, and tugged at the leash. "See? Just a slight correction. Bring his attention back to you."

He seemed to have succeeded at bringing her attention back to himself. And his to her. That scent filled his nose: the spring bouquet freshness of her. The softness of where her skin touched his intensified some feeling of being totally alive.

He could have let go and stepped away, but there were two little old ladies in the distance coming toward them. He didn't want Chance jumping at them.

After they had passed, he moved away from Krissy, aware of his reluctance to break contact with her and annoyed with himself because of it.

The dog immediately sensed she was on her own. It yanked on her, and she lurched forward. Jonas fought the impulse to leap in and rescue her. He couldn't be here all the time. He had to focus on his mission, which was to at least make it safe for her to have the dog, to handle it on her own. The way it was behaving now, she could end up with a broken bone.

"Gather yourself, make him sit, try again."

But now she was rattled and trying too hard, and the dog was confused. Jonas stepped in, took the leash—careful not to touch her this time, Chance was obviously picking up on something agitated—and made the dog sit.

Jonas passed the leash back to her. "No, don't go right away. Make him sit. You decide when to go, not him."

"I'm terrible at this," she decided dejectedly.

"Try this," Jonas said. "Act the part. Shoulders back, long, confident stride. Exaggerate it at first. You're a model on the runway."

She cast him a doubtful look.

"No, really. Just give yourself to it. Lots of attitude!"

He could see the moment she decided she would try it. Her shoulders came back. Her chin went up. With the leash firmly in one hand, she set the other on her hip. She stepped out, long strides, placing her feet one in front of the other, as if she was walking a tightrope with deliberation. Her hips swung. She narrowed her eyes and did a stern little purse with her lips.

Jonas had to bite back laughter. He was tempted to tell her the facial expressions were probably not necessary, at least for the dog's sake, but he was enjoying them too much to stop her.

Chance, sensing the difference in Krissy instantly, came to attention and walked well at her side. Jonas watched from behind them, trying to be teacher-to-student analytical, but he was now aware he was definitely checking her out!

Krissy turned her head back to him. *It's working*, she mouthed, as if it was a big secret they needed to keep from the dog. She seemed to realize he was checking her out. She lost her rhythm and Chance catapulted into her.

Jonas leaped forward and caught her before she fell. The moment intensified around him: her softness, her scent, a pink, plump petal falling from a flowering tree.

Her lips looked as plump and as pink as that petal. A command blasted through his brain. *Kiss her*.

He was so shocked by the impulse that he shoved her away.

"Okay, so modeling material I'm not," Krissy said.

"Actually, I think you nearly had it. But you could try something else. Maybe an actress going up to get your Oscar?"

She made a face at him, gathered the leash and concentrated. He watched her face form into haughty lines. Confident and untouchable, she sashayed forward. Then, really getting into the spirit of the thing, she bobbed her head to the right and left, nodding at her imagined fans. It was hilarious. The dog was taking tentative steps with her, glancing at her face with utter confusion. After half a dozen steps, he sat down in protest.

"I'm not really feeling this," she said. "It's phony—it's not me."

In other words, absolutely the wrong choice for fake mate. She wasn't good at pretending. The dog knew it, too.

"That explains the dog being confused," Jonas said. "But sometimes you can at least fake the body language. Try the queen."

Krissy shot him a look, but gamely recomposed herself. She cupped her hand and marched along with the dog, her face solemn, her hand turning languidly in her impression of the royal wave. The dog was now dragging behind her, shooting Jonas aggrieved looks at what he had created.

"Toodle-loo," she told the dog, in a very bad impression of an English accent. "Come along, now."

Jonas had been trying to hold back, but this cracked him up.

She stopped and looked at him. The dog, relieved, plopped down. Jonas stifled his laughter and moved to them. He tried to convince the dog to get back up. Chance pinned his butt to the ground as if it had been crazy glued.

His stifled laughter broke free. It rolled out of him.

Still with the accent, she said, "Are you laughing at your Royal Majesty the Queen?"

"No, Your Highness." Snort, chuckle, snort.

"The Royal Dog?" she asked, aghast.

"I wasn't laughing, Your Highness. Coughing. See?" He demonstrated a cough, but it didn't work. It turned into a fit of laughter that he had no hope of stopping.

And then she was laughing, too, and the dog got all excited and raced around them, binding them up with the leash.

Somehow, they were pressed together again, and instead of feeling all wrong, a pretense that had gone too far, it felt all right.

She gazed up at him, and he looked down at her. The world—even the dog—faded away. So did the laughter.

CHAPTER EIGHT

HE'S GOING TO kiss me, Krissy thought, dazed by Jonas's closeness, his scent, the glory of his hard, muscular frame pressed against the softness of her curves.

She closed her eyes; she leaned into him. She might have even puckered her lips. Anticipation tingled along every nerve ending. Her heart was beating way too fast. And then...

Nothing happened.

It reminded her, exactly, of his hesitation to accept her offer to be his fake mate the other night in his car. It reminded her how quickly she could be hurt by Jonas when she expected one thing and then another happened. Or didn't happen, as the case might be.

Krissy did what she should have done in the first place. She opened her eyes, sandwiched her hands up between them and pushed. It opened the smallest gap, enabling her to reach down to loosen the leash that was holding them together.

Unfortunately, that required much squirming. The dog, held tight by the wound up leash, cocked his head and looked at them with frank adoration but no cooperation. There was more shared laughter, though now it had the faintest edge to it.

Awareness.

By the time she'd extricated them, Krissy was flushing madly: over the shared merriment and thwarted kiss and the rather intimate contact.

She realized this was exactly what the dog sensed in her all along: a certain reluctance to take control, a certain timidity to take on life on life's terms.

She was with an attractive man. He'd almost kissed her, but then pulled back. She was going to refuse to be a shrinking violet about it.

No! Instead, she would show Jonas what he had missed, what he had said no to. She would make him regret pulling away.

With new determination, Krissy sorted the dog. Once he was sitting at her side, she took a deep breath. She snapped the leash to get the dog's attention, she set her feet.

Krissy didn't want to be an actress or a model. She had never even wanted to be the queen!

This was an opportunity to find her authentic strength in role models she admired.

"I am," she said firmly, "an Olympic medalist going to the podium!"

She strode forward, radiating confidence, strength, victory. She could feel the relief in Chance. He got it instantly, he stepped it up, he aligned perfectly with her.

"What sport?" Jonas asked.

Krissy had never played a sport in her life.

"A woman warrior," she cried. And she reached up with her free hand and grabbed the elastic that held her hair back. She didn't slide it off, she broke it. Her hair fell free, and she gave it a shake.

"That's it!" Jonas said, his voice low and approving. "That's it exactly!"

But she already knew she had found the sweet spot

of confidence she had been searching—maybe all of her life—for. Krissy could feel it in the leash, in the dog's attentiveness to her, in Jonas's attentiveness. She could feel the shift in herself, and she reveled in it.

Thinking of the power and the confidence with which Jonas drove his car, she revved into the next gear. She was the shield maiden going into battle. She was Boudicca, she was Joan of Arc. She stepped out, not with fear. Not with anticipation. Not with awareness of all the bad things that waited to befall her.

With glory! With confidence. With excitement for all the victories that awaited her.

The dog got it. Completely And so did Jonas. Completely.

Krissy felt as if she had stepped out of a shadow she was not even aware she had been standing in. She was enjoying playing the part, and it was wonderful to feel a sense of coming into some part of herself.

That was powerful.

And confident.

And amazing.

And dangerous.

She laughed out loud as she immersed herself in the discovery of her own confidence. She was aware of Jonas looking at her, his smile faintly tinged with trepidation. She was not the same woman who had meekly backed away from his rejection of that kiss a few minutes ago.

They came to a section of the trail where dogs were allowed off leash. Which was ironic, because Krissy was wondering exactly what he had unleashed within her when he had guided her to finding her confidence.

"I don't think he's ready for that," Jonas said.

But she suspected maybe Jonas wasn't ready for things to be completely unleashed, either.

Was she?

"There is a dog park just a little farther up the trail."

"Perfect." He was looking at her as if he wasn't thinking about the dog park, at all.

And somehow that was exactly how it felt. As if this startling, beautiful, electrifying day of discovery was absolutely perfect.

They had the fenced dog park entirely to themselves. They played a game that Jonas said would help Chance learn to come when he was called.

Jonas held the leash, and Krissy went and hid in a small grove of trees. Then she called the dog, and Jonas unclipped the leash. Chance barreled toward her hiding place, ecstatic when he found her, wriggling and ducking and lolling his tongue. But he didn't even attempt to jump on her. Then they reversed it, Jonas hiding and Krissy holding the leash. Chance's joy in the game was utterly contagious. Or maybe it was just a joyous kind of day.

But an hour later, they all lay on the grass, panting, tired, happy. Krissy and Jonas lay shoulder to shoulder.

Like the oldest of friends. Or like lovers. Like any of the young couples out enjoying the park today.

"I think the last time I laughed this hard was at last year's family reunion," Jonas said. "There's a big water fight every year. No restrictions on weapons, just as long as they get you wet. My sister, Theresa, had found this gun that shot water balloons. She was an absolute menace. Mike and I ganged up on her to take it away, and then Simon and Garfunkel—that's what I call the monster nephews—plus their two dogs, were in there, and we were all on the ground, and the rest of the family ganged up on us, until we were wallowing in a mud bog. Those kids and dogs were so dirty, the whites of their eyes were shining."

Krissy tilted her head to look at Jonas. He was smiling slightly at the memory, looking up at the sky, the utter blueness of it reflected in the deep blue of his eyes. Chance had his big head resting possessively on the flat plane of Jonas's stomach, a pool of contented drool darkening a patch of the shirt to black. Jonas toyed with the remnants of that torn ear.

She both liked the way he talked about his family with such warmth and affection, and hated the niggling sense of longing it caused in her.

"Or maybe it was at Gar's birthday that I laughed like this. He was turning four. Simon is six. Gar got a cake shaped like Fuzzy Peter—that's a cartoon character, not something obscene—and then he wouldn't let anyone eat it. He was standing guard over that cake, and Simon sneaked in and grabbed a handful from behind, and then I don't exactly know what happened, but the cake fight was on. Thank goodness we were outside."

His laughter was rich and warm at the memory. That feeling of longing in Krissy intensified. What he was describing was like families she had seen in movies and read about in books, but, except for Aunt Jane, it was the very thing she had never had: connection.

She wanted to know more.

"For research purposes," she said, acting as if her interest in him was purely clinical, so she could play the role he'd assigned, "you really call your nephew Garfunkel? What's his real name?"

"I think it might be Daniel," Jonas said, pretending not to know. "The other one may be Henry. No, Harry."

She laughed, and she could tell that was his intent.

"Boring names to be sure," he continued. "I tried to tell Theresa we could have a family contest to name them, but she's a bit of a spoilsport that way. She seemed to think naming kids was a serious business."

"It is!" Krissy said sternly.

"Uh-huh," he teased her, unconvinced. "When's the last time you laughed like today, Krissy?"

She cast about for an answer. She couldn't find one, which she thought was thoroughly pathetic.

"I teach kindergarten," she said. "There's a laugh a day, for sure."

But his gaze on her seemed to be finding a deeper truth. "You said the other night your family wasn't fun. You said a war zone. I'm really sorry."

She did not want his pity! And yet, his gaze on her, steady, did not hold pity. Sympathy perhaps, definitely compassion. Why did she feel suddenly compelled to tell him the truth?

Maybe so his expectations of her at his family re-union wouldn't be too high.

"The only fun in my family was in the word dys-*fun*ctional." What had possessed her to say that? Did she think he would laugh? He didn't. The look in his eyes, the one that made her want to confide in him, deepened.

"My mother and father did not like each other. They got married because they had to. And the reason they had to was me, the unexpected pregnancy. It was a war zone. They divorced, finally, when I was in my teens, but in some ways that made things worse. I was sud-denly at the very centre of every single disagreement. It seemed I was the club they liked to hit each other with."

He sat up on his elbow. He looked down at her. He traced the line of her cheek with a gentle finger.

"Oh, Krissy," he said. "Oh, Krissy."

And for some reason, the way he said her name made her glad she had told him, instead of sorry.

It was a part of revealing who she really was, the masks coming off. But being totally authentic with another human being created a feeling of intimacy—of trust—that felt even deeper than if they had given in to the temptation to kiss. She was not quite sure she was ready for this.

"So there you have it," she said, trying for a breezy tone. "The reason I, personally, will never get married."

She brushed his finger away from her cheek as if it was a bothersome fly. She leaped to her feet. The dog reluctantly lifted its head from Jonas's lap and gazed at her.

"I had my aunt," she said firmly. "It might not have been the rowdy kind of fun you just described, but she was the one who saved me, and almost everything we did together was pure fun. She unlocked the secrets of New York for me—the Russian Tea Room, Broadway and, of course, Fifth Avenue."

Jonas looked unconvinced, somehow, that adult excursions with her aunt had replaced the joys of a boisterous family.

"Did you ever do kid things? Ride a bike, play in the mud?"

"Oh, uh, occasionally. I should probably get going," she said, flustered, hating it that he seemed to be able to see her deepest longing. "Home. I have things to do."

Jonas sat up lazily, then stood, brushing grass from his slacks. His hair was slightly rumpled, as if he'd had a nap. In such a self-contained man, the mussy hair was adorable.

But then adorable went out the window as he turned his back to her. "Did I get it all?"

She was in bad enough shape without being asked to inspect the seat of his pants. "Yes," she said, her voice a squeak.

"What kind of things do you have to do?" Jonas asked, turning back to her. She was pretty sure he noticed the blush.

He was going to find out the truth! She played it safe. She was boring! But wasn't that part of what today had ended up being about? Revealing truth?

"I'm doing a spring art project with the kids on Monday. It involves some prep."

"What is it?"

"I'm making them into a garden: each of them will be a flower, with a big cutout that they put their face through. They'll sing a song at assembly next week."

He grinned. "I hope there will be a video."

"And I have to get Aunt Jane's affairs sorted out. I've been procrastinating. I have to get back into her office and box things up. I've given notice already, so I have to get out of there."

He nodded. "Okay. I get it."

She thought of his car and the way he dressed. She didn't know, really, anything about him yet. But he looked like he would be at least as busy as she was and probably more so.

"We'll walk back. I just thought ice cream was on the agenda." He said it hopefully, and it was his hopefulness that did her in.

She had revealed so much of her authentic self to him: some strengths, that inner warrior coming out, and some weaknesses, the childhood on a battlefield that didn't include any water balloons.

And he still wanted to spend time with her? Still, he was willing to put his busy life on hold for more time together?

Something sighed within Krissy. A sigh of pure surrender.

"There's always time for ice cream," she decided, and she was rewarded with his smile, a smile that a person could become utterly addicted to—a smile that could make every other activity and responsibility seem dull and uninteresting—before they even knew what had happened.

Jonas wasn't sure why he had insisted on the ice cream. He was already on sensory overload, so aware of Krissy that his nerves were singing with it.

For one insane moment, wrapped up in the dog's leash, pressed into the soft, womanly curves of her, he had found the temptation of her lips nearly irresistible. Somehow—maybe the warning bell in his brain screaming complications—he had managed, but only barely, not to accept the invitation of her lips.

If the dog had wrapped them in his leash after she had declared she was a warrior and let loose her hair, they'd probably be under a shrub somewhere acting like teenagers.

He should have realized, right then, this was a bad idea. That things were not going to go according to his plan.

His plan? Which was what?

Something utterly trivial like pretending to his sister and brother-in-law that Krissy and he were engaged so he could keep his car. That original mission seemed to be wavering like a mirage on a hot desert day.

Now, even the complication of the near kiss was

being blurred with an even stronger desire: to see that playful light come on in her, to see her throw back her head and laugh.

Astonishingly, since he considered himself, unapologetically, the most self-centered of people, he realized it was no longer all about *getting* what he wanted—his car, the satisfaction of winning a bet—but about *giving* Krissy something.

A well-behaved dog. A carefree day. Laughter.

Even if buried in that altruism was an ember of danger that could light his whole world on fire.

They walked down the main street of Sunshine Cove. It was the perfect backdrop for a perfect day: lovely little storefronts under colorful awnings, couples and families, old people and singles made their way in and out of antique stores and bookshops and bakeries. It wasn't summer, but there was enough warmth in the air that the day felt summery and light filled.

Jonas realized the fragrance thick in the air from those abundant flower baskets that hung everywhere was so similar to Krissy's.

"He's never this good," she said to Jonas in that whisper he was beginning to recognize as her keeping a secret from Chance.

"He's tired. You want a good dog? Keep him played out."

"I'm just not sure I have the time."

"Invest three dollars in a Frisbee. That will do the trick."

They arrived at Moo-Moo's. It was under a pink-and-white-striped awning, white painted wrought-iron tables and spindly chairs on the sidewalk patio outside the front door. Jonas realized he had not been here in years, not even with his nephews. It occurred to him he avoided the places where the memories were the sharpest, and that this was one of them.

"I'll stay outside with the dog if you want to go in and order," he said, realizing this had been a mistake. He did not want to go in there. He reached for his wallet.

"I'll get it," she said.

"No, this is my deal." A reminder to them both, hopefully, that this was, in the end, a business arrangement, an understanding between two people.

She looked as if she planned to argue, but then, as he passed her some money, didn't.

"What would you like?"

"Surprise me," he said, realizing handling that small challenge might reveal even more of the secret side of Krissy to him.

Chance flopped down under the table, settling on his feet.

"Hey, buddy, you're cutting off circulation," he told the dog, who ignored him.

Jonas watched Krissy through the window. Studying the menu, looking at the display cases. It was silly, but he couldn't wait to see what she chose.

A few moments later she came out of the ice cream store, laden with a tray. He was not sure why he was so disappointed. It was a small thing. Krissy had decided not to surprise him, at all.

CHAPTER NINE

ON THE TRAY Krissy was balancing was her strawberry shake, served in the old-fashioned way that made Moo-Moo's such a sought-after summer destination. The shake came in a tall thick frosted glass, and extra milkshake that couldn't be fitted into the glass came in the steel mixing container with it.

Jonas saw that for him, she had chosen the Triple Chocolate Volcano Sundae.

And, of course, she had a treat for Chance.

Still, watching her come toward him with that tray, Jonas realized that sundae was one of the reasons he avoided this place.

Krissy carefully set the tray on the table. She gave Chance his treat: a little plop of doggie-friendly ice cream that Chance inhaled in one gulp.

And then came the surprise: she unloaded the rest of the tray, putting the strawberry milkshake in front of him. She took the sundae, and then slid into the seat across from him.

She saluted him with the spoon. "Let's get to know each other," she said.

She dug into that sundae with approximately the same enthusiasm that Chance had used for his treat.

"This is so good."

The memory came, sharper.

His silence made her look up. "Is something wrong?" Krissy asked him.

Jonas could say no. And he should say no. And yet, he thought of her sharing her confidences with him.

He was shocked how much he wanted to tell her this, as if it was a burden he had carried, long and alone, and he needed to set it down.

He took a tentative sip of the milkshake. He could see why Krissy loved it so. It was rich and creamy, and the taste of strawberries was as magical and uncomplicated as a summer afternoon.

"Are you okay?" she asked again. She set down her spoon.

"Just memories," he said.

"But good ones, right?"

He lifted a shoulder. "Bittersweet, I guess. There was never much money growing up. The resort and the dogs were a living for our family, but just. The heyday of the kind of resort they showed in *Dirty Dancing* was well over. So we didn't get much in the way of extras. It was a big treat to come here. A once a year event, usually as our season was winding down.

"I never realized until I was in my teens that my Mom always ordered the cheapest thing on the menu.

"So I brought her here the Mother's Day that I was sixteen. My driver's license was pretty freshly minted in my pocket. I didn't let her order. I bought her that."

He nodded toward the mountain of whipped cream and chocolate sauce and ice cream melting in front of Krissy.

"She tried to smile, but she got these tears in her eyes. I guess there's a day when a mother realizes maybe, just maybe, her kids are going to turn out all right. She was just so pleased. She ate every bite.

"Looking back, it seems so small. And too late. Why didn't I see sooner how much she gave and how little she asked in return?

"Her and my dad died in the winter of that year. A car accident on a slippery road. People say funny things after a tragedy like that. Things like what a blessing that they went together. They loved each other so much."

For a moment, he could not trust himself to speak. "But me and Theresa loved them that much, too. Theresa managed to turn everything they gave us into a gift. She has a life much like the one we experienced as children."

"But you never got over it."

Her words were so quiet.

"No," he admitted, "never. I told myself for the longest time that becoming responsible for Theresa so young made me allergic to being responsible for another person."

"But that isn't it, is it?"

It was unnerving that she got him so completely.

"You love so deeply," she said softly. "So deeply."

And Jonas knew that was it exactly. He had experienced the kind of pain that came from losing someone you loved that much. "I'm not sure I could survive another loss like that."

He glanced up at her. Her eyes were dark and wide, filled with an ache for him that was soothing rather than embarrassing, that made him glad he had confided in her, rather than regretful. Of course, because of her close relationship with her aunt, she would understand like few others would.

After a long time, Krissy nodded. "So here we are," she said. "A match made in heaven. Two people who have experienced the terrible pain of love in very different ways, but with the same result. Sworn off it. Forever."

"Forever," he agreed.

She took a bite of her sundae. For someone sworn off love, he felt inordinately aware of her lips.

He took a sip of his shake. For someone sworn off love, she seemed inordinately focused on his mouth.

She looked away first. They finished their ice cream treats in silence, with eyes skittering everywhere but on each other.

On the walk home, it occurred to him the excursion had been a success only in one area. Chance was coming along nicely.

But really, if the goal was convincing Theresa and Mike this thing was real, there were other issues they should have tackled.

They stopped outside of her cottage.

"Are you still game for this?" he asked her.

"More than ever," Krissy said firmly, as if sharing confidences had strengthened the agreement rather than sending it galloping off in unexpected directions.

"We need to start filling in some blanks," he said, meaning they needed to get it back on track. And that didn't mean sharing vulnerabilities. They needed to stick to the facts!

"How about if I pick you up for dinner Friday night?" he suggested.

"Maybe we could meet in New York? I only work half a day on Fridays, and I was going to go finish up some things at my aunt's office."

"That's perfect. I have a great place in mind."

* * *

Krissy considered that. Jonas would know all the great places. Of course he would. Did she even have the right dress for a great place in New York? Was she really already worried about that? Yes!

"I'll pick you up from your aunt's office around six. Bring a list of questions."

"What kind of questions?" she asked.

"You know. Filling-in-the-blanks kind of questions. Knowing-a-person kind of questions. Who was your best friend growing up? What was your dog's name? What was your favorite subject in high school? That kind of thing."

"Okay," she said, but the funny thing was she felt like she already knew quite a lot about Jonas without having any of those kinds of questions answered. He was a man who would take hours out of his life to drive someone home on a dark night. He was a man who could make a dog mind, firm and gentle by turns. He was a man who had suffered horribly at the hands of fate, and—despite what he said—he had not allowed it to make him hard or bitter.

"You have a bit of chocolate, right…" He touched her lip.

They stood staring at each other for a long time. Long enough that Krissy was well aware that knowing a person had nothing to do with who their best friend was growing up!

He jerked his hand away from her lip, which was a good thing, because she had nearly nibbled it.

It wasn't until he had driven away that Krissy realized he was right. How very little she knew about Jonas. She hadn't even thought to ask him what he did for a living! This fact-finding dinner was a great idea. Essential.

She touched her lip. Good grief! Was it? A woman could redefine what she thought essential was around a man like that!

Late Friday afternoon, Krissy stood in the middle of her aunt's office. She glanced at the clock. It was time to get ready for Jonas. She took one last look around the office.

Finally, all the phone calls had been made, all the files had been closed, all the boxes had been packed. A mover would come, pick everything up and schedule a delivery for a later date when they could combine several deliveries to Sunshine Cove into one. Thankfully, there was a basement under the cottage where she could store this stuff when it finally arrived.

It should have been a relief to finally have this looked after, all these loose ends tied up. Despite the fact June was a busy month for her, with school also winding up, she was ahead of the end-of-the-month deadline for clearing her aunt's office.

She had given notice to the landlord. But instead of feeling relieved, Krissy felt oddly deflated as it hit her she would never come to this office again.

Match Made in Heaven was no more. Her aunt's life mission—to bring lasting happiness through the discovery of love—was no more.

Krissy slipped into the small washroom. Hanging on the back of the door was the perfect little black dress.

She shucked her dusty work clothes and slid the dress over her head, and added a hint of makeup, and finally a simple pair of black pumps and a strand of pearls.

She could feel her eyes misting with tears as she snapped on the pearls her aunt had also given her. She remembered the particular excursion where she had gotten this dress. When Krissy had put it on, they had both known it was special, a kind of a once-in-a-lifetime dress that was so "go anywhere" flattering and so feminine—and breathtakingly expensive.

Aunt Jane, who loved shopping, and loved clothes, had insisted on buying it. She had bought the strand of pearls the same day.

No more Match Made in Heaven, no more shopping with her aunt. So many endings. Krissy burst into tears just as a knock came at the back door. Her eyes flew to her watch. She hadn't even done anything with her hair, yet. Not that it mattered. Her makeup was now a mess.

She dabbed at her eyes, and the piece of tissue came away black. The knock came again.

Obviously, everything had changed. She went and opened the back door a crack.

"I came to the back," Jonas said. "I didn't want to set off the alarm."

"I think we should postpone," she said. "I'm not feeling up to it.

"What's wrong?"

"I can't go. I'm sorry. I just—"

He gently shoved the door open and came inside. He gazed down at her. "Krissy?"

"It's over," she wailed. "Match Made in Heaven. Shopping with my aunt."

"I'm sorry," he said.

"Aunt Jane bought me this dress. I said it was silly. I taught kindergarten. I needed wash-and-wear. I need comfortable, durable clothes that can go in the laundry. I might have even mentioned the forbidden polyester word.

"When I tried on this dress, she told me I looked like Audrey Hepburn in *Breakfast at Tiffany's*. She said it didn't matter if I taught kindergarten. I needed to know what the perfect dress felt like."

He took her shoulders and looked at her gravely. "You do," he said. "You look like Audrey Hepburn in *Breakfast at Tiffany's.*"

"You probably don't even know who Audrey Hepburn is," she sniffed.

"My mom was a huge fan."

"We just loved each other so much," Krissy said. "I didn't like shopping, but with her, I just basked in her enjoyment of it. Anyway, now I'm a mess. I can't wear this dress without feeling heartbroken, so our date is off."

"Okay," he said soothingly.

"Besides, I look like a raccoon."

"I'll call the restaurant and cancel our reservation."

"I do look like a raccoon, don't I?"

Jonas stepped in close to her. He took his thumb and gently wiped mascara from beneath her eye. It was a useless effort, because the tears began to slide again.

He sighed, and his arms wrapped around her. His scent, so rich, so masculine, somehow so familiar, wrapped around her. It felt like a homecoming.

But that's what she had to remember. Home was the biggest illusion of all. The only thing she'd ever had that was even close to it was the love of her aunt, and now that was gone, too.

Krissy pushed away from him reluctantly. "You should cancel that reservation."

He nodded and took his phone from his pocket. He scrolled through and touched a button. She could hear the phone ringing on the other end.

"Why don't we get takeout?" he said. "We'll take it to the park. Oh, hi. I had a reservation. I have to—"

He looked at her. He smiled, that kind of hopeful smile that he had used when he wanted ice cream.

Note to self: Jonas Boyden, pretty much irresistible at any time, but when he gave you the charming smile? Hopeless.

She nodded.

"—change it to a takeout order. Surprise me. Dinner for two. Allergies?"

He looked over at her. She shook her head.

"No allergies. I need plates and cutlery, too. Pull out all stops," he said. "I'm trying to impress a girl who looks exactly like Audrey Hepburn." He paused. "That's no object."

He disconnected and looked at the phone, pleased. "There's an item off my list already."

"List?"

"The get-to-know-each-other list? Allergies. None."

"Well, penicillin, but they hardly ever add that to food."

Despite her deliberate effort to keep her tone light, his mentioning the list was a reminder what this was really about. Getting to know each other for fake mate purposes. She hadn't expected it to be so much like a doctor's appointment. She had thought it might be more personal.

"I'll just go change," she said. It wasn't 100 percent social. She should have remembered that when she put on this dress in the first place. It was like a job interview, only in reverse, since she already had the job.

This was a dress a woman wore when she wanted to get to know someone in a different way. A way that had nothing to do with allergies!

"Don't you dare."

She was going to tell him it was no more practical

to wear this dress on a picnic than it would be to teach kindergarten.

But somehow the words never came out of her mouth. It wasn't just the look on his face, either, though his look made it clear this wasn't 100 percent like an interview for him, either, even if that was what he wanted it to be.

It was as if her aunt was giving her yet another gift: not just the dress, but an ability to be open to life's surprises.

Jonas wasn't dressed for a picnic, either, but for dinner at one of New York's finest restaurants. He looked completely at home in a dark charcoal suit and knife-pressed narrow slacks. The brilliant shirt looked—and had felt—like silk. The tie was also dark charcoal, with a raised pattern of darker swirls on it. The pocket square was a perfect, slender rectangle of white.

"I'll just go wash my face," Krissy said.

An hour later, Jonas had purchased a blanket and they had picked up the food from a restaurant that Krissy recognized as a New York hot spot, where it was nearly impossible to get a reservation. They made their way into Central Park.

He set out the blanket on the gentle slope of Cherry Hill, overlooking Bow Bridge. A confetti of finished pink petals drifted on the ground like snow.

Krissy sat down, thinking she would feel awkward, but no, she tucked her legs to one side and watched as Jonas got rid of the jacket, then the tie, tossing them casually on the blanket and then sitting down, stretching his legs out in front of him.

He began to take items out of the basket. She understood suddenly exactly what he had meant when he'd said, *"That's no object."*

Money, obviously.

"Did they give you *real* plates?"

"So it appears. And, look, *real* wineglasses."

"We're not allowed to drink alcohol in Central Park!"

"Oh, well, they put in a bottle of wine." He looked at it. "A very good bottle, too. And glasses, so we'll live dangerously this once."

"Somehow, I don't think living dangerously is a one-off for you."

For some reason, that made her look at his lips. And suddenly living dangerously felt altogether too enticing!

CHAPTER TEN

"ME LIVING DANGEROUSLY?" Jonas wagged his eyebrows at her. "It seems to me it's you who has nearly gotten us arrested before, not me."

"How do you figure that? It wasn't me knocking on the door in the middle of the night."

"It wasn't exactly the middle of the night. And I did have an appointment."

Krissy enjoyed this teasing, the back-and-forth banter, more than she should have. The setting was just so lovely, the evening light perfect, warmth in the air. A young couple went by in a rowboat, him putting his muscle into moving the boat, her trailing her hand in the water. She splashed him, and their laughter drifted up the hill.

"Remember you asked me if I'd ever done kid things?" she asked him. "How funny we would end up here today. My aunt brought me here once. We rented one of the rowboats. I think that was exactly her intention, to do a 'kid' activity with me."

"And how was it?"

Krissy laughed. "You would have to know my aunt better than you did to know how funny it was. She had on high heels and a Chanel suit. She loved crazy hats and she had on this huge sunbonnet. She tried to row the boat, and she kept going in circles. So then we changed places and nearly capsized the boat. The wind came up and took her hat off, and we chased it all over the reservoir. She nearly fell in half a dozen times reaching to get the hat. Every time her fingers would touch it, it would drift away. I feel like I can hear her laughing now. Even though the hat was ruined by the time we did retrieve it, and we were both sunburned and exhausted, she said it was the best day ever."

"What a great memory," he said warmly.

Jonas finished unpacking the bag: beautiful white cardboard boxes came out, one by one, each with a handwritten label. *Baked Brie with Pecans. Mixed Green Salad with Dates and Goat Cheese. Smoked Crab with Herbed Crème Fraîche. Assorted Dessert.* With a sigh of surrender, Krissy realized it was exactly the kind of meal one would eat in this kind of dress.

He handed her a plate and an appetizer, then put wine in one of the tall, long-stemmed glasses.

"Cheers," he said, and lifted his glass to her.

Somehow, as their glasses clinked and their eyes met over the rims, she knew her aunt would approve of her christening the dress like this.

"Here's to getting to know each other," he said, reminding her that there was a mission, after all. He pulled a list out of his wallet, carefully unfolded it and set it down on the blanket. He took a pen out of his breast pocket and wrote something down.

"What did you write?"

"Knows her way around a rowboat," he said, and the laughter leaped up between them, easy and comfortable.

Krissy took a bite of the Brie. It was incredible.

"I don't even know what you do for a living," she

said. "I mean aside from the fact it involves lawyers and owning all the hotels on the Monopoly board."

Jonas laughed. "I own a company called Last Resort. Basically, I buy properties that are run-down or struggling or both, bring them up to standard, put an operational plan in place, run them until they're making money again and then flip them."

"That's an interesting business."

"I was born for it. I mentioned to you our family resort was pretty hand-to-mouth. When my parents died, there was an insurance policy. I took a chance that I could turn it around. I looked around at all the failing resorts in the Catskills and tried to figure out what to do differently. What would make people come back for that kind of vacation?

"I started researching to see what people wanted when they were looking for a place to have a vacation.

"The hardest issue for them to resolve seemed to be pets. People wanted to holiday with Rover, and resorts did not want pets. And so we became the first pet-friendly resort in our area. I brought the cabins up to a new standard, including dog bath stations outside each one. That first time, I hired Mike, and we did all the work ourselves. And then Theresa and I worked on dog-focused programs like weeklong obedience immersion."

"I'd take that!" Krissy said.

"Exactly. We found a niche people wanted. We made our motto Dog-Gone Fun. My sister loved it—loves it—and was content with it, but I was bored within a year. About the same time Theresa had produced the first little monster. I noticed troubling changes in her. One day, she said to me, *'I always thought I'd be a yummy mommy.'* She went on to say she felt fat and frumpy and like she always had some mystery smudge on the front of her blouse. She said she had days when she didn't know whether to eat lunch or have a shower. Sometimes Mike came home from work, and she realized she hadn't even combed her hair. The resort next door to ours had been boarded up for years, so I went and took a look. I was thinking a health and wellness of some sort, but after talking to my sister, I wanted to target her demographic. So I picked young moms. I revamped the whole place so it had a very spa-like aesthetic. We developed hour, day and weeklong retreats that focused on delicious food, quiet spaces, learning yoga or meditation or music or art. A mom could have a facial or a massage or a long walk or a soak. And then Theresa figured out the thing that really sold it: child care. Moms might not like the day in, day out drudgery of their kids, but they aren't going to leave them for any length of time, either. We called it Yummy Mommy."

"I've heard of that!" In fact, Krissy's coworker, fifth grade teacher Martha Montrose, went every year.

"I sold the majority of the ownership a few months in. I realized my strength was in the concept, but the operational side bored me. And then I went on to the next one. I keep a percentage, I move on. I think I'm over a hundred properties in right now."

"So you do own all the hotels on the game board!"

He laughed. "Working on it."

"And you have no formal training in any of this? No university? No degree?"

"No, I kind of plunged right into the working world and all these massive projects when I was eighteen and never looked back."

"You know what I like the best? That it's about your family. The first one about saving your family business, and then the second one was about seeing a need in your sister. It's about love for you, isn't it?"

He cleared his throat uncomfortably. "Love and business don't mix."

"I think you're amazing." She blushed. "I mean, that's amazing."

Jonas laughed, obviously trying to keep it light. "That's exactly what we want—my fiancée to think I'm amazing. In fact—" he took his phone out of his pocket "—I'm going to take a picture of you looking amazed at me."

"Just a sec." She picked up her wineglass. "Here's to the amazing Jonas." Just as he took the picture she crossed her eyes and stuck out her tongue. "Post that on Instagram."

"I actually don't use social media," he said, still holding up his phone. As soon as she uncrossed her eyes and tucked her tongue back in her mouth, he took another picture. "The company does, and I have a specialist who puts together posts, but I don't have any personal accounts. I don't get the concept of living your life as if it's an open book, seeing every event as a photo op to be posted instead of something just to be enjoyed. This is a great pic."

He turned his phone to her and showed her both photos. The one was quite hilarious, but the other one had a loveliness to it she found startling. She had scrubbed all her makeup off and had never gotten around to doing anything with her hair. Still, there was something about the photo she really liked. There was an expression on her face she didn't see often.

She looked relaxed. Happy. With a faint undertone of hopefulness. Or maybe it was wistfulness.

"Do you do social media?" Jonas asked her. "You want a copy of it?"

She did want a copy of whatever he had captured that she usually did not see in herself, though in all fairness, she did not see many pictures of herself.

"No, send it to my phone. I don't do social media, either. Mostly because of the teaching thing. Even though some teachers use it with a false name, I just don't want my kids—or their parents—snooping around in my life."

"We have something in common!" he crowed. He picked up his crumpled list off the blanket and pretended to write on it. "No social media. The fact that I don't even have your phone number yet shows this is quite an old-fashioned kind of romance. My sister will approve."

It was a much-needed reminder that this old-fashioned romance was really not a romance at all—a hard thing to keep in mind with the delicious food and the wine, and the growing ease of being with him. A hard thing to keep in mind when he talked about his sister.

It was the same as when he had talked about his mom.

He might protest; he might say otherwise, but Jonas was the rarest of things: a decent guy. She could feel herself falling just a little bit in love with him.

A little bit in love with him? She should watch the wine! He seemed to be topping her glass up more than his own. In fact, he might still be sipping his first one.

"I think I'll send her this picture, kind of a little fore-shadowing of what's to come."

"Foreshadowing," she said wryly. "A literary term. Do you like to read, then?"

"Love it. Nothing literary, though. Espionage, suspense."

"Me, too. Murder and mayhem."

Just like that, it was so easy. The food and the wine disappeared as they talked about favorite books and favorite movies, favorite things they had done and planned to do. They talked about childhood friends and pets, naturally, no lists involved.

Jonas, now stretched out, leaning on his side on one elbow, finally flicked open the lid on the dessert box.

She peered in. "Wow."

"They're all individually labeled. Look at this one." He held up a fragile delicacy for her to look at.

She leaned in closer and read the lovely miniature sign that had been planted in the dessert on a toothpick. "Buttermilk panna cotta with raspberry and rose."

"There's only one of each," he said. He teased her by opening his mouth as if he was going to gobble up the whole thing.

She grabbed his wrist, and they pretended to struggle.

"One of the first things I teach in kindergarten is the value of sharing," she said, and then she leaned in, and bit half the dessert right out of his hand. There was a spot of the glaze on the mound below his pointer finger. She blamed what happened next on the wine.

Jonas felt Krissy's lips touch his hand. And then he felt just the faintest flick of her tongue. The intensity of it felt like a burn. Like a brand.

He snatched his hand away and managed to avoid looking at it to see if there was a mark. He popped the rest of the treat in his mouth. She had closed her eyes and was rolling the confection over her tongue. A little sigh of pure pleasure escaped her as she swallowed.

Awareness of her burned in him, more scorching than the brand of her tongue.

She opened her eyes and gazed at him with sudden, unveiled hunger that could not be satiated with dessert.

The sensual tension leaping between them was at least as delightful and at least as delicious as the dessert selection. He took another confection from the box and held it out to her, hoping for a barrier, knowing it was an invitation.

Which she accepted. She nibbled. Her breath tickled his hand. She had icing sugar on her lip.

He had, truth be told, done quite a bit of dating in his day.

Bimbos, Krissy's aunt had proclaimed scornfully.

But still bimbos who knew their way around the art of pleasing a man. And yet, there was something about this—sitting on a blanket on a warm evening with flower petals floating around them—that was infinitely more powerful than just about anything he had ever experienced.

His mouth was dry. His heart was pounding. She reached out with the tip of her tongue and flicked that speck of icing sugar away from her lip. It scorched him nearly as badly as when she had flicked her tongue to his hand.

Her lips were moist and plump. He wanted to taste her. He wanted to do exactly the same thing he had done when there had been chocolate on her lip the other afternoon.

She blinked at him. Her lips parted faintly. The desire that had sprung up over dessert was mutual. Really, this particular spring storm had been coming between them since the first time they had touched, and it had been building like thunderclouds on the horizon.

Jonas leaned in closer yet to Krissy. One part of his

brain tried to remind him that this arrangement between them was going to be complicated enough.

But another part assured him that he couldn't very well fake an engagement without any physical contact.

Better to do it now, his rational mind whispered, in somewhat controlled circumstances. It wouldn't do to be taken totally by surprise by kissing her for the first time in front of Theresa or Mike.

It was like a practice run—that was all.

But when Jonas's lips touched Krissy's, there was nothing about it that was controlled, nothing about it that felt like a practice run, absolutely nothing about it that was for the benefit of convincing his sister of something at some faraway future date.

In fact, those things were wiped from his mind. Completely. Except the part about it being a total surprise.

Even though he had seen hints of passion sparking in her eyes, nothing could have prepared him for this part of her.

Krissy tasted of wine. And of the desserts they had just eaten. But she also tasted of mystery and the unknown, of all that was feminine and of the secret powers of the universe. She was *Breakfast at Tiffany's* but she was also a fresh mountain morning with mist rising off a lake. She was a perfect bouquet of roses and she was a wildflower meadow. She was innocence, and she was seduction.

She was a model, an actress, a queen. She was an Olympian and a warrior. She was as complex and multifaceted as a diamond and as simple, as of the earth, as a fresh-turned shovel of soil. In her was that same ripe promise of being able to give life.

"Oh," she said softly, breaking the contact of their

lips, but staying close enough that she could taste him again in a heartbeat. Her eyes were wide and dazed on his face.

It occurred to him, that she might have consumed most of the wine. Which made this totally wrong, as if it wasn't totally wrong, anyway.

Jonas was glad they were in a park in such a public setting. Because if this had happened the other night outside her door, there was no telling where it would have led.

He got to his feet and stretched mightily before she could lean into him again. Before he leaned into her again. He began to gather up the picnic things from around her. "It's getting late. I'll take you home."

To that front door, where the options were going to be so much different.

He had an hour's drive, he told himself sternly, to gird his loins for the coming battle, to pull himself together. It was not as if he was a callow boy incapable of saying no to temptation.

She got up off the blanket. Her hair was wild and curly, and her dress was rumpled, as if they had done quite a bit more than share a kiss. She was stiff from sitting for so long. She stretched, hands way up over her head, dress riding high up the long delicate curve of her thigh.

"You don't have to take me home," she said. "You can just drop me at the train."

Uh-huh, like he was going to put her on a train looking like that.

She followed his gaze and smoothed her dress. "I could go back to my aunt's office and get changed."

"It's okay. I don't mind the drive."

"Should you be driving? How much have you had to drink?" she asked.

"Quite a bit less than you." In fact, he was not even sure he had finished an entire glass of wine. She, however, with those flushed cheeks and starry eyes, was demonstrating every sign of slight inebriation. Another reason not to put her on the train. She giggled, confirmation of how much less than her he had had.

"I'd like to see Chance, anyway," he said, heading further argument off at the pass.

She smiled at him as if he had declared they shared a beautiful child.

Something happened to Jonas that had never happened to him before. Not ever. He wondered what a child they made together would look like.

It was the most astonishing—and terrifying—thought he'd ever had.

Because here was the thing: Jonas Boyden was *not* a baby kind of guy. His nephews, in that baby stage, had been cute, but messy and demanding. He had watched Theresa's transformation—and Mike's to a lesser extent—from once-intelligent people, now given to discussing what a crayon that had passed through a digestive system looked like. It had been the start of Yummy Mommy but had killed any other parenting ambitions Jonas had, admittedly slight as those had been to begin with.

He made the mistake of glancing at Krissy again, and remembered what he had tasted on her lips: the ripe ability to give life.

He was suddenly so aware, looking at her, that it was what she needed, and probably what she desired, deep down in that secret place, a place protected by the barbwire fence of the hurts inflicted on her by her family.

But Jonas was willing to bet it was those hidden longings that had led her to teach kindergarten. It was those hidden longings that had made her so susceptible to Chance's debatable charm.

She *needed*.

She needed love and stability and something to care about, even as she denied needing those things.

Jonas was self-aware enough to know he was not the man to entrust with those kinds of needs.

And yet still, he now was tangled enough with her to want things for her. To want to change her mind about family, so that she could have what she secretly wanted and what she surely deserved.

A family of her own.

A good family.

Family the way it should be. That safe place. That solid place. That soft place to fall in a hard, hard world.

And there was nobody more qualified to show her what family really was than his own. So, as dangerous as this had become, Jonas felt more committed to getting her to that family reunion than ever. She could just never know it had become about so much more than keeping his car.

He had an hour, he told himself, to get this thing back on an even keel. To get things back on track.

He disposed of the rubbish and put the blanket over his arm. She hesitated for just a moment and then tossed her hair—the woman warrior—and took his hand in hers as if she owned it, as if their hands belonged together.

Such a simple thing, the intertwining of hands.

So why was it Jonas was no longer even sure where the track was, never mind how to get back on it?

CHAPTER ELEVEN

KRISSY FELL ASLEEP on the way home. She was horrified when she woke up as Jonas pulled his sleek car to a gliding halt in front of her house, aware there was a little pool of drool darkening her dress.

She was even more horrified when the memory of that kiss came back to her.

"Oh," she said. "I don't drink very much. It went straight to my head." She scrambled out of the car and headed down the walk.

The wine had made her forget the most important aspect of all this: *it wasn't real.* How could it not be real? Jonas's lips claiming hers had felt like one of the most real experiences of her entire life.

Which, she told herself firmly, spoke to a pathetic life.

She fumbled for her key. Jonas was behind her.

"I guess we shouldn't kiss anymore," she said, as brightly as she could.

"Really? I think it was good to get it over with. You know, before we have an audience. So we both know what to expect."

Get it over with? Know what to expect?

Well, no one should know better than her the value of a good experiment. Still, Krissy had obviously made a complete fool of herself.

"Well, good," she managed to say. "Lots accomplished tonight. I think we've gotten to know each other quite well enough."

"Do you?" he said.

She opened the door, and Chance bounded out, went right past her, his new Frisbee caught between his teeth. He sat in front of Jonas, his tail thumping the ground and his tongue lolling out, begging for just one toss.

"What a good dog," Jonas said.

The dog quivered ecstatically, but did not leap up.

Jonas got down on his haunches in front of the dog and did that massage thing to that huge marred face.

So every living thing felt the chemistry of this man, every living thing longed to be more to him, every living thing longed to feel the warmth of his approval.

"I think we could consider the dress rehearsal over," she said. "If you think of any other details about yourself that I need to know, text me. I'll do the same. And the family reunion. Do we have a plan? Drop by on it for a few hours? Announce our engagement? Look besotted with each other? Leave?"

"Ah, maybe not quite that easy. They'll expect us to stay the weekend."

The dog moaned his happiness and pushed his ear deeper into Jonas's hand. He nearly lost his grip on the Frisbee but managed to keep it from falling from his jaws. It was quite distracting.

"Together?" Did her voice have a faintly hysterical shriek to it?

"Well, yeah, but the cottages are quite large. No one will know if I take the couch. Except maybe you, eh, Chance?"

Aside from the dog, she would know. And after what happened tonight, it just seemed like a really lousy idea to share close quarters with him while they were pretending for his family.

That was her lesson from tonight. She sucked at pretending.

"Maybe we could tell them I have a belief system that precludes sharing accommodations with you?" she suggested.

He looked skeptical.

"I don't look like that kind of girl? I mean, it needn't be overt. I wouldn't carry a hymnal. Or start preaching at the campfire. A small gold cross around my neck. An occasional softly murmured, *praise be.*"

For somebody who sucked at pretending, Krissy realized she was getting into this.

Probably because it was making Jonas laugh. It was an absolute weakness to enjoy making him laugh so much. Which was why they had to call it quits on the dress rehearsals.

"I actually think," Jonas said, cocking his head at her and standing up, though his hand still rested on Chance's head, "you've shown yourself to be more the warrior type. Plus, uh, I'm not sure my sister would ever be convinced that I would go for a Goody Twoshoes kind of gal."

"I am a Goody Two-shoes kind of gal!"

"Not really," he said softly.

"Joan of Arc was a warrior *and* a girl of strong conviction. You better believe she wasn't sharing a cottage with her betrothed."

"Did she have a betrothed?" That gorgeous, sexy smile tickled his lips. "So you're thinking of going in costume, now?"

"Thinking of it," she said solemnly. "We could shop for a sword instead of a ring."

"Chain mail should do the trick if we end up sharing a cottage," he said thoughtfully, his smile deepening wickedly. So he knew sharing a cottage was going to be a challenge for both of them! But it seemed to be one he was anticipating with some delight.

She snapped her finger and thumb together. "Okay, forget Joan."

"As hard as that will be," he said, his tone solemn, but still smiling.

"This is better, and more practical. I'll get a call that there's been some sort of emergency. I'll have to leave."

"Maybe we should just play it by ear," he said. "Come prepared for the weekend, and if you're uncomfortable, we'll pull the plug. But I actually think you'll like it."

That was the problem. She liked playing Cinderella to his Prince Charming just a little too much.

"Chance will love it out there." He took his phone out of his pocket and took a picture of the dog mooning at him adoringly.

Argh! Get to her through the dog!

"And there's one other thing, since you mentioned it. We have to get you a ring."

"No sword?" Krissy said as lightly as she could to cover up what a perfectly awful outing shopping for a ring with him would be. She could unfortunately picture Jonas slipping a ring on her finger for this make-believe engagement.

"No sword," he said firmly.

"Oh, sure, then. A ring. Pick whatever you like."

He cocked his head at her. "You aren't a jewelry person at all, are you?"

"Not really."

"The ring should be sized."

How many rings had he bought for people? Was it his favorite bauble to give?

"I mean nothing would alert to a fake engagement like a ring falling off your finger. Do you want to just go pick one soon? Then it will be sized in time for the reunion?"

"I'll check my calendar," she said haughtily.

"Krissy…" He took a step toward her. She was aware how much she had to tilt her head to look at him. She was aware of the jolt right through to her heart when she looked at his lips, when she remembered the intoxicating, weak-to-the-bone sensation of taking them with her own.

"Yes?" Still with the haughty tone.

"You had fun, didn't you?"

The question took her off guard. For some reason, she thought of her aunt's Match Made in Heaven questionnaire.

What do you do for fun?

There was something ever so faintly imploring in Jonas's tone. He liked having fun. He wanted her to have fun.

Was it so evident she was not really a having-fun kind of person?

"Yes," she said, dropping the you-can't-touch-me veneer, and admitting the truth to herself. And to him. "Yes, I had fun."

She remembered her aunt's *Nothing naughty, please* instruction. Maybe that kiss had been the most fun of all, even though it was the playing-with-fire piece. Or maybe it was so much fun because it was thrilling, because it was playing with fire.

Even now, this simple thing, bantering back and forth with him, was fun.

"Can't we just do that?" he asked, his voice low, utterly charming in its beseeching tone. "Can't we just have fun?"

It was an enchantment. Wearing her wonderful dress to the impromptu picnic in Central Park had made her feel like she was Cinderella at the ball.

And Jonas was suggesting that the clock had not struck midnight, and that she didn't have to lose the glass slipper just yet.

He was right. It had been fun. The whole thing was just fun. She had been invited to take part in some good old family high jinks. Jonas wanted to win a bet, and he planned to have fun doing it. No one was going to get hurt. His deep-seated love for his sister was obvious.

Krissy was along for the ride. A roller-coaster ride, obviously, with lots of stomach dropping dips, long climbs of anticipation, tight, hang-on-for-dear-life twists and turns.

For once in her life, Krissy didn't have to be so cautious. Or know the final result. Or plan everything out to a conclusion that would bring her a sense of safety and security. She just had to buckle up and hang on for dear life, didn't she?

"Can you do that?" Jonas asked. "Can you just have some fun with it?"

Suddenly, she felt she wasn't going to be relegated to the stick-in-the-mud who needed carefree Jonas Boyden to bring her to life. She was not going to be the wilting daisy, waiting for him to water her! She was suddenly not prepared to buckle up and hang on for dear life. Let Jonas buckle up and hang on for dear life!

She leaned over and took the Frisbee from Chance.

Then she reached up and kissed Jonas full on the lips. Any Goody Two-shoes kind of girl that she had ever been, she now banished firmly.

"So," she called to Jonas, she and Chance already running, "let's do it, then. Let's have some fun."

Jonas hardly even hesitated. He ran after her onto the sprawling, carpet-like lawn of the mansion that neighbored hers. She kicked off her shoes.

"Aren't we trespassing?" he asked her, but he was already kicking off his shoes, too, and peeling off his socks.

"They're hardly ever home. I keep an eye on their place, so I'm pretty sure they'd be okay with it."

Chance begged her for the Frisbee. She threw it to Jonas. It was a terrible throw and he had to run really fast and jump really high to beat Chance to it. He grabbed it out of the air. Really, he looked so magnificent that she saw many bad throws in his future!

He threw it back to her. His throw, naturally, was perfect, and, to the distress of the dog, she snatched it out of the air. She deliberately threw quite wide of Jonas, hoping to see that wonderful demonstration of athleticism again, but this time it was Chance who grabbed it out of the air, ecstatic. They ran after him, and finally—if briefly—retrieved the toy. They played until they were breathless with laughter and exertion.

Finally, they could run no more. Krissy collapsed on the grass first, and Jonas came beside her. The dog was content to lay his big head across Jonas's belly and chew on his Frisbee as Jonas toyed with his ears.

In comfortable silence, they lay in the grass as night chased the last light from the summer sky and the stars winked on, one by one.

Jonas leaned up on one elbow and looked at her.

"You're not drunk, are you?"

"Not even a little bit," she whispered. Maybe she had been. She wasn't sure. But if she was drunk now, it wasn't on wine.

He traced the line of her face with his hand. "I can't stop myself," he said with wonder. He dropped his mouth over hers.

She could not stop herself, either. She welcomed him back to her. His mouth was now both familiar and dangerously unknown.

And then the automatic sprinklers came on.

Jonas leaped off her and held out his hand to her. Under a star-studded sky, they ran hand in hand through the sprinklers, gathering up their shoes, laughing joyously.

He never let go of her hand. They found themselves at her front door once again. Her dress was plastered to her. His slacks and shirt were plastered to him.

She reached up and touched the droplets on his soaked face and then took them from her fingertips with her lips. He moaned and dropped his head over hers.

She took the moistness of the sprinkler water from the fullness of his lips with her tongue, one droplet at a time. And then he did the same to her.

And then that was not enough. The kiss deepened exquisitely, tortuously. She could feel every muscle of his body tensing beneath the wetness of his clothing, which was not really a barrier at all. Their kiss deepened yet more. With discovery. With exploration. It was exhilaration. With pure ecstasy.

It was life itself that she tasted when she tasted so fully of him. The force of it rippled through him, surged, enveloped her. Some slumbering part of her stirred awake, sputtered to life and then roared like a fire being fed oxygen. She knew this powerful thing unleashed between them could not be put back to sleep again.

"Are you coming in?" Krissy murmured helplessly against the rough whiskers of his cheek. She wanted him. She wanted him as much as she had ever wanted anything—anybody—in her entire life. No, it was not want. It was need. She needed him with the hunger of someone who had been starving; she needed him like a wintered plant needed sunlight to live.

The kiss between them reflected all of that and became ferocious with the tender violence of their mutual need.

He reared back from her, his eyes taking in her face.

"I thought," he reminded her roughly, "you weren't that kind of girl."

"I'm not," she whispered, "but maybe I have always wanted to be. Maybe the right person never came along before."

And then he scooped her soaked body up in his arms, and she felt deliciously consumed by the scorching heat of him. He found the handle and nudged open the door with his foot.

The three of them. Krissy and Jonas tumbled through it, Chance bounding past them into the house.

CHAPTER TWELVE

JONAS WOKE UP the next morning with the dog laid out across the foot of the bed crushing his feet and Krissy nestled against him, her hair scattered, a sheet covering some, but not all, of her curves.

Her hand was resting on his chest—his naked chest. Something sweetly possessive about that.

Looking at her without her awareness, he took in the thick sweep of her lashes, the delicate roundness of cheek and shoulder, the beautiful bow and slight movement of her lips as the breath moved in and out of her.

Jonas felt the searing and shocking memory of what had unfolded, white-hot, between them last night.

But another feeling overlaid that one, and it was more powerful: he felt the most exquisite tenderness for this woman whose sensuous warmth was pressed against him. And he felt enormously protective of her.

They both knew she wasn't that kind of girl. What had she said last night?

That she had always wanted to be. She had proved that in spades: by turns playful, demanding, ferocious, giving, gentle.

It was the second part of her statement that a better man would have paid attention to.

That maybe the right person had never come along

before. Jonas was well aware he was no one's *right person*.

He waited for panic to set in, and the self-recrimination. What the hell had he done? He hadn't even been drunk. And neither had she.

But intoxicated, yes. On her laughter. On her wet body in that little black dress pressed against his, on the look in her eyes.

And oh, yes, on the taste of those incredible lips.

But, oddly, no sense of recrimination came.

Krissy stirred and then her eyes opened and then opened wider. She didn't look upset; she looked the very same way he felt.

Happy to be waking up beside him in the same way he felt happy to be waking up beside her, as if something that had been missing from their worlds—without their awareness—was suddenly there.

She came fully awake and was suddenly shy. He couldn't resist cupping her face in his hands and kissing her on the lips with all that tenderness he was feeling toward her.

The dog whined.

"I think he needs to go out," she whispered against Jonas's mouth. "Why don't you take him?" she suggested. "I'll make us some breakfast."

There were many things on his mind besides the dog and breakfast, but she was right to put the brakes on this thing unfolding between them before they were both so swept away with it that not one other rational decision could be made. Hopefully a walk would be a great way to get his head back on straight. He put on his crumpled clothes and went out the door. Instead of getting his head back on straight, Jonas found he couldn't wait to get back to her and couldn't stop thinking about her.

He stopped and plucked a flower from a garden that bordered the walk.

When he got back, Krissy was showered and dressed in a pair of yoga pants and an oversize T-shirt. She was very focused on making pancakes. He let the dog off the leash and went up behind her. He wrapped his arms around her and buried his face in the sweet curve of her neck.

When she turned into him, he gave her the flower.

"Oh," she said, blushing crimson, "how lovely!"

That blush reminded him of what he was dealing with. It had been a long, long time since he had been with a woman who blushed.

It was a little late for this, but Jonas realized he needed to take things slowly. He was dealing with grief. He knew from experience how intensely vulnerable she was right now. He should just give her—and himself—some space.

"We should—"

She turned and looked at him, and he saw what she was expecting in the sudden vulnerability of her expression.

If he asked for space right now, she would not see it as being for the greater good of both of them. She would see it as a brush-off.

"We should go get that ring today," he heard himself say.

What? a voice inside him asked, shocked.

"What?" she asked, shocked.

"There's a jewelry store in a little town north of here. It's close to one of my favorite hiking trails. Have you got sturdy boots?"

Krissy stared at Jonas.

He'd brought her a flower. Snatched from someone's garden, but a romantic gesture nonetheless.

Now he wanted to go ahead with the ring? The whole time she had cooked breakfast she had thought he would arrive back with the dog and a zillion reasons to bolt out of here.

She had a zillion reasons she needed him to leave. This was all becoming exactly as he had predicted! Terribly complex.

For instance, she couldn't even look at him without wanting to touch him, kiss him, drag him back down the hall… Shop for a ring when she was feeling some dangerous hope zinging in the air between them. Wouldn't that be utter madness?

Still, he had put ring shopping into perspective really quickly. For him, the ring shopping was a casual outing—it had nothing at all to do with what had transpired between them last night. In fact, it could combine with a hike! Sturdy boots, indeed!

That was the proper outlook.

"Can I use your shower?" he asked. "And maybe pop my clothes into the dryer for a bit to loosen the wrinkles?"

Krissy gulped.

Jonas Boyden had been in her bed. Now he was going to be in *her* shower. Part of her longed to be as bold as she had been last night and get in that shower with him.

But another part of her held back. *They barely knew one another.* Wasn't this how her parents had gotten into such difficulties? They had hurried into a relationship when they didn't even understand each other's core values. Their legacy had been that Krissy grew up fast and learned to depend on herself from a very young age.

She had to take this lesson now and back this thing up. It felt as if it would be way too easy to start depending on Jonas. Already, her safe and tidy little cottage felt as if it would never be the same, as if some part of Jonas would linger here tantalizingly, so could you go backward once you had gone *there*?

She heard the shower turn on. She imagined the water sluicing over that gorgeous body that she had owned last night. But then she also heard the dryer thumping.

Was this a man who was accustomed to waking up in a strange bed? He seemed very practiced at getting wrinkles out of clothes that had been left in a hurried heap by the side of the bed.

Tell him to go home, Krissy ordered herself. But already she wasn't that strong; already she was prepared to ignore the lessons life had given her. She wanted to spend the day with him. She wanted to see where all this was going to go.

No doubt, straight to a heartbreak, she warned herself. But even with that warning inside her head, while he was still showering, she quickly chose a suitable hiking outfit: a pair of denim shorts and a plaid shirt. She braided her hair.

Then she looked at herself in the mirror, hoping she had achieved a nice, casual outdoorsy image. Good grief. A little too Daisy Mae? But it was too late; she could hear him emerge from the shower.

He came out of the bathroom with a towel tucked around his waist and water beaded in the strands of his hair, turned dark gold from water. Her helpless eyes trailed to the perfect, muscled body.

He paused and looked at her. He smiled. "Hey, you look awesome in braids. Very wholesome."

A reminder to them both that they were in totally different leagues?

He got his clothes out of the dryer and put them on. It was his business attire from yesterday—minus the suit jacket—and yet he looked like a poster boy for an outdoor excursion being featured in *Men's Fitness*. There was nothing Li'l Abner about him, except maybe for the broadness of his shoulders.

Considering what had occurred between them last night, did she want to look wholesome? Considering that, wasn't it the safest thing? Considering their mission today—an engagement ring—wasn't it a good thing he was setting the tone by treating the hike as the main event?

Soon Chance was loaded into the back hatch. The dog was over the moon to be having an outing with them.

As they took to the highway, Krissy felt some tension leaving her. It was that perfect kind of day that only late June had: warmth without too much heat, the crispness of summer, spring freshness still in the air, the world bright green with growth and lushness that sang of possibility.

The vehicle filled with the heady scent of his shower-washed body.

He glanced at her, smiled that smile that made her feel cherished, as if she *mattered* to him. "Cat got your tongue, Krissy?"

She didn't think any talk of tongues was a very good idea right now!

"Tell me something wonderful about your week," he said to her, and she loved it that he had sensed her awkwardness and was prepared to work at easing it.

Well, there was the picnic. And then there was something quite wonderful crowding out all the other wonderfuls.

"Something I don't know about," he said softly, reading her mind. "Maybe something from work."

So Krissy found herself telling him about Georgie, her very adorable five-year-old class miscreant.

"He brought worms for show-and-tell. Then he chased Emily all over the class with one. I think it's the five-year-old way of saying I like you. But then, when I told him to lose the worm, he ate it. I think his chances with Emily are over for good now."

"Note to self—don't eat worms in front of the girl you are trying to impress."

Krissy gulped. Was *that* girl her? "I think you're way past the eating worms stage of impressing a girl," she said. She thought of his mouth. *Way* past.

"You are way overestimating the sophistication of the male species," he said, and the laughter that rose up between them was deliciously comfortable and companionable.

"What about you?" she asked. "Best part of your week."

He gave her a lazy, sexy smile that turned her insides to mush and made her happily aware there was no question about what had been best about his week.

"I acquired a resort about a year ago that's been an extraordinary challenge. It's in the Florida Keys, more run-down than we thought it was going to be. Usually, I have a pretty good sense of how the resort will feel specialized, but for this one every single thing about it has been a grind, including the mission statement. But it all came together last week. I haven't run a resort in conjunction with a charity before, but one of my executives is a military veteran, and he was telling me about some of the challenges military families have during— and sometimes especially after—their service.

"So we're going to work with veteran's groups, and provide getaways for these really stressed and sometimes not very well off families."

Krissy could not even look at him. She was sure the admiration she had for him—the growing sense of connection, the desire to know this man, completely, to be a part of his life—would just be too evident in her face.

"You should come," he said after a moment, "to the opening."

She nearly quivered with pure longing. He had just opened the door to a future beyond this, and beyond the weekend with his family.

"Wouldn't that be, um, kind of complicated?" she asked, trying to strip the helpless sense of longing from her voice. "It would mean extending the charade, wouldn't it?"

They needed to address that. Didn't they? The charade part?

She was hoping he would say it wasn't a charade, not anymore. But he didn't.

He frowned. He sighed. "Yes." And then almost to himself, "It's not as if I didn't see it coming. Complications."

The silence between them did not seem comfortable anymore.

The town that was their destination was a village, much like Sunshine Cove, only smaller. The day was cool enough to leave Chance in the vehicle with all the windows open, but now that they were actually in front of the tiny jewelry store, sandwiched in between a bookshop and an antique store, Krissy felt reluctant to go in.

"Are you sure you want to leave the vehicle unsecured?" Krissy said. She suddenly did not want to do this. It was too personal. Too crazy. Too much a lie.

There was too much potential to feel things she did not want to feel. Especially after last night.

Like her growing attachment to Jonas. There was this sense in her of wanting to know him so completely. And that was without the further complication of the fact that she couldn't look at his lips without thinking of kissing him. Of his hands claiming her. Of her hands exploring him. Like how much she enjoyed making him laugh.

How could she possibly go look at a ring with Jonas—an engagement ring—and not have the lines she had drawn around him blur even more than they already were?

She could not do this!

CHAPTER THIRTEEN

"MAYBE WE SHOULD go hiking first," Krissy suggested to Jonas.

He gave her a puzzled look. "The store is right there."

She snapped her fingers. "I have an idea. You go in and pick out the ring, and I'll take Chance for a walk. Then you can lock the vehicle."

"I'm not sure why you're so worried about that. It doesn't exactly look like a hotbed of criminal activity," Jonas said, looking up and down the sleepy main street.

She acted as if it was decided. "And then, after you've picked the ring, I'll go in and get it sized."

There. That seemed like a safe way of getting out of a totally awkward situation.

"He'll be fine for a few minutes in the vehicle with the windows down." Was Jonas deliberately missing the point of Krissy's reluctance?

She made one last desperate effort. "Someone could steal Chance!"

He looked back at Chance and made a face. "Now that seems highly unlikely. Come on. Half the fun is going to be seeing what you pick."

Fun, Krissy reminded herself sternly. She got out of the vehicle, took a deep breath and went around to where Jonas waited by the door. *Sanderson* was etched into the glass. A bell jangled as he opened it and held it for her.

She hesitated, her reluctance to do this deepening. Jonas put his hand on the small of her back and gave her a firm push.

It took a second for her eyes to adjust to the light. They were the only customers. In fact, they were the only people. The store appeared to be unmanned.

"I told you it wasn't a hotbed of criminal activity," Jonas said quietly. He took her hand and tugged. "Come on, why don't we start over here?"

She let him guide her over to the display case. The rings glittered up at her. She felt as if she couldn't breathe. She recoiled when she caught sight of the price on one.

"That seems a little much for a ruse," she said, shocked.

"Just play along. Show me the ring you would get if money was no object."

She glanced at him. Could he not see they were messing with a moment most women spent a good deal of their lives dreaming of? Could he not see that after last night this felt like the worst kind of lie?

Not that Krissy had ever indulged such fantasies, but now that she was here, it was hard to ignore the longing. The wish that it was all different.

The wish that she had entered this store with a man that she loved. That they were looking for a ring that symbolized their commitment to each other, a ring that shone with their hopes and dreams for the future.

Jonas was the kind of man who inspired exactly that kind of fantasy.

"What's wrong?" he asked her softly. "Don't be so serious. You're going to get a permanent line, right here."

And then he gently touched her brow with the knuckle of his hand, and she could feel the line of tension evaporate under his touch.

Of course, he was right. She didn't need to be so serious. She could have fun! She could! She pointed at a ring with a huge solitaire diamond. The tag said it was one karat. And that it was worth ten thousand dollars.

"How about that one?"

She had hoped he would reward her choice with shock, and that they would both have a good laugh to break some tension she still held, despite him erasing it from her brow. But Jonas tilted his head and regarded the ring as if it was a serious contender.

"I don't think you could lift up your hand with that thing on it," he said. "How about this one?"

She gazed at the one he was pointing at. It was a smaller diamond, flanked by two emeralds. The price made her gulp.

"It's too much money."

"We weren't going to think about money. Yet. It's just preliminary, to see what you like."

She peered at the display cases. It was making her head ache. There were too many rings, and they represented too many things, and she was pretty sure the frown line was burrowing in deep between her eyes again.

Get it over with, Krissy ordered herself. "How about this one?"

"You're picking it because it's cheaper."

"It's good enough."

"Why do I think the ring out of a candied popcorn box would be good enough for you?"

"Because it would be. It's a game," she reminded him tersely. "You could buy this less expensive one and donate the rest of your budget to a holiday for veterans."

"You really aren't getting into the spirit of this," he chided her. "Most women like shopping for jewelry."

"And you are an expert on that, why?"

He didn't need to answer. She could see it in his face. This was not his first shopping excursion in a jewelry store with a woman.

And probably not his first one the morning after, either. What on earth was she doing?

As the tension snapped in the air between them, a little old man came out from the back. He looked surprised to see customers. He was wearing a jeweler's loupe on a chain around his neck. "My hearing isn't what it used to be. Didn't hear the door." He sized them up, smiled. "Sam Sanderson. How can I help?"

"We were just leaving."

"We're looking for an engagement ring," Jonas said, firmly.

"Inexpensive," she said.

"Ignore her," Jonas said.

Sam's eyes went back and forth between them. Krissy was pretty sure he was thinking *This will never work*.

"My favorite thing," Sam declared happily. "I can feel the hopes and dreams in the air."

She felt a shiver go up and down her spine. Wasn't that exactly the thought she just had about what an engagement ring shopping excursion should be?

"It reminds me of when my Sally and I found the perfect ring," Sam said.

Krissy had the terribly uncomfortable sensation of treading on something sacred.

"She's gone now," Sam continued, "but she still helps

sometimes. But you have your own helper already, don't you?"

"Sorry?" Krissy said. It was so much like something that her aunt Jane would have said that she didn't even feel shocked when the man appeared to be nodding at someone over her shoulder.

Jonas, though, turned around, frowning, to look.

"Anything catching your eye here?" the man asked.

"Something inexpensive," Krissy said again, at the same time Jonas, turning back to them, said, "Price is no object."

The man looked back and forth between them again. A smile tickled his lips. He moved to a different case and came back with a small navy-blue velvet box.

He pushed it slowly across the countertop to Krissy.

She hesitated, feeling as if she was part of a spell. Jonas was the one who reached past her and opened the box. The lid creaked open.

Both of them stared at the ring.

"Wow," Jonas said. The truth was he had spent quite a bit of time—and money—in jewelry stores.

It was just the easiest way to say *I had a great evening* or *Here's a little something to remember us by*.

He realized now he was the go-to of a guy who had unabashedly defaulted to superficial in his love life. He was career focused and commitment phobic, and he made no bones about either. Basically, everyone knew the rules going in.

He followed a pretty predictable pattern. There were going to be a few really nice dinners, classic wining and dining, maybe a Broadway show, or a beach or ski weekend trip. The relationship—if it could be called that—was going to be casual, a few good times, some easy laughs. And then it was *adios, señorita.*

A certain kind of woman went for what he offered. Krissy's aunt had gotten it in one glance at him. *Bimbos.*

That seemed a little harsh to him. Still, buying a bauble for a that kind of woman, even an expensive bauble—or maybe especially an expensive one—soothed something in him and satisfied something in her.

Unfortunately, standing in this little store with Krissy put the whole thing in a different light, and made it seem he had engaged in a series of tawdry business transactions. It all seemed embarrassingly superficial.

So here was the irony: this relationship with Krissy had been 100 percent fake from the outset. And yet everything about it—from getting to know her dog, to eating ice cream treats, to picnicking in the park felt real.

Last night had been one of the most real experiences of Jonas's entire existence, though in all honesty, last night was quickly crowding out memories of his past existence!

But here was the truth: there was an authenticity about Krissy that was shining right through the lie he had convinced her to participate in.

Buying this ring was proving no different.

It was supposed to be part of the game, but it didn't feel like it. Jonas felt invested. He wanted this gift to mean something. He wanted Krissy to love what they bought and remember this time they'd had together forever.

Forever? There was a word Jonas Boyden avoided. Obviously, it had been a bit of a slip asking her to the opening of his newest resort at the end of summer. This was a one-off.

Still, as he had watched her face as she looked at the jewelry, it was more than obvious that Krissy was not a jewelry person and never had been. She hated this exercise.

And yet the ring she was looking at now had transformed her features. It was an exquisite ring.

It was so *her* in the same way that little black dress had been so her. Classic. Timeless. Understated. Beautiful. The engagement ring was simplicity itself, a circle of perfect diamonds, all the same size, with no central stone.

"There's no price on it," she said hoarsely.

"Good," Jonas said. He lifted the ring from its velvet cushion. As he held it up, it sparked, the diamonds capturing the light and then shooting out blue flames.

Too late, he got how wrong this was, particularly in light of the intimacy they had shared last night. It was taking the whole thing a little too far, but of course, that was something he was known for. He could spend months setting up an elaborate prank.

But as he held out his hand, he was aware this did not feel like part of a prank. He could not take his eyes off her face, the light in it. Krissy caught her tongue between her teeth—that was cute—and then as if caught in the spell, she placed her hand, palm down in his. Her hand felt feminine and soft, and yet there was strength in it, too.

He took a deep breath.

He tried, a little desperately, to remind himself it was a game.

But when he slipped the ring on her engagement finger it felt as if the entire world—and his heart—stood entirely still.

The ring went on easily. It settled at the base of her

finger, snug, but not tight. It felt as if it would never come off. It also felt as if it was radiating a strange warmth. Krissy stared at it. He stared at it.

It fit her absolutely perfectly.

"It looks as if it belongs on my hand," she said, stunned. "I've never even worn a ring before."

She looked up at him, something tremulous in her gaze. *Trusting him* to somehow turn this debacle he had started into something with redeeming value.

Jonas realized, stunned, they could see where this was going to take them. It didn't have to be a one-off.

"That's the one," Sam said, not with any question in it at all.

She nodded. Jonas nodded.

She slipped her hand from his. He was aware of not wanting to let it go. Krissy never even took the ring off her finger as the old man rang it up. Sam put the empty box in a little silk bag and handed it to her.

"When's the wedding?" he asked.

"The long weekend," Jonas said.

"That soon! But what about the wedding band?"

Jonas did not often find himself in situations where he was not in control, where he was caught off-balance, but this seemed to be spinning out of his control. Sam fetched the matching band for the ring and showed it to them.

Jonas found himself nodding that they'd take that, too, and the ring was put it in a box and handed to him.

Sam wagged a stern finger at him. "Don't put that on her finger until you've said your vows. It's bad luck. If it doesn't fit properly, bring it back then."

Jonas found himself nodding like an obedient schoolboy. He needed to remind himself that second ring was never going on her finger.

Unless they decided to see where this would take them. He could feel his heart beating unreasonably.

"Have you got your license? You should run over to the town hall and get it here. It's just on the corner over there. There's never a lineup. One more thing off the list."

"I'm sure they're not open Saturdays," Jonas said uncomfortably.

"Yup! Yup, they are. Closed Sundays and Mondays."

Krissy shot him a look that said they weren't going to get a license! They stepped out of the store and checked on Chance. He was snoring in the back seat.

Jonas rocked back on his heels and looked down the street.

It had all become a bit too serious for him. Even his own thoughts were veering into deep into uncharted territory. He needed to get this back to a light place, a place where he was comfortable, where they both were aware it was just a game they were playing. It was supposed to be fun!

Then a plan hatching—and maybe feeling a little pressured by Sam, who was watching expectantly from the window—he took her hand and headed for the town hall.

"We are not going to the town hall," Krissy told Jonas firmly, trying to extricate her hand. "That's taking it all too far. It's going to be awful enough when you return the rings."

"I'm not returning the rings."

"Of course you are! What use would you have for a ring like this? And the wedding band?"

"None whatsoever. You can keep it."

"Wh-what?"

"I get the car. There should be something in it for you."

"I'm not keeping a ring from a phony engagement," she said. "And I certainly don't want a fake wedding band."

"The band itself is not fake," he pointed out.

"I deduced that from the price."

"You can have them made into something else, then," he said, dismissing it.

"We are absolutely not going to the town hall!"

CHAPTER FOURTEEN

SUDDENLY IT FELT imperative to Jonas to get Krissy into that town hall to apply for a marriage license.

Not to make it more real, but to make it less so, an essential piece of an elaborate—but fun—stunt.

"Why not?" he said persuasively. "It's just a piece of paper. It's a marriage license, not a marriage. Just think if I can show Theresa and Mike a marriage license. It's the coup de grâce!"

"Coup de grâce is actually a French term that translates to killing blow."

Who knew things like that? She did. This wonderfully complex, smart, sweet, sexy woman, who was wearing his ring. On her engagement finger.

He had to keep the scam part of this exercise in the forefront. But hadn't it moved out of that territory last night? Hadn't he just been thinking they could take it beyond the weekend reunion—after he'd won the bet—and see where it went?

He was never confused! He was not going to let confusion rule now, not this late in his life.

He was keeping his eye on the prize! But his eyes moved to her.

His hand in hers was a mistake. He loved touching

her casually like this, as if it was the most natural thing in the world.

Come to that, it felt like the most natural thing in the world.

How was that possible? He was on the town hall steps, about to fill out paperwork for a life commitment, and it felt natural. And good.

He let go of her hand as if it had burned him. He thrust his own offending hand deep into his pocket.

"You're right," he said, coming to his senses. "This is taking it too far, even for me, master of the elaborate prank."

He felt an uneasy awareness that the prize did not feel like his car, no matter how hard he tried to make that the focus.

The prize felt like her.

Krissy frowned at Jonas's sudden uncertainty. It seemed very unlike him. For the first time since she had met him, he seemed a little off. Uneasy. Distracted. No doubt the cost of that excursion in the jewelry store had caught him a bit by surprise.

"No," she said firmly, "Let's go get the license. You're right—it's just a piece of paper. And if it will help convince your family, it's a good return on your investment in this."

She held up the ring. It caught the light and winked at her and made her heart do a delicious flip-flop.

Silly as it was, she felt totally different since he'd put that ring on her finger. Not just connected to Jonas, but alive. Bold. Aware of life sizzling with the potential for surprises, for delight, for amazement.

At the best of times, life was all just a game, wasn't it? Why not just enjoy it?

"I'm prepared to earn the ring," she told him decisively. "How much was it, again? The whole *'Now you need a wedding band'* thing distracted me."

He didn't say anything, still looking warily up the steps.

"I'll start earning it right now," she decided. "I will play the part of your absolutely besotted betrothed. I'll reprise my queen role."

"You sucked at being the queen."

She pretended offense. "I could tone it down a notch. Princess."

"Would I have to be a prince?"

"Let's not get carried away. A frog will do."

She was relieved when he smiled and shrugged his shoulders as if he was rolling out from under a big weight.

He did a surprisingly good impression of a frog, and when she laughed, he did it again. And then they were both laughing, and that strange tension she had seen in him was gone.

"You have to stop being a frog now, or I won't be able to keep a straight face while we do the paperwork. I would imagine a straight face is required."

They went up the steps, and he opened the front door of the town hall for her. He leaned in close to her ear.

"Ribbit," he croaked.

"Stop it!"

"There's only one way to turn a frog into a prince," he reminded her.

"Never mind being a prince." She did not want to think about kissing him. "You can be a knight to my princess."

"As long as you don't expect shining armor," he told her.

"Tarnished will do."

He grinned. He opened the door to the inner office for her. "Milady," he murmured as she went through.

He seemed to Krissy's great relief to be back to his normal self. They found themselves standing in a dusty and poorly lit town office. The laughter must have still been shining between them, because the clerk, her gray hair in tight curls, looked faintly disapproving as she slapped the paperwork down in front of them and checked their identification.

She was immune to Jonas's rather substantial charm.

"You can't use it for twenty-four hours," the clerk told them sternly. "And you have to use it within sixty days or it's void."

See? Jonas mouthed to Krissy, *Void.*

"It's forty dollars," the clerk told them, as if that was a great deal of money, and they should have thought more carefully before spending it, "but that includes the issuance of the certificate of marriage. The officiant—the person who performs your ceremony—can send it to me—the address is here—and then the record of your marriage will be on file."

"That may have been the best forty dollars I ever spent," Jonas said, standing at the top of the town hall steps.

They both stared at the document for a moment before he folded it and put it in his pocket.

"What do you think? Something to eat and a hike?"

Marriage license, check. Time to think of food. Such a man thing! So delightful!

She thought, if she was sensible, she should just go home.

But somehow it seemed a little late to be applying good sense to this situation. Besides, Jonas was taking the whole thing lightly, treating it like a lark. He had regained his equilibrium; in fact, he was practically clicking his heels as they left the town hall.

Why be the stick-in-the-mud? Why let on that there was something terribly unsettling about playing with these sacred institutions? Something terribly unsettling about the fact they had shared such powerful intimacies, already, and no doubt would again, before this was over.

Over.

In a little more than a week—after next weekend— the game would be over. She'd probably never see him again. No sense paying any attention to the downward swish in her stomach at that thought. Wasn't there at least a chance that it didn't have to end?

Last night had been incredible. If Jonas didn't like where it was going, wouldn't he have hightailed it and run today?

No, he had made a choice to ignore the *complications*. It could even be argued he had complicated things further by buying those rings.

The marriage license, their names joined together on a single piece of paper, complicated things even more. Though they had thought they could escape the implications of such a solemn piece of paper, the very process of applying for it, the fact it was nestled in his pocket, created connection between them.

Obviously, they had incredible chemistry. Obviously, they shared a sense of humor. Obviously, they had fun together. Plus, they both loved the dog!

Was there going to be an awful price for accepting the invitation in his laughing eyes? To let go? To have fun? To embrace the joy life offered?

Krissy faced an awful truth. There was a terrible

chance of falling in love with her fake fiancé. She was pretty sure she was halfway there already.

And as powerless to stop it as she had ever been over anything in her entire life.

She surrendered to it.

He did, too.

The rest of the day, they acted as if there were no complications between them at all.

They acted as if they were exactly what they were: fresh young lovers in the throes of discovery. They ate crunchy croissants at a dog-friendly patio outside a bakery not far from the town hall.

When they got back in the vehicle, an ecstatic Chance was somehow on her lap instead of in the back. His huge head was out the window, his tongue lolling happily as they drove through the beautiful countryside, the spring air flowing through her window—the utter happiness of these moments—felt like she was breathing in wine.

Jonas parked in the lot at the head of the trail that he had obviously hiked many times. They held hands as they hiked a winding trail that went up a mountain. He was not dressed for hiking, and his shoes were terrible for it.

The trail was steep and challenging in places. Jonas pulled her over slippery rocks and piggybacked her across a rushing creek, probably wrecking the shoes completely. The trail ended at a waterfall and a turquoise pool. The water was frigid, but they splashed each other, took off their shoes and chased barefoot through the mud. They threw sticks for Chance, who would bring them back and shake all over them.

Between Chance and the mist from the falls, they were soon soaked, their clothes clinging to them, a reminder of how things had gotten out of hand last night.

But it didn't feel out of hand as their lips met. It felt as if life had conspired to give them each other. In the rainbow hues of its mist, they kissed until they were breathless with it.

Jonas picked the tiny yellow wildflowers that grew in abundance on the banks of the pool, and he decorated the dog's collar and then he threaded them through her hair. And then she picked wildflowers and added them to the dog's collar and threaded them through Jonas's hair.

They laughed until she felt as if she couldn't breathe.

They'd stopped for dinner at a little roadside hot dog stand, that Jonas claimed had the best hot dogs ever. He still had a flower in his hair, and she didn't tell him.

The stand featured more varieties of hot dogs than Krissy had known existed. She ordered a chili dog, Jonas ordered the hot dog version of a Triple Chocolate Volcano Sunday. Chance had two plain dogs, no bun.

Halfway through she traded hot dogs with Jonas.

Funny how wonderful it felt, just one of those little intimacies that couples shared. They lingered over refills of sodas until the sun went down, laughing, chatting, teasing.

Krissy never wanted this day to end. And then it didn't.

Because when they got back to her house, Jonas walked her to the door and leaned into her.

She thought he was going to kiss her. Again. She ached for the taste of his lips. Even though they had been kissing all day, she felt she could not get enough.

His lips had become her drug.

But it was even better than a good-night kiss.

His voice raw with need, he said, "Can I come in, Krissy?"

* * *

Jonas woke up the next morning to his feet asleep under the weight of the dog, and Krissy nestled into his arm.

He was aware of the sound of rain hammering the roof of her little cottage, and contentment unfolded in him like a cat getting up from in front of the fire to stretch.

He slipped out of bed before her, found her washing machine and tossed his clothes in. With a towel tucked around his waist, he made coffee and brought it to her.

She blinked at his towel. "Is that what you're wearing today?"

"I certainly hope not," he said, and let the towel slip.

After that, they drank coffee gone cold, and they shared a real newspaper in her bed. Jonas usually read his on his tablet, so reading the paper like this felt old-fashioned and delightful. But as they read snippets of articles to each other, he wondered what didn't feel delightful with her.

They had cereal for breakfast and put his clothes in the dryer. She walloped him at Scrabble. They finally got dressed. They squeezed under one umbrella and took the dog for a walk. Being wet again had the same predictable effect on them.

They showered the chill away; they ate macaroni and cheese for lunch and then baked cookies and ate them in bed, warm chocolate from melted chips dripping down their lips and inviting the most delightful cleanup.

Jonas was a man whose life had taken him in many unexpected directions and given him many surprising adventures. The nature of his work led him to experiences most people would never have, perfect tens on the scale of excitement.

He had traveled the globe, to some of the most exotic places in the world.

He had helicopter skied in the Rocky Mountains and been on beaches in Saint-Tropez. He had zip-lined and been on a photo safari.

He had been a guest at castles and estates and ranches.

He had hobnobbed with royalty and some of the world's most celebrated stars and athletes, been to their galas and games and award shows.

And all of that—every single bit of it—paled in comparison to a rainy afternoon, with the dog smelling damp and Krissy in her robe, sprawled across the bed reading him the funnies from the Sunday morning paper and sharing a chocolate chip cookie with him.

CHAPTER FIFTEEN

"WHAT THE HECK is that?"

It was Monday morning, and Krissy was in the school staff room. It was the last week of school and there was a certain giddiness in the air.

And a giddiness inside of her, unlike anything she had ever felt. Jonas had left late yesterday afternoon.

And so far, she had received half a dozen texts from him and a video of him doing an impression of Kermit and making frog sounds. In the video, which Krissy had watched more times than she could count, she caught glimpses of the sumptuous apartment he lived in.

Fellow teacher Artie Calhoun grabbed her hand and hooted. "Engaged! Look guys, Krissy is engaged!"

Shocked, she realized she had not taken off her ring. Shocked, she realized the ring already felt like part of her. She had not even considered removing it this morning. But now she was swarmed by her fellow teachers, congratulating her, asking questions, excited for her.

"I didn't even know you had a boyfriend!" Martha Montrose crowed. "Who is it? What's his name?"

Krissy wasn't sure of the wisdom of making any of this public. It would have been such a simple thing to take off that ring! In September she'd come back to school. She'd still own the ring, but would she still wear it? Explanations would be needed.

On the other hand, was it possible she and Jonas would still be going out as summer wound down?

After the weekend together it seemed impossible that they wouldn't be! It felt as if her life could no longer be complete without him, and from the nature of his texts, he was feeling the very same way.

"Jonas," she said. "Jonas Boyden."

Martha's phone came out of her purse, and she plucked at it furiously. She squealed. "Krissy, he's gorgeous! Look at this," she called to the other staff members. "Krissy's guy is a multimillionaire. He owns a company called Last Resort. Good grief, he is part owner of Yummy Mommy."

Thankfully, the bell rang, and Krissy was able to get away from the awed well-wishers all around her.

Excitement was high in the classroom, and she found herself relaxing into it, instead of trying to control it. She giggled with the kids. She played games with them. They sang songs together.

At the end of the day, Georgie came and regarded her thoughtfully. "You're so happy," he declared.

After he and the other children had gone, she contemplated that her happiness was so obvious that even a child could see it.

And what did that mean about the way she had been before? She hadn't felt unhappy.

But she hadn't felt like this, either.

Caring about someone just made everything better! The flowers looked brighter, and the air smelled fresher, and the world seemed funnier and friendlier. The week passed in a flurry of texts and phone calls between her and Jonas, but both their schedules precluded meeting.

The last week of school was always crammed with activities and responsibilities. Normally, after that final Friday afternoon of tears and hugs and kisses from all her kindergarten students, Krissy would go home and feel bereft for days, summer looming large and empty.

But this year, all she felt was excited. Jonas was coming tonight, and tomorrow they were going to his reunion. She was meeting his family.

It was crazy to be so excited.

It was crazy for her heart to beat so hard every time the phone rang, every time a text pinged.

When she opened the door to him that night and looked into Jonas's face, saw the hunger in his eyes and the tender smile on his lips, the truth hit her.

The truth was Krissy was crazy in love.

With her fake fiancé.

But when he reached for her, when he pulled her into him, when his lips claimed hers and lit that now-familiar fire within her, it was the most real thing Krissy had ever felt.

The weather was glorious the next day as they made an early start to the Catskills, but the feeling inside of her put the sun to shame.

She loved his family resort from her first glance of the log arch over the road. A sign swung from it: Boy's Den. Underneath that hung a smaller sign that promised Dog-Gone Fun. Because Jonas had told her the story of the rebirth of the resort, when Krissy recognized the motto she already felt connected to it in some way.

"I told my sister to change the name from Boy's Den, but she wouldn't. My dad named it, and he thought it was such a clever play on the family name. None of us had the heart to tell him it was a terrible name, that it

sounded like a Boy Scout camp or worse, a den of ill
repute."

"I love it," Krissy said firmly, and what's more, she
already loved his sister for keeping it.

They drove down a curving driveway, shaded on
both sides by enormous sugar maples, into a clearing
where a small river crashed over rocks into a large body
of water that was not quite a lake, but too big to be a
pond. There was a sandy beach and a raft bobbed up and
down out on the water. Though it was before lunch, the
day promised to be hot, and there was already a group
of teenagers on the raft, boys showing off for girls by
pitching each other in the water.

"How many people come to your family reunion?"
Krissy asked. There were people everywhere.

"It varies. More than a hundred. Less than two."

"A hundred people in a family?"

He laughed. "That's how many come. My dad was
from a huge family—six brothers and two sisters. My
mom was like you, an only child, and I bet she had
that same look on her face when she was introduced
to this mob."

Jonas stopped the vehicle in front of a rustic log
building that must have been the main lodge, and a
woman Krissy knew instantly was his sister came off
a large covered veranda to meet them as they got out of
the car. Two little boys tumbled down the steps behind
her, and Jonas swept one up in each arm.

"Simon. Gar!" His arms full of children, he leaned
over and kissed his sister on the cheek.

The boys squealed their delight, insisted their names
were Harry and Danny, but Jonas acted baffled and
told them they were mistaken, and that he had a long-
standing relationship with Simon and Gar and knew

who they were. He bantered with them until the laughter of the boys filled the air.

Krissy could not take her eyes off the three of them, a light of love and joy shining from them. She was totally aware this was the kind of daddy Jonas would be. Strong, engaged, fun-filled. It filled her with the most exquisite tenderness she had ever felt.

She was aware of his sister watching her. "He's great with kids," she offered. "Do you think you'll be having any?"

"Hey!" Jonas said, giving his sister a warning look and putting down the boys. "You haven't even been introduced yet."

Danny and Harry switched their rambunctious affection to the dog, who was thrilled.

Jonas introduced them and Theresa greeted Krissy as if she had known her all her life. She was warm and unpretentious, and Krissy's feeling of loving his sister was already deepened.

"Now how did Jonas keep you secret?" she asked, folding Krissy into a firm hug. "Oh, look at that ring! Mike and I thought he was toying with us when he called and told us he was engaged, but he's not, is he?"

Thankfully, before Krissy answered, the boys started fighting over who the dog liked best, and Theresa calmly pulled them apart.

"And look at you!" Theresa said. She got down in front of Chance and took his face in her hands, kissed him right on his ugly snout. "I can tell he's got a great soul."

Krissy's feeling of homecoming intensified.

"Do you want a tour of the place?" she asked when she got back up. "Jonas, take the boys and find Mike. He's building a mud pit. We thought we'd add a tug-of-war to the water fight this year."

"Do you think we could unpack first before you put me to work?" Jonas groused, but shrugged ruefully at Krissy, called his nephews, and they headed off. "Do not interrogate her," he warned his sister.

Chance looked momentarily torn before giving Krissy a guilty look and taking off after Jonas and the boys.

Theresa laughed. "Dogs always love him. Of course I'm going to interrogate you," she said. "I want to know everything about the woman my brother has fallen for."

But as it turned out, the interrogation, thankfully, had to wait. The resort was a cluster of about a dozen adorable weathered gray log cabins. They were on a slight hill behind the lodge and were in a wide horseshoe that faced the lake. The cabins were also called dens, each named after a wild animal. Bear, Rabbit, Deer, Beaver, Skunk and so on.

"Believe it or not, Skunk Den is our most requested cabin. My dad named them," Theresa said with rueful affection. All seemed to be occupied by members of the Boyden clan. There was also a growing tent city on the edge of the lake. They could not walk two steps without Theresa being stopped, greetings exchanged, questions asked, introductions made.

There were cousins, aunts, uncles, great-aunts, great-uncles, until Krissy's head was spinning with names.

Every time she was introduced as Jonas's fiancée, instead of feeling guilty about the lie, it seemed to become more real. She was embraced and kissed and congratulated and welcomed completely into the ranks as if she'd been born to this large, loud, happy clan.

The sound of happiness was in the air: children laughing, the low hum of conversation, the call of a name, an occasional shout, splashing and shrieking at the beach. Dogs barked and birds sang.

It was family as Krissy, as a child, had longed for, family like she had read about in books and seen in movies.

"There are so many people," Krissy said.

"We always have the family reunion first before we open for the year," Theresa told her. "It could be a very lucrative weekend, but its family first for us."

Family first, Krissy repeated inwardly, and something sighed within her. Perfect contentment.

Jonas watched Krissy. This was his moment: mission accomplished. She was currently on the opposite team of the tug-of-war. She was pulling with all her might, but still his team was inching them toward the mud bog in the middle.

Children were shrieking and dogs were barking, but it felt as if his whole world suddenly went silent, his focus sharp around her.

Her head was thrown back with laughter. Her every muscle was braced. Her hair was free and tumbling around her face, her nose sunburned.

His team made their move, a sudden jerk and the other team was flying toward them, then stumbling over each other, and then falling in a tangle of limbs and shouted laughter into the mud.

Krissy was screaming with laughter. She pulled herself up—her clothes absolutely plastered to her—grabbed mud balls in both fists and came after him. He ran, and she ran after him, pelting him with the mud. He turned on her, scooped her up in his arms. She twisted and tried to free herself, but to the cheers of his family, he stomped into the middle of the mud bog and released her.

Except she didn't let go. She wrapped her arms tight

around his neck, and he lost his footing in the greasy muck, and they went down in the slop together. His nephews led the charge of children who were suddenly all around him, squishing mud into his hair and down his shirt.

"Enough," he finally roared, rising to his feet and shaking children off him like a dog shaking off water. He held out his hand to her and she took it, and to the wild cheers of his family, he pulled her hard against himself and kissed her muddy lips. And then he scooped her up again, and with the children racing after them shouting encouragement, he ran into the lake and tossed her and then dived in behind her.

She emerged clean and dripping and he stared at her.

"My weakness," he said in a voice only she could hear, "seeing you wet."

The water had been freezing, but the sudden heat in her eyes warmed him through to his core.

He didn't care who was watching. He scooped her up again and took her to the cabin they would share.

Later that night, they sat at the campfire, sparks shooting up into an inky dark sky. Krissy's mouth was smeared with melted marshmallow and chocolate from the s'mores she had taken from his fingertips. Jonas decided he'd better not look at her lips anymore.

Chance was nestled between his nephews on the other side of the fire. All three of them were utterly exhausted.

The guitars came out, an accordion, a tambourine, a harmonica. His brother-in-law, Mike, had a good voice, and he led the sing-along.

The sing-along was a disaster as always: people sometimes knew the chorus, but not the words. His uncle Fred had too many beers and was singing too loudly and totally out of tune. The kids were getting tired and querulous.

Including his nephews, who began a fistfight over which one of them Chance loved best.

Jonas got up from beside Krissy and picked up Danny. His sister was right beside him and picked up Harry. Both boys were asleep on their shoulders before they reached the lodge.

He tucked Danny into his pint-size racing car bed, and his sister did the same with Harry. She disappeared for a minute and came back with a facecloth, which she handed to Jonas. He brushed the worst of the s'more remains from Danny's face.

"You're going to be a good dad, Jonas. And she's going to be a good mom. I love the two of you together."

He realized, not once had either his sister or his brother-in-law mentioned the bet or the stupid car. They were just genuinely happy for him.

And when he looked inside himself, he didn't find a lie.

He found genuine happiness, too.

"When are you going to get married?" Theresa asked him. "If this afternoon was any indication, you should make it soon."

"This afternoon?"

She rolled her eyes. "Disappearing into the cabin for an hour."

"Oh, yeah, this afternoon," he said. He was blushing. You didn't talk about stuff like that with your sister. "We have the license," he heard himself saying, as if he had to excuse his afternoon excursion to her.

"You do?"

"Yeah. We'll just, ah, slip away one weekend and quietly tie the knot. You know, just the two of us."

He wasn't prepared for the look of devastation on his sister's face.

"You mean without family? Without me?"

He realized he should tell her the truth, right now, right this minute. But he could hear laughter drifting up from the campfire. And Jonas was suddenly aware he wasn't quite sure what the truth was.

He heard a loud popping sounds.

"Somebody is setting off fireworks," she said.

"I hope it doesn't wake the boys."

"It won't."

They walked back out of the lodge. Down at the edge of the lake, the fireworks were starting. He found Krissy. Someone had given her a blanket, and she opened it up, inviting him to sit on the bench beside her.

A firework exploded in the sky above them, and she leaned into him.

"This one's called Bite Your Tushy," he told her.

"Fireworks have names?" she said skeptically.

"They do."

"You're making that up."

"Nope. And this one is called Chasing Booty."

"Are you serious?"

As the fireworks went off, he named them for her— One Bad Mother, Hot Dog, Loyal to None—loving her giggle at the crazy, slightly off-color names, her sighs of awe as the night sky lit up and reflected in the lake.

It seemed there was so much that he wanted her to know, so much that he wanted to show her, so much that she knew and that she could show him.

A lifetime wouldn't be nearly long enough, he thought, and his lips found the top of her head and kissed it.

CHAPTER SIXTEEN

"WHAT'S GOING ON down there?" Krissy asked Jonas the next morning. They were sitting out on the small deck of their cabin, sipping coffee, the dog at their feet. Krissy was not sure she had ever felt like this: such a sense of belonging, of happiness, a pure contentment.

The perfection of the morning was marred only by the staccato pounding of a hammer.

"My uncle Fred is a minister. He holds a church service the Sunday of the reunion. He appears to be building something."

"Are we going?" she asked. "To the church service?"

"Huh? Why wouldn't we? Everybody goes."

"I've never been a churchgoer, but I'm pretty sure the devout would regard what has been going on between us as a sin."

"You know the guy leading 'Ninety-Nine Bottles of Beer on the Wall' last night? After having consumed at least that many? That's Uncle Fred."

"And he's a minister?"

"Yeah. So you know what they say about stones. Not that what has been going on between us feels anything like a sin." He smiled at her with bone-melting wickedness. "Feels more like heaven to me."

"Fred, the leader of drinking songs, is also a minister?"

"Welcome to that crazy, convoluted thing called family."

She laughed, but then grew serious. If what had been going on between them didn't feel like a sin—and it certainly didn't—something else did.

"That's how I feel, Jonas. I feel welcomed to your family. I don't know how we're going to tell them it has all been a charade."

"Has it felt like a charade to you, Krissy?" he asked quietly.

"No," she said. "It hasn't."

"Not to me, either," he said, his voice a low growl that tickled along her spine like his touch. "I think we should see where this could go."

She stared at him. She could feel tears pricking her eyes. "Me, too," she whispered.

He reached out and put the back of his hand against her cheek. He leaned into her, but something below them crashed, and was followed by some pretty liberal cussing.

"Is that your uncle Fred?"

"None other," he said drily. "What the heck are they doing down there? They're building something. That's strange. What would they need to build for a service?"

Krissy got up with her coffee and stood at the deck railing. She craned her neck. "It's an arbor," she said.

"Really? That's—

"Good morning, lovebirds."

It was Theresa coming up the steps to their cabin. "Jonas, I've had the best idea!"

"Oh-oh," he said, raising an eyebrow at his sister. "Why are you making me nervous?"

"I couldn't even sleep last night, thinking about what you told me. That you and Krissy are just going to go and get married by yourselves somewhere. It doesn't make sense. It's something we all want to celebrate with you. Why not do it here?"

Krissy sneaked a look at Jonas.

He looked utterly gobsmacked. His eyes met hers. He looked away. They had agreed they were going to see where this was going, but he was not prepared for this. How could he be?

"Krissy, what do you think?" Theresa asked. She was so excited. "He'd never forget your anniversary. It would fall on the reunion weekend and his birthday!"

"You mean have a wedding?" Krissy asked, not sure she could be hearing right. "At next year's reunion?"

"No! Right now!"

Krissy's heart was nearly pounding out of her chest. She dared not even look at Jonas, afraid her heart would be broken in two by his reaction to his sister's crazy suggestion.

"Look, I know you mean well, Theresa, but Krissy doesn't even have a dress. You don't just get married in your shorts. Do you?"

Krissy shot him a look. All the things he could have said, and he was worried she didn't have a dress?

"I have a dress," Theresa whispered.

"Nobody has an extra wedding dress just lying around," Jonas said. "Look, you're ambushing us, and—"

"Ambushing you? You said you were going to do it anyway. You said you had the license. I bet you even have a wedding band, don't you? I mean, probably not with you, but—"

"I have it with me," he said.

Krissy felt her eyes go wide. He did?

"I haven't taken it out of my pocket since I bought it," he confessed, his voice low.

There was something in his voice—uncertain and

pained—that Krissy heard. He'd been carrying that ring around with him?

She looked at his face. He was looking at her. He had the look on his face that she had seen ever since the first time they had made love.

It was the look of a man who couldn't believe his luck. It was a look that was protective and tender and awed. It was the look of a man who had been swept away by an unexpected current in his life.

By a river.

And the river was called Love.

She knew it, suddenly, to the bottom of her bones. Jonas loved her. And she loved him. There were people who would say that they hadn't known each other long enough, that they could not know if it was love after such a short period of time. There would be people who would say it was an infatuation. Chemistry.

But there was a place in her soul that *knew.* She knew deeply and completely. She might have known from the moment she laid eyes on him outside the front door of Match Made in Heaven.

She belonged with this man. He belonged with her. To her.

This was what her aunt had believed. This was what her aunt had always tried to tell her. That love was a cosmic force, powerful and immutable. That there were people who were made for each other, and Aunt Jane had believed it was her calling in life to find those people and bring them together.

Had this been her aunt's final match? What if even death could not stop her aunt from doing what she felt was her sacred duty?

"What do you think?" Theresa asked, looking back and forth between them.

"What do you think?" Jonas asked Krissy. And she heard the oddest thing in his voice. He was the most confident, self-assured man she had ever met.

And yet there was no mistaking that was fear in his voice. Jonas Boyden, millionaire, self-made man, was afraid that Krissy Clark, a schoolteacher, did not feel the same way as him right now.

"I think that's the best idea I've ever heard," she said.

Jonas let out a whoop. He turned from where he'd been standing at the deck to lift her out of her chair.

But Theresa inserted herself between them. "Uh-uh. After you're married."

"It's just a little late for that," Jonas said grouchily, gazing over his sister's shoulder at Krissy's lips with such wanting that she shivered from it.

"Come on," Theresa said to Krissy, "we've got lots to do. And you," she said to her brother, "go see Mike. And make sure you have that ring with you."

"Yes, ma'am," Jonas said meekly.

Jonas felt as if he was in a dream. The best dream he had ever had. Somehow, this crazy family of his had, in a matter of hours, put together a wedding.

The arbor that they had been building that morning was now so thickly braided with balsam fir boughs that he could not see the structure underneath it. As the summer sun drenched it, the fragrance enveloped him. Beyond the arbor, the lake where he had grown, where the days of his boyhood had unfolded, winked and sparkled.

Mike was at Jonas's side, and his family was slowly filling up the chairs that had fragrant boughs attached to them with burlap bows. He was aware, as perhaps he never had been before, how this gathering of aunts and uncles and cousins and nephews all held the spark of his parents' blood. His parents were gone, and yet here, too.

For the first time, Jonas understood. What was best about them had gone on. What was best about them demanded he be brave enough to accept this gift that had been given to him. Love.

Their love was here, standing with him, in each of these people gathered, and that love went on and on.

With that realization, everything around Jonas took on a shimmering radiance: birdsong, bees humming, blades of grass, the wrinkles on his aunt Martha's carefully folded hands, the cobalt blue of his uncle Hal's shirt.

His cousin Shandra placed a flute to her lips, and the sound that came from that flute increased Jonas's sense of being on heaven's door. The melody lifted and soared, dipped and fell, rose again.

Harry and Danny came first: in shorts and little plaid shirts, with ties. Harry's tie was already askew, and Danny's cowlick already defied Theresa's efforts to tame it. Chance was sandwiched in between them, burlap pack bags slapping him on either side. The boys were pulling leaves and wild white daisies from the sacks and throwing them in the air and at the assembled with just a little too much enthusiasm. Aunt Vera caught Harry's arm and said something stern to him that subdued his flower tossing.

Jonas smiled at that, and then the smile faltered. His breath died like a breeze would die in the hottest part of the day. Down a shaded path that curved through beech and hemlock and oak, he caught a glimpse of Krissy coming.

She was wearing a short white dress that pinched at her waist and then flared out and flowed over her like water. Her shoulders, sun-kissed, were bare. So, too, were her feet, he noticed. She was wearing a ring of flowers on her head, the snowy white of Queen Anne's lace interwoven with waxy green leaves and the soft lavender of dame's rocket. In that intricately woven ring, he saw the hands of the matriarchs of all these clans weaving her into the family.

Her hair flowed free, untamed, gorgeous, from under that ring of flowers. Her hands were clasped in front of her, and in them was a bouquet of deep blue lupines, his mother's favorite flowers.

Jonas had never seen anything, or anyone, as beautiful as the woman gliding toward him.

Confident.

Not a queen.

And not a warrior.

Not even a princess.

Something better.

A woman who did not have to play any role at all. Who had found herself and had found her way of being in the world. So sure of herself, so genuine, so authentic that it shone from her. She was pure love.

She was a goddess.

Her eyes never left his face.

And in those eyes was every man's deepest dream, a dream he did not even know he had, until it walked toward him with sun kissing delicate curves and joyous tears streaming down a serene face.

Jonas marveled at the glory of a world that could bring him someone like her.

Krissy arrived beside him and they looked at each other. He saw the wonder in her gaze, a look a man could die to receive.

Fred cleared his throat, reminding them they could not get lost in each other and block out all else just yet.

Jonas noted that his happy-go-lucky uncle had somehow transformed into a man of quiet authority.

The age-old ritual of two people joining together in front of the community that would love and support them began.

Jonas, because of his large family, had been to dozens of weddings. And yet never had the words resonated so deeply with him, never had he felt the sacredness of the vows so intensely as when he was saying them. It felt, not as if the words were leaving him, but as if they were entering him, becoming part of his muscle, his cells, his bones, his soul.

For better, for worse.

For richer, for poorer.

In sickness and in health.

To love and to cherish.

Till death do us part.

And then, just when he thought the experience could not intensify anymore, Krissy, so beloved to him in such a short time, was saying those words to him, her voice strong and sure, her gaze steady on his face.

He could feel the promise, weaving together with his promises to her, making something brand-new in the world, strong, invincible.

And then they were declared husband and wife, and to the cheers of the assembled, they kissed each other.

A kiss that said welcome home.

A kiss that promised it would stretch toward eternity.

A kiss that filled every void that neither of them had known they still carried.

After a long, long time, they came up for air. Jonas rose out of the silence of their joined lips like a swimmer coming from the bottom of a body of water, breaking the surface. His family was cheering. His sister was crying. Mike was grinning ear to ear. Chance was moaning. His nephews were pelting the gathering with flowers and leaves.

He took Krissy's hand. It felt so right in his, a perfect fit. He gazed down at her, and she drank him in with wonder. Finally, they turned and walked down the aisle. The gathering had been waiting, and daisy petals floated around them until it felt as if they were walking through a blizzard.

How right his sister had been that this was the kind of moment that was not just about two people.

This moment, this celebration of hope, this confirmation of love, this confidence in the future, was not just for Krissy and Jonas.

It was for all of them.

Love was a gift that radiated outward to the whole world.

CHAPTER SEVENTEEN

KRISSY AWOKE IN the morning, sun pouring through the red and white oaks that shaded their cabin and dappling her face. Her feet hurt, in the best possible way, and a smile tickled her lips as she remembered dancing into the wee hours of the morning.

No doubt that was why she was exhausted, despite having slept soundly.

In her husband's arms.

She realized the place beside her in bed was empty, but she turned to the rumpled sheets and touched them. Buried her nose in his pillow and drank in the scent of him.

She was married to Jonas Boyden.

It was almost too big to comprehend. Ever since they had driven under those gateposts onto the resort, it felt as if enchantment had unfolded.

An enchantment where love was fanned to life, where every moment shone brilliantly, where the impossible became possible, where what was considered *normal* was suspended.

Krissy realized she needed to see Jonas to make sure she was not having a dream. She climbed from the bed, showered, pulled a comb through her hair and tossed on some shorts and a T-shirt.

There was always coffee on the front porch of the main lodge, and she was sure she would find Jonas there.

She heard him before she saw him, among the deep rise and fall of male voices. She stopped, loving that she knew him so well that she could tell which voice was his. She loved the sound of it, the pure masculine vibrancy, and she felt a quiver as she remembered how his voice had worshipped her last night.

Beautiful.

My heart.

My love.

But then he stopped talking. And she heard the other voice. Mike?

"I have to give it to you, buddy, you went the extra mile to keep that car."

Just as she had recognized his voice, now she recognized Jonas's shout of laughter. Everything in Krissy's world felt as if it was crashing down around her. She did not wait to hear his response.

This was what the enchantment had kept her from seeing, had kept her from remembering, had kept her from focusing on.

From the beginning, it had been a deception.

Her eagerness not to be alone on a weekend that would have intensified her sense of having lost her family and best friend, her aunt Jane, had clouded out reason, had clouded out fact, had clouded out *everything*.

And now that the first doubt had wiggled its way past the shining walls of the enchantment, others crowded in.

What kind of idiot followed through, turning what was supposed to be a game into reality? What kind of fool got married on an impulse?

Sickly, Krissy realized exactly who got married on an impulse.

Her parents had. An impulse, and because they had to. Because momentary passion had led to a permanent situation, an unwanted pregnancy.

She suddenly saw her exhaustion this morning in a completely different light. She counted back to the first time she and Jonas had spent the night together. She realized her cycle was off.

She had been so swept up in the magic of what had been unfolding between her and Jonas that she had forgotten that stark possibility.

She was a science major! How could she, of all people, have forgotten the biology of what a man and a woman together could produce? How could she have been so reckless? She had acted without reason, swept away in a tsunami of passion. She hadn't asked him to take precautions, and he had probably assumed she was on the pill.

But she wasn't. She'd given up on love. She knew better. She'd made the very reasonable decision, based on facts, that love was a whirlpool that sucked in everything around it and tossed the wreckage back out when it was done.

Was she pregnant?

The fear that overtook her made her heart pound.

Because this was her parents all over again. A marriage that should have never been held together by a poor baby, born with a job, a responsibility.

Krissy turned quickly away from the lodge before anybody saw her. She started to run through the trees toward the cabin, panic driving her.

Calm yourself, she said as she arrived back at the cabin. She had to make rational decisions. And that was never going to happen as long as Jonas was in the picture, clouding her reasoning processes.

She had to get out of here, before she saw him again. Where was Chance? She had to get her dog and go home, buy herself some breathing space, find out if she really was pregnant or if she was just being hysterical.

Decide for herself—away from the hypnotic presence of her beautiful husband—if any of this was real, or if it was all part of his game. It was not as if he hadn't warned her.

That it would be complicated. That he was master of the elaborate prank.

The thought that those vows they had spoken might be part of a prank made her sick to her stomach. It was all too much. Too much had unfolded over the last month, and especially these magical days at Boy's Den.

All Krissy's old fears around family swarmed to the surface. She realized she had made a terrible mistake. She had let herself be seduced—literally and figuratively—into thinking make-believe was real. She had been pulled into a fairy tale when she of all people should have known better.

Where was Chance? The last she had seen him had been last night. He had been trailing Mike, a sleeping boy over each shoulder, to the main lodge.

The boys who had called her auntie with such excitement last night.

Her sense of loss deepened. She was not their auntie, not really. None of it was real.

She couldn't risk going to find her dog and bumping into Jonas. Besides, her dog loved it here. He loved having little boys to play with. Chance was better off without her.

Just like she was better off without Jonas.

She threw things into a bag. She paused at the white dress. She couldn't take it, this poignant reminder of the most incredible day of her life.

But she couldn't resist it, either. She stuffed the dress in her bag, scribbled a note to Jonas and went out the door. She slid through the trees like a ghost to the main gate and then the main road.

She did something she had never done before.

She stuck out her thumb. She wasn't afraid.

Jonas looked at his watch and smiled. Krissy was sleeping late. Well, who could blame her? It had been quite the night. Dawn had been breaking when they had finally collapsed into each other's arms and slept.

He grabbed her a coffee, taking great pleasure in making it exactly how she liked it, and then he made his way up to the cabin. He was going to kiss his wife awake.

He kicked open the cabin door. "Hey, Mrs. Boyden, time to—

The bed was empty. The cabin was completely empty. He thought she must have gone in search of him, but how could he have missed her? And then it occurred to him the cabin had a strange aura of abandonment clinging to it. And that her things were gone.

Even the dress that had lain in a crumpled heap by the side of the bed this morning was gone.

He felt a sense of panic rising in him. And then he saw the note, tucked under a jar that she had put her bouquet of lupines into.

Jonas raced over and picked it up, sank into a chair.

Jonas,
I am just feeling entirely overwhelmed. I feel we've been swept away by passion and realize

that may not be the best way to make this kind of momentous decision. Please respect my need for some time and space.

She signed it simply *Krissy*. And then added a PS asking him to give Chance to his nephews.

His nephews. Not her nephews, as if those vows they had spoken yesterday, that joined them so completely, did not matter. As if they were not married at all.

He sank into the chair and the note trembled in his hand.

Of course she didn't trust love. She'd told him about her parents. But now he saw she didn't trust it so much that she didn't even want to risk loving her own dog.

His heart felt as if it was shattering.

For himself.

But for her, too.

And this was a truth he'd always known about love. It left you open to the worst kind of pain. A pain that felt insurmountable, as if it would never end, a gaping wound that would never heal.

Krissy was right.

They had not thought this thing through nearly enough. He was shocked at himself for allowing himself to be exactly as she had stated, *swept away by passion*.

But for him, it wasn't passion. He was no newcomer to passion. If he'd been swept away by it in the past, it had been temporary. A moment, and then he'd found his feet, himself, his equilibrium.

This was not passion that was sweeping him away.

It was love.

What did love do? Did it go after her and insist on having its own way? Did it try to convince her? Throw itself at her feet begging for mercy? Or did it respect her need for space and time, and trust that she would come to know the truth as surely as he did?

If he had to convince her that what had leaped up between them was good and real, maybe it wasn't quite as good and real as he thought it was.

Besides, who knew love's dagger more intimately than him? If he felt this bereft about losing Krissy after only knowing her for such a short time, didn't that prove what he had felt since the death of his parents? That love could cripple the strongest man?

Jonas tried to convince himself it was good that she had taken this step—declared a need for space—before it deepened even more.

He had the awful thought she might be hitchhiking. If that was the case, he had to find her for her own safety.

Besides, he realized, after the joy of last night, he could not face his family. He quickly packed his things and made his way out to the parking lot. He got in his car—the car he suddenly hated—and drove away before anyone could see him, ask painful questions, put him on the spot.

He scanned the road for Krissy. She couldn't have been gone long, and she could not have gotten far. But she was nowhere to be seen.

When it became apparent he would not find her, he finally stopped and sent his sister a quick text.

Something has come up for Krissy.

He remembered her planning an exit strategy well before all this had unfolded into such a spectacular disaster.

She's had an emergency. Can you look after the
dog for now?

Then he turned off his phone before Theresa could
answer. He resisted, just barely, the impulse to toss it
away in a fit of fury and frustration.

CHAPTER EIGHTEEN

KRISSY LAY ON her couch. She was in her wedding dress. She had developed a terrible habit of wearing it around the house, as if she was taking some satisfaction in the fact it made her feel even worse, if that was possible.

She hadn't combed her hair yet today, and the dress had an ice cream splotch on the front of it. Prone, she trailed her hand with the spoon in it over the edge of the sofa until she hit the rim of the ice cream bucket. She dug the spoon in and lifted it to her lips.

Another splotch melted onto the dress.

She had to pull it together. Ice cream for breakfast wasn't good for the baby. The drugstore earliest alert pregnancy test kit had confirmed what her heart already knew.

A baby.

She was going to have Jonas's baby.

It made her so happy, and so sad at the same time. She would not repeat her parents' horrible story, a baby binding them together long after the passion had fizzled to ugly, wet embers.

Still, she had thought Jonas would call or drop by unexpectedly, hadn't she? Just to check on her? Just to make sure she was all right? Just because he loved her to the moon and back and couldn't stay away?

She had told him to leave her alone. He was just following instructions. She burst into tears and then tried to staunch the flow. All this emotion could not be good for the baby!

Krissy heard a vehicle pull up out front. Could he have come, after all? She got up off the sofa and flicked back the curtain. The sunlight hurt her eyes.

Not Jonas. It was a moving van. How could she have mistaken that deep rumble for the sound of his car? That was the nature of hope, perhaps, wanting something so badly it filled in the blanks with imagination. This was what her secret longing, her secret hope, had always been, even when she denied it: someone to love her. Someone to give her the family she longed for.

Two burly men were getting out of that van, sliding open the rolling door on the back of it. Good grief. Today was the day they were bringing the boxes from her aunt's office. Had she known that? Did she have it marked on a calendar somewhere? It was summer. There was no school to keep her on schedule. No routine. The days were sliding into one another, and her responsibilities—keeping her grass cut, opening her mail, answering messages—had fallen completely by the wayside.

No one missed her.

That was how totally pathetic her life was. Why try to hide it from complete strangers? She went and opened the door. If her state of dishevelment, and her wedding dress, shocked the deliverymen, they certainly didn't show it.

She showed them where the basement door was, then ignored them as they carried boxes up and down the stairs. When had she become this person? She simply didn't care what they thought of her as she took up her reclining position on the couch.

"Ah, miss?"

"Yes?"

"We're all done. If you could sign this?"

She sat up and took the clipboard and signed.

"This fell out of one of the boxes," he said, handing her a file. "Sorry."

"It's okay." She had some money lying on the coffee table left over from a pizza delivery, and she handed it all to him as a tip.

Then they were gone, and she stared at the two items in her hand. One was an envelope, and the other was a file that had Jonas Boyden written across the front of it in a thick black Sharpie in Aunt Jane's block printing.

Krissy realized how *hungry* she was for any smidgen of information about Jonas. How had he answered the questions on the Match Made in Heaven application? What did he do for fun? What did he consider the most important attribute in another human being?

But she forced herself to be disciplined, to calm the hammering of her heart by opening the envelope instead. Inside it was the purchase agreement for her little carriage house.

She remembered how pleased her aunt had been when she had found it and brought Krissy to see it, how excited they both had been when it was priced reasonably, well within Krissy's minuscule budget.

Now, she saw exactly why her aunt Jane's business account had been so meager. Her aunt had spent all her money when she had paid for the majority of the cost of the carriage house.

Stunned by this gift, her fingers trembling, Krissy opened the file with Jonas's name on it. She was not sure if she was relieved or aggrieved that there was no application form inside the thin file.

There was nothing there at all, except a carbon copy of a receipt for five thousand dollars with words written across it: *Satisfaction guaranteed.*

She was going to close the file when she realized something was written on the back of the receipt.

She turned it over.

In her aunt's spidery, oh, so familiar handwriting, were the words *Krissy's perfect match.*

Her house. And her husband. Aunt Jane looking after her. Except the husband part had gone so terribly wrong.

But there was the baby. Someone to care about. Someone to lavish love on... She heard another vehicle stop in front of her house. That was more traffic in the last hour than she'd had since she arrived home from the Boyden family reunion.

Krissy went and peeked out the curtain again.

Finally he had come. Her relief was instant and acute. It was real, after all. They could figure this thing out.

But as she watched, it wasn't Jonas who got out of the car. First it was Chance, racing toward the door, and then it was Theresa.

She might have been able to keep that door closed to Theresa, but the dog? She cried harder as she saw how fast he was running to the door. He was scratching on it, now, whining, giving hysterical little barks.

Krissy went and opened the door. She collapsed in a puddle of feeling, threw her arms around the dog, who lavished her with kisses and whined his admonishment for being abandoned.

Theresa's feet moved into her range of vision.

"Oh, my," Theresa said sadly.

And Krissy realized the sight she must make, in her

crumpled, stained wedding dress, hair uncombed and eyes puffy from crying.

"Let's go in," Theresa said gently. "I'll make you a nice cup of tea." Once they were in the door, Theresa took her in solemnly, and said, "Where's your bathroom? I'm going to run you a nice bath and make you tea while you have a soak."

Stop this, Krissy ordered herself, but the truth was, she was so relieved to have someone take charge that she just pointed the way to the bathroom. While the bath ran, she shucked the wedding dress and put on her robe.

Minutes later, she was soaking, the dog was hanging his head woefully over the side of the tub, looking at her accusingly, and she could hear Theresa humming away in her kitchen.

It was the first time Krissy had felt sane since she had left Boy's Den. Feeling restored and stronger, she finally pulled herself from the tub, wrapped herself in her robe and padded down the hall.

"How do you like our new car?" Theresa asked her, setting a cup of tea down in front of her and taking the seat across from her.

"He told you about the bet."

"Bet?" Theresa said, cocking her head at Krissy. "No, he told us he hated that car. He didn't want it anymore."

"Oh," Krissy said.

"Just for the record, he looks as bad as you. Maybe worse."

She couldn't even be offended that Theresa thought she looked bad. Her heart twisted at the thought of Jonas in pain. Somehow, she had pictured him shrugging the whole thing off, getting back to normal quite quickly, leaving the whole debacle behind with a certain ease.

"Maybe you'd better tell me about the bet," Theresa suggested.

"The bet. The one where Mike would get the car if Jonas turned thirty and wasn't in a committed relationship."

"That wasn't really a bet," Theresa said. "It was a joke between the three of us."

"Well, he didn't see it that way. And neither did Mike. They were laughing about it the morning after the wedding. I heard them."

"You better tell me how our silly bet relates to you," Theresa said quietly.

And suddenly Krissy needed to tell someone, as if in the telling of the entire story, she would herself be able to figure out the truth. She started at that night they had set off the alarm at Match Made in Heaven and told Theresa the entire story.

"And then today," she finally finished, nearly half an hour later, "I found this."

She went and got the receipt her aunt had written and flipped it over so Theresa could see the back of it.

Her almost sister-in-law looked at it, then sighed. "Do you think I would have pushed you two to get married if I didn't think this very same thing, Krissy? You two, together, were something to see. You know, Mike and I have the best relationship. It's as solid and as comfy as an old T-shirt you love to wear around the house.

"But you and Jonas have something else. It's the same thing I saw in my parents. It's like a light goes on in both of you when you're together, and it makes the very air around you shimmer with radiance."

"But we barely know each other!" Krissy wailed. "It started over a bet!"

"Maybe that is how it started," Theresa said, "but you can't possibly believe he married you because of that! I saw the look in his eyes. And our bets go back and forth all the time. They're games, that's all. He might have lost the car. Mike would have enjoyed tormenting him for a week or two and then made sure he won it back on a bet about a hockey game or something. So what's really going on with you?"

Krissy faced what was really going on with her. It felt like a relief to say it. "I don't want to be like my parents."

"Your parents?"

And so she ended up telling Theresa about that, too.

"And now you're going to have a baby," Theresa said.

Krissy went very still. "How do you know?"

"I'd like to tell you I can see it in you, and I can, now that I know. But I saw the test strip in the bathroom. Did you suspect it at the reunion?"

"Yes."

"So that explains the fast exit."

"Are you going to tell him?" Krissy whispered.

"No, Krissy, I'm not. You're going to have to make that decision."

"What if I tell him, and he feels obligated to make our marriage real because of a baby?"

"Just like your parents?"

"Yes."

Theresa sighed. "This isn't about the baby, not really. It's about whether or not you love him. Because that would involve a level of trust in him. And you can't decide that based on what your aunt thought, or what I think, either. Your heart is telling you the truth, and I think you are brave enough to listen to it. But I can't make that decision for you."

As Theresa spoke, as her words washed over Krissy, it felt as if a dark curtain was being lifted and the sun was dancing back into her life.

That thing that would not be killed and would not be quelled, no matter how hard she tried. It winked back to life, an ember that had been blown on.

Hope.

A sudden illuminating realization came to her. The level of trust she needed, she realized, was not in Jonas. She needed to trust herself.

"I need to see him," Krissy said. And then she laughed. "I don't even know where my husband lives."

"Luckily for you," Theresa said, grinning, "I do."

Jonas's face itched from not shaving. His hair was too long. He could smell himself, for God's sake. His breath could make a train take a dirt road. Added to that, Jonas had the headache of all headaches. He wished he could blame it on alcohol, but no, it was heartache pure and simple. He wasn't eating right. He was barely sleeping.

How well he remembered this kind of pain from the loss of his parents.

He counted back to the day he had first met Krissy. Barely a month. If she could do this to him after one month, wasn't it for the best that she was gone? What if they'd been together a year, and she decided to pull the plug? Or two years. Or ten.

Or maybe she wouldn't make a decision to pull the plug. Maybe she would die in a terrible accident, just like his parents had.

This was what he'd forgotten when he was falling for her and falling so hard. The pain, not so much of loving, but of losing that love.

It was why he had wrestled down the desire to phone

her. A thousand times he had looked up her number, thought of calling it just to hear her voice. But then, no.

He'd get through this period of grief.

He'd white-knuckle his way through it. Go cold turkey, like an addict leaving behind their drug, their source of pleasure, their *one thing* that made them want to live, that gave them the impetus to get up in the morning.

But he wasn't strong enough to go completely cold turkey. Well-meaning relatives—who had no idea his marriage was over before it had really begun—kept sending him pictures from the reunion.

The tug-of-war, her face caught in the reflected light of the fireworks, her expression as she ate her first s'more and of course, her coming toward him with those flowers in her hair and that look on her face.

That was the problem, really.

The look on her face. Nobody could make up a look like that, could they?

He groaned, back on the merry-go-round, revisiting all those things he needed to stop revisiting.

He glanced at the clock: 10:00 a.m. Today, he'd go to the office. Today, he'd make those phone calls, today he'd answer emails.

He took his phone out.

He ordered himself to look at his emails, to return a call, to look for a new resort to buy.

But instead, he opened the pictures of Krissy, felt his heart fall all over again and realized he would not be getting back to normal today.

CHAPTER NINETEEN

JONAS WOKE UP, feeling groggy and out of sorts. His teeth felt as if they were wearing socks. He glanced at the clock. It was two o'clock in the afternoon.

What kind of self-respecting person was napping at two in the afternoon?

He realized someone was at the door. You practically had to have secret service clearance to get in his building so he knew it must be Theresa.

"Go away," he called.

She knocked at the door again. He knew his sister. She wasn't going away. He got up and went to the door, flung it open.

It wasn't his sister.

Krissy stood there, with Chance.

The dog apparently had forgotten all the good things they had taught him, because he leaped at Jonas, put his paws on his shoulders and cleaned his face.

"Get off me," he bellowed.

"If I were you," Krissy said, slipping in the door completely uninvited and shutting it behind her, "I'd take kisses where you can get them. You look terrible." She wrinkled her nose. "And you smell."

He managed to get the dog off of him. "Sit down!"

The dog did so reluctantly. Jonas stared at Krissy.

His wife. Unlike him, she looked at the top of her game. Not the least heartbroken, apparently. Radiant.

Beautiful in a pair of jeans and open-toed shoes and a clinging T-shirt. Her hair was flowing free around her shoulders, and he had to shove his hands in his pockets to keep from touching it.

He looked away from her so that he didn't have to see her lips. How could he look at them without remembering? Wanting? Longing?

"Sorry," Krissy said. "I had to bring Chance. He won't leave me since I left him at Boy's Den. He has anxiety now, every time I go out the door."

Perfectly understandable, Jonas thought.

"What do you want?" he asked hoarsely.

"This came in the mail," she said.

She handed him a piece of paper, and he unfolded it, frowned at it. So much easier to study it than to look at her.

It was their certificate of marriage.

"Yeah," he said gruffly, handing her back the piece of paper without looking at her, "about that. What do you want to do? Annul it?"

"Hmm, I think you can only annul an unconsummated marriage," she said mildly.

She was going to bring *that* up? He dared a look at her. Memories of being with her in that way stormed him.

"Well, what do you want to do, then?" he managed to ask her.

"I want to give it a try," she said.

He stared at her.

"If you want to."

Want to? He wanted to throw himself at her feet and scream yes. He wanted to pick her up and swing her in circles until they were both dizzy from it.

But what if it didn't work out? What if all those scenarios he had played out in his mind over the last few days came to fruition? He would be a destroyed man.

Though, truth to tell, he was nearly a destroyed man now.

"Why?" he asked her.

Her words were so simple.

"Because I love you. Madly. Unreasonably. It feels like the air is gone from my world. The color. The reason."

But that was how he was feeling.

"I know you're scared, Jonas."

He wanted to deny he was scared, but when he looked at her, she was the one who would always know all of him.

And who would accept it. Maybe even cherish that which he tried to hide from the rest of the world.

"I am, too," she said. "Terrified. Both of us have been so wounded by love. In very different ways, but it still makes it hard to say yes to it. I think that's why I was so quick to reach the wrong conclusion when I overheard you talking to Mike on Sunday morning."

"What?"

"He was congratulating you on the lengths you'd gone to to get your car back."

"It stopped being about the car a long, long time ago."

"I know that," she said softly. "I needed it to be about the car. Because I had to run. I was so afraid, Jonas."

"Of me?" he asked, appalled.

"No, Jonas. Of repeating history. I'm going to have a baby. Our baby."

He could feel something rising within him, phoenix-like, out of the ashes of his destruction.

He stepped toward her, and then closer.

"A baby?" he said. "Our baby?"

She nodded, and it was all there. Her terror. Her uncertainty.

He put his hands on her shoulders and rested his forehead against hers. The moment he touched her, his strength began to flow back into him. She was Samson's hair and Arthur's sword.

"I was born for this," he told her softly.

"To be a daddy?" she asked.

"Maybe that, too, but no. I was born to take that fear from you, and that uncertainty. I was born to show you a world that can be trusted. I was born to show you what love can do, and what it can make and how incredible the world can be because of it."

She was crying now. He wrapped his arms around her and held her tight.

"Jonas?"

"Yes, my love?"

"You really stink."

And just like that, they were laughing. And the dog was barking, and the world and the future stretched out in front of them, illuminated.

Illuminated by the one light that had illuminated the world forever. Sometimes it flickered, sometimes it was hard to see. Sometimes tumult and the unexpected and uncertainty threatened it.

And yet it always fluttered back to life, it always gained strength, it always proved itself more powerful than any darkness.

There it was, shining.

A beacon for all to follow.

Love.

EPILOGUE

"ARE YOU SURE?" Jonas asked Krissy.

"About?"

"Leaving her with the boys."

"Jonas! We are not leaving Jane with the boys. We're leaving her with your sister. I think she can be trusted with a baby."

Jane-Paulette was named after Krissy's aunt Jane, of course, and after Jonas's mother. She was nearly four months old.

And so tiny. And so perfect. Jonas had never felt anything like what he felt the first time he had held that baby. Protective. Besotted. Enchanted. And you would think that feeling would go away—the newness would rub off the awe—but no, it deepened.

"You told me you were going to take away my fear and uncertainty," Krissy reminded him. "You told me you were going to teach me the world can be trusted."

"And haven't I?" he demanded.

"Oh, yeah, you have. But honestly, Jonas, when it comes to the baby, I have to teach you all those things."

"She's little! Simon and Gar are rambunctious. You can't be too careful."

"You can, actually, be too careful. If she's survived

Chance, the probability of her surviving our nephews is pretty good."

The reunion was starting tomorrow. But Jonas and Krissy and Jane and the dog had all arrived early. Because Krissy had announced to him, her eyes shining, that she finally had figured out where to spread her aunt's ashes.

When she had told him, he'd had his doubts.

"But you said she wanted them spread in the place she loved most. She's never even been to Boy's Den."

Krissy smiled at him tenderly, that smile that could still melt his heart, even as they approached their one-year anniversary.

"What she loved most was love," she told him. "That's where she would want to be."

So Jonas reluctantly surrendered the baby to his sister and followed Krissy down to the rowboat. She had the urn of ashes on her lap.

"Where to?" he asked, gathering up the oars.

"You know," she said.

And then he did.

They had honeymooned here, last year, after all the vacationers had gone home. And they had taken out the rowboat and found the most beautiful private cove overlooking the lake. It had its own beach and was only visible from the water.

And it had a For Sale sign on it.

They had wandered that piece of property most of the day, deciding where to put the road and where their cabin would go, where they would put the tire swing over the water, where a good place for a sandbox would be.

Now he turned the boat in that direction and rowed through quiet waters.

They came to the cove. Their new house was rising out of the ground, the framing nearly done.

Already, Jonas could feel the long summer days that would unfold here. He could hear children laughing and dogs barking. He could smell campfires burning and marshmallows cooking. He could see Krissy reading on the deck and a little girl with blueberry stains around her mouth. He could see himself and another child carrying a string of fish up from the dock. For one brief, incredible moment, he could see the future.

"Are you ready?" he asked softly.

With reverent fingers, she unscrewed the lid from the urn. She held the open mouth over the water and the ashes spilled out in a silver trail across it.

He thought of that strange woman whom he had only met once, how he had felt she had seen his soul and known things about him no one could know.

He thought of how she had loved Krissy, how she had kept that little spark of belief in love alive in Krissy, when her childhood experiences could have snuffed it out for good.

He knew he owed this woman in some way. Jonas was well aware he did not know how these things worked, but that did not stop him from being grateful, daily, that it had worked. That Aunt Jane had, from heaven, made them, Jonas and Krissy, her most perfect match.

"Thank you," he said softly, and Krissy smiled.

It was that smile that lit his world, and that he saw on his child's perfect little lips. It was a smile that let him know, over and over again, that the world was full of distractions. Wealth and success, toys and games like the ones he used to play.

But in the end, all that mattered was what that smile told him.

Jonas knew Krissy had been absolutely right about putting these ashes in this tiny lake where her aunt had never visited.

Aunt Jane would want to be right here. In her favorite place.

Where the love was.

* * * * *

HIS SECRET
STARLIGHT BABY

MICHELLE MAJOR

To Dutch— Thanks for being a fantastic father-in-law and for raising one of the best men I know (and love!).

Chapter One

Cory Hall approached the man who'd just exited the darkened bar, trying not to be intimidated by his size and strength. He was well over six feet tall with an athlete's build, the body of a former NFL star.

In the dim glow of the streetlamp overhead, it was hard to make out his features, although she knew his dark hair was shot through with streaks of burnished gold, the kind of natural highlights that pro-athlete wives and girlfriends spent gobs of money to re-create in the salon. Cory could see that his angular jaw was muted by several days of stubble, and the canvas jacket he wore strained to envelop his massive shoulders.

He turned back toward the door without noticing

her. At this point in her life, she was used to being invisible, so that wasn't a surprise.

"We're closed," he said, his voice reverberating in the quiet of the hour. So he'd noticed her after all. He didn't bother to turn from the door he was locking. Either Jordan Schaeffer didn't expect trouble late at night in a small town like Starlight, Washington, or he wasn't worried about handling himself.

It could be either option. Yet Cory was about to dump a whole heap of trouble into his life that might make him wish he'd taken more care.

She certainly would have made different choices if someone offered her a do-over on the past few years. More care with her heart and a sharper focus on what she wanted her life to look like. Instead, Cory had let the people around her dictate her choices and her self-worth, and they hadn't given a single damn about her. Now she was ready to begin again at twenty-seven years old. There was only one thing that mattered—her baby—and she'd do whatever it took to be the mom he deserved.

After a quick glance over her shoulder at her grandmother's old Buick, which was parked at the curb, Cory swallowed and took another step forward.

"Hey, Jordan."

His hand stilled on the set of keys he held, and his broad back went stiff. For a moment Cory didn't think that he recognized her voice. A spike of panic zinged across her middle at the thought he might not even remember her.

They hadn't exactly parted as the best of friends.

A bitter wind whistled along the empty street, and she hugged her arms tight across her body. She'd left her big coat in the car when the anticipation of this meeting left her drenched in sweat. The late-March temperature was cool but not frigid, not like the biting cold of her hometown in Michigan. This part of Washington, an hour east of Seattle in a valley at the base of the Cascade Mountains, had appeared both temperate and picturesque when she'd driven in earlier this afternoon. In fact, it seemed perfect. A quaint, quiet place to start fresh.

Cory needed a fresh start like she needed her next breath.

Jordan went back to locking the door, and if it weren't for that initial rigidity and the tension currently radiating from him, Cory might have thought he hadn't heard her greeting.

When he turned, she realized what a fool she'd been—nothing new there. Jordan's pale green eyes blazed with an emotion she couldn't name, although it definitely wasn't friendly. Not that she expected a warm welcome back into his life, although she had to admit, in the two and a half days it had taken to drive halfway across the country, her mind had wandered down the path of silly fantasy more than once.

She fisted her hands, the sharp pain of nails stab-

bing into the flesh of her palm a much-needed reminder to stay grounded in reality. Cory was in
Starlight to take care of business, not to indulge in
ridiculous daydreams. Single moms didn't have time
for that sort of nonsense.

"How are you?" she asked, clearing her throat
when the words came out on a croak. She tried for a
smile. "It's been a minute."

"What are you doing here?" He pocketed the set
of keys and rocked back on his heels. His eyes raked
over her in a way that left her wishing she hadn't forgotten her flat iron back in Michigan. Or had she deserted that particular styling tool when she'd taken
off from Atlanta? She hadn't given much thought
to making herself look pretty in what felt like ages.

"I was…um…in the area, and I thought I'd stop
in and say hi." She gave a limp wave. "Hi."

Jordan stared at her like she'd lost her mind.

"I didn't know if you'd remember me." She pushed
away a stray lock of hair that blew into her face. "I'm
sure you want to—"

"I remember, Cory." His voice was a deep, angry
rumble. "I remember everything."

She swallowed. "Oh. Okay, well, that's good. I
think." She gestured to the bar he'd exited minutes
earlier. "You own this place, right? It looks nice."
She inwardly cringed at her inability to stem the tide
of inane babble pouring from her mouth. She wasn't

here for pleasantries but couldn't quite bring herself to get to the point.

"It's after midnight." He ran a hand through his thick hair. She still couldn't see its true color, but it was longer than he'd worn it when he'd played football in Georgia. Untamed and a bit wild, much like the man himself.

"Right." She took a slow, steadying breath. "I need to talk to you, Jordan."

"I got that."

"It's about what happened when you left."

"From what I saw on ESPN, Kade got one hell of a contract offer. Forty million for four years. He got it all. You both got exactly what you wanted."

She winced at the accusation in his voice, even though she deserved every bit of judgment and condemnation Jordan Schaeffer could dish out. "Kade and I aren't together," she said, as if that explained everything when it was only the tip of the iceberg.

"Not my concern, Cory. In fact, right now my only concern is getting home and into bed for a decent night's sleep. I wish you well in whatever you choose for life after Kade Barrington, if you're telling the truth about that."

"I never lied," she said, trying and mostly failing to keep the pain out of her voice. Trying and completely failing to stop an image of Jordan asleep in bed from filling her mind.

"You went back to him."

Cory sucked in a shaky gulp of air, because she could have sworn she heard an answering pain in Jordan's tone. That couldn't be possible, because...

"After you took off." She bit down on the inside of her cheek until she tasted blood. "You left without even saying goodbye."

He laughed, a harsh scrape across her fraught nerves. "Sweetheart, we barely said hello."

Oh no. He wasn't going to do that. Not now. Not after everything Cory had dealt with in the past year. She might have had only one night with Jordan, but it had meant...something. To her, it had turned out to mean everything.

Her gaze darted to the gas guzzler her grandmother had given her before she died last month, and Cory was tempted to walk away. She could climb back in the car, spend one night in the local inn where she'd rented a room and be on the highway by first light.

Then she looked at him again, at those unique eyes she saw staring back at her every day, and realized she had to see this through. If not for herself, then for her baby.

"We said plenty," she told him, straightening her shoulders. "We did plenty. Enough that I have a six-month-old son in that car." She hitched a finger at the Buick. "You have a son, Jordan."

Jordan stared at the little boy gazing up at him from his mother's arms for several long seconds, then resumed pacing back and forth across the scuffed hardwood of Trophy Room, the bar he owned.

His mind continued to race at a thousand miles an hour, and adrenaline pumped through him so hard he thought his head might actually explode. Jordan had grown up an athlete. He could handle adrenaline. On the football field, he'd loved the spike of heat through his veins. It meant he was ready for action. He was in control. It didn't matter whom he was facing in the lineup or what the stakes were, from his chance at a college scholarship to a national championship to a televised playoff game.

He rose to meet every challenge and welcomed each new opponent, unwavering in his faith that determination and dedication would see him through.

Cory Hall had nearly felled him with four simple words.

You have a son.

Of course he remembered her. The thought that he could forget the sweet, beautiful woman who'd been the girlfriend of Jordan's jerk-wad quarterback was preposterous. She was different from a lot of the other girlfriends and wives on the team. She didn't seem to care much about the trappings of the lifestyle, only about keeping Kade happy, which turned out to be no easy task.

Jordan had played with Kade Barrington in Atlanta for two seasons and had been more than a little shocked that a woman like Cory could be so devoted.

Kade had talent in spades, but he'd been released from the team that drafted him out of college due to his inability to get along with the coaches and other players.

He landed in Atlanta with an attitude and something to prove. He and Cory had rented a big house in an expensive neighborhood, and Kade had loved to throw huge team parties. Cory had never seemed all that comfortable in big groups, which was how she and Jordan had ended up talking late one night out by the pool.

Their talks had become a bright spot in his otherwise dark life. Then he'd been injured and hadn't seen her for months. Until the night she showed up at his condo after breaking up with Kade. She'd asked to sleep on his sofa, and he still believed that was what they'd both intended.

It wasn't what had actually occurred.

"I'll arrange a paternity test if you want," Cory offered, her voice quiet. She'd changed from how he remembered her in his mind. Her dark hair was shorter, just skimming her shoulders. Her slim build, rosy lips and the sprinkling of freckles across her nose remained the same. But there was something different about her deep brown eyes. They were guarded now and looked world-weary, as if she'd seen things and experienced feelings that changed her at a cellular level. Somehow it made her even more appealing.

He'd barely been able to speak after she dropped

that bombshell on the sidewalk. A part of him, the shadowy fragment that never planned to become a father, had urged him to send her away.

Jordan had a good life in Starlight. He liked the town and the people living in it. He liked owning a local watering hole and had worked hard to elevate Trophy Room from a dumpy dive bar to a popular hangout for locals and visitors alike. His existence was simple and straightforward, and he worked hard to keep it that way.

Cory Hall was ten kinds of complicated. That was without a baby thrown into the mix.

Jordan didn't want complications.

Instead of sending her away, he'd told her to bring the baby into the bar. He'd unlocked the door, flipped on the light and reentered the space he knew like the back of his hand.

With Cory following close on his heels, he saw the bar through her eyes. Through the lens of someone who'd known him when he was a big deal in the world, or at least had a monster-size attitude. He'd changed, and because of that, he couldn't send her away without at least hearing her out.

Then the baby, who'd been sleeping soundly in the car-seat contraption Cory carried him in, had woken. She'd quickly made a bottle while Jordan stared out the bar's front window into the peaceful night and said a fond farewell to the calm he'd known in life.

"He looks just like me," he said through clenched teeth.

"Yeah." Cory smiled down at the baby, who was beginning to drift off once again. "He has your eyes. I've never seen eyes that color on anyone else."

"They're my father's eyes," Jordan said, then clamped his mouth shut. He wasn't going to bring his dad into this conversation. "Why didn't you reach out to me right away, Cory? I can't believe I'm just finding out about him."

"I'm sorry." Her delicate brows drew together. "I was reeling after you left Atlanta. I thought…" Heat crept into her cheeks, and she shook her head. "It doesn't matter what I thought."

"You went back to Kade."

"Not right away. We gave it another try after I found out I was pregnant," she admitted. "It seemed like the best thing for the baby. I had a few complications at the start of the pregnancy. When the doctor did the early ultrasound, I realized that, based on the date of conception, the baby wasn't Kade's."

"And there was no one else other than me?"

She closed her eyes for a moment, and he could see how much the question hurt her. Damn it. Even now, he didn't want to hurt her.

"Forget I asked that," he said, lowering himself into a chair across from her. "I know this baby is mine. Did you tell Kade?"

Her mouth tightened. "I told him I'd been with

someone else during our breakup. He wanted me to give him a name, but I wouldn't."

"And he just let you go?"

"That's not exactly how I'd describe it. He kicked me out of the house with nothing but the clothes on my back. I stayed with a friend for a couple of days and managed to get one of the other guys' girlfriends to help me retrieve some of my belongings. But most of what I had, he'd bought for me. The clothes, the car, the jewelry."

"Did those things mean a lot to you?"

She rolled her eyes. "I'm pretty sure you know they didn't. I never cared about that stuff."

"I thought I knew you," he said quietly, the ache in his chest expanding with every moment that passed. "But now I wonder. The woman I knew wouldn't have kept a baby from me."

"I get it." She adjusted her hold on the child, cradling him more snugly against her. "With how you left, I was afraid you wouldn't want anything to do with me, and it would have broken my heart. I'd planned to contact you after he was born, but with the surgery and follow-up visits, there was so much happening."

"What surgery?" Jordan sat straighter in the heavy oak chair.

"Ben had a congenital heart defect. The doctors discovered it shortly after he was born," she explained. "He had surgery when he was five days old."

"What kind of defect?" Jordan demanded, then took in a calming breath when the baby startled. "Sorry, I didn't mean to shout."

"It's okay." Cory gave him a hesitant smile. The smiles he remembered from her had been wide and beaming, like she was a character in that old TV show his grandma used to watch, turning the world on with her smile. "It was a narrowing of the aorta, and his lower extremities weren't getting enough blood flow, so they had to do surgery to correct it. It was scary, but he came through like a champ. According to the pediatric cardiologist, he's healthy now. And he's perfect." He watched as she drew in a shuddery breath and then added, "To me, he's perfect."

Jordan pressed two fingers to his chest in an attempt to rub away the deep ache that surfaced at the obvious love in her voice. Questions and accusations surged through him in angry waves. He had a child. His baby had been through something as significant as heart surgery, and he hadn't been there. He'd had no idea. "You dealt with all that on your own?"

Cory shook her head. "I went back to Michigan and moved in with my grandma. Mom didn't want much to do with me. She was too mad that I'd thrown away my 'meal ticket.'" It was clear by the sharp air quotes she made what Cory thought of her mother's opinion.

Jordan agreed. Despite his frustration, Jordan had

to admit it said a lot about her character. He'd had his doubts about that part when he'd left Atlanta. Somehow the knowledge that he hadn't been wrong about her priorities softened the sharp edge of anger he seemed to be skating at the moment.

"Gran was great, but…" Her gaze went dark. "She passed away last month."

"I'm sorry," he said automatically.

"I was happy to be with her at the end, and I'm grateful she got to meet her great-grandson. In fact, Gran was the one who made me promise I'd seek you out to tell you about Ben."

"Thanks, Gran," he said, glancing up at the ceiling.

"I don't expect anything from you." Cory gave a quiet laugh. "Lowering my expectations has become par for the course these days. If you want to be a part of his life—"

"Who do you think I am?" Jordan demanded, temper flaring again. "Hell, yes, I want to be a part of his life, Cory. He's my son. I don't know how we're going to figure this out, but I can guaran-damn-tee you I'm not letting him go."

"Okay," she said. "We'll find a way to make it work. Gran always said everything is figure-outable. I believe that."

She spoke softly, her tone calm, like she was trying to gentle an angry bear. Jordan sighed when he realized he was the bear. Another benefit of his simple life was that it allowed him to stay in control of his emotions. When he didn't feel much of anything, he couldn't get himself into trouble.

Tonight a bomb had gone off, blowing apart the simple life he'd crafted in Starlight. Despite Cory's vow to make it work, he had no doubt his moratorium on trouble had just been lifted.

Chapter Two

Cory woke early the next morning, light just beginning to make its way through the edges of the heavy curtains she'd pulled tight over the window of the inn the night before. She turned on her side to watch Ben asleep in the crib the inn's owner had helped her set up when they'd arrived yesterday afternoon.

She'd shared a bedroom with her son since the day she finally brought him home from the hospital, almost a full week after he was born. Last night, she'd explained the baby's heart condition to Jordan with the calm of hindsight, but there was no way to describe the terror she'd felt watching her newborn being taken to the operating room in that sterile hospital.

She wasn't sure if she'd ever adequately be able to communicate all the reasons she'd taken so long to reach out to Jordan and tell him he had a son. He'd been angry and shocked, both of which she'd expected, but he'd also been surprisingly quick to commit to being a part of Ben's life.

Cory didn't have much experience with men and commitment. Her own father had left town when Cory was barely a toddler, and she'd had virtually no relationship with him since then. She'd thought Kade, whom she'd met her sophomore and his senior year at the University of Michigan, was committed to their relationship. He'd certainly demanded her devotion, begging her to leave school early when he was drafted. Despite her doubts, she'd done what he asked and believed him when he told her she could transfer to a different college once they were settled.

Then she'd been swept into the world of being a full-time girlfriend, always available to cater to Kade's never-ending list of needs.

She'd worked at a small boutique owned by one of the coaches' wives and tried to ignore the fact that every aspect of her life was set up to revolve around a man. It shamed her to think about how much of herself she'd given away in those years. When she'd driven away from Atlanta, hand on her belly like she could draw strength from the life growing inside her, she'd promised herself she would never give away her power or conform to a man's desires in lieu of her own dreams.

Now she was in a strange bed in a strange town, unsure of what the future held because she was waiting for a man to decide what he wanted from her. Her gut tightened painfully as a familiar wave of regret rolled over her.

The unexpected friendship with Jordan had been a bright spot in her life. Because he was a veteran player with an impeccable reputation, team management had asked him to mentor Kade on his behavior, both on and off the field. Jordan made an effort, but Kade didn't like to be told what to do. Still, Jordan became a regular part of their lives.

For Cory, who always felt alone despite being constantly surrounded by people, Jordan's easygoing charm and lack of interest in the postseason party scene held a powerful appeal. They'd talked for hours and fallen into an easy rhythm of sharing parts of themselves that no one else saw. She'd come to depend on his steady presence, and when things fell apart after their one night together, it had been a huge loss.

What would they be to each other going forward? She couldn't imagine a way back to the connection they'd once had. For all she knew, based on how he'd left Atlanta without a word to her, all of those feelings had been one-sided anyway.

She and Jordan hadn't discussed next steps last night. In truth, Cory had been so exhausted from a mix of the adrenaline crash and plain old fatigue that she wasn't sure she would have lasted through another heated conversation. Ben had saved her from having to admit how overwhelmed she was by fussing enough that she knew she needed to get him to bed.

They'd exchanged numbers and agreed to meet today to make a plan. Cory reminded herself that she wasn't waiting for Jordan to call the shots.

Gran might not have had anything but the Buick to leave her, but she could start over and make her way in the world however she saw fit. Cory had spent most of the months after Ben's recovery nursing her grandmother until the cancer stole Gran's life. Despite the lingering guilt at keeping father and son apart for a time, she would fight for whatever she deemed best.

Unfortunately for her, she had no money, no home and very few prospects to provide for her son on her own. Gran had left her the car, but Cory's mother had taken everything else.

Determination. She had a soul-deep determination to give her baby a good life. However that unfolded, Cory would make it work. Of course, it would be a lot easier if Jordan had gone bald or ended up with a beer belly in the time since she'd last seen him.

They'd spent only one night together, but her body still seemed to be tuned to his like some kind of powerful radio frequency. The last thing she needed was to be distracted by her son's father.

She continued to watch Ben sleep, his little chest rising and falling in steady breaths. Not a day went by that she didn't think about what he'd been through and the gift she'd been given when he recovered from the surgery.

Cory might not have much now, but she could imagine what the future would bring if she continued to work toward her goal of providing a good life for him. She saw him as a toddler and then a young boy, playing in a backyard with green grass and pretty potted flowers. Maybe they'd adopt a puppy one day, a furry beastie that would love Ben best of all, just the way she did.

She quietly showered and got dressed, an expert at getting ready in silence so as not to disturb him. When he woke an hour later and gave her a radiant smile, her heart filled with hope and her eyes with tears. She would do anything to ensure her child had a better, happier childhood than hers. Not a high bar to surpass, but one she planned to leapfrog just the same.

She changed his diaper, fed him a bottle and a bit of rice cereal, then changed him from pajamas into one of her favorite outfits—a striped shirt under tiny overalls. He was her little man, and she believed without reservation that he was the cutest baby ever. Most moms probably felt that way, but it was important to Cory that Jordan also recognize it.

He hadn't even held Ben last night, and she'd been

too nervous to push the issue. As he'd walked her to her car after they agreed to meet today, he'd reached out and traced a finger along Ben's temple. She'd heard his sharp intake of breath, like the touch had sparked him in some way.

There'd been no text from Jordan this morning, and she wondered if he was a late sleeper because of long nights at the bar. She figured she'd get coffee and a pastry at the coffee shop she'd passed in town and then call him once she was fortified with caffeine and a hefty dose of sugar.

Ben had been crying when they'd arrived back at the hotel last night, so she'd left the infant seat in the car and carried him in her arms to their room.

Instead of waiting for the elevator, she took the stairs to the lobby. The inn's lot had been relatively empty both times she'd parked. She guessed a weeknight in late March wasn't a popular time for tourists.

If she'd done the math right, she had two more nights to stay at the hotel before she maxed out her remaining credit card. Hopefully today's conversation with Jordan would help clarify next steps. She hadn't really thought beyond carrying out her gran's request. Cory had gotten used to taking things one day at a time, especially in the last weeks of her grandmother's battle with cancer.

It was time to start planning for her future and to figure out what role a sexy, grumpy, definitely off-limits man might play in it.

She exited the heavy door that led to the lobby and stopped in her tracks, her heart beginning to beat an uneven clip in her chest.

As if she'd conjured him with her unwelcome thoughts, Jordan sat in one of the cozy space's over-stuffed armchairs, clearly waiting for her. And not looking the least bit happy about it.

"Do you actually think I would have skipped town?" Cory gave Jordan a sidelong glare as he ma-neuvered the hulking SUV he drove along the wind-ing mountain road that apparently led to his house. "I sought you out in the first place."

"Because your grandma made you promise," he reminded her. "I'm guessing you didn't think I'd want to be part of my son's life."

She chewed on her bottom lip. "I didn't not think you would."

He snorted.

"The past few months haven't exactly been a cake-walk for me," she said, trying not to sound as over-whelmed as she felt. "Of course I hoped you'd want to get to know Ben. I want my child to grow up with a father in his life."

"Our child," Jordan corrected.

"Ours." She nodded. "You have my phone num-ber. Why didn't you just call to make plans?"

"I wasn't sure you'd answer," he said, and she appreciated his honesty. "As I remember, you weren't great with the follow-up."

Annoyance burned her stomach like someone had dumped a bottle of acid down her throat. She knew he was referring to the one night they'd spent together, when she'd left his bed early the next morning before he woke up.

At that point, Cory had thought she was done with Kade, and to fall for another guy—let alone another football player—went against everything she'd thought she wanted for herself.

It didn't matter that Jordan was completely different from Kade, both in how he approached his career and how he treated her. She ignored the fact that he seemed to want to be her friend as well as her lover. Cory had been too raw from the breakup and unwilling to trust her heart again.

By the time she'd gotten up the nerve to go to his condo later that week, he'd moved out and moved on. His Atlanta number had been disconnected, and she'd taken that as a fairly concrete sign that he had no inclination to hear from her.

"As I remember, you cut and ran pretty quickly when things weren't easy to manage." She glanced into the back seat and smiled at Ben, who laughed, kicked his feet and then went back to staring out the window at the pine trees flanking either side of the road. "A baby isn't easy, Jordan."

"I understand," he said quietly. "I googled his surgery when I got home last night. He went through a lot for such a little guy."

"The hardest thing I've ever had to deal with was knowing I had no power to take away his pain."

"I'm sure you did everything you could to make sure he got through it."

She shrugged. "The doctors and nurses had more to do with that than me. All I did was spend those hours in a hospital waiting room, wondering if he'd survive and what I'd done wrong that he'd been born with that sort of complication."

Jordan's fingers tightened on the steering wheel. "It was a congenital defect. That had nothing to do with you."

"Mom guilt is a powerful thing." She laughed without humor. "You'd be amazed at the dark paths where the mind of a mom can wander."

"Did your mom ever feel guilty about the way she raised you?"

Cory shook her head. "She was too busy trying to land another boyfriend or husband to spend much time thinking about me. I'm guessing your mom didn't have much time for guilt, either." She glanced out the window. She and Jordan had shared a lot about each other's childhoods during the football season when they became friends.

"She was too busy keeping my dad happy," he answered without emotion.

They fell into a silence that should have been

30   *HIS SECRET STARLIGHT BABY*

awkward. Cory guessed he was as entrenched in unwelcome childhood memories as she was. She certainly had a treasure trove from which to choose. Her mom had made it clear over and over that Cory had changed everything about her life, and not for the better. Cory had done her best not to be a burden and had learned from an early age how to make herself smaller so her mom—and later her boyfriends—wouldn't have to deal with the weight of her love.

Her stomach churned at the thought of how she'd lost herself trying to be what other people wanted—or maybe she'd never been found in the first place. Jordan's fingers were tight on the steering wheel, and she wondered what dark path his mind was traveling along.

The air seemed to hold a thousand unspoken regrets, but it wasn't uncomfortable in the quiet of the car, the thick forests of the Pacific Northwest surrounding them. For the first time since she'd found out about the pregnancy, Cory felt a sliver of peace doing its best to bloom inside her heart.

Maybe because no matter what kind of arrangement she and Jordan made, at least she knew she was no longer alone in raising her child.

"I want to be a good mom," she said as he turned onto a narrow driveway. "I don't want to make him feel the way I felt as a kid. Like I was an inconvenience that held her back from the life she wanted.

Even if she didn't say it out loud, I always understood I was the root of the problems in her life."

Jordan slowed as he steered the SUV up the winding gravel drive. "You won't do that."

"How do you know?" She knew she sounded weak, needing confirmation, but she couldn't stand the thought that she might fall into the same pattern as her mother. Although Gran and Mom had been estranged for the better part of Cory's life, her grandmother hadn't once spoken an ill word about her difficult daughter.

"She did her best" was all she would ever say. Cory didn't want to believe that her mom had tried her best at parenting, because that might mean Cory could do her best and still end up hurting Ben. The thought terrified her more than she could explain.

"I just know," Jordan said as he pulled to a stop.

Well, that wasn't very reassuring. Then her gaze switched from him to the truck's front window. She'd been so focused on watching Jordan, searching his face for confirmation as to whether he was telling her the truth or blowing sunshine up her proverbial skirt, that she hadn't noticed the house.

It was magnificent, a two-story log cabin with an expansive wraparound deck, large windows and a burnished slate roof that made the cabin look like it had been in these woods for generations.

"Wow," she murmured. "The bartending business must be treating you right."

He chuckled. "More like the NFL retirement business after having my knee blown out on national television."

She tore her gaze from the house and focused on him again. "I'm sorry that happened to you."

"Not your fault," he said and climbed out of the vehicle.

She exited and then unhooked Ben's infant seat and lifted it out, as well.

"I can take it," Jordan said as he came to stand a few feet away.

Some tiny part of her resisted handing the carrier over to him, which was ridiculous. She'd sought out her baby's father. Of course he'd want to hold the boy.

"Thanks." She gave Jordan the carrier, and he hooked an arm under the handle, then headed for the house.

"Did you have to do a lot of work on this place when you moved in?"

He shook his head. "I bought it from a Seattle couple who'd used it as a weekend retreat. They'd totally remodeled the interior, although I added an outdoor living area in back."

"Divorce?" she guessed.

"After twenty years," he confirmed. "It was sad, actually, although I got lucky with the property."

"I wonder if the statistic that people throw around about fifty percent of marriages ending in divorce is accurate. Sometimes it seems like it should be higher.

Can you imagine being with someone for two decades and then walking away?"

He shrugged. "Some people stay married even when divorce is a better option."

Was he talking about his own parents? She knew he'd had a difficult relationship with his father, which had led to challenges with his mom due to her loyalty to her husband.

"I heard a rumor Kade is getting married," she said, then wished she'd kept her mouth shut.

Jordan's gaze cut to hers. "Does that bother you?"

"No. He called a bunch after I left Atlanta, trying to convince me to come back, and…" She shook her head as she thought about what her ex-boyfriend had suggested she do to handle the pregnancy. "It doesn't matter. I didn't want to return to that life or raise a child in the midst of it."

Jordan didn't say anything in response as he opened the front door and then stepped aside to let her enter first.

"No lock?"

One corner of his mouth lifted into a smirk. "I'm too far out of town for locks. Actually, I'm not sure if anyone in Starlight locks their doors. It's the kind of town where a person feels safe."

Cory had trouble imagining a world where she'd feel safe. Safe from heartache, disappointment and the constant worry about providing a good life for her son. But she was more than ready to try.

Chapter Three

Jordan filled two glasses with water and tamped down the maelstrom of emotion surging through his veins. He glanced over his shoulder to see Cory lifting the baby—his baby—over her head. She grinned and cooed sweet words, bringing Ben close enough to shower him with kisses and then lifting him again.

The boy loved the game, laughing and waving his arms before curling his chubby fingers into his mother's hickory-colored hair.

She'd been beautiful when he first met her in Atlanta. One glance at her soft caramel-colored eyes and that sweet smile, and he'd lost a bit of his hardened heart. She seemed more herself now in a casual sweatshirt and faded jeans with no makeup and her hair holding a bit of natural curl. But to witness her so filled with love for her child took his reaction to a whole new level.

One that wasn't smart for either of them.

He'd told himself his night with Cory had been a fling, although somewhere deep inside he knew that was a lie. But it had been easier than admitting he'd fallen for a woman he had no right to want.

She clearly hadn't wanted anything to do with him after sneaking out of his bed the morning after. He might not be the sharpest knife in the drawer, but she'd given him a pretty straightforward hint as to what being with him meant to her.

Jordan's plan had been to leave Atlanta when his lease ended. He'd known his injury would end his career. It said something about his commitment that after seven seasons with the same team, he was still renting a basic condo near downtown instead of buying a place of his own. So it was easy to move up the time frame for leaving. His injury during the playoff game that season signaled the end to his NFL career, which he hadn't found as upsetting as he probably should have.

By the time he got to that point, he'd lost much of his love of the game. It had simply become a job for him, and since Jordan didn't care for the trappings of pro-athlete fame, it hadn't been hard to walk away from his career and start over. He'd returned to Washington but come to Starlight because he liked

the small-town feel and the bar was an easy business to manage. Jordan discovered that after so many
years of pushing himself, he appreciated ease.

Forgetting Cory had been anything but easy.

He'd managed eventually—or so he'd thought—but
now here she was, sitting on his leather couch, looking
like she belonged in his world. He didn't want to admit
how much he liked seeing her in his space, how her
reaction to the unique beauty of his home had made
his chest ache with yearning.

She was there because they needed to work out
plans for raising a child together. Nothing more.

Sleep had been elusive last night. Jordan had
spent hours combing the internet to learn the specif-
ics about Ben's surgery. He'd finally drifted off only
to wake in a cold sweat an hour later, panic gripping
at the thought that Cory might change her mind and
leave town.

He would have tracked her down, of course. She
might not expect much from the men in her life, but
Jordan would never shirk his parental responsibility, even though he didn't know the first thing about
being a father.

The only certainty was that he would do it differently than his own father had. Looking into Ben's
eyes—his gaze both familiar and not—had upended
Jordan's world. He'd never intended to start a family
of his own, but he would do his best no matter what.

"He's happy this morning." Jordan placed the

two waters on the coffee table and started to take a
seat in one of the chairs across from the sofa. He'd
hosted the bar's holiday party at his house last year
but otherwise hadn't had many visitors to his home.
It hadn't felt lonely before. He liked the solitude. But
he had the feeling he'd notice the silence in a different way once Cory and the baby went back to town.

"Do you want to hold him?" she asked, her gaze
both expectant and hopeful.

"I might break him," Jordan answered automatically, but he straightened and took a step closer, heart
thudding dully.

"You'll do fine." She shifted on the sofa to make
room and then reached out and tugged on his hand.
The gentle touch made Jordan's lungs squeeze as he
remembered how soft Cory's skin was—everywhere.

Keeping his features steady so she didn't realize
her effect on him, he sat down next to her. She transferred Ben to his arms, and he felt the baby tense
slightly, like he was unsure about being handed off
to a stranger.

Jordan didn't blame the kid, but he also hated the
thought that he was a stranger to his own child. The
reminder that he'd been robbed of the first six months
with his boy was the splash of cold water his heart
needed to go icy again.

"Relax," Cory urged in her sweet voice. "He's
an easy baby. Last night he was overtired, which is

why he fussed so much. Normally he has a sunny attitude."

"Are you a ray of sunshine?" Jordan asked, amazed at how solid such a small creature felt in his arms. Ben's green gaze locked on Jordan's as his mouth widened into a toothless grin.

Jordan held the baby's torso and turned him. Ben planted his feet on Jordan's denim-clad legs and bounced up and down, smiling the entire time.

"He's really active, too," Cory said with a laugh. She rose from the sofa. "Shoot. I left the diaper bag in your truck. His toys and a blanket are in there. We can put him on the floor to play while we talk."

"Wait. You aren't leaving me alone with him." So much for steady. Even Jordan recognized the panic in his own voice.

"Only for a minute." She patted his shoulder as she moved past him. "You'll be fine."

Jordan wasn't convinced, but arguing would make him sound like a complete wussy. He'd faced off against the toughest defensemen the NFL had to offer, so why was he terrified of one small baby?

"Don't cry," he told the child, who shoved a fist into his mouth in response. "Please."

To his great relief, Ben seemed content to bob up and down and stare at Jordan.

"I like to see you starting squats early," Jordan told him when he finally started to relax. "They're important for overall leg strength. You might want to give it a rest on chewing your own hand. I'm not sure if you realize it, but the sleeve of your shirt is already soaked in drool."

"He's teething," Cory explained as she returned.

"That diaper bag–retrieval mission took five hours," Jordan stated. "But Ben and I managed just fine, so you know."

She laughed again. "You're a natural."

Hardly, based on the relief he felt when she took the baby from him. She placed him on his back on the colorful fleece blanket she'd spread across the rug and handed him a plastic telephone that played obnoxious, tinny music.

"Have you introduced him to Luke Bryan?" Jordan asked as she sat next to him.

Her brows drew together. "Not officially, although we listened to a lot of country stations on the drive out here."

Jordan nodded. "Music is important. He needs to know the classics of country, rock and blues. Also how to swing a bat the right way and how to change a tire. I see too many kids around town who don't know the first thing about car maintenance. It's a sad turn of events."

"Whoa, there." Cory held up a hand. "He's six months old. Right now we're working on solid foods. Car mechanics come a bit down the road."

"Right." Jordan scrubbed a hand over his jaw. "But I'm going to be there for all of it. I want to be clear on that, Cory. Ben is my son, and I'm going to be a part of his life forever."

Cory wasn't sure how to describe the riot of feelings that comprised her response to Jordan's declaration. Her body's response to him. A day of stubble darkened his jaw, and the laugh lines around his green eyes captivated her. Everything about him appealed to her, and that was not good. Of course, his willingness to step up as a parent was what she wanted for her son—a father who would be there for every phase of his life.

When she'd made the promise to her grandmother that she'd introduce Ben to his father, she hadn't thought about what it would mean for her own life. Yes, it was a relief to think about having a partner in parenting, but having Jordan involved also meant she'd be relinquishing control. It meant that Ben would spend time with his dad away from her. There would be custody arrangements and co-parenting challenges.

She might be giving up as much as she was gaining.

The thought didn't sit well.

At the same time, she was humbled by Jordan's immediate acceptance of the situation and the sincerity of his commitment. There was no doubt in her mind that he'd be a great father. He had financial security, owned his own business and lived in a town that was just about picture-perfect.

Cory had her gran's old Buick and a trunk full of everything she owned in the world. No college degree, no career to speak of and not one friend she could call for moral support.

The idea her son could grow up to be disappointed by her strengthened her resolve to make something of her life. She refused to go down the same path her mom had traveled, constantly scrambling and struggling to make her romantic relationships work. Her mom had terrible taste in men. She picked boyfriends who were selfish and treated her like an afterthought.

Cory thought about everything she'd done to fit into Kade's world. She'd wanted him to love her in the same way he loved football and the fame that came with it. But that was never going to happen, and she wished she'd accepted the truth long before she did. She felt a bone-deep commitment to protecting her heart going forward so she'd have more of it to give to Ben.

"I'm here so you can be a part of his life," Cory said, relieved when her voice didn't tremble. "I want you to have a relationship with him, Jordan. The next step is to figure out how that's going to work for all of us."

Jordan nodded and looked at her in a way that had awareness zinging along her nerve endings. The weight of his gaze seemed to hold the promise of what might have been. "I don't mean how you and I will work," she clarified. "There's no you and I, of course."

"Of course," he murmured in that rumbly tone. "Also, I assume you're planning to stay in Starlight. This is my home and I want Ben close."

Her first instinct was to argue, because somehow the assumption grated at her. With the few details she'd given him about her life since he'd left Atlanta, Jordan didn't know that she was basically on her own and homeless with little savings and fewer prospects back in Michigan.

She'd told him about the promise to Gran, and he knew about her strained relationship with her mom. But that was it. As far as he was concerned, Cory had a great life in Michigan. Her grandmother might have left her a secret fortune in the old car's glove box.

Never mind none of that was anywhere near the truth.

Before she could answer, the shrill ring of his cell phone sounded from the kitchen counter. Ben moved his head in the direction of the noise, overly loud in the silence that had settled in the house.

"Let me check who it is." Jordan stood and stepped over the baby's blanket, easy with his long legs. Cory did her best not to notice how the faded denim conformed to the muscles of his thighs. She almost smiled as she thought of the fact that tight end, his football position, was the perfect description of the man himself.

She got up off the couch and went to sit on the floor next to Ben, surreptitiously watching Jordan's reaction to whoever was on the other end of the line. He sent the call to voice mail, and the phone almost immediately began to ring again.

He hit the mute button and then quickly punched in and sent a text. A moment later the phone dinged with a response, and he frowned at the screen, his thick brows drawn together.

"Persistent girlfriend?" she asked, trying to sound casual when he returned to the family room.

"My mother," he said tightly.

"Is everything okay?"

He shrugged. "I have to make a quick trip to my hometown tomorrow morning. Family function. I'll be gone for a couple of days."

"Okay." She nodded, unsure what to make of his darkening mood. "I have the hotel room booked for another night. After that, I need to figure out where to—"

"You should go with me," he said suddenly.

Cory blinked. "To your family function?"

"Yeah." Jordan nodded as if he was working out the details in his mind. "I grew up outside Spokane. It's about two hours from here. If we leave around eight—"

"I haven't agreed to anything," Cory protested.

"Even if I was willing to go with you, won't your family think it's odd?" She smoothed a hand over Ben's soft forehead. "You were the one who said he has your father's eyes. Your dad might be a bit shocked when you show up with a baby who looks like him."

"My dad won't be shocked," Jordan answered, his tone frigid enough to freeze water. "I haven't seen anyone in my family since I moved back to Washington. They don't know a thing about my current life, other than I own a bar in a town they have no intention of visiting. This is actually perfect. You and Ben come with me, and that will distract everyone. They'll be too busy focusing on the baby to remind me how badly I screwed up my life by having the stupid luck to be injured in that game."

"They can't blame you for the injury," Cory told him, her brain firing on a dozen cylinders. There were things Jordan wasn't telling her about his relationship with his family and what this trip meant. Despite her reservations, she didn't like the thought of anyone trying to make him feel guilty for something he had no control over. She'd dealt with plenty of that in her life, and it was awful.

"Please come with me." He closed his eyes for a moment, then opened them again, and the pain she saw in their depths sliced across her heart.

His eyes were so similar to her baby's, and she hated the thought that anything would ever cause

Ben to look that way. "This situation is complicated, which isn't exactly my comfort zone. It might be helpful if we could spend a couple of days getting to know each other again before we make any definite decisions about the plan for going forward. You can think about whether you want to stay in Starlight."

He offered a tentative smile. "I hope you decide you will. I can't imagine a better place to raise a child."

"Do you have a girlfriend?" she blurted, then pulled her bottom lip between her teeth. It was none of her business, but the thought of Jordan raising children with some gorgeous mountain woman made an unwelcome pit of jealousy open in her stomach.

He frowned and shook his head. "Do you have a boyfriend?"

She rolled her eyes. "I barely have time to brush my teeth. Men are way too much work for me right now."

"Good to know." He drew in a deep breath, his chest rising and falling under the flannel shirt. "Will you go with me, Cory? You and Ben. I promise I'll make sure you have time for teeth brushing while we're away."

That simple vow made her smile. It was ludicrous to agree to it. She and Jordan needed to come up with a custody agreement, not get to know each other. But for the first time in as long as she could remember, Cory didn't feel the heavy weight of stress and responsibility. Her life wasn't much to speak of at the moment. What would be the harm in delaying decisions about the future for a few days? She could attend whatever wedding or family reunion he had to make an appearance at, and it might even be fun. At least there would probably be lots of free food.

"Do you want to go on a road trip with your daddy?" She lifted her son into her arms and cradled him close. Ben made a high-pitched squealing sound.

"Sounded like a yes to me," Jordan told her.

"Okay," she said. "We can work out plans for co-parenting on the drive."

"Whatever you want."

"I left most of my nice clothes in Atlanta," she told him, trying not to sound bitter. "So my wardrobe choices are limited. If it's a fancy wedding—"

"It's not." Jordan turned to gaze out the picture window that overlooked the pond behind his house and then back to her. "It's a funeral. My father's funeral."

Chapter Four

Jordan winced as a bony elbow jabbed him in the ribs later that night. "Hey," he protested. "Unnecessary roughness."

Tanya Mehall, Trophy Room's primary bartender, arched a brow as she turned her back on the customers sitting at the bar to face him. "You're scaring people with tonight's perma-scowl," she said in a low voice. "I've got enough to handle with the attitude coming from the kitchen. You need to fix your face."

Before he could answer, she lifted a hand and patted his cheek. "Let's see those dimples, boss," she commanded, then moved around him to pour a round of pints for a group near the end of the well-worn mahogany bar.

Tanya was a Starlight native, a few years older than Jordan. From all accounts, she'd spent her teen years babysitting almost every kid in town. Although she remained single, she liked mothering people—customers and coworkers alike.

But she was wrong about Jordan. He didn't scare people, not anymore. A quick glance around the bar's crowded interior had him swallowing back a sigh. The regulars facing him seemed to be collectively attempting not to make eye contact, like they were nervous about how he might react if they had the audacity to meet his gaze.

Damn. He needed to fix his face.

Drawing in a deep breath, he forced a smile and stepped forward. It only took a few minutes of small talk for the line of customers to visibly relax. They discussed the game broadcasting from the television hanging behind the bar, and Jordan made a point to ask Ray Monning about his new grandchild, a girl who had been born the previous week.

That launched his crew of regulars into a heated discussion about whether girls or boys were tougher to raise. Jordan found himself listening with more interest than usual. He wondered in what ways Ben would challenge him. His son. Of course, he didn't mention the bombshell that had been dropped into his lap the previous night, although people around town would learn about it soon enough, especially if he convinced Cory to stay.

He had to convince her to stay. Jordan might still be reeling at the thought of being a father, but that didn't mean he wasn't committed to figuring out how to manage it.

He'd already ordered a half dozen books on parenting and had spent most of the afternoon watching instructional online videos on everything from diaper changing to developmental milestones. He was going to get this right on some level.

Nick Dunlap, Starlight's police chief, appeared at the far end of the bar and lifted a hand to wave at Jordan, who nodded in response. It was Thursday, which meant Nick was picking up dinner for his fiancée, Brynn, and her son, Tyler. With a ten-year-old boy and a baby daughter at home, the couple rarely spent much time in the bar, but Brynn was a bit addicted to the Trophy Room wings, which Jordan appreciated.

"I'm going to grab Nick's food," Jordan told Tanya as he headed for the kitchen.

"Keep smiling and tell Madison not to make anyone else cry tonight."

"Someone cried?" Jordan asked automatically, then shook his head. "Do I want to know?"

"Probably not. Smile," Tanya repeated.

Simple, Jordan told himself as he entered the bar's refurbished kitchen. He could keep his life simple and his emotions on an even keel, despite the changes.

"Are you having a good night?" he asked Colleen,

one of the servers, as she placed plates on a large serving tray.

She glanced up at him, then over her shoulder, and rolled her eyes. "Sure," she said, sounding totally unconvincing.

"Her customers would have a better night if she could get the lead out," a feminine voice said from behind the industrial range positioned on the far side of the kitchen. "No one wants lukewarm burgers."

Colleen flashed a patently fake smile. "That's my cue." She moved past Jordan, muttering under her breath as she went.

"No one is complaining." He walked forward until he faced his surly chef, then flinched as Madison Maurer fixed him with a glare that could sear a rib eye. He'd hired the edgy blonde chef despite her spotty résumé. There were periods of unemployment, and she readily admitted she'd left at least one former job because she didn't get along with the restaurant's owner.

But the caliber of kitchen she'd cooked in throughout the Pacific Northwest was stellar, and she had five-star reviews to spare. He hadn't delved into why she wanted a job running a bar kitchen, but he was glad she had. With her skill and creativity, Madison had improved Trophy Room's menu. Unfortunately, they were going to run out of potential servers for that food if she continued to scare off his staff.

"Because people in this town are too nice." Madison Maurer gave an order to one of the kitchen workers, then stepped closer to Jordan. "That doesn't excuse lack of effort."

"Colleen makes an effort," Jordan countered. "Everyone on staff does. We should make sure we appreciate and recognize that effort."

Madison narrowed her icy blue eyes at him. "Tanya got to you."

He crossed his arms over his chest. "Did you make someone cry?"

"Not exactly."

Danny, one of the line cooks, poked his head around the fryer. "She told that new waitress you hired she was a waste of space."

Jordan groaned. "Where is Samantha now?"

"She quit," Danny offered. "That's why Colleen is so frazzled."

"Everyone knows you have to have thick skin to work in the restaurant industry," Madi grumbled. "I did you a favor."

"Not so much," Jordan said, shaking his head. "Right now I need Nick's food. I'm heading out for a couple of days tomorrow. We'll discuss this in more detail when I get back."

Madison's full mouth pressed into a thin line as she handed him a large brown paper bag. "I don't think there's anything to talk about. I put extra sauce in the bag because Brynn likes her wings wet."

"We'll discuss your opinion, as well," Jordan told her. "Thanks for taking care of Brynn."

"See." Madi held up her hands, palms out. "I'm all about customer service."

Danny let out a loud cackle.

Jordan smiled tightly but didn't answer his surly chef. There was no denying that hiring Madison Maurer was one of the best things he'd done to elevate Trophy Room from a standard bar to the gastropub he envisioned. But to say she was prickly made a cactus seem as soft as a kitten.

Normally, Jordan took a hands-off approach to managing his staff. He hired good people and stayed out of their way so they could do the job. But if he couldn't hold on to staff because Madison chased them away with her bad attitude, that was a problem.

Add it to the list.

He handed the bag to Nick and mentioned the extra wing sauce.

"Brynn will be thrilled," the police chief confirmed with a smile. "You okay, Schaeffer?"

"Yeah. Peachy keen." Seriously, what was wrong with Jordan that everyone could read his emotions so easily?

"Nice crowd for a Thursday," Nick commented, still studying him.

"It's the food, without a doubt."

"No one can resist Madi's wings and sliders."

"She's got skills, that's for sure."

"If you need anything, man, reach out. Okay?"

"I'll do that," Jordan said, a bit of the tension in his chest loosening. He appreciated the reminder he wasn't alone in facing the sudden complications of his life. He mainly kept to himself when he wasn't working, but as a bar and restaurant owner, Jordan had gotten to know a lot of people in town. Good people. Caring people. People who would help build a community around his son.

"How's Remi?" he asked just as Nick turned for the door.

The police chief grinned. "Sweeter by the day. She's almost sitting up on her own. We're hoping the adoption is finalized in the next couple of months."

Jordan leaned forward. "You made it seem so effortless, the instant family deal."

Just before Christmas last year, Nick and Brynn had taken in an abandoned baby, the child of Brynn's late husband and the man's mistress. The way Jordan understood it, Nick and Brynn had been close friends growing up, but they'd had a falling-out during high school. It had taken the baby to bring them together again, and now Jordan couldn't imagine a happier family.

He also couldn't imagine that kind of future for himself, although becoming a father made him committed to try.

"There's definitely a lot of effort," Nick answered

with a laugh. "But it's worth every moment." He waved over his shoulder as he headed for the door.

Jordan rubbed at his chest, where his heart seemed to beat an unsteady rhythm. Would he ever seem that comfortable with his role as a dad? He wanted to ask Nick how he'd managed instant parenthood, but things were still so tenuous with Cory. Maybe after the trip to Spokane, he'd have a better handle on what came next. Although, deep inside he knew his estranged father's funeral wasn't exactly the ideal place to gain emotional clarity.

A couple approached the bar, and he greeted them with his usual smile. Even that took some effort, but it was his job. He just had to get through the next few days. He could imagine turmoil in his hometown since he'd been estranged from his family for years, but he'd manage it. Then he and Cory could work out their parenting arrangement. Things might feel complicated now, but they didn't have to stay that way. He'd make sure of it.

"Are you sure this isn't going to be weird?" Cory asked the next morning as they drove past a sign that announced they'd enter the town of Spokane in thirty miles.

"I'm counting on it to be weird," Jordan said, shooting her a *duh* glance. "That's what's going to take the attention off my return."

"Oh. Great." Cory swiped her hand across the side

of her mouth. "Now I'm really nervous. Any chance you packed a barf bag?"

"No, but I can pull over if you're going to puke."

"I was joking."

Jordan winked. "Me too. By the way, the dried drool is on the other cheek."

Heat infused Cory's face as she pressed the sleeve of her sweatshirt to her cheek. "I didn't sleep well last night," she told Jordan. "Sorry I wasn't a better driving companion."

"You were fine," he said in that deep, rumbly voice. "Plus, it gave Ben and me time to get acquainted."

Cory huffed out a laugh and glanced into the back seat, where her son was racked out in his car seat.

"Until he dozed off, as well," Jordan admitted, one side of his mouth curving in a way that did funny things to her insides.

"You're quite stimulating," she told him, earning a deep chuckle. She wasn't sure whether the nerves zinging along her spine had more to do with anticipation of meeting Jordan's family or the way he made her feel.

"I'll have to work on that."

"We need to get our story straight," she reminded him.

His smile faded. "It's best not to offer too many details. We met in Atlanta, and now we have Ben."

She turned to face him, adjusting the lap belt as

she shifted. "Your family's not going to question you showing up with a six-month-old baby? Like maybe you would have mentioned it to them prior to now?"

One bulky shoulder lifted and lowered. "I told you we aren't close."

"Your mom not knowing she has a grandchild is a bit more than 'not close,'" Cory felt compelled to point out. "Will she be upset we aren't married?"

"I'm not sure."

Her stomach tightened at his response. "Will she want to have a relationship with Ben after this weekend?"

"Good question."

"I have a million of them where that came from," she said. "I don't even know how your father died."

"Heart attack."

"Sudden." She worried her lower lip between her teeth. There were so many potential potholes for her to tumble into this weekend, and based on the tight set of his jaw, Jordan was in no shape to help her navigate through it. In fact, she had the feeling she'd be the one supporting him and he'd need solace well beyond a distraction.

"Can you answer a question with more than two words?" She was careful to make her voice light and was rewarded when his posture gentled somewhat.

"I suppose so."

"A bonus word. Nice. I'm sorry about your father's death," she said, giving in to the urge to reach out

and place her hand on his arm. Of course she should
have expected the hard muscles under his jacket. He
was a big guy and clearly still in great shape even
after his injury and retirement from football. But
the touch unsettled her just the same, although she
didn't release him. Cory knew what it was like to
go through grief alone, and she didn't want that for
him. "For your loss."

He said nothing for several moments, and she
wondered if she'd already overstepped the bounds
of whatever nonrelationship they had.

"It wasn't a loss from my perspective," he said
tightly. "We didn't have a relationship."

"Then I'm sorry for that."

He looked at her sharply, like he wanted to rebuke
her for the expression of sympathy, but then shook
his head. "My mom is sad. She sounds lost, and I
don't want that for her. I want her to know how much
better off she is without him."

"How long were they married?"

"Thirty-five years."

"And you're thirty, right?" He'd told her his age
when they met in Atlanta.

"Yeah."

"Do you have siblings?"

"One brother. Max is twenty-five. My mom had
trouble getting pregnant after me, and my parents
had long stretches where they weren't exactly close."

She wanted to ask more, but the air was already

so charged. She feared he might shatter as he fought against the emotions she could almost see gripping him. Maybe asking about his brother would defuse some of the tension. "Does he play football?"

Jordan shook his head. "No. He's smart."

Cory wasn't sure whether Jordan meant his brother was smart for not engaging in such a violent sport or was referring to Max's intelligence in some other manner. Either way, she knew it was an implied criticism of himself, and that didn't sit well.

"I think we should stick to the truth as much as we can." She lifted her hand from his arm, immediately missing the warmth that radiated from him like a space heater. "You might not be close to your family, but I'm not looking to cause them more pain or upset by getting caught in a lie. If we simply tell the truth about how we met—"

"A party at your boyfriend's house?" Jordan asked wryly.

"We met in Atlanta during your football career," Cory explained as if he hadn't spoken. She didn't want to revisit those nights of talking to Jordan out by the pool while everyone else partied inside the house. Her time with him had meant more than it should to her.

He'd been kind and sweet, diametrically opposed to how Kade treated her. It had been too easy to fantasize about how different her life might be if she was with someone like Jordan, and even then she'd realized how dangerous that train of thought could be.

Even more now.

"I think we stick with the story that Ben was a surprise—"

"The understatement of the year," Jordan muttered, flipping on his blinker to exit the highway.

Heat crept up Cory's neck, but she ignored it. "But he helped us realize we want to be together. That we're a family."

Her words seemed to reverberate in the silence that followed.

"Sure," Jordan said finally, his voice barely above a whisper. "We'll be in and out for the service so quickly, the details won't really matter."

Cory didn't argue with him, although in her experience, the details always mattered.

"This is a pretty town," she murmured as he turned into a residential neighborhood of modest rows of homes, all with neat yards and fresh paint. "It must have been a big change for you coming to the South after growing up here." She knew that before being drafted to Atlanta, he'd gone to college in Alabama.

"The heat and humidity were hell my first preseason," he admitted with a chuckle. "I must have puked during every practice, but I didn't care. I was so damn happy to be away from here."

"And your dad?"

A stiff nod.

"We'll get through this." It was the mantra Cory had repeated to herself countless times in the past year and a half, but it felt strangely comforting to replace the singular pronoun for the plural *we*. It felt good not to be alone and to be able to offer support instead of being the one who needed it.

She could see Jordan's broad chest rising and falling in shallow breaths and wondered at his reaction. During the football season when they'd been friends, he'd shared enough of his family history that she understood he hadn't remained close with his parents. He'd never mentioned having a brother. His reaction told her he'd left out some of the details of how bad it had been with his dad.

"I've booked two rooms at a hotel downtown," Jordan told her as he pulled to a stop in front of a red-brick rancher with white trim and gutters. "There's no way I'm staying in this house."

"Okay," she answered automatically. This wasn't her homecoming, so she didn't pretend like she had any opinion on how he handled things.

As he turned off the car, she glanced in the back seat to where Ben still napped. Her sweet, handsome boy was about to meet his grandmother.

Cory's mother had only seen the baby twice, and both interactions had been overshadowed by Tracy's disappointment with her daughter. Ben was only a physical reminder of the future Cory had thrown away, according to her mom.

It was silly to pin her hopes on a complete stranger, but Cory hoped Jordan's mom was at least kinder than her own. She couldn't help but want that for her son. A loving family.

She woke Ben and lifted his still-limp body into her arms while Jordan stood next to her, glowering and tapping an agitated toe on the asphalt.

"Do you want to carry him to the house?" she asked as she straightened, the baby cradled against her chest. "It might help relax you a bit."

"I'm relaxed," Jordan countered.

"Like a man about to face the firing squad is relaxed." She offered an encouraging smile. "It's going to be okay, Jordan. You're not alone."

He stared at her like she was speaking a foreign language. "Thanks," he mumbled finally and then smoothed a hand over Ben's downy hair. The boy blinked and lifted his head to study his father, shoving his fist in his mouth.

But Cory noticed that Jordan's shoulders eased ever so slightly and felt a huge sense of accomplishment. She might not know what they were walking into, but she knew how to be useful.

"I'll let you hold him," Jordan said and led them up the narrow walk. "It would be kind of embarrassing if I dropped him or something. To show my mom that I don't even know how to hold my own baby."

"You'll get more comfortable," Cory promised.

The front door opened just before they got to the porch, and an older woman watched from the doorway, hand clasped to her mouth. She was small and delicate, reminding Cory of a fallen leaf that might blow away in a strong gust of wind.

"You came," she whispered as her hazel eyes filled with tears.

"Yeah," Jordan answered simply. "I told you I'd be here." He reached for Cory's elbow and tugged her closer. "I have a couple people for you to meet. My fiancée and my son."

Cory felt her jaw go *clack* and quickly snapped shut her mouth as his mother also tried to hide her shock. Maybe Cory should have pushed for more details from Jordan on the plan, because she wouldn't have guessed in a million years that his suggestion for keeping it simple might involve a fake engagement.

Chapter Five

"A grandson. I still can't believe I have a grandson."

Jordan pressed his lips tight together as he watched his mother smile at the baby she'd been holding in her arms for the past hour.

"It's obvious he likes you," Cory said from where she sat next to Jordan on the pale blue damask sofa in the house's formal living room. Although the home was small, his mother had decorated it with as much pride as if she were holding court at Buckingham Palace. As a kid, Jordan had hated the stuffy decor and the fact he was constantly being told to remove his shoes or to stay out of rooms other than the cozy study off the kitchen.

But his mom had insisted that he and Cory sit with Ben in the once off-limits room at the front of the house. Jordan couldn't help but wonder if he would have been allowed into the precious space if he'd shown up alone.

He swallowed back a yelp when Cory pinched the back of his arm. "Isn't it obvious how much Ben likes his grandma?" she asked.

"He's a baby," Jordan said, earning another squeeze, although her bright smile remained in place. His mother glanced up, and he could clearly see the hope in her gentle gaze. "But, yeah, he likes you, Mom. Of course he does."

"I can't get over how much he looks like your father."

"You mentioned that," Jordan muttered.

"He would have loved to know his grandchild."

Jordan recognized and ignored the soft admonishment.

"If there's anything we can do to help with the service," Cory told his mother, sitting forward, "please know we're here for you."

"Thank you, dear." His mom sniffed. "My book club has handled most of the arrangements. They've been such a help since James passed. I'm not sure how I would have survived without their support."

Jordan fidgeted. Was that a subtle reminder he hadn't been any help to his mom?

He didn't know who was responsible for the distance in their relationship, so he'd always allowed his father to shoulder the blame. His parents' marriage had been tumultuous when Jordan was a kid, but his mom's devotion to her husband never wavered. So when James came down hard on Jordan or pushed him in sports beyond what was safe for a developing boy, she didn't step in to defuse the intensity of his dad's expectations.

James was so seduced by Jordan's innate athletic talent that success on the field or in the gym was the only thing that mattered. He didn't just want to promote Jordan's glory. He wanted to share in it, and Jordan understood that without the all-encompassing excitement of sports, he had no value to his father.

Cory took his hand in hers, and her soft touch was more comfort than it probably should have been. Although she'd meant something to him when they'd grown close in Atlanta, at this point she was a virtual stranger. One with whom he shared a child, but a stranger nonetheless. How odd that she seemed to be able to read his mood and what he needed before the longing truly gelled inside his mind.

"How long has your book club been meeting?" Cory asked, effectively distracting his mother from thoughts about all the ways her older son was lacking.

"Over twenty years," his mom said with a smile. "Several of us have known each other since high school. We've been through a lot together. I'm lucky to have such amazing friends."

"That's wonderful." Cory nodded. "I always wanted to have lifelong friends." She gave a tight laugh. "Or any real girlfriends. I've never seemed to manage it."

"Are the women in Starlight not nice?" his mother asked, her gaze darting between Cory and Jordan. "I thought you said it's a close-knit community."

"It is," Jordan said, once again on the defensive. "Starlight is a great town."

His mother's feathery brows furrowed. "Then why—"

"It's probably my fault," Cory said quickly and slipped her hand from his. "I've been so busy with Ben that I haven't made much of an effort."

"You need to take care of yourself so you can take care of the baby," his mother advised, then pointed a finger at Jordan. "Are you not taking on enough of the childcare and household responsibilities?"

He felt his mouth drop open.

"Jordan is…um… It's not his fault." Cory glanced at him, her big eyes going even wider. "I need to take responsibility for my own happiness."

"Nonsense." Kathy rolled her eyes. "He's your partner and Ben's father. You know what they say—'happy wife, happy life.'"

"I don't think Dad ever said that," Jordan said, then sighed when his mother's back went rigid. He'd told himself he wasn't going to bring up the past and his father's behavior. His mom had made her choice, and it was none of Jordan's business.

"You might be right," his mom said after a moment. "But he never prevented me from having friends."

Jordan threw up his hands. "I'm not stopping her from having friends."

"He's not," Cory added. "At all."

"You seem like a sweet girl," Kathy told Cory. "I imagine it's a bit awkward being a new mom but not a wife. Maybe after the two of you are married—"

"Mom, stop." Jordan stood and stalked to the fireplace, where the oak mantel still held framed photos of Jordan and Max as kids. "Cory can handle her own life, and no one is shunning her in Starlight because we're not married."

"Have you set a date?" his mom asked, undeterred. "Am I invited?"

Jordan felt his temples start to pound.

"What would you like Ben to call you?" Cory asked before Jordan could respond. "Grandma or Grammy or—"

"Mimi," his mother said, almost shyly. "I always thought my grandchildren would call me Mimi."

"Mom, that's—"

"Adorable," Cory interrupted. "I think that's so cute. Ben and his mimi are going to have so much fun together. I can already tell."

Jordan gave her an arch look he transformed into

a smile when he realized his mother was grinning broadly.

He couldn't remember ever seeing his mother smile like that. Just as he started to relax again, the back door opened and shut with a slam.

"Mom?"

"In the living room," Kathy called.

"Seriously?" Max's voice got louder as his footsteps sounded in the hallway. "Did someone else d—" His voice trailed off as he came to stand at the room's threshold, his hazel eyes taking in the scene. "Jordan. You're back."

"Why does everyone sound so shocked?" Jordan said. "I told you all I'd be here." He closed the distance between him and his younger brother in a few strides. His brother was taller now and had filled out from the gangly, bespectacled teen he'd been when Jordan left for college. Max had dark hair and their mother's gentle eyes. Her gentle spirit, as well. "You look good, Max. All grown-up."

"Five years will do that to a person," Max answered and returned Jordan's hug with a half-hearted embrace.

"You're welcome to visit Starlight anytime," Jordan said, ignoring the animosity in his brother's voice. "I have plenty of room."

"Some of us care about home," Max muttered, and Jordan hated the bitterness in his brother's gaze. He wished his relationship with his younger brother hadn't been a casualty of breaking away from his father's choke hold on his life, but there was little he could do to change that now.

"Come and meet your nephew," their mother said, as always trying to smooth over any friction that appeared between the brothers. Max had regularly been sick as a kid and stayed home with Kathy, while Jordan and his dad spent hours together through the football, wrestling and baseball seasons.

Max drew in a sharp breath. "You have a kid?"

Jordan wanted to explain the whole situation, to reveal his shock and worry over his suitability as a father. If anyone would understand, it was his brother.

"He has a fiancée, as well." Kathy stood and gestured to Cory. "Your brother must have forgotten his manners. Jordan, introduce your Cory to Max."

His Cory. Jordan scrubbed a hand over his jaw and tried not to think about how right it would feel if she were actually his.

"I'm Cory. It's nice to meet you," Cory said as she came to stand next to him, holding out a hand to his brother. "I'm sorry about the circumstances."

Max stared between the two of them and then glanced at Ben. "You two have a baby. But you aren't married?"

Jordan heard Cory's sharp intake of breath and shook his head. "Since when did you become the morality police?" he demanded of his brother.

"No disrespect." Instead of taking Cory's hand, Max stepped forward and gave her a hug. "Welcome to the nuthouse," he told Cory.

Wasn't that just the truth, Jordan thought. Honestly, he wouldn't blame Cory if she rented a car and headed back to Starlight and as far away from him as she could get.

"I'm glad to be here," she told his brother, although Jordan knew it must be a lie.

"We should check into the hotel," Jordan said as Max took Ben from their mother. The boy gazed up at his uncle for a long moment, then grinned. It embarrassed Jordan to no end that even his stuffy younger brother was more comfortable holding the baby than Jordan. What did that say about him? Nothing he wanted to admit.

"You aren't staying here?"

He couldn't make eye contact with his mother, not after the hurt in her voice.

"We'll see you tomorrow at the service," he said by way of an answer.

Max bounced Ben for a few more seconds before handing him to Cory. She gave both his brother and mom another hug. It felt as though she was as confused as Kathy about why they were checking into a hotel. To Jordan's eternal gratitude, she didn't question him.

In fact, she spoke very little on the short drive to downtown. That worked for him. There was nothing

he could say that would adequately explain the riot
of thoughts tumbling through his mind and heart.

Cory wasn't sure what she was thinking, knocking on the door separating her room from Jordan's
later that afternoon. He'd made it clear he wanted to
be alone. After the strange and surreal visit to his
mother's house, she didn't blame him.

No one spoke directly about his father, although
it was clear the man's presence continued to loom
large for both Kathy and the two sons he'd left behind. Cory had never been so grateful for Ben, whose
sweetness was about the only thing that made the
time go by quickly.

She felt almost guilty she'd liked Jordan's mom. It
was nice to have someone fussing over her son and
talking about the baby like he was something more
than a burden.

The good memories Cory had from spending time
with her grandmother still meant the world to her,
so of course she wanted that for her son. It definitely
wouldn't come from her side of the family.

But she couldn't include Kathy in their lives without Jordan's approval. There had to be more to why
he was so distant with his mom than simply time
and the impact of Jordan living across the country.
After all, he'd been in Starlight long enough to plan
a visit to his hometown.

He opened the door after a few seconds, his hair

wild like he'd been pulling at the ends and his gaze shuttered.

"I talked to the lady at the front desk," she said with a bright smile. "She said there's a really good place to eat around the corner. It's not too cold, so Ben and I are going to walk over for an early dinner. Would you like to join us?"

He squinted at her like he was having trouble making sense of her words. Yes, she'd said them all on one rush of breath, but the invitation had been clear.

She pantomimed bringing a fork to her mouth. "Food. Eat. You and me."

"Why?"

Her turn to frown. "I'm hungry and figured you might be, as well."

"I was such a jerk earlier."

"At least you can admit it," she said with a laugh. "I get how hard it can be to go home, especially under the circumstances you're dealing with, but I'm not the enemy."

"I know." He ran a hand through his hair, and her stomach clenched as the muscles in his bicep flexed. She needed to get a grip on her awareness of this man. No point being distracted by his physical perfection when nothing could come of it. "In fact, I'm stellar at being my own worst enemy when it comes to being around my family."

Cory placed a hand on her stomach when a growl

escaped. "Grab a jacket and let's discuss your jerki-ness over dinner."

"Dinner is a yes. Talking about me being a jerk, hard pass." His voice was stern, but she could see his lips tugging up at the corners. And suddenly she desperately wanted to coax a smile from him.

They made their way to the nearby diner with Ben riding contentedly in his stroller. The air was chilled, so Cory had tucked a blanket around him and placed a wind barrier over the stroller's hood.

"Babies don't travel light," Jordan observed as Cory lifted Ben into her arms outside the restau-rant, and he folded the stroller to stow it near the front door.

"Not at all," she agreed with a laugh.

An older woman led them to a booth in the cor-ner and placed a high chair alongside it.

Cory sat the baby in it, supported from behind by his blanket. Ben looked around with his gaze wide, every experience and place new and fascinat-ing to him.

"I wish I could see the world through his eyes," Jordan said, echoing the thoughts in her head.

It both disturbed and delighted her that they were on the same wavelength. "I hope he never loses his curiosity," she said. "He's going to have the kind of unconditional love and support that makes him know he can do or try anything and still have a soft place to land with his mom."

"And his dad," Jordan said. "Although, I hope he doesn't try all the stupid stuff I did when I was younger."

The waitress appeared at the table and took their orders—a chicken club and side salad for Cory and a cheeseburger with sweet potato fries for Jordan.

She studied the man across the table for a long moment, then asked, "Were you a rebel back in the day? In Atlanta, you seemed like the mature one of the team, always guiding and mentoring the younger players."

"I learned some hard lessons that I didn't want to see other guys repeat." He glanced around the restaurant. "Most of my hell-raising was done in high school. Once I got out of Spokane, I lost the need to cause trouble."

"Because you didn't have to antagonize your father any longer?"

"I like to think I grew up, but I guess that had something to do with it." He shrugged, then turned his attention to Ben. "I was a master at pushing the old man's buttons." He wiggled a hand in front of the baby. Ben grabbed on to his father's finger, and Cory's breath caught in her throat at their two matching smiles. "I'm not planning to give this little guy a reason to cause trouble."

"Do boys need a reason?" Cory asked with a chuckle, which faded quickly at the look on Jordan's face. "You and your dad had a lot of problems."

"He was never satisfied with anything I did. No matter how much effort or energy I put into training, it wasn't enough. But at least if he was harping on me, that kept his focus off my mom. It's not going to be like that with Ben." He closed his eyes for a moment, like whatever he was thinking caused him pain. "I don't know how to be a dad, but I like to think I learned a lot about what not to do."

"That's a tough lesson."

When he looked at her again, he seemed miserable. "Would now be the appropriate time for you to point out how badly I messed up the reunion with my family today? I hadn't expected being back in that house to hit me the way it did. And then seeing my mom with Ben and how happy she seemed..."

"I'm glad she felt that way," Cory admitted, trying not to let too much emotion seep into her tone. "I know you aren't close with her, but maybe Ben can help change that. It's obvious she loves you."

He inclined his head. "Is it?"

"Yes. In fact—"

The waitress returned to the table at that moment with plates of food. Cory immediately regretted her choice of a salad instead of fries. The mountain of crispy sweet potatoes on Jordan's plate looked almost too good to resist.

"Go ahead." He handed her a ketchup bottle when they were alone again. "I remember that you're a food thief."

She wasn't sure what it meant that he remembered her habit of coveting food the people she was out to eat with ordered. They'd been at any number of team dinners together, but she couldn't remember ever "borrowing bites," as she liked to call it, from Jordan. Maybe she had without even thinking about it. She'd certainly tried to sit next to him when she could, because she always had more fun that way.

Her habit had bothered Kade to no end. By the end of their relationship, he seemed to relish pointing out that her inability to stick with the menu item she'd chosen said something about the inherent indecision built into her character.

She bit down on her cheek to hide her grin. "*Thief* is a harsh word." Her fingers brushed Jordan's when she took the ketchup from him, and awareness sparked across her skin. "I like options."

"The options from other people's plates," he countered.

"Sometimes."

Jordan pushed his plate closer. "Take a fry."

She tipped her chin and placed the condiment bottle on the table without opening it. "I'm happy with my salad."

"But you want a fry."

Her mouth watered as he popped one into his mouth. "So good. Crispy on the outside and fluffy inside, just like a good fry should be."

"Stop tempting me," she muttered.

"It's too much fun." He forked up a couple of fries and placed them next to her sandwich. "Now I'm going to have my feelings hurt if you don't eat one."

She wanted to say no, but they were too much to resist. The fry was indeed done to the perfect golden crispness, with the center remaining light and just the right amount of salt sprinkled on top.

"That a girl," Jordan coaxed with a smile, placing a few more on her plate. "It was worth giving in, right?"

Cory rolled her eyes. "I still have ten pounds of baby weight to lose. Salads are going to make that happen a lot quicker than fries."

"You look great."

"Sorry, I wasn't fishing for a compliment." She grabbed the ketchup and dumped a small pool onto her plate. If she was going to enjoy the fries, might as well add her favorite condiment into the mix.

"I know," Jordan told her, his deep voice once again sending her nerves into overdrive. "It's true, though. Motherhood agrees with you."

She tried not to read too much into his words, although she appreciated them. Being a mom wasn't the most glamorous, and with her grandmother sick on top of everything else, Cory had all but given up on self-care. "Thanks. You're going to get through your dad's service. I know it will be hard, but it's clear your mom is happy to have you here."

Jordan took a slow sip of the beer he'd ordered.

"I haven't been a very good son to her in the past few years."

"I saw the way she hugged you, Jordan. She's just waiting for an invitation back into your life."

"It's strange how I can hold on to my bitterness. She never once defended me when my dad was coming down hard or being an overbearing jerk. When I was twelve, I passed out in the middle of a wrestling tournament from dehydration and exhaustion. He got a doctor he knew to give me IV fluids, then put me in for the next match."

He set the bottle on the table and picked at the edge of the label with his thumbnail. "We were in town, so my mom happened to be there that day. She watched it happen and didn't say a word. She'd always bring me an ice cream sandwich later in my room. We wouldn't talk about whatever lecture I'd received or my aches and pains or the way he expected me to play through any injury without complaint. We'd just sit together in the glow of my nightstand light and eat our ice cream. That's when I felt the closest to her, although now I hate ice cream."

"No one hates ice cream," Cory argued gently.

"With the passion of a thousand burning suns." Jordan chuckled. "His behavior wasn't her fault, but I couldn't untangle her from him."

"Now you have a chance. With your brother, as well."

"I barely know my brother. My dad and I spent

so much time away from the house at games and tournaments and sports camps, it felt like we were two different families living under the same roof."

"Do you want that to change?"

He was quiet for several seconds before he nodded. "Yes."

"Then you'll make it happen."

"You make it sound easy."

She shook her head. "I gave up on easy a while ago. But worth it is a different story." Cory wanted to help him mend the tattered fabric of his bond with his mother. Both for Jordan's sake and for their son's.

Chapter Six

The late-winter sun lit a burnished sky the next day as Jordan's father was buried. It was still hard to believe the old man was gone, and Jordan couldn't quite shake the feeling of his shadow looming over the ones he'd left behind.

But Jordan had taken Cory's words to heart and made an effort with both his mom and his brother. He half expected them to rebuff his attempts to make peace. In this case, the prodigal son returning didn't feel worthy of any type of welcome home.

Instead, they'd shifted to assimilate him without question, as if everything that had come before was simply water under the bridge. He couldn't imagine it would be that easy to find balance and function bet-

ter than they had before. But he was so damn grateful to think he might have a chance that he didn't
examine or question their acceptance too closely.

With Cory at his side, he'd even managed to en-
dure a number of awkward conversations with people
who knew him as a kid, many of whom wanted to
talk about his days in the NFL. Jordan was shocked
how many of them had followed his career with avid
interest, and he was reminded again of how much he
appeared to have given up when he retired.

For him, he'd walked away without a second
thought, the love of the game waning so much that
staying wasn't worth it. Not with egocentric, fame-
hungry guys like Kade becoming the ones who appeared to be the future of the league. Men who were
more interested in being featured in highlight reel
videos on the various sports channels each week or
the size of a sponsorship payout their agents could
negotiate as opposed to playing the game they were
supposed to love.

Jordan's father had urged him to do more adver-
tising and schmoozing with company execs and less
enjoying his life on and off the field, only solidify-
ing Jordan's understanding that he wasn't a match
for the sport any longer.

Since leaving football, he'd gotten into an easy
routine of working at the bar and taking advantage of
the outdoor recreational activities around Starlight,
but Cory and Ben had already changed his focus. If

one thing had become clear during this trip, it was that he wanted them in his life. How that would look and whether she'd agree to it were a different matter entirely.

He exhaled a long breath as his mother wrapped him in a tight hug after walking them to the car. It amazed him how well she seemed to be coping with his dad's death. There were still a few women in the house, friends from book club who'd stayed to help her clean up after the reception that followed the funeral service.

Jordan was glad she wasn't alone.

"I'll call you in a couple of days," he said, pulling back. "If you need anything—"

"Having you here is what I needed." She patted his cheek, then glanced at Cory, who'd just strapped Ben into his car seat. "And meeting my grandson. You both have given me a reason to smile again."

"I'm glad, Mom."

"Now we just need to plan a wedding."

Jordan heard Cory's sharp intake of breath and resisted the urge to cringe. He might appreciate the progress he'd made in repairing his relationship with his mother, but he couldn't deny that the gains were built on a lie. He and Cory weren't together, and she'd given no indication she wanted a relationship with him.

If he had to guess, he'd say that if not for the

promise she'd made to her grandmother, she might not have even told him about his son.

He swallowed back the anger that clogged his throat at the thought. He'd missed the first six months of Ben's life and supporting his son through the trauma of his heart surgery, but Jordan was determined not to miss anything more.

"We're taking our time," he said, not exactly an outright lie. The more of those he could avoid, the better.

"Well, I've learned time is precious," his mother said with a glance at the back seat of the car, where Ben was chewing on his fist. "I'm not losing any more of it. In fact, I've made a decision."

"Okay." Jordan hoped his smile was encouraging as opposed to apprehensive.

"I'm coming to Starlight."

Cory made a choking sound next to him, and he purposely widened his smile. "I'd love that, Mom. Let me check the calendar when I get back home—"

"I'll be there on Friday," his mother told him with a nod. "I've already arranged for Marylou to water my plants."

Jordan swallowed. "How long are you planning to stay?"

"At least a week. Maybe longer." His mother reached out a hand and squeezed his arm. "I hope it's okay. I want to spend time with you and my grandson." She glanced around Jordan to smile at Cory. "And my future daughter-in-law."

"I mean…" Jordan searched his mind for an appropriate response. One that didn't involve him hurting his mom's feelings. That was the last thing he wanted. Well, maybe not the last. The last thing he wanted was his mother in Starlight for an extended stay.

He could see her eyes begin to dim as he tried and failed to formulate his words. She'd just buried her husband of over three decades. Jordan couldn't reject her outright, no matter the trouble he was about to get himself into.

"We'd love to have you stay with us." He pulled Cory closer to him, ignoring her squeak of protest. "Right, honey?"

"Of course," she murmured, and he was impressed her voice didn't waver. "We'd love to show you around town, and it would be wonderful for Ben to spend more time with his mimi."

Kathy's face brightened. "I can babysit while you two have date nights. I know it's hard to find time for romance with a little one around."

"Romance," Cory repeated, sounding not quite as sure as she had a few moments earlier.

"I promise I won't be an imposition," his mom said, then looked over her shoulder. "I should let you all start the drive. The timing is a bit strange, but the book-club ladies and I are having a meeting. They're such a comfort to me."

"What book are you reading?" Cory asked, apropos of nothing.

Jordan stared at her. How could she think about anything other than the fact that his mom was coming to town?

"Oh, it's an amazing personal development book." Kathy's gaze darted to Jordan, and she gave a sheepish smile. "Mainly geared toward women. It's called *Me First*. The ladies chose it because they figured I needed to learn how to make myself a priority after your father's death. I spent too much time giving away my power to him."

And the hits just kept on coming. Jordan had never thought of his mother other than as a helpmate to his dad. He would never have guessed that she possessed the self-realization to want to change and grow. Had that always been a part of her, a piece he'd overlooked because of his own anger?

Cory nodded as if everything coming out of his mom's mouth made complete sense. Impossible when his world was spinning out of control. "I'll have to check that out."

"Yes." Kathy reached out and squeezed Cory's hand. "We can have our own mini book club while I'm in Starlight."

"I'd like that."

"We need to go," Jordan said, unable to stand in

the front yard of his childhood home and feign things being normal for one more moment.

After another round of hugs from his mom, they got in the car and started toward the highway that led out of town.

He could feel Cory's assessing gaze on him but kept his eyes firmly on the road. There was no way he could mask the emotions swirling through him, and he wasn't ready to share them.

"What are we going to do?" she asked after checking on Ben in the back seat.

A quick glance in the rearview mirror showed the baby happily gumming the plastic ring of keys Cory had given him when she put him in the car.

"Apparently," Jordan grumbled, "you and my mom are going to start your own book club."

Out of the corner of his eye, he saw Cory stiffen. "It sounds like a good book."

"My mother didn't do one ounce of self-reflection during my childhood. So now I'm supposed to believe she's suddenly ready to be enlightened by some pop psychology tome?"

"I think it's nice she's trying to grow and change." Hearing Cory stand up for his mom both annoyed him and made him feel petty because of his irritation. "People can change, you know."

"Well, it's the opposite of nice that she's coming to Starlight and expecting to stay with us." He flicked a glance in Cory's direction. "You understand, right?"

"Of course," she answered tightly. "There is no us."

"So what are we supposed to do?" He shook his head. "What am I supposed to do? My mom wants to get to know a baby that I've just met. She wants to form a relationship with a fiancée that I don't have."

"Those are valid points." Cory turned to him. "We'll figure it out. It's figure-outable, just like my grandma always said."

Jordan blew out a long breath. "I sure hope your grandma knew what she was talking about."

Cory stood outside the coffee shop where she and Jordan were scheduled to meet the following day, nerves fluttering through her stomach like a renegade gang of spastic butterflies. After last night at the hotel, she was out of money and options.

They'd spent most of the drive home from Spokane working out how to manage his mom's visit. In the end, they'd come up with a plan to continue acting like they were a couple. Cory would be introduced in town as his long-distance girlfriend turned fiancée, and she'd stay in that role until his mom left town. She'd spent one final night in the hotel but would move into his house later that afternoon.

In fact, Jordan had suggested they plan their fake engagement to last for a full month. After that, they could break up but remain friends, or at least tell that story to the close-knit community of Starlight.

She'd considered Jordan a friend at one point and

wanted him to be more. But she had the feeling he didn't trust her or her motives at this point. Not that she blamed him. Wives and girlfriends of professional athletes sometimes got a bad rap because of the behavior of a select few. Most of the women Cory had met from the team were nice, although some of them got a little too caught up in the lifestyle.

She told herself that it didn't matter what he thought of her. Ben was the priority, and this temporary farce would ensure her son spent plenty of time with his father. It was a bonus that Ben would get to know his grandma, as well.

Cory had gotten used to putting the needs of her son above her own. Every time she thought of those first few days in the hospital and the terror of being told he'd need heart surgery, she knew that she could make it through anything as long as her child remained healthy and happy.

So what if her body seemed to be strangely aware of Jordan? Every move he made caught her attention in a way she didn't want or appreciate. It was going to feel like torture to pretend to be close to him but keep her emotions—and even more so her desire—out of the equation.

But she'd do it for Ben. Anything for her baby.

She balanced him on one hip as she entered Main Street Perk, amazed by the crowd of people filling the café tables in the middle of the afternoon. Clearly the coffee shop was a popular part of Starlight's downtown business scene. Ben looked around with wide eyes, and she smoothed a hand over the back of his head to ground herself before heading toward the table where Jordan sat near the front of the shop.

"Hey, babe," he said as she approached, his voice carrying across the room.

Cory felt color rise to her cheeks as the two baristas behind the counter openly stared at her. Oh yes. The women of Starlight were well aware of Jordan. She'd always hated the attention she received as Kade's girlfriend and the way other women would eye her up and down like they were trying to assess how easy it would be to poach her man.

She reminded herself Jordan didn't belong to her, even as she reached out to hug him when he stood. To her utter shock, he dropped a lingering kiss on her mouth, a public claiming, so to speak.

The butterflies took flight again, and Cory did her best to smother them. This was all an act, she told herself. They had only a few days to make their relationship believable to the people of this town before his mom arrived.

No time for subtlety.

Ben cooed and reached for his father, making Cory's breath catch. "Come to Daddy," Jordan said, a little too loudly.

Cory laughed. "Maybe find a different way to say that next time."

The blush that rose on Jordan's cheeks loosened

some of her nerves, but she realized he was truly disconcerted. He glanced around to make sure no one could overhear him. "I don't know what the hell I'm doing being a dad."

"You've got it." She transferred Ben to his arms. "It would be more believable if you didn't look like you were going to throw up."

Jordan's jaw tightened. "I'll get used to it."

"It's not like a toothache." She took the seat across from him. "I promise you'll be a natural before you know it."

Two cups of coffee and a plate of muffins sat on the checked tablecloth.

"I got you a sugar-free latte," he told her as he sat down again. "Although, I guess I don't know if that's still what you drink."

"It's great," she whispered, blown away he remembered her favorite coffee drink from the time they'd spent together in Atlanta. Seriously, how was she going to walk away from this man in a month?

A woman approached the table, curiosity obvious on her pretty features. She was tall and lithe, her chocolate-colored hair pulled into a loose bun. To Cory, she looked more like a high-end professional than a woman who belonged in a small-town coffee joint. "Hey, Jordan."

"Hi, Mara," he said calmly, like he showed up in the coffee shop every day with a strange woman and baby. "Nice muffins today."

"Thanks. I appreciate a guy who appreciates my muffins." She flashed a saucy grin before her gaze turned serious. "Parker said he stopped by Trophy Room last night for a drink with Nick and Finn. Tanya mentioned you were out of town for your dad's funeral. We're all sorry for your loss."

Cory watched Jordan's reaction closely. He started to go tense, but Ben patted a chubby hand on the tip of his nose. One side of Jordan's full mouth pulled into a smile, and relief coursed through Cory.

"I appreciate that," he answered, then gestured to Cory. "Have you met my fiancée? This is Cory Hall."

Cory choked on the swallow of coffee she'd just taken as the other woman's mouth dropped open.

"I don't believe I have," Mara said, eyebrows lifting almost to her hairline.

The grin he bestowed on Cory was filled with tenderness. "Sweetheart, this is Mara Johnson. She runs the coffee shop and is Starlight's master baker."

"I've heard a lot about you," Cory lied, because that was the plan. Jordan had told her most people in Starlight came through the coffee shop at some point during the week, so it made sense to have their first date there.

"Interesting." Mara glanced between Cory and Jordan. "I've heard nothing about you, but I'll admit I'm quite curious. Apparently, our friendly neighborhood bar owner has been keeping his private life very private."

"I can't wait to get to know all of Jordan's friends." Panic made Cory's chest tighten. She didn't like to lie, so she had spent a lot of time working out how to explain her sudden appearance without outright falsifying information. "You can blame me for the secrecy." She licked her suddenly dry lips. "Ben had some health issues when he was born, so I needed to stay in Michigan until the doctors cleared him for travel."

Mara made a soft tsking sound and touched Ben's arm. "Oh, sweet boy. You look perfect."

"He is perfect," Jordan said, and Cory blinked away tears.

"He had heart surgery five days after he was born to repair a narrowed aortic valve."

"Jordan." Mara's hazel eyes widened. "Why didn't you tell us anything? People would have happily pitched in at the bar to take care of things so you could go back. How old is Ben now?"

"Six months," Cory offered before Jordan could speak. His eyes had gone dark, and she could imagine what he was thinking. How angry he must feel that he wasn't told about the baby, so he missed the chance to be with them during the trauma of surgery and recovery.

"Jordan flew back to Michigan whenever his schedule allowed. I really wanted to keep everything private." She gave the other woman a watery smile she didn't have to manufacture. Just talking about that time made her emotional. "To be honest, Jordan and I have been through some ups and downs. We needed to get to a solid place before…" She drew in a deep breath. "We needed to be solid."

"And now we are." He covered her hand with his big one, the callus on his palm tickling her skin, and then looked at Mara. "I'm hoping you, Brynn and Kaitlin will help her get her bearings in Starlight."

"And a job," Cory added.

"You have a job," Jordan countered, thick brows furrowing. "It's called being a mom."

"I can be a great mom and also work if that's what I choose." Cory spoke slowly, like she was talking to a toddler. Of course, they hadn't discussed her working yet. The list of things they needed to go over seemed never ending.

Before Jordan had a chance to respond, Mara chuckled. "That's exactly right. Brynn is balancing work and motherhood, and she has little Remi plus a ten-year-old. I managed most of my daughter's life. Don't worry, Cory. We'll help you figure it out." She pulled a cell phone out of the back pocket of the jeans she wore. "Although, I'm not babysitting. Babies aren't my thing."

Jordan frowned. "You have a six-year-old. Evie was once a baby."

"I barely made it out alive," Mara said with a mock shudder before winking. "Just kidding. I love my daughter, and she was adorable. Your little guy is adorable, too. I can admire him from afar." She handed her phone to Cory. "Go ahead and put your number into my contacts. I'll arrange a time for all of us to get together. I'm sure Tanya has made you feel welcome already."

Cory darted a questioning glance at Jordan.

"She hasn't met everyone at the bar yet," he said, almost apologetically. "Tanya's going to give me a ration of grief for not telling her about this."

Mara laughed again. "Good luck with that." She turned her attention to the counter when one of the baristas called her name. "It was nice to meet you, Cory. Welcome to Starlight."

"Thanks," Cory said quietly, then stared at the half-eaten pastry on her plate as the other woman walked away. Her mouth felt like it was filled with sawdust, and her stomach cramped from anxiety.

"I don't know if I can do this," she told him. "It's too much. If she's an example of the type of people who live in this town, I don't want to lie to them."

Jordan scrubbed a hand over his jaw, then closed his eyes when Ben rested his head on his shoulder. "It's for Ben. We're doing this for our son. You'll move into my house today, right? Are you comfort-able with that?"

Cory blew out a long breath. Hadn't she just re-minded herself that she would do anything for Ben? "Okay, yes," she whispered. "But just know I hate every part of it."

Chapter Seven

Jordan did a double take when Cory walked into the bar later that night. She wasn't carrying the baby and looked as beautiful as he'd ever seen her. Her dark hair had been curled at the ends, and she wore a pair of fitted jeans that hugged her curves, along with a red sweater in a material so soft he wanted to reach out and touch it. He wanted to touch her, and the knowledge their pretend relationship gave him the freedom to do just that made it hard to concentrate on anything but his desire.

They'd agreed that he would mention her and Ben to his employees before formally introducing them so that he could answer questions and get everyone

Jordan nodded and averted his gaze. "Duly noted," he said through clenched teeth.

It was going to be a long few weeks pretending this was her life and not desperately wishing it to be real.

used to the idea of the boss having a secret family before they met.

He'd talked to Tanya, Madison and the rest of the crew earlier that afternoon during an impromptu staff meeting. The announcement that Jordan had a fiancée and a baby had been met with a range of reactions—from straight-up shock to gentle teasing to hearty congratulations. Tanya had grilled him on the situation while Madison stared with amused astonishment. True to her form, his prickly, if talented, head chef seemed to enjoy watching him squirm under a barrage of pointed questions.

But he'd gotten through it, and although Tanya sent him admonishing looks as she served drinks to the regulars, he knew she'd make sure the rest of the staff fell in line to support Cory and make sure there were no rumors spread about her.

Jordan didn't quite understand his protective streak when it came to Cory. He still held plenty of resentment about her keeping his son from him. He wasn't sure if he could truly trust her, despite his attraction. The attraction part had him swallowing back a growl as several male heads turned to check her out as she approached the bar.

He hadn't been kidding when he said motherhood agreed with her. To his deep consternation, Jordan wasn't the only one who seemed to notice.

He ran a tight ship at Trophy Room. The bar might look like a throwback to a small-town tavern with its paneled walls and scuffed wood bar, but he wanted everyone who walked in the door to feel comfortable. He didn't tolerate rude and offensive comments from customers or rowdy crowds, although he couldn't exactly stop his patrons from admiring a pretty woman.

Certainly he couldn't give in to the urge to knock some heads together until they stopped looking at his fiancée.

His fake fiancée, he reminded himself.

"Hey, ba—" He cleared his throat, then lifted a hand to wave. Cory had told him in no uncertain terms she would not answer to the term *babe*, which made him smile and also tempted him to call her that all the more just to elicit a reaction.

Her mouth quirked at the corner like she was trying to hide a smile. "Hi, hon," she said, smooth as his favorite single-malt scotch. She placed her hands on the bar, elegant fingers spread over the burnished wood, and leaned forward.

Like a moth drawn to a flame, he bent his head, heart hammering when she pressed her soft mouth to his.

He barely registered the gasps that came from the patrons around him and had to resist the urge to lift her over the bar and into his arms, caveman style.

"This is a surprise," he told her when she pulled back.

Her thin shoulders lifted and lowered. "Mara put me in touch with her friend Brynn, who recommended a babysitter." She bit down on her lower lip and then offered him a smile. "I missed you, so once I got Ben down for the night, I thought I'd stop in for a visit."

Blood roared through Jordan's brain. He knew she was playing a part right now, but the look in her eye made him believe every word. It was hard as hell not to want her to be speaking the truth.

"Are you going to introduce us?" a feminine voice asked behind him. "Or just stand there making googly eyes all night?"

He turned to see Tanya and Madison staring at him with twin smirks on their faces. Of all the times for his chef to make an appearance at the front of the house, it would have to be this moment.

"I vote for googly eyes," Ray Monning said from his bar stool. The older man winked at Cory. "I mean that in the most respectful way, ma'am."

"Understood," she said with a wide grin and held out a hand. "I'm Cory, Jordan's fiancée." She hitched a thumb in Jordan's direction. "Googly eyes aren't usually my thing, but I make an exception for this guy."

Jordan's heart melted just a little bit as Ray shook her hand with wide-eyed astonishment. He was one of the regulars, but his history in town was spotty at best. He had trouble holding down a job and stuck mostly to himself since his wife had left him several years earlier. Jordan rarely had to refuse to serve customers, but he would if someone got out of hand.

Ray never got out of hand, but most people in town overlooked him. He was just an old-timer who'd fallen through the cracks when it came to living a life society deemed successful. He wore the same ratty flannel every day and was often in need of a shower. Jordan mostly felt sorry for him and did what he could to be a sympathetic shoulder, but Ray wasn't much for conversation.

Now he was looking at Cory like she was the sun shining down on him. Jordan certainly understood the feeling.

"I didn't know the barman had a fiancée," Ray said, drawing out the syllables of that last word as he glanced between Cory and Jordan.

"He kept the secret from all of us," Madison added. "Sneaky schmuck."

To her credit, Cory didn't flinch at the other woman's snarky tone. If anything, her smile grew brighter. "I'm here now, and I'm looking forward to getting to know everyone." Her gaze zeroed in on Madison. "I hear that your food is amazing. Fries are my favorite, so I can't wait to try yours. It probably sounds strange, but I'm a little bit of a connoisseur. A perfect French fry is difficult to master."

Jordan flinched as his chef narrowed her eyes. She tended to be just shy of outright confrontational when anyone even hinted at judging her culinary skills. "Well, then. It's my dearest hope I can live up to your high standards."

"Be nice," Tanya whispered under her breath.

Cory only continued to smile, not offering an antagonizing reply but not backing down, either. Add backbone to the list of things that Jordan found attractive about her. The list was getting longer by the second.

A couple gestured to Jordan from the far end of the bar. It was easy to get distracted by Cory, as well, but he needed to keep his wits about him.

"I'll be right back," he said, tossing a towel over his shoulder.

"Come to the kitchen with me," Madison ordered Cory, crooking her finger. "I'm working on a new dipping sauce for the manchego cheese croquettes. I need a discerning palate to taste test for me."

"Unnecessary," Jordan said as he moved past, throwing a beseeching glance toward Tanya. "Help," he mouthed.

She shrugged in return. "You should have mentioned her earlier."

The wife of the couple waved to him again. Thirsty patrons he couldn't ignore. He gave one last glance over his shoulder. "You can wait for me," he called to Cory.

"I don't bite," Madison said.

Cory nodded and stepped forward. "I appreciate that. Lead on. You had me hooked at the word *cheese.*"

Worlds colliding, Jordan thought, his heart still

beating at a rapid pace as Cory followed Madison into the kitchen and out of his sight. He hadn't expected his worlds to collide so soon.

Anxiety pounded through him like a fierce thunderstorm. Maybe he needed to serve himself a drink along with his customers. Tanya gave him a funny look, and he forced a steadying breath and pasted a smile on his face. As if he didn't have enough dealing with the shock of being a father, he'd never imagined how stressful it would be to have a fake fiancée.

Cory was used to being underestimated.

Her mom had done it for most of Cory's life and then she'd spent her relationship with Kade being either coddled or condescended to, so she didn't misinterpret the willowy chef's invitation to her kitchen as anything but the gauntlet it was.

If she had any question, Jordan's terrified glance had confirmed her suspicions. Even Tanya, the spirited bartender, had squeezed Cory's arm as she walked past. "Good luck," the other woman murmured. "Just don't cry. Tears are like blood in the water when the sharks are circling for Madison."

A dire warning for sure.

"Sit," Madison ordered when they entered the bar's kitchen. The woman flicked her wrist at the line cook currently chopping vegetables on an oversize butcher block. "Out," she told him.

He swallowed and nodded, then dropped his knife and practically raced out of the room.

"Is everyone around here afraid of you?" Cory asked conversationally as she took a seat on the metal stool positioned in front of the stainless-steel counter. Despite all of her bluster, Cory liked Madison. As far as she could tell, they had very little in common, but somehow the prickly woman felt like a kindred spirit.

"Fear and respect go hand in hand in my kitchen," Madison said simply.

"They aren't mutually exclusive, you know."

The other woman shot her a glare. "Big words. Are you some kind of fancy scholar?"

That made Cory laugh out loud. "Hardly. Are you a classically trained chef?"

Madison's mouth thinned. "As a matter of fact, yes."

"What do you like most about cooking?"

"No one has ever asked me that. I like your earrings. They're unique."

Cory touched a finger to one of the thin gold hoops with multicolored stones strung through them. Pride snaked along her spine. "Thank you. I made them. But you're avoiding my question, and it's a fair one for someone who makes her living in the kitchen. I read the online reviews of the bar and the food you serve. People rave about it."

"I'm good."

"I'd say you're more than good. When you have

that much positive feedback for doing work that's so personal, it must be because you have a true passion for it. I'm curious what that is."

"You know this is supposed to be an interrogation of you." Madison crossed her arms over her chest. Her white chef's coat and black pants were basically shapeless, but it was clear she had an enviable figure, all long legs and slim curves. It didn't look as though she was wearing makeup, which in no way detracted from her creamy skin and rosy mouth. A mouth that was pressed into an unforgiving line, something Cory could almost appreciate. She had a feeling this woman wouldn't take grief from anyone.

"You're interrogating me?" Cory inclined her head. "I wouldn't have guessed. I thought I was just here to eat."

"Jordan gave us a convoluted story about your long-distance relationship. He wasn't convincing."

Cory drew in a breath. "It's complicated."

"That I believe." Madison took a trio of perfectly round cheese balls out of the fryer and plated them. She poured two different kinds of sauces into matching ramekins, then placed them in front of Cory. "Tell me more."

"Oh, that smells divine." Cory dipped a piece of fried cheese into one of the creamy sauces and bit into it. The flavors exploded on her tongue, a kaleidoscope of savory and spice with just the hint of smoky sweetness. She closed her eyes so she could concentrate more fully on the bite. She didn't consider herself a foodie but could appreciate Madison's genius with flavors. "Is that paprika?"

"I have it shipped in from Hungary. The local grocery in Starlight doesn't carry anything worth buying as far as spices go."

"I didn't realize it made such a difference." Cory took another bite. "Wow. I could swim in a vat of that."

She glanced up as Madison let out a rusty laugh. "That would be disgusting."

"But worth it." Cory looked past the other woman. "Didn't I see that chicken satay skewers are the special tonight? My taste buds are advanced." She tried hard not to laugh as she said the words. Her idea of gourmet during her pregnancy had been fast-food chicken nuggets with a large fry and a strawberry milkshake. "I can definitely give you a worthwhile opinion on those, as well."

"You just told me you want to swim in garlic aioli. That's not exactly discriminating."

"You never told me why you like to cook," Cory said with a shrug.

"You never told me the real deal with you and Jordan."

Cory thought about how to handle this situation. She knew what Jordan would tell her. Lie. She needed to keep up the charade of them being a couple until his mother came and went. That was the agreement.

But she didn't want to lie. It had been hard enough when they were together in the coffee shop. Madison's gaze on her was far too knowing. Cory got the feeling the other woman would sniff out the deception, and Cory wouldn't get to be any sort of taste tester if she got on the chef's bad side.

"We have a baby together," she said because that was the truth.

"And you're engaged?"

"In a manner of speaking." Cory kept her focus on the plate. "Can I have a piece of chicken now?"

"Explain the manner of which you speak and I'll give you the best satay you've ever had."

"That's blackmail." Her mouth watered.

The other woman shrugged. "It will blow your mind." She glanced toward the kitchen door. "But I want the scoop before Jordan comes back here like some knight in shining flannel to rescue you."

"It's kind of wrong to look that good in flannel," Cory mused.

"Stop trying to change the subject."

"You're bossy," Cory said, pointing a finger. She felt oddly comfortable with the caustic chef.

"You're tougher than you look."

That compliment made a lightness infuse Cory's chest, but she didn't answer the question about Jordan. "I've heard you have trouble keeping your employees happy. Do you think that is a result of your bossy nature?"

"It's my kitchen," Madison reminded her.

"But you need people to want to be here with you. You can't do it alone."

"I hire good people and train them well."

"Are they loyal to you?"

"They respect my skill."

"Okay, Ms. Chef Miyagi." Cory made a face. "Wash on and wash off with your bad self. Who cares if people like you as long as they're afraid of you?"

"Do you want the chicken satay or not?"

"Of course I do. It smells amazing, and I'm hungry."

"Then tell me about the engagement."

Cory threw up her hands and then looked around the kitchen to make sure they were alone. She didn't need to tell this woman anything. They were strangers, and Madison worked for Jordan. That should tell Cory everything she needed to know about the other woman's loyalty.

Yet… Cory had no one in her life now that her grandmother was gone. Nobody in her corner. No friends. No support system of her own. She didn't think for a minute that she and Madison were destined to become besties and braid each other's hair or skip off to Vegas for a girls' weekend. There was something about the woman, however, that made

Cory believe she could be trusted. And Cory desperately wanted someone to know the truth. "It's fake, okay?" she blurted before she thought better of it. "Until I got to town this week, I hadn't seen Jordan since the one night we spent together."

"The night where you made the baby?"

"Yes, that night. Now please give me the satay."

"Okay, Ms. Sassy-Pants." Madison plated the food and placed it in front of Cory. "First, your strange little secret is safe with me. I'm trying to figure out why the two of you are bothering to make all of this up. Did Jordan know about the baby and he didn't want to be involved?"

Cory shook her head and cut off a sliver of chicken. "No. The complicated part was the truth. We were friends and then had one night together after I broke up with my long-term boyfriend. The next day Kade told the guys we were back together and getting engaged. He hadn't bothered to mention it to me, but Jordan believed him." Her chest ached at the memory, but she forced herself to breathe through it. She was leaving the past behind for the sake of her baby.

Instead she focused on Madison's food. As soon as the chicken hit her tongue, she moaned out loud. "This is obscene," she said after finishing the bite. "Does the Michelin-star guy know about you?"

"Small-town bars don't get Michelin stars," Madison said with a laugh.

"They should when the food is this spectacular." She pointed her fork at the chef. "You should get five stars."

"And that's not how the rating system works."

"Seriously, what are you doing here? You should have your own restaurant in some fancy upscale town or big city."

Madison's eyes went dark. "Been there, done that. The pressure didn't agree with me. Stop trying to change the subject. We were at the part where your boyfriend—"

"Ex-boyfriend," Cory corrected.

"Your ex-boyfriend," Madison amended. "When you call him Kade, does that mean Kade Barrington, the bad-boy darling of the NFL?"

"You makes him sound a lot more charming than he actually is."

"So what happened next?"

"Kade showed up at the hotel room I'd rented while I was looking for a place to stay. I tried to avoid him, but he eventually tracked me down. I'm pretty sure the girl at the reservation desk alerted him. He could be a real charmer when he wanted to."

"Sounds more like a real stalker," Madison observed.

Cory shrugged. She'd gotten so used to her ex-boyfriend's overbearing personality that it hadn't seemed odd at the time. But, yeah, Kade had crossed the line, and she'd let him. "I hadn't talked to Jordan since I left his place. Everything was too over-whelming, and I thought I had time to figure out my feelings. After Kade told me what he'd announced to the guys, I kicked him out of my room and went to find Jordan."

"Don't tell me he believed you'd gone back to that guy or used him for a night."

"He was gone," Cory murmured, placing her fork on the plate. As amazing as the food was, her stomach twisted into uncomfortable knots. "It was the postseason and there was already a question as to whether Jordan would return because of his injury. I don't know if the business with Kade had anything to do with it, or the timing simply worked out, but he left Atlanta and announced his retirement the following week."

"You didn't go after him?" Madison asked, curiosity clear in her tone.

"No." Embarrassment added to the uncomfortable feeling roiling in her gut. "I figured we were just together one night and he realized he didn't want anything to do with me. That's how it felt, anyway." She ran a hand through her hair, regretting the fact that she'd tried so hard to look nice tonight now that emotions from that time had risen to the surface. Jordan had walked away without even talking to her. That had been a clear indication of his feelings. There was a good chance she was imagining everything else—the connection and attraction that seemed to shimmer in the air between them.

"Then you realized you were pregnant," Madison added quietly when Cory didn't say anything else.

"I knew after the first ultrasound the baby wasn't Kade's." Cory pressed her lips together. "He tried to convince me to get back together with him anyway, but it wasn't going to work. I didn't want that life for my baby. The timing of the pregnancy…" She shook her head. "The baby was Jordan's. I know I should have tried harder to track him down, but I went back to Michigan and things just seemed to spiral out of control. My grandma was sick, so I moved in with her. I could barely process the thought of being a mom, let alone trying to negotiate it alongside a man I'd been with one time."

"That's a lot to deal with."

"I'm not proud of the choices I made, but I'm trying to make amends for them."

"Oh, honey." Madison chuckled. "Welcome to the club. We all have things we'd like a redo on. My list is a mile long."

Cory did her best to smile, although it felt a little wobbly at the edges. At the same time, she felt more at peace than she had in ages. She'd shared the truth of her circumstances with someone who didn't seem inclined to judge her for her mistakes. It felt like the first real step she'd taken toward the life she wanted to have. In fact, she wanted more of this feeling.

Madison was obviously wrestling with her own demons. What if they could be actual friends? What if Cory could put together her own tribe of women the way Jordan's mom had in her life? What if she made Starlight her home even after she and Jordan ended their pretend engagement?

"We should start a book club," she blurted, and Madison took a step back.

"Do I look like the joiner type?"

"You look like someone I want to hang out with."

"No one wants to hang out with me." Madison scoffed, but Cory saw color bloom on her cheeks. "Unless it's because I'm cooking for them."

"Then we'll start a cooking club," Cory said with a nod. "That's perfect."

"You're crazy."

"Crazy about me." Jordan's voice came from the door leading to the bar.

Madison looked at Cory, brow raised.

"Not a word of what I told you," Cory murmured. "We're friends. Friends don't snitch."

She thought the other woman might laugh in her face, but Madison only inclined her head. "Because snitches wind up in ditches," she said with a soft laugh.

"Not exactly my train of thought, but let's go with it." She climbed off her chair and turned to Jordan. "You're lucky to have someone with so much talent in your kitchen."

"Agreed," he said, then ran a hand through his hair as he glanced around. "By the way, Louis quit on his way out. He said he'd rather flip burgers at a fast-food dump than have you order him around."

"He's an idiot," the chef muttered.

"Also the fourth kitchen employee we've lost this month. We're going to run out of candidates in Starlight."

Madison's whole demeanor changed in an instant. "Then I'll do it all myself."

Jordan shook his head. "That won't work when we're busy on the weekends. You need help."

"I'm looking for work," Cory offered as she took a final bite of chicken. "Madison and I are going to start a cooking club, so the more I learn about the kitchen, the better. I can wait tables, too. I've done it before."

"No way." Jordan looked almost horrified. "I won't have my fiancée toiling away in the kitchen."

Cory felt her mouth drop open. "Um, what year is this? Did I miss the time traveling to Downton Abbey, where you're the lord of the manor and I'm the lowly servant wench?"

"Sounds like some kinky role-playing to me," Madison said, clearly enjoying Jordan's irritation.

"No, thanks," Cory told the chef, then turned fully to Jordan. "For your information, if I can work out childcare for Ben, I can apply for whatever job I want."

"It's my bar," he countered.

"It's my kitchen," Madison said. "Remember, our deal was I got full control of the food and my staff."

"You don't want to hire her." Jordan hitched a finger at Cory. "She has no experience, and she can barely boil water."

Cory narrowed her eyes, even though he was right. She regretted sharing funny stories with him about her long list of kitchen failures, never guessing that they would be thrown back in her face this way.

"You take two days off a week," Madison reminded Jordan. "I'll arrange her shifts so she works those nights as well as the weekend." Her crystalline blue gaze switched to Cory. "That way you'll have less childcare scheduling to manage."

"That sounds great." Cory couldn't hide her smile.

"*That* sounds like the worst idea in the history of ideas," Jordan said, sounding exasperated.

Madison gave a thumbs-up to Cory and ignored Jordan. She grabbed a small pad of paper and a pen from a nearby counter, scribbled something on it and handed the paper to Cory. "Here's my number. Think about the logistics. Discuss it with your fiancé if you need to."

"Doubtful," Cory muttered.

"Call me tomorrow if you want to talk more about what I'd expect. I don't go easy on the people who work for me."

"I'm not looking for easy," Cory said. "We can make plans for the club idea, too."

"This is not happening," Jordan said, arms akimbo.

"I'm heading back home." Cory turned and planted a smacking kiss on Jordan's cheek. "We'll talk later, hon. Nice to meet you, Chef."

Madison chuckled. "It's been interesting."

Ignoring Jordan's heavy scowl, Cory walked away, looking forward to this new challenge.

Chapter Eight

"I'll help you find a different job," Jordan said a few days later as he watched Cory making a list of instructions in her neat penmanship. "One that will make you happy."

She didn't look up from her writing as she answered, "I think working with Madison will make me happy."

"Said no one ever. I don't know a single person who would say Madison Maurer makes them happy, other than through her food."

"Her mom might argue with you. Most mothers are made happy by their children." Cory straightened, her brows furrowed. "Except maybe mine, but most others. At least that's what I want to believe."

He felt his mouth open and close in stunned shock at her eternal optimism. Other than when she was giving him grief, Cory always tried to look at the bright side of a situation. It made him feel like a regular Eeyore in comparison. "That's an argument for another time. Once we finish this one."

"We aren't arguing, and there's no need for discussion." She glanced at her watch. "I need to leave in fifteen minutes. Don't want to be late for my first day on the job."

He closed his eyes for a moment, trying to figure out if it was worth making one last-ditch effort to change her mind. He'd been trying all day. Cory had been asleep when he got home last night, or at least her door remained closed. The door of the room across the hall from hers had been cracked. He'd crept in to watch Ben sleeping in the soft glow of the night-light plugged in next to the makeshift changing table.

Jordan's heart had tightened almost painfully as his son's chest rose and fell with steady breaths. The boy wore fire-truck pajamas, and his arms and legs were spread out in a great imitation of a starfish. Jordan tended to sleep the same way even as an adult, and he wondered if something like that could be passed down. It still amazed him that he'd helped create this beautiful baby.

Of course, Cory had done the heavy lifting so far, which was often the way with mothers, in his experience. But he'd become part of the equation, even though he wasn't yet comfortable with his abilities.

"It's probably too soon," he told Cory, taking a different tack. "Ben needs to be more settled here before you start work. What if he needs something?"

She inclined her head as she studied him like she couldn't understand a word coming out of his mouth. "Even way out in the woods, you're only fifteen minutes from town. If there's an emergency, call me."

Before he could answer, the baby monitor on the counter crackled, and he heard the sounds of Ben's quiet fussing. The boy had such an easygoing temperament but always woke with a few minutes of postnap crankiness. Another thing he could have inherited from Jordan.

Cory held up the paper with the instructions she'd been writing. "I have a list for you here with his feeding schedule and other pertinent details, but let's start with the first lesson." She winked at him. "Diaper changing."

Jordan shook his head slowly. "I've never changed a diaper."

"I figured as much by the way you conveniently disappear any time he needs to be changed."

"It's not convenient. It's purposeful."

She laughed as she walked past him and squeezed his arm. "Get ready to become an expert."

Jordan had never considered becoming an expert on diapers, or anything to do with fatherhood, but he dutifully followed Cory. She was right. He did tend to pick and choose the parenting duties he was comfortable performing.

Mostly he liked being in the role of entertainer, making both Ben and Cory smile with his funny faces or games of peekaboo. Although Cory told him Ben was big for his age, the baby still seemed so breakable to Jordan, especially after what he'd been through.

As soon as they walked into the bedroom, Cory began to talk to Ben, telling him in her soothing voice that he'd be spending the afternoon and evening with Daddy and she knew they'd have lots of fun.

Jordan found her words oddly reassuring, as if hearing her say them out loud made him able to believe they were true.

She stopped in front of the crib that Jordan had borrowed and put together. He needed to do more to make this room welcoming. Before Ben, it had been an overflow storage room, and it certainly didn't look like a nursery. No doubt Jordan's mom would notice that immediately.

"So you have to pick him up to change the diaper," Cory explained in a patient voice.

"He likes you to get him up from a nap," Jordan argued. "That's what he's used to."

"He'll get used to his daddy."

Jordan felt like the biggest fool. How hard was it

to be a father? He had plenty of friends who raised kids, both in Starlight and back when he was in the NFL. Huge, hulking bruisers on the field who'd cradle their babies in their arms, mostly like a football, in Jordan's opinion. But they'd done it.

What the hell was wrong with him?

He swallowed back his irrational fear and leaned over the crib. "Don't cry," he commanded, earning a chuckle from Cory.

Ben shoved his fist in his mouth and stared as Jordan lifted the baby into his arms. "Okay, that was easy enough." He made a face as a rancid scent rose in the air. "Oh no. I think something crawled into the crib with him and died."

"He probably woke up because he pooped." Cory smoothed a hand over the boy's head. "Did Mommy's big man make a big poopy?"

"I hope Mommy's not going to make Daddy run the poopy gauntlet his first time out of the gate," Jordan said, matching her singsong tone.

"One hundred percent you are changing this diaper. Don't be a wimp."

He raised a brow. "I have never been accused of being wimpy."

"I think I just made the accusation."

"Fine." He gripped the baby's torso and held him at arm's length. "Let's do this doo-doo duty."

"So clever," Cory murmured with a soft laugh.

Jordan shouldn't like making her laugh as much

as he did. Or take so much pleasure in the way she smiled at him. She smiled a lot. He needed to keep reminding himself that he wasn't special. Not to her.

He placed Ben on the changing pad Cory had brought with her, which sat on top of the pine dresser in the baby's room. The boy kicked up his feet like he wanted to give Jordan easy access to his dirty bottom.

"I believe in you," Cory said, placing a hand on Jordan's lower back. The words were said in a teasing manner, but they meant something. Like her laugh, the vote of confidence made him feel like he could do anything.

He unbuttoned Ben's one-piece romper but frowned as he pulled the baby's legs out of the soft fabric, exposing his chest. "He doesn't have a scar." Jordan glanced at Cory. "If he had heart surgery…"

"They went in through his back," she explained, her tone tight. "After you finish the diaper, you can undress him and see it."

"I wasn't doubting you," Jordan quickly told her. "It just surprised me."

"I understand."

But it didn't sound like she understood. "Grab a few wipes," she told him and proceeded to walk him through changing a dirty diaper while Jordan did his best not to gag or make faces at the mess and the smell.

"How does a kid that small produce so much

poop?" he asked as he placed the final wet wipe into the bag Cory had given him.

"You should have seen the blowouts he used to have when he was really young. At least the poop is somewhat contained now."

Jordan cringed, then picked up a clean diaper as Ben continued to wriggle on the table. He seemed in a much better mood now that the mess had been taken care of, and Jordan couldn't blame him.

As he started to place the diaper under the baby, Cory moved forward and turned it around. "Tabs go from back to front," she told him, but he was struggling to focus because she was so close that she was pressed against his side. Awareness zipped through him. They might have only spent one night together, but his body remembered hers.

Damn, he needed to get out more. There was absolutely nothing sexy about changing his baby's diaper, but he couldn't seem to stop his reaction. He wanted to be closer to her. He wanted more—more than he knew was right based on their arrangement, and he'd guess far more than she was willing to give.

As they made it through the diaper-changing lesson, Cory patted Jordan's arm. "Nice work for a newbie," she said, not meeting his gaze. "I'll take him while you wash your hands." Had she sensed his awareness of her or noticed the unexpected intimacy of the moment the way he did?

While he finished washing, she took Ben into

the family room, where he sat on a blanket playing with a toy piano in front of him. She'd taken off the baby's romper, and Jordan sucked in a breath as he noticed the one-inch scar from an incision that ran next to the boy's spine. "I can't believe what he went through." He dropped down on the blanket next to his son and traced one finger along the scar. It had healed but was still pink and looked tender, but Ben didn't react to Jordan touching it. "He couldn't have understood what was happening to him."

"No," Cory agreed. "But at some level he had to know it was a huge trauma. He fought for his life, Jordan, and he survived. Your son is a survivor. I know you think he's fragile, which in some ways all babies are. But he's tough, too. Think about his strength and determination instead of his size or that he's helpless." She crouched down next to Jordan and kissed the top of the boy's head. "I think he gets a lot of that strength from his father."

When their gazes met, hers was tender. Once again, she seemed to understand exactly what Jordan needed to hear—reassuring him both that the baby was strong and that Jordan had a place in his life. He didn't understand how Kade had let her go. The guy might have a hell of a throwing arm, but otherwise he was a complete fool.

With her so close that he could feel her breath against his face, it seemed the most natural thing in the world to lean in and brush a gentle kiss across her sweet mouth. It was different from the way he'd kissed her at the bar. This was a vow, a quiet promise that they were in this together. It was a question about what they could mean to each other if they tried.

A question that was answered when Cory pulled away so fast she fell on her bottom, then scrambled to her feet.

"I'm sorry," he said immediately, even though he didn't regret kissing her. He couldn't regret it.

She pressed two fingers to her lips as if his touch had burned her. "I need to go. The instructions are written on the paper on the counter. Call if there's a problem."

"Cory, I didn't mean to upset you." Jordan made to stand, but she held out a hand.

"It's fine. I'm fine." She flashed a wan smile. "Have a fun boys' night in." With a last look at Ben, she hurried from the room.

"A customer at table five wants to talk to the chef."

Cory looked up from where she was chopping a celery stalk two hours later as the waitress, Misty, ducked her head like she thought the boss might throw something at her.

Cory didn't blame her. Madison didn't speak to her staff as much as she did growl and command. She rarely raised her voice but didn't need to. Her rigid tone reminded Cory of a military commander—one who wouldn't tolerate being questioned.

Cory had discovered that the hard way when she'd asked a series of questions about how the different menu items were prepped. Madison had looked at her like she was the biggest fool on the planet. Cory wasn't sure what it said about her that she didn't flinch in the face of so much silent condemnation. If the surly chef was trying to chasten Cory, she'd have to work a lot harder. Cory'd grown up with a mother who enjoyed tearing her down for sport. She could handle almost anything.

The same couldn't be said for Misty, who'd told Cory she'd taken the part-time waitressing job while attending a nearby university. Misty was the first in her family to attend college and wanted to give her parents a little relief on tuition by making extra money.

Cory knew what it was like to work to put herself through school, so she admired the younger woman's dedication. Actually, Misty was only a few years younger than Cory, although Cory felt decades older. But Misty had also confided that she was thinking of looking for work elsewhere just so she didn't have to deal with the woman who ran the kitchen.

"Why?" Madison's eyes narrowed as she pointed a spatula at the waitress. "What did you do?"

"N-nothing," Misty stammered.

"Are they complaining about the food?"

"I'm not sure. It's a woman. She seems happy enough. Maybe she wants to pay her compliments to the chef."

"The chef doesn't need or want compliments."

"I'll go." Cory wiped her hands on a towel and stepped out from behind the counter. "I can accept a compliment on your behalf and explain that the chef is so humble and shy she doesn't like to leave the kitchen."

Misty smothered a burst of laughter as Madison glared at Cory. "I don't have a shy bone in my body."

"Or a heart," Chuck, the other line cook, called from where he was deep-frying wings at the far side of the kitchen.

Cory saw the briefest instant of pain in Madison's blue gaze before she shuttered it again. "My heart goes into the food. I don't bother sucking up to customers," she shot back, then flicked her fingers at Cory. "See what Ms. High-Maintenance wants. If she complains or asks for a comped meal, dump a beer on her."

"Interesting tactic," Cory said as she headed for the front of the bar. "But I think I can handle this. Point me to table five," she told Misty.

The bar was even more crowded than last night. She liked the energy of the place, groups of people together laughing and having fun.

Tanya, who was tending bar on her own tonight, gave her a questioning gaze as she walked by. Cory waved and smiled, then placed a hand on Misty's arm. "You're doing a good job handling Madison," she told her.

"She's awful." Misty shook her head. "I know she cooks great food, but is it worth it?"

"Have you tried the fried cheese?" Cory sighed. "It will change your world."

"I heard you were Jordan's fiancée," Misty said as she glanced at Cory. "You must be titanium strong. He's scary, too."

"Jordan?" Cory chuckled. "Nah, he's a big teddy bear."

Misty snorted, then pointed to a two-topper in the corner. "That's her. I'm sorry I didn't figure out what she wants. I got flustered when she said she wanted to talk to the chef, knowing I'd have to ask Madison to come out."

"It's fine." Cory approached the woman with a smile. She'd worked at a diner just off campus all four years of school. There was no customer complaint or irritation she couldn't handle.

"Hi, I'm Cory. Is there something I can help you with?"

"You aren't the chef." The woman frowned at her. She had long, wavy brown hair and was dressed in a bulky cable-knit sweater and leggings. She looked comfortable and still stylish, with understated diamond hoops in her ears. Cory guessed she either had or came from money.

"No," Cory agreed. "I'm one of the sous-chefs." To be honest, she didn't exactly know what that meant, but it sounded better than glorified slave in the kitchen. "The head chef is in the middle of something, so if I can be of assistance—"

"I need a recipe." The woman pointed to her bowl of beer-braised chicken stew, of which there were only two bites left. "This recipe, to be specific."

"I'm not sure that's how it works at a restaurant." Cory had watched in awe earlier as Madison toasted anise seeds and then blended them in a food processor with a variety of other spices, bathing the kitchen in their heavenly aroma. She'd put together the seemingly simple chicken dish, tonight's special, in a way that seemed effortless but would have been impossibly demanding to a chef with lesser talent.

The woman shook her head and narrowed her hazel eyes. "Trophy Room isn't a restaurant. It's a local dive bar that happens to currently serve the best food I've had on three continents." She held out a hand. "I'm Ella Samuelson. I grew up in Starlight, and I guarantee you can't get a meal like this anywhere else in town."

"We're glad you like it, but I highly doubt the chef will share her recipes. What would keep you coming back?"

Ella's jaw set in a hard line. "You don't understand. I have to cook something this amazing in two days. It's imperative."

"Why?" Cory asked, and Ella frowned.

"The reason is private."

"So is the recipe."

Ella closed her eyes for a moment and drew in a deep breath. "I have a friend coming to town. Toby doesn't think I can cook. He doesn't think I can do anything remotely wifeish."

"Is that a bad thing?" Cory asked, genuinely curious.

"He sees me as one of the guys," Ella said, her shoulders slumping slightly. "We worked together."

"Doing what?"

"I'm a nurse. I was a nurse. I'm not anymore."

"You're the woman Mara mentioned," Cory murmured. "Her friend who works as a nanny."

"Sometimes," Ella admitted, almost sheepishly. "I'm trying to figure out what my next move is going to be."

"And you want to put the moves on your former coworker?"

"That sounds pathetic." Ella scooped up another bite of chicken. "But maybe. Can you get me the recipe?"

Cory opened her mouth to say no, then had an idea. "I might be able to if you join our cooking club."

Ella blinked. "I gave up clubs in middle school."

"Don't be silly." Cory clapped her hands together. "It will be great."

"I just need a recipe to make before my friend gets here."

"Are you normally a good cook?"

"I've been a traveling nurse for the past five years. Cooking skills weren't much of a priority for me."

"Then learning to cook the dish will be the perfect start."

"By Saturday?" Ella looked skeptical.

"Our first meeting is this week in the Trophy Room kitchen."

"Jordan is letting you use his bar for your club?"

Cory laughed, hoping it sounded casual and not manic. "I'm his fiancée. He can hardly say no."

"And the chef will agree to teach me?"

"All of us," Cory said, nodding.

"How many of us are there?"

"Well, just you and me for now. But Madison's reputation is huge in Starlight."

"Her reputation or her food's reputation? They aren't the same thing."

"Do you want to learn how to make the dish or not?" Cory glanced over her shoulder. She was going out on a limb. In fact, she half expected Madison to come charging out of the kitchen to see what was taking her so long.

"I'll be here to learn to cook."

"You have to commit to four meetings. Twice a month."

"Are you making this up as you go along?"

"Maybe."

"I respect your honesty. Two months of a cooking club. If things work out this weekend with Toby, I'll need more than one recipe."

"Yay."

"Don't say 'yay.' You sound like you're twelve."

Ella handed Cory her cell phone. "Text me the details and I'll be there."

Cory clasped her hand to her chest as she turned back toward the kitchen. For a person who didn't like to lie or be assertive, she was certainly turning over a new leaf in Starlight.

It was a leaf she quite liked.

Chapter Nine

"Thanks for coming," Jordan told Josh Johnson as he stepped back to let the local contractor into his home. Josh had done some work at the bar, and he was Mara's brother-in-law plus a Starlight native. Although everyone in town was a fan of Josh's easygoing nature, Jordan didn't know him well. He'd been somewhat surprised at Josh's willingness to help with the project Jordan had planned.

"I have insane painting skills," Josh answered, holding up a bucket filled with brushes and rollers. "My employees are going to love having a staff appreciation happy hour at the bar. That woman you hired is a unicorn in the kitchen. Everything she makes tastes like sunshine and roses." He grimaced.

MICHELLE MAJOR   133

"Although, I saw her the other day in the grocery and tried to give her a compliment about the mango salsa she served with her fish tacos. She practically ripped my head off."

"She's working on her people skills," Jordan admitted. "She has a ways to go on the lessons."

"Yeah. She scared the hell out of me. I thought chefs liked compliments."

"I'm not sure we've discovered anything Madison likes other than cooking." Jordan tried not to let frustration seep into his tone. As amazing as his chef's skills in the kitchen were, her attitude was becoming a problem. If her temper and surly demeanor overshadowed her food, he was going to have to make a change. Or convince her to make a change. Maybe Cory and her never-ending supply of positivity could help with that.

All she'd said when she came home from her first shift was that it had been "fun," and then she'd checked on Ben and gone straight to bed. Jordan didn't know if she was exhausted or simply intent on ignoring him after he'd made the mistake of kissing her for real yesterday.

He still couldn't bring himself to regret it, but he also couldn't stop thinking about her softness and how good it felt to be that close to her.

"Did you get the paint?" Josh asked, pulling Jordan from his thoughts.

"Two gallons of natural, nontoxic paint. Thanks for the recommendation."

"Of course. A couple guys from my crew are on their way. Let's get any furniture moved out of the room, and we should be able to knock this job out in an hour."

"Perfect. Cory said she'd be back before Ben's nap time at one, and I'd love to surprise her with a finished nursery."

"I have some stuff I saved from when Anna was a baby, too. We were surprised about the sex, so everything's neutral in color. It will make the room look finished, at least until Cory does her own decorating. Do you want to tell me about the new fiancée?"

"I'm a dad," Jordan said simply.

"I got that with the request for help painting a nursery." Josh followed Jordan through the house. "Apparently, you're also going to be a husband. There's keeping things close to the vest, and there's being downright spy-worthy secretive."

"It's more complicated than that. I don't feel like I can say much else, other than I'm going to do my best to be a good father. Maybe you can give me lessons, because I don't know the first thing about it, and you're an expert."

"Hardly," Josh said with a laugh. He was a big bear of a man, an inch or so taller than Jordan, with light brown hair that looked like it hadn't been trimmed in months and at least two days' worth of stubble darkening his jaw. He was dressed in a long-sleeve Henley and tan work pants, which Jordan imagined was his standard contractor uniform. "The most important part is showing up every day. I know that for sure. Everything else you can figure out as you go. Kids are resilient. Anna taught me that. She's way tougher than I could have ever been."

Jordan had moved to town shortly after Josh's young daughter, Anna, had been diagnosed with leukemia. Apparently, Josh's wife had left Starlight and divorced Josh, unable to handle having a sick child. So Josh and Anna had managed through her chemo treatments together, and she was now a precocious and healthy kindergartner.

Jordan spent time with Josh when he occasionally came into the bar for lunch with his brother, Parker, and a couple of Parker's friends, police chief Nick Dunlap and Finn Samuelson, whose family ran the local bank. Jordan had never heard him complain about being a single father or the added responsibility. Anna was the center of his world, something Jordan hadn't been able to understand until Cory and Ben came into his life.

As they moved the crib and dresser into Jordan's bedroom, Josh continued to give little tidbits of parenting advice while asking subtle questions about Cory and Jordan's relationship. Jordan hadn't thought about how much to share of the details of his son's trauma but figured if anyone could understand, it would be Josh.

"Ben had heart surgery when he was less than a week old," he said as they spread drop cloths over the floor.

"Are you serious?"

He looked up to find Josh staring at him, wide-eyed. "Yeah. They had to fix a narrow valve. It was critical." Bile rose in his throat like it did every time he thought of Cory and Ben facing that trauma on their own.

"He's okay now?"

Jordan nodded.

"Then why don't you look okay?"

"It's hard for me to talk about or even think about what he went through," Jordan admitted. "And what his condition could mean down the road. He's healthy now, but what if that changes? What if I can't protect him?"

"Oh man." Josh scrubbed a hand over his face. "If I had a nickel for every time I worried about Anna's future, I'd have a lot of nickels. One of the biggest lessons cancer taught me was there are no guarantees on anything. Anna will see the oncologist annually for scans, and I can't imagine ever sleeping a full night in the week leading up to her appointment. The relief I feel when she gets a clean report is indescribable."

"How do you deal with it?" Jordan asked, genuinely curious about a father's point of view. "I don't want to talk to Cory about my fears. She doesn't need to deal with my anxiety when I'm sure she's got plenty of her own. I should be the strong one."

Josh blew out a breath. "And you think being the dad means you can never show any emotion? Let me guess—you learned that lesson from your old man."

"Pretty much," Jordan admitted.

"Mine was the same way," Josh said, "although he had a mile-long mean streak when he drank. Parker was better at not letting anything faze him, or at least he had a better poker face than I did. My dad saw me as weak because of it."

"My dad saw me as a way to finally live out his own dreams of sports fame. I was his second chance, and I still resent the hell out of it."

"Do you want to be like your dad?"

"Not in any way."

"Then don't." Josh shrugged. "That part is easy."

"None of it feels easy," Jordan said. "Although, Cory makes being a mom look so natural."

"Then you're lucky. Don't make her handle parenting alone." Josh gestured to the empty bedroom. "All it takes is a little work to make your future into something special."

"You're like the Dr. Phil of contractors," Jordan said with a laugh. "Do you charge extra for the life advice?"

"On the house this time."

They both turned as the doorbell rang. "That's my crew," Josh said, patting Jordan on the shoulder as he walked by. "Let's make your boy a nursery."

"Maybe ordering food and putting it in a pan so I could pretend it was my own would have been easier." Ella glanced at Cory, who tried for a reassuring smile.

Both of them winced as another crash came from the Trophy Room kitchen. After her conversation with Ella, Cory had returned to the kitchen with the goal of convincing Madison to agree to the idea of a cooking club. It had taken a lot of cajoling and begging, but the chef had finally said a reluctant yes. She hadn't seemed happy about it, but Cory figured a bit of time would soften her attitude.

Instead, Madison had stormed into the bar fifteen minutes earlier, complaining loudly and with an impressive stream of curses about wasting her morning off. She'd told both the women that they would have to wait until she got things set up in the kitchen, because she wasn't going to be slowed down by two amateurs.

"She'll be fine once we get started on the recipe," Cory said, then turned as the front door to the bar opened, sunlight streaming into the empty space. She certainly hoped it wasn't Jordan, because she didn't need to hear another round of I-told-you-so about whether Madison could play well with others.

"Is this the cooking class?" a petite woman asked as she stepped into the bar. Her timid voice was at odds with her flaming-red hair. "I saw a flyer posted over at the coffee shop this morning. Is it too late to join?"

Cory felt her mouth open and shut in surprise. "It's not too late." She jumped out of her chair and moved forward, holding out a hand. "Your timing is perfect. We were just about to get started. We're calling it a cooking club. But the Trophy Room chef will be teaching the rest of us."

Another crash, this one louder than the last.

"Oh yes," Ella said, shaking her head. "This is shaping up to be a ton of fun."

Ben gave a soft cry when the pacifier slipped from his mouth. Ella immediately bent down to unstrap him from the infant seat and lift him into her arms. "I'm totally using your baby as a shield."

"Why does she need a shield for a cooking class?" the redhead asked, eyeing the door to the kitchen warily.

"It's a joke." Cory smiled at the woman. "I'm Cory Hall. The cooking club was my idea, although I'm not teaching it. I want to learn to cook."

"She's got a hot fiancé to impress," Ella called out.

"Not really." Cory shook her head, then frowned. "I mean, he's hot, but I'm not trying to impress him."

"I'm trying to impress a guy." Ella lifted Ben

above her head, and he kicked excitedly as he took in his elevated view.

"I don't have a guy to impress," the new woman admitted, sounding a little disappointed. "Is that part of the deal with this club? Women trying to impress men?"

"Not a bit," Cory assured her. "I'm actually new to town and wanted to meet some other women. What's your name?"

"Oh." The flame-haired beauty ducked her head like she was embarrassed that she'd forgotten to introduce herself. "I'm Tessa Reynolds. I'm new to town, too. My aunt had a cabin here that I moved into a couple of weeks ago. I work from home, so I haven't had a chance to meet very many people. That's part of why I wanted to learn to cook. I also just need an excuse to get out of the house."

"I grew up here, so I know everyone," Ella announced, turning Ben around in her lap.

"So you have a lot of friends in town already?" Tessa asked.

"I know people," Ella clarified. "Which is different than having friends. I don't want friends."

"Everyone wants friends," Cory argued.

"I definitely do," Tessa said, almost under her breath.

"I don't want friends."

All three of them turned toward the kitchen, as Madison came through the swinging door and crossed her arms over her chest. "And it feels like a colossal waste of time to teach a trio of losers how to boil water."

Ella snorted. "We aren't losers."

"You can boil water in the microwave," Tessa said.

"I don't use a microwave," Madison answered with a dismissive sniff. "I've never found a use for one."

Cory found that hard to believe. Her mother had heated up a wide array of frozen foods in the microwave and taught Cory to fend for herself with the ubiquitous kitchen appliance from a young age. Heaven help her if she'd eaten the last Lean Cuisine pizza when her mom went looking for an easy dinner.

"Jordan was impressed you agreed to be part of our cooking club." The lie rolled off Cory's tongue so smoothly she wondered if she should be worried at how effortless it was becoming to not tell the truth. She'd always believed without question in the importance of the truth. "He thinks it will be good for your image and great PR for the bar."

"Stop calling it a club," Ella demanded even as she snuggled Ben closer. "I told you I'm not a joiner. We're taking a class."

"I like the idea of a club." Tessa tucked a long strand of hair behind her ear. "Do any of you play Bunco?"

"No," the other three women answered in unison.

"My mom had a great Bunco group," the redhead

shared. "I used to watch when the women were over. I could teach you all if you want."

"Let's get through one meeting at a time," Cory advised gently.

"Right."

Madison glanced at her watch. "I've got two hours before I'm leaving, so if we're going to do this, we need to get started. No messing around." She pointed a long finger at Ben. "And no babies. I don't like babies."

"I love babies," Tessa said. "He's adorable."

"Ben stays," Cory told the chef, hands on her hips. "Unless you want me to call Jordan and tell him you hate his son."

Madison narrowed her eyes, then turned on her heel and stalked back to the kitchen.

"Well played," Ella said, straightening from her chair. "You look like a wimp, but you've got moxie."

"Thank you, I think." Cory shook her head.

"Moxie is a compliment," Tessa told her. "Do you want me to take him?" She held out her hands toward the baby.

Ella shook her head. "Human shield, remember. She can't hurt me if I'm behind the baby."

Tessa looked genuinely shocked. "Is she going to hurt one of us?"

Madison leaned around the kitchen door. "She is if you all don't get your butts into the kitchen so we can get started."

* * *

"I take back every mean thing I said to you."

Madison arched a brow at Ella, who was forking up bites of the baked pasta dish like she hadn't eaten in days. "You didn't say anything mean," Madison told her.

"Maybe they were just mean thoughts," Ella admitted. "But never mind. All is forgiven thanks to this amazing food."

Cory quickly clinked a fork against her water glass. "A toast to our amazing instructor. Thank you for taking the time to teach us how to make this dish."

"If Toby doesn't want more than friendship after this," Ella said, shaking her head, "he might not be the one after all."

They sat around one of the tables toward the back of Trophy Room, four women with little in common but an unspoken need for companionship and an appreciation for great food. The sausage and broccoli rabe dish they'd made seemed simple, but the flavors were complex and multilayered. It was truly the best pasta Cory had ever eaten.

After a less than auspicious start, Cory had been concerned that she'd made a huge mistake in bringing together the group. But once they got into the kitchen, Madison relaxed into her element. Even Ben seemed fascinated watching the talented chef work her magic. Between sautéing the vegetables and adding fresh herbs to the dish, Cory, Ella and Tessa had followed her instructions to the letter.

Tessa had pulled a pad of paper out of her tote bag and taken copious notes on each section of the recipe. She'd promised to transcribe and distribute them to the other two, which Ella had definitely appeared to appreciate, since she was going to try to re-create the dish for her potential boyfriend.

Cory thought things might get tense again once they were all around the table, but the pleasure of the food mellowed each of them.

"Why do you want a guy who's put you in the friend zone anyway?" Madison asked, tipping her glass toward Ella. "It's not like you're horrible to look at, and you seem to have an okay personality— a little annoying, but nothing out of the ordinary."

Ella blinked at the backhanded compliment.

"Moxie was better." Tessa turned to Ella. "But she does have a point."

"You don't understand the pressure we were under when we met. We were in a combat zone working to vaccinate children in rural villages against a measles outbreak. There was no time for anything but friendship. We were too busy keeping kids alive."

"That's a huge responsibility and must have taken an amazing amount of commitment," Cory said quietly. "So why aren't you working in nursing now that you're back in Starlight? Trust me, I'm not complaining. If you can help out with Ben a couple nights a week, it would be just a godsend for me. I can't imagine anyone more qualified to take care of my baby."

"I need a break," Ella said simply. "Plus I'm not sure whether I'm going to stay in town long term."

"This place is amazing." Tessa dabbed a napkin at the corner of her mouth. "Anyone would want to live here."

"It's a little off the beaten path," Madison noted. "Certainly isn't the easiest place to find really fresh ingredients."

"I think it's perfect." Tessa grinned. "And now I have friends, which makes it even more perfect. I've never been part of a club before."

"You aren't now," the chef told her. "I taught you all to cook something impressive because this one—" she pointed at Cory "—has influence with the boss. Somehow I've gotten the reputation of having a bad attitude."

"I can't imagine why," Ella muttered dryly.

Madison sniffed. "If you get some action from making my recipe, you won't care about my attitude."

"I don't care about it now." Ella shrugged. "I'd rather you be grumpy than fake nice." She bit down on her lower lip. "My dad and brother seem to think there's something wrong with me because I came home and didn't immediately jump back into nursing. Like I'm fragile and need them to coddle me."

"I hate being coddled," Tessa said, and the bitterness in her tone shocked Cory. The redhead had seemed like a regular Pollyanna before this moment.

Madison and Ella seemed just as surprised. All three of them stared at Tessa until she shifted uncomfortably under their scrutiny.

"Spill it," Madison commanded. "I can tell you have a story to share."

"No." Tessa fidgeted.

Madison tapped a finger on the tabletop, and no one spoke.

"I had a kidney transplant two years ago," Tessa blurted. "It's not a big deal."

Ella pointed a finger in her direction. "In fact, a new organ is a big deal."

"I'm fine now. I take my medicine every day, and my health is better than it's ever been. But my parents treat me like blown glass, as if I'll shatter under the slightest pressure. It's why I moved to Starlight. I had to get away. I was suffocating." She drew in a shaky breath. "I'm creating a new life here. One that I live on my terms."

"That makes two of us," Madison said, offering a surprisingly gentle smile.

"Me three," Ella added.

"It's official." Cory drew in a shaky breath. "We're a club."

"Yes." Tessa pumped her fist in the air.

Ella shrugged. "I guess hanging with you all is

less pathetic than spending every night with my dad and his girlfriend."

They all looked toward Madison. "Fine," she grumbled. "I'll teach you all to cook for your little club. We're also going to have some ground rules. I'm willing to do it twice a month like Cory suggested, but not here every time. You all are going to have to open up your kitchens. I have a reputation to protect as a professional."

"Actually, I think your reputation is something you need to fix," Cory reminded her. "At least the customer-service part."

"So we're doing you a favor," Ella said, then smothered a laugh when Madison threw her a dirty look.

"Chop It Like It's Hot." Tessa nodded. "That's our name."

"You're joking," Madison muttered.

"I like it." Cory grinned at Tessa. "Every good club needs a name."

Madison sniffed. "I've changed my mind."

"No take backs," Tessa said in a firm tone.

Even Madison couldn't hide her grin at that. They finished the meal and cleaned up the kitchen until no one would be able to tell anyone had been there. Ben began to fuss and rub his eyes, a sure sign that the baby was ready for his nap.

Cory exchanged numbers with the women before heading back to Jordan's house, hope blooming in her chest for the first time in ages. The idea of no take backs tumbled through her mind. So far she didn't want to take back a single thing about her decision to come to Starlight. She sent up a silent prayer of gratitude to her grandmother. This truly felt like starting over, and Cory was one step closer to creating a life she could be proud of.

Chapter Ten

Jordan met Cory at the door of his house, a nervous smile playing around the corners of his mouth.

"How was your cooking class?" he asked, stepping back into the entry to let her pass.

"I brought you lunch." She held up the take-home box of leftovers. "Madison is truly talented."

"Yeah," he agreed, scratching his jaw. "I just hope that will be reason enough to keep her around despite the attitude." He reached out a hand for the infant carrier. "Let me take him."

Cory tried not to look stunned. This might have been the first time Jordan had offered to take the baby from her. Not that he wasn't willing to pitch in when she asked, but he still seemed too uncomfortable to do it on his own, even though he'd stayed with Ben during her first shift at Trophy Room without incident.

"You can't fire her," Cory said simply. "She's actually quite nice."

Jordan arched a brow. "Right. She's cuddly like a grizzly bear."

"She's working on it," Cory insisted. "I'm helping her."

"You barely know her."

"She gave me a job. I owe her."

Ben interrupted whatever Jordan was going to say with a loud cry.

"Did I do something wrong?" Jordan immediately placed the carrier on the counter and took a step back like he'd hurt the baby.

"He's tired. A nap will make everything better."

"Right." Jordan unclipped the boy from the seat and lifted him out. Ben whimpered and rubbed his face against the soft fabric of Jordan's T-shirt. "About that…"

Cory frowned. "About a nap?"

"I have something to show you."

"That sounds ominous."

"It seemed like a good idea at the time," Jordan said cryptically. "Now I'm not sure. If you don't like it, I can make any changes you want. I probably should have waited or gotten your opinion, but—"

"Show me." Cory put a hand on his arm, unsure

whether to be amused or alarmed by his sudden case of nerves. This was a new side of Jordan, one that was strangely appealing. Other than with Ben, he always seemed so sure of himself. She'd envied that confidence back in Atlanta, where she'd spent the better part of her life second-guessing every decision she made.

She followed him through the house toward the hallway that led to the bedrooms. When he flipped on a light in the spare room where they'd set up the crib, Cory gasped and placed a hand to her chest.

In the few hours she'd been gone, the space had been transformed into a soothing sanctuary. Instead of plain beige walls, the room was now painted a soft sage green that reminded her of Ben's eyes when he woke in the morning. Two free-floating wooden shelves hung next to the crib, and a new bookcase sat on the other side of a wooden rocking chair.

"What did you do?" she whispered, awed by the transformation.

"I figured Ben needed a real room before my mom arrives," Jordan told her, his big hand rubbing gentle circles on the baby's back as he held him. A faint blush colored his cheeks, and the image of this giant man blushing made her heart skip a beat. "A friend of mine in construction came over with a couple of guys from his crew, so it only took about thirty minutes to do the walls. I made sure to get the natural, nontoxic paint, so there are no fumes."

"I can't even smell it," Cory confirmed. She brushed away the sudden tears that sprang to her eyes. "It's perfect."

"Then why are you crying?" Jordan asked quietly. "I don't want you to cry, Cory."

"Happy tears," she said with a watery laugh. "Ignore them."

Ben gave another cry, arching his back and rubbing his eyes.

"He's going to sleep so well in his new room."

"Josh told me that he'd be fine in here because it's environmentally safe paint. If you're not comfortable, we can move the crib."

"Lay him down, Jordan." Cory tried to keep the emotion from her voice.

As Cory turned off the overhead light and closed the shades, Jordan placed the baby in the crib, which was now covered with a striped sheet that matched the throw pillow on the rocking chair.

Ben fussed for a brief second before relaxing to sleep.

His own room, decorated specifically for him. Something she'd only dreamed of providing for him.

She kept her gaze averted as she led the way back to the family room, still trying not to reveal how much the gesture affected her. As if her tears weren't a giveaway.

Her legs felt like jelly, so she lowered herself to the sofa and took a deep, hopefully calming breath.

"You should really eat the pasta before it gets cold. Even I'm amazed I could make something that tastes so good."

"Did I mess up with the paint?" Jordan sat down next to her, so close that his leg brushed hers, sending awareness shivering all the way to her toes. "You've been dealing with so much for Ben. Everything, in fact, and it's amazing. You're an amazing mom, Cory. I just wanted to play a part. Stinky diapers might not be my comfort level, but I can slap on a coat of paint with the best of them. Like I said, if you want to change it, that's fine. I'll have the guys back out here tomorrow."

Now she felt like an even bigger jerk for making him feel bad when he'd made such a wonderful gesture. Yet Cory still didn't trust herself to speak without losing it completely. The last thing she wanted was to burst into loud, hiccuping sobs. If Jordan wasn't freaked out by her behavior already, that would do the trick.

Instead of using words, she did the only thing she felt capable of in the moment. She wrapped her fingers around his large, calloused hand and lifted it to her mouth, pressing a kiss to his knuckles. And then another and another, ignoring that her tears were slowly dripping all over both of them.

Cory didn't like to cry.

After Ben's birth, when the shock of having him whisked away overwhelmed her, she'd given in to one night of self-indulgent weeping. She'd spent hours in her hospital bed crying until she had no more tears inside her, then dry heaving over a hospital basin as the medicine from her C-section moved through her body and she tried to process her new reality. But that was it. After that night, she'd met with the doctors and begun the process of figuring out how to best help her precious boy, even when she felt helpless. She stayed positive in the face of whatever life handed her.

In some ways, it felt as if she'd poured out all of her tears and had nothing left to give. Even in the last few difficult weeks of her grandmother's life and at the funeral. Or when her mother had callously informed Cory she had two days to vacate her gran's house. Although tiny and cramped, it was the only home Ben had ever known. His crib had been shoved against the wall in the spare bedroom, and Cory had slept on an old twin mattress with no box spring only a few feet from him.

Sometimes late at night when she couldn't sleep, she'd hack into the Wi-Fi of the couple next door and spend hours looking at houses on the internet. Homes with bright white kitchens and family rooms with vaulted ceilings and stone fireplaces. Master suites with beds so big they looked like they could fit an army of people, and nurseries that felt like harbingers of a happy childhood.

She'd lived in a huge house in Atlanta with Kade,

but his taste had been modern and streamlined to the point it felt sterile. Her closet had been filled with clothes he'd picked up for her, and she'd had no say in any part of their home. She would have slept on that twin mattress for her entire life if the alternative was giving up so much of herself for a man's whims and desires.

Jordan had decorated that room for Ben, but Cory was the one shattered by his thoughtfulness. She'd spent so long being strong and pretending like nothing fazed her, but what she hadn't been able to give her son festered like a wound that wouldn't heal. It stung at odd times, forcing her to block out the pain so she could keep going.

The simple act of creating a real space for Ben in his home had simultaneously helped to heal her and created a new, deeper cut across her heart. It brought her to her knees.

"You're killing me," he whispered, his voice rough with pain. "They don't seem like happy tears, Cory. Please don't cry."

How could she explain what he'd unleashed inside her when she barely understood it herself? She lifted her gaze to his, ready to do her best, but the intensity in his brilliant green eyes unlocked another layer of the defenses she'd built around her heart.

Without thinking about the consequences—Lord, she was so sick of thinking—she leaned in and kissed him. Purposefully and with an open mouth, not wanting him to mistake her meaning. This wasn't an accidental brush of the lips or her being swept up in the moment. The emotion pounding through her demanded a release, and this was the only way she knew to relieve the pressure.

Their breath mingled, and Jordan groaned low in his throat, as if her touch was as painful to him as her tears. But when she started to pull back, not wanting to make him uncomfortable, he cupped her cheeks in his big hands and shifted closer.

The kiss deepened, warm and wet, and Cory hummed her pleasure against his lips. He overwhelmed her senses, his soapy scent swirling around them and the scratch of his stubble at odds with the impossible softness of his lips. Cory gave herself completely to the moment, to the desire that blotted out everything until she couldn't even remember her own name.

The longer they kissed, the less she felt anything but the deep satisfaction of his mouth against hers, his hands cradling her like she was something precious. No anger or guilt or worry could push its way through the bubble of desire that surrounded them. This might not be real, but it was now and it was everything.

So when he pulled her closer, it felt like the most natural thing ever for Cory to climb into his lap and press herself against him. His hands squeezed her arms and she moved her hips, just enough to feel that he was as moved by her as she was by him.

The realization only fueled the fire that had started deep inside her.

"Cory." His voice rasped against her jaw as she ran her fingers through his messy hair.

"Are you reminding yourself who you're with?" She tugged at the soft strands.

"I could never forget." As if to prove it, he took her mouth again, a claiming more than an exploration. One she wanted with her whole being.

She grabbed the hem of his T-shirt, lifting it up and over his head. So much heat emanated from him, and she'd been frozen for so long.

Of course, she'd seen his body before. Hard planes and six-pack abs that distracted her from the simple task of breathing. She'd seen plenty of athletes without their shirts on at the pool parties Kade liked to throw during the hellish heat of summer in Georgia. But Jordan was different. This moment felt different.

It felt as if he belonged to her, even though it was only temporary and mostly pretend. Completely pretend, she reminded herself, but even that didn't dull her desire the way she'd expected. Not when he seemed content to give her whatever she needed, like he understood she was a stick of dynamite and he held the match.

She ran her palms across the dark hair that covered his skin. His heart beat a frantic pace, and she could see his chest rise and fall in shallow breaths. It felt essential that she taste his skin, so she kissed the place where his clavicle dipped at the base of his throat. He rewarded her with a low groan, and she kissed his mouth again.

He tasted like all the things she'd convinced herself she shouldn't want, not when her priority was Ben. As if sensing the emotions warring inside her, he gentled their connection, but Cory didn't want gentle. She wanted to escape for a few minutes, to forget about everything but the way her body felt pressed to his.

"More," she whispered against his lips, and bless him, he gave it to her. The air around them was filled with their wanting.

Her shirt was gone in an instant, and her skin felt hot everywhere he touched. She wanted him everywhere.

He rose from the sofa, lifting her in his arms like she weighed nothing. They continued to kiss as he carried her through the house, and she laughed softly at his ability to walk without running into anything. Cory wasn't sure it was a feat she'd be able to manage.

"Normally women don't laugh when I'm taking them to my bed," he said, his voice hoarse.

"Do you make a habit of taking women to your bed?" she asked, then immediately regretted it. Did she really want to know about the other potential women in his life? He didn't owe her anything, but the thought of Jordan with someone else made jealousy spike inside her.

He paused at his bedroom's threshold, pulling back enough to look into her eyes. "No." His gaze was clear on hers. "There have been no women in this house, Cory. Only you."

Well, if that didn't just slay her.

She wrapped her arms more tightly around him and nipped at his earlobe. There was no way she was going to allow him to see what those words meant to her.

The room was furnished with a bed and dresser crafted from some type of reclaimed barn wood, sturdy and clean. It was a perfect reflection of Jordan.

He pulled back the covers and placed her on the soft sheets, his hands smoothing along her torso. His thumbs caught in the waistband of her leggings, and he tugged them, along with her panties, over her hips.

"You're beautiful," he said even as she automatically covered the C-section scar with one hand. His fingers tugged hers away. "Everywhere."

She normally didn't care about the three-inch line across her lower belly. Ben had been born as a result of that incision, and he was worth any trauma her body had to take. But it wasn't exactly a signal of sexy times ahead, although under Jordan's intense gaze, every part of her felt desirable.

"Do you want this, Cory?"

"Yes." She wanted this more than she wanted her next breath. "But you're wearing too many clothes," she teased, needing to keep what was between them light. Hiding what was in her heart.

"Easily remedied." He straightened and shucked off his jeans and boxers, taking a wallet from his back pocket before dropping his pants in a pile on the bedroom floor. He removed a condom from the wallet and then joined her on the bed, warmth radiating from his body like he was her personal space heater. She liked the thought of this man belonging to her, keeping her warm when the world got cold.

It was a fantasy she shouldn't allow herself to entertain, and she pushed all thoughts of the future aside as he settled over her, one knee nudging her legs apart.

Jordan stilled, and their gazes met. She read the question in his eyes. Even now, he was giving her a choice. The recognition of having control moved through her like a cloud of fairy dust, making her feel light-headed with the joy of it.

"Yes," she whispered, unable to put together a more coherent thought.

"Thank God," he said with a rough laugh, his forehead against hers. He took her mouth with his, tongues melding as he pushed inside her. Cory gasped at the pleasure of it, the way her body awakened with longing and recognition.

She could feel the rapid cadence of his breath, like he needed a minute to get himself under control.

But she didn't want control. This wasn't a time for restraint or composure. She wanted to forget everything other than the sensation of the moment, and she didn't want to go there alone.

She skimmed her nails down his back, taking hold of his hips and pressing him closer as she wrapped her legs more tightly around him. They'd only been together once before this, but somehow his body felt familiar to her. He was her perfect fit.

Jordan let out a low moan, and then they moved together, setting a pace that drove her out of her mind in the best way possible. Desire spiked inside her as she realized she couldn't tell where he ended and she began. She held tight to his strong biceps as she arched up to him. Minutes— or hours—later, the pressure built to an erotic peak, and she felt like she might lose herself completely if she didn't get a release from it.

Lose her heart if she wasn't careful.

But it wasn't the time for doubt or reality. Her heart pounded and goose bumps erupted along her skin as Jordan's scratchy jaw traced a path down her neck. His breath was warm on her ear, and he whispered the sweetest words to her. Words that made her feel beautiful and wanted and drove her to the edge of her desire and then over. A thousand sparks broke over her like the bright light of a meteor shower, and a guttural cry tore from her lips.

A moment later, his breath caught and she felt his body tremble with release. She held this big, strong man in her arms as they rode the last waves together, and it was a million times more satisfying than the first time she'd been with him.

Because she wasn't coming to him broken and angry the way she had before. She'd made the choice to give her body to Jordan from a place of power, and that changed everything.

For Cory, this moment changed everything, and that sobering thought was terrifying enough to have her shift under him. She needed to remember the boundaries. The temporary nature of their relationship—the fact that everything between them was pretend.

Except it didn't feel pretend.

The way he dropped gentle kisses in her hair and continued to hold her close. It felt real. It felt like he cared, like she wasn't alone.

Cory hadn't realized how lonely she'd been until the warmth of him reminded her.

But she was still alone. A tumble in the sheets didn't change that, and she couldn't afford to believe it had.

She pushed at his shoulders, and he immediately rolled off her. She sat up and tugged the sheet around her, trying to control her rioting heartbeat.

"What's wrong?"

Jordan's big hand on her back burned like a brand.

"Nothing." She glanced over her shoulder with a patently false smile. "I need to get dressed." How she wished she hadn't left her shirt and bra in the other room. "Thanks for…" She waved a hand toward him, looking ten kinds of a Roman god stretched out next to her on the bed. "I needed that."

"Cory."

"Ella is coming over later this afternoon. She's agreed to watch Ben on the nights we're both working. If your mom wants to stay with him, I guess we can—"

"Cory, stop. Please." His hand moved to her shoulder, and he brushed her hair over to the side before leaning up to kiss her bare skin. "This was more than a physical release. You know that, right? We aren't going to pretend—"

"This is all pretend, Jordan." She yanked the sheet off the bed as she stood and took a step away. "Let's not make more of it than it was. We're two consenting adults, and this was…nice."

"Nice," he repeated with a wince. "I'm losing my touch if you describe the two of us together as nice."

"I don't want to describe anything," she said, fisting her hands in the sheet's soft fabric. "I don't want to talk about this. We have a baby together, and we have to find a way to make things work for his sake. Your mom arrives soon, and your friends—my new friends—think we're a couple. But we're not, Jordan. This is all for show."

He sat up, pulling the comforter over the lower half of his body. "You coming apart under me wasn't pretend." His voice was tight.

"You're right." She shook her head. "Which is why it can't happen again."

"I disagree."

"You don't get a vote."

"Seriously?"

"Please, Jordan. I can't do this right now. I'm working on myself so I don't repeat the mistakes I made in the past."

His mouth pressed into a thin line, but he nodded. "I won't be a mistake for you, and I respect whatever choice you make. For Ben or for yourself. I know this isn't easy."

That was the understatement of the century. She looked down at her painted toes, because if she met his gaze he would see everything she felt. No way she could hide.

"Thank you," she whispered, then backed away and added, "For all of it."

Chapter Eleven

The Friday lunch crowd at the bar was the biggest Jordan had ever seen, although he took little comfort in it. Not with the black mood he'd woken to earlier after a night of tossing and turning and wishing Cory was in his bed and not the guest bedroom down the hall.

He should be thrilled about his full bar. Ever since Madison had started offering a Friday special of fish tacos on the menu, Trophy Room had been slammed from the moment he opened the doors.

There was no denying her expertise with the tacos. The fish, which she had delivered each week from Seattle, was served with a beer-batter coating that she fried to a golden brown and a tender, flaky inside. She accompanied the fish with a homemade slaw and pico de gallo and served the mixture on tortillas made fresh each week by a local woman in town. The bar smelled delicious. Laughter and conversation rang out through the room. When he'd bought the bar, Trophy Room had a been a redneck watering hole that was lucky to have a half dozen customers a night.

He'd transformed the business into something vibrant, a pub he could take pride in that was also part of the community. He'd made this place his home, and it would continue to be no matter what happened with Cory. So why was it so hard to get over her ease in walking away from his bed?

Jordan hadn't lied when he told her that she was the first woman he'd shared it with, but that didn't mean he'd been a monk since moving to Starlight. He preferred the term *discerning*. He dated casually, with women who understood he couldn't offer them more than some mutually beneficial companionship.

Which should make Cory the perfect choice, since she loved to remind him that their arrangement was both temporary and pretend. Yet he couldn't stop thinking about how right it felt to have her in his arms, distracted like he was some lovesick schoolboy. He'd messed up three drink orders in a row, which never happened.

Josh approached the bar after finishing lunch with Parker. The Johnson brothers were Friday regulars, always arriving well before noon since they knew that once the kitchen ran out of fresh fish, the tacos were gone until the following week.

"Have you swapped personalities with your chef?" he asked, arching a thick brow.

Jordan rolled his eyes as irritation filtered through him. Finally, an outlet for all his pent-up frustration. "What are you talking about and what did she do now? I told her that if she didn't adjust her attitude—"

"She personally served our food with a genuine smile." Josh held up a hand to stop Jordan's out-of-character rant. "We even had what one might call a civil conversation. I was shocked."

"Are you sure it was Madison?" Jordan glanced over his shoulder toward the kitchen. "Normally, the waitstaff doesn't let her interact with customers. It's ended badly more than once."

"She brought me extra salsa."

"I don't believe it. She doesn't give extras." A customer at the far end of the bar rapped his knuckles on the countertop to get Jordan's attention. Jordan flicked a glance in the man's direction. "Make a noise like that again, and I'll kick you out of here. I'll be there when I get to you."

He turned back to find Josh grinning at him. "See what I mean? It's like Freaky Friday with you and Chef Maurer. She's sweet as cherry pie, and you're as ornery as a bear coming out of hibernation."

"I'm not ornery."

"Grumpy."

"Or that." Out of the corner of his eye, he saw Tanya take the order of the man he'd just snapped at. "First drink on the house," he called to her.

"Ya think?" she responded.

"How did Cory like the nursery color?" Josh asked.

Jordan's heart clenched as he thought about the emotion that had filled her gaze. "It was good. Thanks again for your help."

"Anytime. I'm having Parker and Mara and her daughter over for a cookout this weekend, if you and Cory want to bring the baby? We try to do a regular Sunday supper a couple times a month."

Jordan blinked. He liked Josh but rarely hung out with people other than when he was behind the bar. It felt strange and somehow nerve-racking to be included, even for a casual get-together.

"My mom comes into town tonight for a visit," he said instead of directly declining.

"Bring her along," Josh said easily. "We might not be cutting-edge fun, but it's family friendly for all generations."

Jordan had barely spoken more than a few sentences to his mom in the past decade. It was difficult to imagine making her part of a social group he wasn't even sure he belonged to.

As if on cue, the door to the street opened, and his mother walked in. He glanced at his watch, because she wasn't supposed to be arriving until closer to dinner.

She patted her neat bob and clutched her purse tight to her side like she was afraid one of his customers might reach out and snatch it from her.

"Appreciate the invite," Jordan told Josh, already moving to the end of the bar. "I'll let you know if we can make it."

Without waiting for a response, he headed toward his mom. It only took a few seconds before she spotted him. He tried to ignore the catch in his heart as her shoulders relaxed and her features gentled.

"Hey, Mom." He stopped in front of her, unsure whether to lean in for a hug or what. His parents had never been demonstrative with affection, and he didn't want to assume that had changed. Although, some quiet place inside him wanted it to.

"Hi," she said, glancing around. "Your bar is crowded for noon. Are there a bunch of alcoholics who live in Starlight?"

He barked out a shocked laugh, then shook his head. So much for considering a hug. "We serve food. Fish-Taco Friday."

"I thought bars served bowls of peanuts or stale popcorn." She swallowed, then glanced up at him. "Do you know this is the first bar I've been to?"

"Since when?"

"My whole life."

"Oh." He thought about how little he truly knew

about his mother and tried for a reassuring smile. "Well, welcome to Trophy Room."

"It smells in here." She sniffed the air. "It smells good, like food."

"Fish tacos," he repeated and led her toward the bar. "Are you hungry? How was your drive? Are you doing okay?"

He wasn't sure how to stem the anxiety that had bloomed inside him or bridge the gap between them. His father had been such a huge presence in their household, it was as if his mother automatically shifted to the shadows. Even now, as they walked past a table, a man scooted his chair out to stand. The edge of the chair bumped her hip, and she recoiled with a gasp.

"You're fine, Mom." Jordan moved behind her, using his body to form a makeshift shield as they moved through the clusters of people. "I've got you."

She smiled a little at that. "You always were a gentleman. I'm sorry if I'm acting like a ninny, Jordie. It's strange to become accustomed to life without your father. One moment I think I'm going to be strong and independent, and the next I realize I'm the same wimp I've always been."

"Mom, you're not a wimp." He rubbed two fingers against his chest. Her use of his childhood nickname hit him square in the solar plexus. "Don't say that." He waved as someone across the room shouted a greeting. "Let's get you some lunch. It was a long drive, and you'll feel better after you eat."

His mother turned to him suddenly. "Are you happy, son?"

And the hits just kept on coming.

"Mostly." He shrugged. "I'm proud of this place and what I've done with it. I know Dad hated when I left football, but it was the right choice for me."

Kathy's gaze focused on him more intently. "Does Cory make you happy?"

"Yes," he answered before he could think better of it. Not that it mattered.

"Tanya." He gestured to the bartender. "This is my mom, Kathy Schaeffer."

"Mrs. Schaeffer, it's nice to meet you." Tanya seemed to have no problem giving his mother a tight squeeze. "It's hard to believe this big oaf came from someone so lovely."

His mom giggled at that. "He was over ten pounds at birth," she said with a nod. "We were convinced I was having twins."

"Ouch." Tanya grimaced at Jordan. "You owe her, buddy. Big-time."

"Yeah," he agreed. "Yeah, I do."

He saw the hitch in his mom's shoulders. There were so many things they needed to talk about if they were finally going to get on the right track. It was difficult to believe that could even happen when he'd started off this new chapter on a lie.

"Why don't you have a seat?" Tanya said to his mom, shooting him a look full of censure when he didn't move. "I'll have the kitchen make up a special plate for you."

He gave himself a mental shake and held the chair still while his mom climbed up into it.

And the scene he never could have imagined—his mom visiting the bar he owned—came to life like it was always meant to be.

Cory was on her hands and knees when she heard the front door open.

Well, knees and one hand, since the other was throbbing in pain and nowhere near able to bear her weight.

Jordan let out a soft curse, and she called out a chipper "It's fine. We're fine" in response. The horrible scent of burned food and the gray plume of smoke coming from the oven told a different story.

She'd opened the windows and turned the vent above the stove on high, but smoke still filled the air.

"What the hell happened?" Jordan asked as he came into the kitchen. He looked completely shocked by the scene in front of him. Cory winced as she sat back on her heels.

"A little mishap with dinner," she said, trying to keep the smile on her face and her voice light. She could feel the wobble in her chin and hated that she'd messed this up, even more so when his mother followed close behind him.

To make a horrible situation even worse, Ben began to whimper from where he sat in his high chair. He'd actually seemed fascinated by the smoke and the mess his mommy made in the kitchen, but now, with an audience, it felt like her baby was throwing her under the bus. As if his cries were voicing what should be clear to all of them—Cory couldn't handle even the simple task of making dinner while taking care of her child.

"Hello, Kathy. I hope you had a good trip." Cory stood and moved toward the high chair. "Sorry about all of this. I'll have it cleaned up in a jiffy."

"A jiffy?" Jordan murmured, his eyes going wide as he looked around at the destruction that included mixing bowls and a sauté pan filling the sink, in addition to the broken casserole dish and food exploded all over the floor.

"Absolutely," Cory answered with more confidence than she felt. She felt no confidence whatsoever. "I have the bed made up for your mom in the guest room, if you want to take her there."

With the embarrassment pouring through her, Cory forgot about the fact that she'd burned her hand grabbing the scorched casserole dish from the oven minutes earlier. She gasped with pain as she put her hands on Ben's torso to lift him up.

Jordan cursed again but moved to her side with

lightning speed and pulled the baby from the high chair. Ben's whimpers turned into full-blown cries.

"Let me take him," Kathy said gently. "I've been looking forward to spending time with my grand-son all week." She offered Cory a gentle smile as she took Ben from Jordan's arms. "I can find the bedroom on my own. You get that hand under cold water. Jordan will help you clean up."

She turned and headed for the hallway with Ben's fussing already gentling as she held him close.

Cory wanted to argue. She wanted to apologize again, to both Kathy and Jordan, but was too afraid the sobs she was doing her best to hold back would break free if she tried to speak.

She turned for the sink, but Jordan was already there. He flipped the faucet to cold, held his own hand under to test the temperature and then reached for her.

"I've got it," she whispered.

"You should have had water on that immediately."

She didn't argue because he was right. She also didn't pull away when he took her hand and turned it over to reveal two angry red welts on her fingers.

Out of the corner of one eye, she saw his jaw tighten, but his touch remained gentle. She sucked in a breath when the water sluiced over her skin. "I burned dinner," she said through clenched teeth.

"I don't care about dinner." He didn't take his hand off her wrist, although it was no longer necessary to continue holding her. "You hurt yourself. You have to take care of you."

"I'm fine," she said again, even though it had to be clear that she was anything but okay.

His thumb made circles on the inside of her wrist, the pressure featherlight. "Do you want to tell me about it?"

She shrugged as the water made her skin numb. It was easier to breathe, and she didn't know whether it was the relief from the cold or Jordan's comforting presence next to her.

"Ben went down for a late nap. He woke just as I finished the casserole, so I didn't have time to clean up the kitchen. I put it in the oven and then went to get him."

She pulled her hand out of the stream of water and flipped off the faucet. "Honestly, I lost track of time. It's so stupid. I knew I needed to watch the oven and should have set a timer on my phone." She glanced up at him and grabbed a dish towel from the counter. "He rolled from back to front for the first time. I got distracted."

"It's okay, Cory."

"No." She shook her head. "Moms aren't supposed to get distracted. Babies get hurt. Houses burn down." She broke off and looked away, unable to meet his gaze.

"Cory."

Could he tell this was more than what had happened here this afternoon? She'd wanted this night to prove something, but not like this.

"I wanted to make a good impression on your mom," she said with a soft laugh. "She must think I'm crazy, or at least incompetent."

"Mom will understand. Accidents happen."

She started to bend down again, but Jordan stopped her. "Let's get ointment for your burn. I can handle the cleanup later, and we'll take Mom into town for dinner. She'll like that."

"I hate having you clean up my mess," Cory murmured. "I want to take care of myself."

"You do." He reached out and tucked a strand of hair behind her ear. "Look at how you took care of Ben when he needed you most. I'm still amazed that you managed to handle his surgery and recovery on your own after just giving birth. You're stronger than I could ever imagine."

"You haul kegs around and manage partiers for a living," she reminded him, appreciating his words even if they didn't exactly ring true. She'd only done what any parent would have in the situation. "I bet you could bench-press me."

He flashed a wide grin, stealing her breath in the best way possible. Jordan smiled but not often with this wide, disarming openness. "I could totally bench-press you."

The thought of his hands on her in that way did funny things to her insides. "I'm going to check on your mom and Ben," she said. She looked around him with a frown. "You can leave the kitchen, and I'll clean it later."

"I have aloe in the medicine cabinet under the master bath sink. Take care of your hand and Ben. I'll handle the kitchen, and then we can head out for dinner. We'll make it some place quick and casual, so Ben doesn't get bored."

She bit down on her lower lip, suddenly shy. "I moved my things into the master since your mom is here now."

"That's fine," Jordan said, massaging a hand over the back of his neck. "All part of the plan."

"Yeah," she agreed on a puff of nervous breath.

"Nothing has to happen," he told her. "You made it clear this is just for pretend. Nothing about you and Ben being here is real."

She'd made that clear to him? Good to know, because her mind and heart were a jumbled mess of conflicting emotions. "I appreciate your help with the kitchen." She nodded. That felt like a safe enough conversation. "That's real."

"Okay, then. I should get to it."

Something flashed in his eyes that looked like disappointment. She wasn't the only one who'd agreed to this fake arrangement. Jordan had given her no indication he wanted more.

Unless you counted sex, but Cory didn't. In her experience, men were much better than women at separating physical from emotional intimacy.

She thought about the way he'd held on to her wrist under the faucet, like she was precious to him. Did that count as intimacy? It had certainly felt that way to her.

Unwilling to push him for clarification, she turned and headed toward the bedroom. If he wanted something more from her, he'd tell her. And why would he? Yes, they had Ben in common, but otherwise there was nothing special about her.

She had no career, no college degree and no friends or family looking out for her. She had an old car that probably should be traded in before it conked out completely, all of her worldly possessions fit into a couple of suitcases, and if she lowered her pants, she'd see the iridescent stretch marks that had erupted across her skin during her final trimester of pregnancy, along with the C-section scar.

Oh yes. She was quite the catch.

Plus, she'd burned dinner and practically set his kitchen on fire. First thing tomorrow, she was texting Madison, Tessa and Ella and insisting on another meeting, this one focusing on kitchen basics.

Ella might want to impress a man with a few delectable recipes, but Cory would be happy if she could put an edible dinner on the table without incident. Baby steps, she told herself, then channeled her inner Gran. She could figure this out, she reminded herself. If only she knew how.

Chapter Twelve

"You almost burned down his kitchen? That's hilarious," Ella told Cory the following week as the four unlikely friends met in the small kitchen in Tessa's cabin.

"It's pathetic," Madison said with a sniff. She wore skintight black jeans and a fitted T-shirt fashionably ripped at the collar, looking every inch the force of nature Cory knew her to be. "If you're forgetful, set a timer."

"I meant to." Cory covered her face with her hands. "I forgot."

Tessa patted her shoulder. "It sounds like Jordan was there to save the day."

"I don't want him to save the day," Cory argued.

"I want to be able to save myself. I spent too long feeling indebted to Kade, not to mention all those times growing up when my mom reminded me how choosing to bring me into the world was the beginning of the end as far as her life was concerned."

"A real peach, your mom," Ella said with a grimace.

"She did her best."

Tessa leaned closer. "Sometimes even a person's best can hurt."

"Isn't that the truth," Ella agreed, then turned to Cory. "How is it with Jordan's mom?"

"I like her." Cory smiled. "She's sweet. There's a lot of unspoken tension between the two of them, though. He had problems with his dad growing up, and it seems like that resulted in problems with his mom."

"Families are complicated," Ella murmured.

Madison sniffed. "Families are a pain in the butt. Let's talk food. That's less nauseating. You need to understand some basic techniques that will allow you to make a variety of dishes."

"You also need to learn how to set a timer," Ella told Cory. "That's kind of cooking 101."

"I realize that." Cory shook her head. "It doesn't matter. Once Jordan's mom leaves, it will just be Ben and—" She broke off, remembering that Madison was the only one who knew the truth of her arrangement.

Tessa frowned at her. "Ben will be eating solid food soon enough, and you'll want to cook for Jordan. Or with Jordan."

"Food is love, they say." Ella grimaced. "I don't, actually, and I don't know who 'they' are, but it's a good line."

"It's a ridiculous line," Madison said, pointing a wooden spoon in Ella's direction. "The food itself doesn't have anything to do with love. It's what goes into the preparation that counts. When you put your heart and soul into something as essential as feeding another person, that's a fundamental gift. You're giving part of yourself to someone else."

Cory glanced around to find the other two women staring at Madison with the same shocked look that Cory knew was reflected on her face.

"There you have it," Ella said softly. "She's got a heart after all."

Color crept into Madison's cheeks. "Of course I do. I just don't wear it on my sleeve the way some of you do." Her gaze caught on Ella's. "And I would never cook for a man who didn't deserve the passion I put into my food."

"Speaking of that…" Cory sat forward on the bar stool where she was perched, happy to distract herself with something other than her own issues for a few minutes. "How did it go with your big date?"

Ella concentrated for a few seconds on tracing a drop of condensation down her water glass before offering a fake smile. "Turns out Toby came to town to ask me in person…"

"Ask you to be his girlfriend?" Tessa clasped her hands together.

"To ask me to be his best man—or woman, in this case. He's getting married to his high school sweetheart. They had been corresponding while he was traveling with the agency." She blew out a harsh laugh. "While he was there with me."

"Do you know laxatives can be put into food without anyone knowing?" Madison asked without missing a beat.

Ella's brows furrowed. "Are you suggesting I poison him?"

"Just enough to have him hugging the porcelain throne for a couple of days."

"It's a good idea," Tessa agreed. "Sends the right message."

"You all are demented," Ella told them, but she said it with an authentic grin. "I appreciate demented right now. If I can't be happy like Cory with her cute baby and hot bartender, then I might as well turn myself into some sort of supervillain."

Cory drew in a breath but kept her features neutral, refusing to meet Madison's assessing stare across the kitchen. She knew the other woman wouldn't discuss the truth of Cory's situation without her permission. And there was no way Cory could tell the other women the truth. She had too much at stake.

The real truth was she felt happy. Because of Kathy's presence in the house, Jordan and Cory were playing the roles of loving couple without question. Cory liked the pretend arrangement far more than she should.

As she watched Madison demonstrate a few basic cooking techniques, from making a roux to frying an egg, and explain how to use specific kitchen appliances, Cory realized that for the first time in forever, she felt normal. It was easy to forget her entire life was a sham and simply revel in the good moments. And there were so many of those.

In the past few days, she and Jordan had fallen into a routine. The mornings started with Jordan up early to make coffee and cut up fresh fruit before Ben woke. The baby would begin to gurgle, and either Cory or Jordan brought him out from the nursery. The three of them had breakfast in the sun-drenched kitchen with the scent of the surrounding pine forest coming in through the windows Jordan liked to crack open.

Jordan's mom usually joined them about a half hour later, and Ben absolutely adored his grandmother. It made Cory's heart soften with memories of her own relationship with her grandma at the same time her gut clenched thinking about how her son would never have that special bond with her mother.

They spent time hiking in the woods or checking out antiques stores around the area or browsing the wares of local artists at the Dennison Mill shopping area. On the days Jordan went to work, Cory kept his mom company. She was quickly coming to love his mother and the way she took pleasure in every activity—whether a walk around the property or a trip to town for groceries.

Kathy was a kindred spirit of sorts. The woman never spoke badly about her late husband, but Cory definitely got the impression that Jordan's father had been a harsh taskmaster and a bullish sort of man. It was obvious that Kathy regretted the distant relationship she had with her older son, and although Jordan was kind and courteous to his mom, the emotional gap between them remained.

Cory wanted to help them grow closer, both for Ben and for Jordan's sake. Especially because she knew she'd be relying on Kathy to help Jordan with parenting once he and Cory ended their arrangement.

It was going to break his mom's heart, and Cory felt like the worst sort of heel for agreeing to the whole fake-relationship farce in the first place.

"I'm not sure you have the market cornered on supervillain," she told Ella without humor.

"Trouble in paradise?" the other woman asked,

looking confused. "I thought things were going great between you and Jordan."

"They are," Cory quickly amended. "For now, anyway. I'm sure it's just a phase."

Madison barked out a laugh.

"I should go," Cory said as emotion clogged her throat. "Kathy and I are driving over to that paint-your-own-pottery place in Claremont this afternoon. I want to get Ben's food and clothes ready before we leave."

"I'll walk out with you." Today's lesson finished, Madison gathered the measuring cups and utensils she'd brought for a sort of cooking-club show-and-tell into a canvas bag.

"No need."

"I have to get to the bar anyway." The chef wiggled her eyebrows. "We're serving eggplant lasagna for the special. The lumberjack-type guys who live around here act like they hate it, but there's a wait for a table every time it's on the menu."

"Thanks for hosting the kitchen basics lesson," Cory told Tessa. She should really be thanking her new friend for giving her a place to go for a group therapy session.

"My pleasure." Tessa nodded. "You're my first houseguests."

"The decor is very you." Madison's voice dripped with sarcasm as she glanced around at the mounted animal heads hanging from the walls.

"My uncle was a hunter." Tessa cringed. "I haven't had the heart to take them down yet. They sort of keep me company."

"Don't say that." Ella made a face. "It makes you sound kind of odd."

"She is odd," Madison muttered. "You all are."

Instead of arguing, the three of them laughed. "Hey, Pot, this is Kettle calling," Cory said over her shoulder as she reached the front door. "Face it, Chef Fancy-Pants. You're as strange as the rest of us."

The other woman snorted as she followed Cory into the early-spring sunshine. Today was almost balmy, and Cory couldn't help but compare it to the constant gray of Michigan at this time of year. Once again she appreciated the surroundings, from the blue sky overhead to the fresh evergreens scenting the air. How would her life have looked if she'd taken a different path? Would she have found her way to this sort of charming setting on her own? As a kid, she'd kept scrapbooks filled with photos cut from the travel magazines her grandmother subscribed to that displayed beautiful scenes of exotic locales and destinations closer to home.

Cory had been fascinated by every spread on the national parks and other nature escapes, so to be living in this beautiful, rustic town made her feel like she was in a dream come true.

Other than the fact that it was all based on a lie.

"You're falling for him," Madison said, bumping Cory's shoulder. "You want it to be real."

"No," Cory lied without hesitation. "I know it's temporary and not real."

"You're playing house and you like it."

"Stop being mean." Cory crossed her arms over her chest with a huff. "You're supposed to be my friend."

"Since when?"

Cory had reached her car, and she turned to face the chef. "Why do you push us away?" she demanded. "It's not as if you have people coming out of the woodwork to wax poetic about your amazing personality. You know you were on the verge of being fired, right?"

"Jordan isn't going to fire me. My food brings in customers."

"The rest of the staff can't stand you. Every one of them warned me not to work with you, that you'd suck my soul from me and serve it as a daily special." Cory squeezed her hands into tight fists. "I defended you. Maybe I was wrong."

"I don't need you to defend me." Madison's voice was a reedy line of indignation. "I don't need anyone. If everyone at Trophy Room is so bothered by my presence, maybe I'll put them out of their misery and quit." She leaned closer. "Because I don't want to be where I'm not wanted or where I have to pretend to be something I'm not. I don't lie."

Cory felt the words like a blow, but she wasn't in the mood to back down. She'd done that too many times in her life before now, and it had gotten her nowhere she wanted to be.

"You're lying right now," she said, proud her voice remained steady. "You say you don't need anyone, but that's not true. You like us, and you like that we like you, even if you won't admit it. No one serves the kind of food you do without putting their heart into it. You said so yourself. We've already determined you have a heart, one that I'd guess was treated poorly by someone."

Madison looked away, blinking rapidly.

"Maybe we can both be honest, at least with each other. Yeah, I like Jordan. I wish I didn't. It would be easier for both of us. I'm an emotional train wreck, and I need to focus on getting myself together before I worry about being in a relationship." She blew out a breath and pointed a finger at the chef. "You want people to like you for more than just your food."

"Not true," Madison argued, then shook her head. "Okay, maybe true. But it's also easier if I don't care what people think of me. Things are easier with no expectations. I have a tendency to hurt people who care about me."

"You don't have to," Cory told her gently.

"You don't have to work out your relationship issues with Jordan."

Cory laughed at the shocking truth of the words. "That's a good point."

"You're too nice," Madison muttered.

"Probably," Cory admitted. "But I'm learning to like myself. And this is just the start of who I'm going to be."

The satisfying sound of logs splitting broke the quiet silence of the morning. A cold front had moved in a day earlier, bringing frigid temperatures and a layer of frost across the ground. Still, sweat dripped between Jordan's shoulder blades as he swung the ax in a familiar rhythm.

The hills around Starlight stayed cool enough most nights that he could have a fire well into late spring, but at this rate he'd have enough firewood to last a couple of years.

Physical exertion seemed like the only thing that calmed him. There weren't many moments when he missed his time on the gridiron, but this was one of them. He would have liked a productive outlet for the frustration and confusion pounding through him.

Frustration at sleeping next to Cory every night, her heat and her scent tangling in his brain and body until his fingers itched to reach for her. He stayed on his side of the bed, of course, because she was doing him a favor by pretending to be in love with him while his mom visited.

It had seemed like such a good idea to bring her to

his father's funeral as his date, a simple way to take the attention off himself and the feelings he should be able to muster about losing a parent. Feelings he couldn't access.

Nothing about Cory was simple, especially the way she made him want things he'd never dreamed of for himself. How could Jordan ever expect to be a decent father when he'd had such a poor example of one?

He remained constantly terrified of doing the wrong thing with Ben. The boy was just a baby, yet there were already so many ways Jordan could hurt him. He wondered if his mom had picked up on how much Jordan tried to avoid holding his son. It was easy to do with Grandma staying with them. His mother loved cuddling her grandson, and Jordan couldn't help but wonder why he had no memories of her showing that kind of affection with him or his brother when they were younger.

He turned to grab another log. As if he'd conjured her with his tumultuous thoughts, his mother came around the side of the house. Cory had taken Ben to town, and Jordan thought his mom had gone with them.

"That's a big pile of wood," she said, frowning at the huge stack.

"I like a fire," he said with a shrug.

"You like to burn off energy with physical activity," his mom countered, her features softening.

"I can remember you in the backyard flipping tires until well past dark most nights. You never stopped moving."

"It's what Dad expected."

Jordan cursed himself when his mom's posture went stiff. They'd had a good visit, easy and fun. He didn't want to bring up the past or memories that were difficult for both of them.

"He expected too much of you." His mom drew closer. "He pushed you too hard, but you never complained. I used to watch the two of you out the kitchen window, and I was in awe of your ability to stay strong under his coaching style."

"What choice did I have?" Jordan lowered the ax to his side as he remembered how badly his body hurt back then. Constant aches and undiagnosed injuries, which were typically unheard-of for a kid his age. "He wanted me to be perfect. You both did."

"I wanted you to be happy," Kathy said softly. "I did a bad job of letting you know it." She held out a hand. "Show me how to chop wood."

Jordan raised a brow at his fine-boned mother. "I'm not sure that's a great idea."

"Do you think you were the only one who felt like they had to be strong back then?" She leaned in and took the ax from his hand. "Oh, this is heavier than it looks."

"Mom, you're going to hurt yourself."

"No, Jordan." She leveled him with a steely stare.

"I'm healing myself and becoming stronger, things I should have started a long time ago. Something I should have managed for you and your brother."

"Did Dad hit you?" Jordan blurted, then immediately regretted the question.

His mother's eyes widened. Jordan had always wished he'd inherited her gentle eyes instead of his father's piercing green ones.

"Not after you were born," she said, almost sadly. "We got in a few knock-down, drag-out fights the first year of our marriage. I knew it would end badly for me if I kept pushing him, so I stopped. And after you were born, things seemed to get better. He was so happy to have a son, and then another when Max came along. I became like window dressing. I didn't matter to him."

"That's not true," Jordan argued. "He cared about you."

"He needed me to play a role, but you were going to be his crowning achievement."

"What a disappointment to him." Jordan laughed without humor.

"I'm not sure he would have ever been satisfied," she said instead of contradicting him. "But I knew he wasn't just pushing you. He was pushing you away. It's the biggest regret of my life that I didn't stop him."

"I allowed it to happen," Jordan told her. "Even when I was old enough to know better." He sighed.

"Even though I saw the toll it was taking on the rest of the family. We weren't really a family."

His mother blinked rapidly as she looked down at the ax, the vivid pink of her nail polish particularly bright against the worn wood of the handle. "I want to chop something."

Jordan felt a smile tug the corner of his mouth. Maybe he wasn't so unlike his mom after all.

He placed a piece of wood on the full round, showed her how to hold the ax with two hands and swing it over her head. The first time she missed the mark completely and the ax stuck in the base. But the grin she gave him made her look ten years younger, and he remembered the times he'd seen her smile like that when he was a kid. All those times involved him or his brother and their happiness.

After a few more tries, she split the log down the middle and let out a loud whoop of delight.

"You're a regular Paul Bunyan," he told her and was rewarded with her deep belly laugh.

She handed the tool back to him. "Thanks. I've got that out of my system. I see why it's so satisfying for you."

"Satisfying," he repeated, turning the word over in his head. He wasn't sure he would recognize fulfillment. He'd been trained to keep reaching, striving for more. Even after leaving football, those early lessons had continued to hold sway in his life.

He'd turned his attention toward the bar and making it into something better. But he hadn't thought about taking satisfaction from the work. He just needed to keep moving and stay busy.

"You're a good father," his mom said as they walked back to the house.

He snorted. "You've been here for less than a week. You can't possibly know that. What if…?" He pressed his lips together.

"Your dad had a lot of demons." His mother placed a hand on his arm. "He was private, and there's no point rehashing his unhappy childhood and how it manifested into the type of dad he became to you and your brother. But I see the way you look at Ben. I see how careful you are with him, Jordan. Too careful sometimes, like you can't be trusted."

"How can I be anything else?"

"Cory trusts you. She chose you, and that means something."

Those words burned in his gut. Cory hadn't chosen him. She'd chosen to walk away the morning after they were together. Even now, he didn't know how much she wanted from him, and it scared the hell out of him how much he wanted from her. Jordan liked hard work and he was fine with giving maximum effort, but he wanted control. There had been too many years when he hadn't been in charge of any aspect of his life. Unfortunately, he'd never felt more out of control than he had since Cory and Ben showed up in his life.

But he couldn't tell his mom any of that. They'd mended a piece of their relationship in her time here. He wouldn't take the chance on ripping that apart so soon.

"I want to do the right thing by my boy," he said, because that was the truth.

"Then that's what you'll do," his mom said, and the unwavering faith in her tone made his throat sting.

He hoped he could be the man to deserve that faith.

Chapter Thirteen

"Don't look now, but the boss is coming this way, and he looks mad as a cat in the bath."

Cory glanced up from where she was stirring a marinara sauce to see Jordan moving toward her.

"Did I just say don't look?" Madison nudged her hip as she walked by.

"Everyone looks when someone says 'don't look.'"

"Another example of why I stay away from people," the chef told her, then waved to Jordan. "Hey, there. What brings you to my fair section of this fine establishment?" She threw up her hands when Jordan frowned at her like she'd just kicked him in the shin. "Come on, Jordan. Don't tell me you've had more complaints about my attitude. I've been flippin' sunshine and roses lately."

Cory hid her grin as Madison turned toward the line cook and servers gathering plates of food. "Tell him my mood is set to unicorns pooping rainbows all the time now."

"A hundred percent unicorn poop," Misty said with a cheeky grin.

"I appreciate the effort," Jordan told Madison. "You even got mentioned in a Yelp review yesterday."

Her eyes narrowed. "What did they say?"

"That the quality of the food was enhanced by how professional and lovely the chef was when she came out of the kitchen to personally greet them."

"Professional and lovely. Exactly." Madison nodded. "I remember that sniveling couple. The husband had some hang-up about how none of his food could touch, so we had to serve everything in individual bowls. Pain in my—"

"Unicorns," Cory reminded her friend, then felt joy flutter through her. She really did consider Madison a friend. Misty, Tanya and the other Trophy Room employees, too. Ella Samuelson was watching Ben tonight since Kathy had left yesterday. Cory would miss Jordan's mom, especially since she wasn't sure when or if she'd have a chance to see the other woman again.

"Can I talk to you for a minute?" Jordan crooked a finger at her. "Out back."

"Kind of busy," Cory said with a wooden smile. She absolutely did not want to speak with Jordan. She wasn't sure if he noticed that she'd been avoiding him without his mom in the house to act as a buffer. By the look on his face, he had.

"It's fine." Madison grabbed the wooden spoon from her hand. "Take all the time you need."

Cory shot her a death glare, which Madison responded to with a wide grin. "Unicorns," she said in a singsong voice.

"Thanks," Cory muttered, then glanced at Jordan. "I need to wash my hands."

"I'll wait."

Heat crept into Cory's cheeks as she felt the rest of the kitchen staff watching her. She washed her hands under the big industrial faucet, then dried them with a paper towel, careful to make her movements measured and not like she was nervous or dreading whatever conversation Jordan wanted to have.

He didn't talk or joke with his employees the way she'd become used to. One of things she appreciated most about the way Jordan ran his business was that he remembered personal details about each person who worked for him. Birthdays, anniversaries or even when someone's dog had been to the vet. But now he stood in stony silence, and Cory couldn't help but feel like she was being called to the proverbial principal's office.

She followed him through the kitchen to the hallway door that led to the alley behind the bar.

"You're embarrassing me," she told him as the door shut behind her. He inclined his head but didn't respond other than a slight hardening of his gaze. Cory rubbed her hands against her arms to ward off the evening chill. After the scents and sounds of the busy kitchen, the quiet of the dark night felt almost ominous. "Seriously, everyone is going to think we're in some huge fight or came out here for a quickie. Either way, it makes me look bad. You're the boss, and I'm your fiancée."

"You're not my fiancée," he said, his voice a low growl. "If you were, I wouldn't pull you into a dank alley for a quickie."

She blew out a breath. "You know what I mean."

"Actually, I do." He ran a hand through his hair. "Parker stopped in tonight on his way to pick up Anna from gymnastics class. He heard from one of the Realtors in town that you were looking at apartments on the other side of Starlight yesterday afternoon. He wanted to make sure we were doing okay."

"Oh." Cory cringed. "I wanted to give you some time with your mom before she left, and I thought it would be good to have a plan for when…" She waved a hand in the air. "The breakup."

"Do you think that's something we should have discussed?"

Cory didn't know how to discuss the end of this pretend relationship without making a fool of herself. She didn't want it to end—heck, she dreaded moving her things out of his bedroom—but wasn't about to admit that to Jordan. She couldn't stand the potential of seeing pity in his eyes.

She'd left the house, hoping Jordan and his mom would talk before Kathy left. The pain on the other woman's face was clear each time she looked at her son. She desperately wanted to be closer to Jordan, and although he wouldn't discuss it, Cory knew he wanted the same thing.

Her intention hadn't been to look for a new place to live, but when she'd passed the two-story brick house with a For Rent sign in the yard, she'd called. She'd hoped that looking for a place to call her own would help ease the ache that came every time she thought about leaving Jordan's home. The cabin in the woods felt like her home, as well, and that would only add to her heartbreak when her arrangement with Jordan ended.

"I'm sorry," she said simply. "I don't know how to make any of this okay. We barged into your life and turned it upside down."

She dashed a hand over her cheek when a tear escaped. Damn, she didn't want to cry right now. "I know you were doing fine before this, Jordan. You have a home and a business. I've already come to love Starlight…"

She swallowed when the words *and you* almost fell from her mouth. Admitting her feelings for this man would lead to nothing but agony. She didn't want to scare him off when she wanted so badly for him to be a part of Ben's life. Their son was the most important part of their relationship. "It's obvious you don't want us at the house, and I—"

"What do you mean, I don't want you there?" He took a step closer to her, and longing skittered across her nerve endings. "Hell, Cory. I painted a damn nursery for the baby. I can barely keep my hands off you at night. Do you know how little I was sleeping with you next to me?"

"You never want to hold him," she whispered, pain slicing through her heart. The small rejection of her son felt like a rejection to her, as well.

Jordan's gaze shuttered, and he glanced away.

"It's okay," she said quickly, because letting people off easily was her way. "I know you never expected to be a father. I'm hoping that as he gets older and can do more, you'll want to be a part of his life. Ben deserves to have two parents that love him."

"Of course he does. I want to be a part of his life. He's my son. I just don't want to screw him up the way my dad did me and my brother."

"You're not going to," she told him. "You're a good man and you'll be a great father."

"Did you and my mom get together and rehearse what you were going to say to me?" he asked, then laughed softly.

"I didn't talk to your mom about this. I haven't talked to anyone."

He reached out and linked their fingers together. "Talk to me."

Oh, if only it were that easy. "You know I was raised by a single mom. When I got old enough to ask about my dad, she told me he left when I was a baby because it was too much trouble to be a parent."

She forced a steady breath. "I took that to mean I was too much trouble. I don't want you to leave. Or in this case, to tell us to leave. I like it here, Jordan. We don't have to be a couple to raise our son together. But I'm trying not to put pressure on you for more than you can give."

"You're not."

"Why don't you want to be a dad?" she asked.

He started to release his grip on her, but Cory held on. No way was she going to let him go at this moment. "It's not that I don't want to. I don't know how. You're a natural, and I feel like a bull in a china shop trying to take care of a baby."

"You stayed with him and you both survived."

He sighed, and there was so much emotion packed into that breath. "I want Ben to do more than survive. Surviving is the easy part. He's my son. I want him to thrive."

"We'll make sure he does," Cory said. She pulled him closer and wrapped her arms around his waist. In the intimacy of the dark alley, it seemed easier to let down her guard. Her rational mind might know it was better to keep her distance, but she put those thoughts aside for a moment.

His heartbeat was a steady rhythm as she rested her head against his chest. Once again, he cradled it like she was precious to him. Oh, how she wanted to be precious to this strong, steady man. Even if it ended with her heart in tatters.

They stopped serving food at the bar at ten, so Cory had made it home several hours earlier than Jordan the previous night. He'd returned in the wee hours to a quiet house, a big part of him hoping that Cory would be waiting in his bed.

He shouldn't want her there. He should know enough to keep his distance. Yet even though each night of his mom's visit had been torture to lie in bed next to Cory without touching her, even that tiny bit of closeness was something he'd come to crave.

His bed had been empty, and his heart ached at the realization their days together in this house would quickly come to an end. Hell, did he need another sign besides her looking for rental properties?

She'd gone along with the pretend relationship because he'd asked her to, but it wasn't what she wanted. He wasn't what she wanted.

He'd crawled into bed and fallen into a restless sleep, catching faint whiffs of her perfume clinging to the sheets as he tossed and turned. Even his bedding didn't want to give her up.

As soon as the first rays of light filtered through his blinds, he'd gotten up and started the coffee. He had to be back at Trophy Room for a late-morning meeting with Brynn to discuss the upcoming Maker's Market weekend at the Dennison Mill. He was making the bar an integral piece of the community. More than just a local watering hole. He wanted his establishment to mean something to the people of Starlight.

Jordan was on his second cup of coffee when he heard Ben babbling from the nursery. The boy usually woke from his nap grumpy, but mornings were the baby's happiest time. He greeted each day with a gummy grin and feet pumping. One of Jordan's favorite moments each day had quickly become when Cory—or his mom—brought Ben to the kitchen. The baby would grin and reach for him, effectively melting Jordan's heart.

But his mom was gone, and the babbling continued with no other sound. Was Cory testing him? Had his admission about his fear of being a father made her want him to prove his mettle?

It was silly. His nerves were silly. As she'd pointed out to him, Jordan had stayed with Ben on his own. He'd managed it a few times now. He'd changed diapers and only once put the baby's pants on backward. Not a huge mistake in the grand scheme of things.

He could handle the morning if she needed him to. He would have to handle it, because Cory wouldn't be with him forever.

The ache in his chest as he thought about that on the way to the nursery had him drawing a slow breath. He opened the door and flipped on the light.

"Good morning, bud," he said as he approached the crib.

Ben was on his back, holding his pajama-clad feet and rocking from one side to the other like some sort of miniature yogi. He threw his hands over his head when he spotted Jordan.

Okay, that was a good start.

Now he just needed to deal with the rest.

As Jordan picked up the baby, Ben darted a glance around the room. "Mommy is sleeping in today," Jordan told the boy, although secretly he wondered if Cory was listening to his conversation with their son through the baby monitor.

Great. He could add paranoid along with terrified to his list of go-to emotions for fatherhood.

"Let's start with a clean diaper." He flipped off the monitor, then put Ben on the changing pad.

"I can do that," a rough voice said behind him.

He looked over his shoulder, almost surprised to find Cory standing in the doorway. Or propped against the doorway, was more like it.

"Are you okay?" he asked as she pressed the heel of her hand to her forehead. "Big night once you got off work?"

Jordan knew the younger members of his staff sometimes partied together at the end of their shift. The thought that Cory had joined them shouldn't bother him.

He respected her right to make whatever decisions about her life she wanted.

But he wanted to be a factor in that process almost more than he wanted his next breath.

"Head cold," she muttered, then took an unsteady step forward. "I could feel it starting with a throat tickle yesterday, so I took some zinc and vitamins. They didn't work."

"Don't take this the wrong way, but you look like hell."

"I feel worse," she admitted, then coughed into her elbow.

"Go back to bed."

"I need to take care of Ben." She tried for a smile, but it looked more like a grimace. "Moms don't get the day off. It's not that kind of job."

"It is when the dad can pitch in."

"You have things to do." She coughed again. "Important things."

"I'm doing the most important thing right now." He turned to Ben. "Tell her we've got this."

The boy cooed in response, earning a soft chuckle from Cory.

"You sound like a two-pack-a-day bourbon drinker," Jordan told her. "Go to bed, Cory. I'll wake you if we need anything."

"Okay." She came forward and grinned down at Ben. "Mommy's not going to get too close because she wants you to stay well. Take it easy on your daddy, sweetheart. I'll see you soon." She placed a hand on Jordan's arm. "Thank you. I'm glad he has you. I'm glad we both do."

"Sure," Jordan said. If only he felt confident telling her how much of him she truly had. "I'll put a glass of water and a bottle of cold medicine on your nightstand once I get him changed. If there's anything else you need, let me know."

"Thank you." She backed up, sneezed into her elbow, then disappeared out the door.

Jordan felt her absence like an itch he couldn't reach but reminded himself he wasn't truly alone. If something happened, Cory was available. And it was a morning. He could manage on his own.

After dressing Ben and delivering the supplies to Cory's nightstand, he fed the baby breakfast and then checked the time. He felt a bit foolish toting the baby along to a business meeting. Not because he didn't want to have Ben with him, but he worried that it would be clear to everyone how out of his league Jordan was as a father.

He was used to succeeding. He liked that people in town knew him as someone in control of his life.

Clearly a baby would change all of that. He just wondered how much of a change he'd be in for today.

Turned out Jordan's fears were unfounded. Ben was more enticing than an adorable puppy or free rein in a candy store.

Jordan had shown up to the meeting with Ben harnessed to his chest. The baby seemed to like the carrier. Although Jordan's first instinct was to apologize for bringing his son along, he didn't have a chance to speak before the other business owners descended on him like a swarm of oohing and aahing locusts.

Several of the women—Brynn and Kaitlin in particular—offered to hold Ben, but to Jordan's great surprise, the baby fussed each time someone reached for him. Ben buried his face into Jordan's shoulder and held on for dear life. The sense of accomplishment Jordan took from that was ridiculous, but he couldn't seem to stop it.

He didn't want to stop it.

As the meeting progressed, he took Ben out of the carrier, bounced the boy on his knee, walked around the room with him and generally multitasked in a way that would have seemed impossible just a few short weeks ago.

Jordan felt like a real parent. The kind he never could have imagined becoming.

Once things wrapped up, he started to strap Ben back into his front pack when the most god-awful noise came from the boy, followed quickly by an equally god-awful smell.

Jordan realized he'd made the rookiest of all rookie mistakes. He'd left the diaper bag at home. Such a small issue in some respects, but it seemed to represent everything he doubted about his ability to handle fatherhood.

His palms started to sweat as Ben fussed and squirmed. "Little buddy, I'm going to get you home as soon as possible."

Although if he drove a maximum of five miles over the speed limit, it would take twenty minutes to reach his house. Long enough for that mess to be hardened and caked onto the baby's soft bottom, with Ben crying the entire way.

Oh, he was a terrible dad.

"You're a natural," Josh said as Jordan walked by where the other man stood with Brynn. They were looking at something on her laptop, situated on the table in front of them.

"I'm the opposite of that," Jordan muttered. "I forgot the damn diaper bag, and Ben needs a change in the worst way."

"I've got extra in my car." Brynn pushed back from the table. "Ben looks like he's around the same size as my daughter, Remi. They might not be the perfect fit, but better than a stinky bottom."

"Extra," Jordan repeated. "Is that a thing parents do? Keep extra supplies on hand for emergencies?"

Brynn glanced at Josh, who shrugged. "It's mainly moms who take care of that kind of stuff, although as a single dad, I learned to become equipped for emergencies."

"I need to get equipped." Jordan smoothed a hand over Ben's downy hair. "But I'll gladly take a diaper from you. Next round of wings is on the house in return."

"That's a great trade," Brynn said with a grin. For being a tiny woman, she could put away wings like nobody's business.

She closed the laptop and dropped it into her tote bag. He followed her and Josh out of the meeting room.

"I'd be happy to bring over some chicken soup for Cory," Brynn offered. "Ella says great things about her. Finn and his dad were worried when Ella left her traveling nurse agency so suddenly to return to Starlight. She didn't seem interested in making friends. But it seems like she's already gotten close with Cory and the other two women in their little cooking club."

Josh nodded. "Your scary chef has a kinder, gentler side. Cory has brought it out."

"Apparently," Jordan agreed, although inside he chided himself for not asking more about Cory's new friends. "Cory texted me at the start of the meeting.

She said the extra sleep helped her feel better. I'll let you know about the soup."

Brynn opened the back door of her car and handed Jordan a fresh diaper and a small package of wipes. "I like extra ranch with my wings," she said, winking.

He nodded. "Done."

"You and Cory should come to our weekly friends' dinner this weekend."

"Yeah, maybe." Jordan took a step back. "Josh invited us last week, but my mom was in town."

"Well, I'm not just inviting. I'm insisting."

"Listen to her," Josh advised. "Brynn tends to get what she wants. She talks soft and carries a big stick."

"Good to know." Jordan held up the diaper. "I'm going to go take care of business."

"See you later, then." Brynn climbed into her car as Jordan turned away.

"Hey, barman." Josh grinned. "You're not alone in this parenting thing. You know that, right?"

"You gonna change this diaper?"

"That's not what I'm talking about, and hell, no. But I'm here for you. All the guys are here for you."

"Thanks." Jordan cleared his throat. "I appreciate it."

Unfortunately, he'd never felt more alone in his life.

Chapter Fourteen

The following week, Cory lifted on her toes to return a serving bowl to a high cabinet in Jordan's kitchen.

"You don't have to do that," Jordan said as he walked into the kitchen. "I told you I'd empty the dishwasher once Ben went down for his nap."

"I had a cold, and it's gone now," she reminded him. "I'm totally healthy and able to pitch in again."

"I know," he said, coming to stand behind her and taking the bowl from her fingers. At his height, he barely had to stretch to place it on the top shelf. "I like taking care of you and Ben."

Cory felt the breath whoosh out of her lungs at his comment. Or maybe it was the heat of his body so close to hers. She would have liked to blame the moment on a sudden recurrence of the fever that had plagued her the first twenty-four hours of her illness. Delusional would be a good excuse, not to mention a perfect description for her reaction to Jordan.

"As much as I appreciate it, that's not your job." She forced herself to move away from him. "I've been taking care of myself for a lot of years."

She grabbed the utensil holder from the dish washer rack and busied herself with putting more items away. Anything so she didn't have to look directly at Jordan. Not when she feared she wouldn't be able to hide her emotions.

Since she'd woken last week feeling like someone had taken a sledgehammer to her head, she'd seen a different side of him. Cory didn't know if he'd really lost his fear about being a father or was stepping into the role because she needed him, but either way, he was doing a darn good job of making her fall even harder for him than she had been before.

He'd taken off work so that Ella wouldn't have to come by and had single-handedly parented Ben while simultaneously playing nurse to Cory. She hated being sick and feeling weak and helpless. She'd spent too long feeling helpless.

"You don't have to do everything on your own," he reminded her. "You're not alone."

But she was. In some ways she always had been. Growing up with a single mom who resented her daughter and while in a relationship with a man who saw her as nothing more than an extension of himself. She'd surrounded herself with people who didn't care about her the way they should. It left her feeling as alone as if she were in solitary confinement. In some ways, that was how she felt most comfortable.

Jordan made her question everything. His low-key way of caring made her want to release her defenses and her habit of isolating herself emotionally. It had been a means to self-preservation, but now it just felt like she was being a coward.

"We should come up with a plan for ending this." A spoon slipped from her fingers as she said the words, clattering to the floor and grating against her already worn nerves.

She and Jordan bent to pick it up at the same time.

"Why?" he asked softly. "We've got a good thing going here, Cory."

"It's not real." She quickly grabbed the utensil before he could.

He didn't respond to those three words, and she hated that she wanted him to. She wanted him to tell her it was real. Or it could be. Because being here at this house with him felt like every dream of a perfect life she'd ever imagined coming true.

"I'll do whatever you want," he said quietly.

Did she hear disappointment in his tone?

She blinked against the sudden rush of tears to her eyes. Wasn't that just the problem? She couldn't tell him what she wanted, because that might make her seem weak. But she didn't have the strength to risk her heart again.

"We can give it a few more days," she offered, unsure of how to navigate this minefield of emotions.

Jordan nodded. "If you're really doing okay, I'm going to head into the bar for a few hours. I need to get caught up on some things and work out the staff for the beer tent at the Maker's Market."

"Sure," she agreed as she felt the distance between them grow. It was a distance she should cling to, but she hated it. "I'm really feeling much better. Thank you for everything, Jordan. I promise you don't have to take care of me."

Tell me again that you like it, she thought, but he didn't say anything. Just turned and grabbed his keys from the counter, then headed out the door.

She spent the rest of the day wishing she'd handled that conversation better. Ben woke after his nap, and she strapped him into his carrier and took him for a walk on the trails that bordered the property.

The clean scent of pine and the crunch of old leaves beneath her feet seemed to relax her enough that she was able to draw a deep breath and think about her situation in a more rational way. It was difficult to keep her wits about her around Jordan, when everything about him made her want to lose herself.

She couldn't lose herself again. Not when she was on the verge of truly finding who she was. The time had come to decide who she wanted to be and go after it.

Jordan texted late in the afternoon to tell her the bar was slammed. He'd sent Tanya home with the start of a similar cold to Cory's.

U okay?

That simple question gutted Cory, because despite how they'd left things earlier and the tension about the future, he cared enough to ask. She could imagine how busy he was on a hectic night at the bar and everything that entailed. Being pulled in a dozen different directions. Yet she knew without a doubt he would drop everything and return to her if she gave him any indication she needed him.

She wouldn't do that.

After returning his message, she fed Ben, gave him a bath and read him stories until bedtime. With the house to herself, she pulled out the jewelry supplies she'd brought with her from Michigan and began to craft a series of gemstone earrings using the labradorite chips she'd bought from a thrift store in her hometown.

The way the women she'd met in town seemed to love the earrings and necklaces she wore reminded her how much she'd loved the art of making jewelry. She'd picked up the hobby in high school and even sold some of her pieces at a local gift shop during college but hadn't seemed to find time for the practice when she moved to Atlanta. It was nice to have the space to finally think about who she wanted to be. To finally get to the place where she could figure out who she was because she didn't have to be anything else.

But the one thing she wanted to be—with Jordan in truth—was something she couldn't have the way things stood between them now. She hadn't earned her happy ending with a man like him, but the more time she spent with him, the more she wanted to try.

It was nearly two in the morning when Jordan let himself into the quiet house. Cory had left the copper fixture on over the sink, so he didn't bother to flip on any other lights as he moved toward his bedroom.

She did that every time he closed the bar, and he'd quickly gotten used to taking the last turn on his winding driveway to see the glow beckoning to him from the front window. It made his house feel like a home in a way that shocked him for such a small change.

But it was more than the light, he knew. It was the feeling that someone was waiting for him. Someone cared about his return. He wasn't alone.

He'd thought he'd liked living alone until Cory and Ben. Now he realized he'd just gotten used to the solitude because it was easier than anything else.

He'd never thought of himself as someone who took the easy path, but he'd done that in his emotional life.

As had become his habit, he cracked open the door of the nursery and spent a few minutes watching Ben sleep. The bar had been host to two bachelorette parties plus one reunion of high school friends, and Jordan hadn't stopped moving, pouring drinks or talking to customers since the moment he walked in.

He didn't realize how keyed up he was until the stillness in his son's room eased the tension that filled him. He wanted to slip into Cory's room the same way, but he was afraid that might make him an inappropriate creeper.

He'd just taken off his watch and set it on the tall dresser in the master bedroom when a sound caught his attention.

Cory lay asleep on his bed, on top of the covers, as if she'd dozed off there without meaning to.

Every nerve ending in Jordan's body went on high alert. It was like his fantasy life had thrown a party, and this was his dream come true. Like most dreams, once achieved, he wanted more. Suddenly it wasn't enough to watch her. He wanted to hold her in his arms, to bury his face in her hair and breathe in the citrusy fragrance that always clung to her.

He wanted so much more.

Not a creeper, he reminded himself. He wasn't sure what had led her into his room, but he had a feeling she could easily be scared off again. He still couldn't believe how much his feelings had changed in the past couple of weeks. He tried and failed to access any of the initial anger he'd felt when she'd shown up in his life with a baby he hadn't known about. Maybe the anger could protect him.

He still wished that she would have told him about Ben earlier, but Jordan understood she hadn't been in the best place emotionally. He also took responsibility for the way he'd left Atlanta without speaking to her.

Walking away and changing his number had seemed like the simplest course of action if she'd gone back to Kade. If he'd stayed, he would have spent months waiting and hoping for her to call. Too much time devoted to wondering if he should reach out to her.

But he hadn't known what would result from their night together.

Now he did. What was the saying?

When you know better, you do better.

He had to do better for both of them.

He stripped off his clothes and put on a fresh T-shirt and shorts. No way was he going to wake her smelling like stale beer.

Hell, he wished he didn't have to wake her at all.

Maybe the right thing to do—the better thing— would be to retreat to the couch for the night and leave her in peace.

He wasn't quite that much of a better man.

The mattress sagged with his weight as he sat on the edge of it. Cory's skin felt like silk as he gently shook her arm.

"Sweetheart, wake up."

She mumbled something incoherent, then shifted and snuggled against his pillow. He felt a smile tug the corner of his mouth. Cory didn't wake easy and sunny like Ben.

Okay, he'd tried. Maybe not the most valiant effort, but he'd made some attempt.

He moved to the other side of the bed and pulled back the sheet and comforter. His hands fisted as he resisted the urge to draw Cory closer, his own personal soothing blanket. She made him feel secure in a way he hadn't realized was lacking from his life. Like she was some sort of lighthouse in the storm of whatever might come his way, a true north that would always guide him home.

Except there was no always between them. There was just a temporary arrangement that she seemed more than ready to end.

He never wanted it to end.

With a deep breath, Jordan closed his eyes and willed his body to relax. A moment later he heard a startled gasp and turned his head to find Cory staring at him in the faint light of moon glow that came from his bedroom window.

"I tried to wake you," he said immediately.

She didn't answer for a moment, then said softly, "I like your bed."

Her voice was sleep-rough, her eyes heavy, and it was all he could do not to groan in response.

"Then stay," he managed and did his best to gather all his gentlemanly instincts. "I can move to the couch if you want."

"I want you to stay," she answered without hesitation.

Then, as if every one of his dreams was coming true, she leaned forward and pressed her mouth to his.

Jordan's body went into overdrive, but he tamped down the need to move too quickly. He let her set the pace. This was a gift, and he was smart enough to cherish it.

His measured response must have been the right one. Cory shifted closer, her small frame pressed against the length of him. He inwardly cursed the layers of bedding that separated them.

"How was your night?" she asked between kisses.

"This is the best part of it." He threaded his fingers in her hair, reveling in the feel of the soft strands.

She moved again, lifting herself to straddle his hips as she balanced her weight on her hands on either side of his head. Her hair fell around him like a cocoon, and he wanted to stay in this moment forever.

"Can I tell you a secret?"

"Yeah, sweetheart. You can tell me anything."

"I was dreaming about you before I woke up."

"The kind of dream where you're naked and in front of a crowd of people?" he asked with a smile.

She shook her head, the ends of her hair tickling his neck. "The kind of dream where you and I are alone and we're both naked."

"I like your version better," he said, not bothering to keep the desire from his tone. He was so damn tired of hiding how much he wanted her. For all he knew, she was sleep seducing him, but he'd take whatever she was willing to give him.

"Me too." She sat up and tugged the pajama shirt over her head.

To his eternal gratitude, she wasn't wearing a bra.

He lifted his hands and drew his thumbs over the tight peaks of her nipples before holding the weight of her breasts.

She moaned low in her throat and leaned forward to kiss him again, but he shifted her forward so he could take her breast into his mouth. He gave attention to one and then the other, savoring the sweet and salty taste of her.

Then she leaned down to kiss him again, deep and long. He lifted her up and off him so he could pull down the covers. He needed to be closer to her, to feel her skin against his. To be inside her.

But maybe he should have turned on the night-stand light, because suddenly they were tangled in covers, arms flailing and legs kicking as they tried to get to each other.

Cory's laughter rang out in the dark room. "I'm stuck in the sheet."

"Damn sheet," he muttered and turned his attention to freeing her.

She laughed again, and the sound made Jordan's heart feel like it was filled with champagne bubbles, light and fizzy. He'd never thought of sex as fizzy. He was the down-and-dirty type. As with everything else, Cory helped him see a new perspective that made something already awesome even better.

They were both breathing hard and laughing just as hard by the time he untangled her and threw back the covers. She flopped on the mattress next to him. "Wow, that was a bit of a mood dampener, huh?"

"Not one bit." He took her hand and brought it to his mouth, kissing each of her knuckles. "I can't imagine anything that would dampen my desire for you."

She squeezed his hand. "Then you'd best get naked, my friend. Because I've got some dreams, and you're just the man to make them come true."

With that kind of a command, how could he do anything but follow it? Minutes—or hours—later, he sheathed himself in a condom and slid inside her. The sigh she let out was like music to his ears, and it felt like coming home.

They moved together, all thought of laughter put

aside for the moment. As good as it had been with Cory before, something was different this time. Jordan wanted more, and he got it. Their connection seemed deeper, and he couldn't imagine how or why they would end their arrangement in any way but making it real.

If she needed time to get used to the idea, he'd give that to her. If she needed space, it was hers. But whether or not she wanted to talk about it now or pretend otherwise, they belonged to each other.

Of that he had no doubt.

And when they went over the edge of desire together, holding each other tight, it was as if the universe was giving him a sign of how right this was. They were meant to be.

As he held her close while their breathing went back to normal, she smiled against his mouth. "That was better than any dream I ever had."

Filled with hope and an overwhelming sense of peace, he couldn't agree more.

Chapter Fifteen

Sunday evening, Jordan parked the car on the street in front of Nick Dunlap's Craftsman bungalow. "You don't have to be nervous."

"I'm not nervous," Cory lied.

"They're nice people."

"Of course you think that. They're your friends."

She closed her eyes and tried to steady her breath, knowing she was being ridiculous but unable to stop herself. When Jordan had suggested attending the Sunday supper party at Nick and Brynn's house, it had seemed like a great idea. Mara and Parker would be there, along with her daughter, Evie. Josh and his daughter, Evie's best friend, Anna, were coming, as well.

"Actually, they're not really my friends."

She glanced toward Jordan. "What do you mean?"

"I mean, they're my customers. They come into the bar on a regular basis for a drink and a meal. I like all of them, and they seem like the kind of people who would make good friends. But I don't have friends. I have coworkers and customers."

"That's not true," she argued. "Josh gave up an entire morning to help you redo the nursery."

"And I'm comping his employees a happy-hour game night at the bar."

"Everyone in town likes you, Jordan. At least everyone I've talked to."

"I'm the local bartender," he told her with a laugh. "I pour beer. Who doesn't like the guy who pours beer?" He took her hand. "This is new for me, Cory. I'm not much for socializing. It's out of my comfort zone. Hell, don't forget how we met. Most of the team was inside whooping it up at the party, and I was sitting alone on the side of your pool."

"I'm glad you were there," she said softly, running a thumb over a scar on his pointer finger. "And that you're here. I'm glad we're doing this together, even if it's hard for me to open up to these people."

He frowned. "Everyone who meets you loves you. You already have a foursome of friends, and you're thick as thieves, from what I can tell."

She shrugged. "Those women are like me, not quite broken but definitely a little banged up and bent in places. The people in that house have their lives together. I feel like they're going to take one look at me and know I don't belong. That everything between us is fake."

"Not everything. At least I don't think you could have faked me making all those dreams come true last night."

"I'll give you that," she said, feeling a blush creep up her cheeks at the memory of how many times he'd made her dreams come true.

"You gave me a lot more." He leaned in and brushed a kiss across her temple.

Ben let out a happy shriek from the back seat, making Cory grin. Was it possible a baby could pick up on the connection between his parents? She'd noticed that Ben seemed to express his happiness every time he saw his parents touch.

"We should go in." She looked toward the house again. "I just hope these people don't turn on me if I'm no longer a part of your life."

"We have a son together, Cory. We'll always be a part of each other's lives."

She nodded and got out of the car, unwilling to let Jordan see how much the thought affected her. Of course, they'd always have a part in each other's lives. But the idea of Ben being the only thing that held them together hurt her heart. She didn't want to believe that. There was no way to believe it when the truth was so much more for her.

Cory wasn't pretending to be in love with Jordan. She'd fallen for him, and she knew how badly her heart would break when they ended this.

Nick opened the front door with a wide smile. "Good to see you out from behind the bar," he told Jordan with an enthusiastic handshake before turning to Cory. "I hear we have your better half to thank for the change in everyone's favorite solitary bar owner."

"I'm Cory," she said, offering her hand. "It's nice to meet you."

"The pleasure is all mine."

Jordan held up a couple of the growlers of beer he'd picked up from the bar on their way over. "You can take a bartender out into the real world, but lucky for you, I travel with beer."

"Thanks, man." Nick led them into the house, and Cory followed, trying to tamp down the nerves that bubbled up again.

Nick seemed nice enough and not as intimidating as she would have imagined for an officer of the law, but his casual comment about Jordan being the favorite reminded her once again that she would be the outsider when their arrangement ended.

It would end because it had to. Her feelings for Jordan were already too overwhelming. They threatened to outstrip her good sense and her commitment to making herself a priority.

She pasted a smile on her face despite her tumbling emotions as Nick led them into a bright kitchen painted in a soft yellow with maple cabinets and a beautiful granite counter. She greeted Mara and Brynn and was introduced to Mara's husband, Parker. She also finally got the chance to personally thank Josh for his help with the nursery.

"The girls are in the basement playing Ping-Pong," Brynn told her as the men went into the family room to watch a basketball game. Brynn held a baby girl who looked to be near Ben's age. "This is our daughter, Remi. She's seven months now." The baby was adorable—although not nearly as big as Ben, she seemed just as happy.

Cory held her baby a little tighter. "Ben is almost seven months old, as well."

"They'll grow up together." Brynn grinned. "Best friends, I'm sure."

As much as Cory loved the thought of those kinds of lifelong friendships for her son, she could also imagine a future where she'd be alone with only Ben. What if Jordan eventually found a woman to settle down with? Someone who wasn't her. What if her son had half siblings and she had no one other than her cooking-club friends and whatever job she ended up finding once she left the bar?

"Did I say something wrong?" Brynn asked gently.

"Because you look like she just kicked your puppy," Mara added, earning an eye roll from Brynn.

"Ignore her," Brynn said.

"She works with Madison Maurer," Mara reminded her friend. "My level of snark is nowhere near hers."

The easy banter between the two helped Cory to relax the tiniest bit. "It's nothing. I just didn't exactly grow up in a tight-knit community. Sometimes the easy camaraderie of this place overwhelms me."

"Girl, same." Mara pointed to herself. "Sometimes it's overwhelming, and sometimes it's nauseating."

"It's never nauseating," Brynn argued. "But it can be a lot to handle."

Cory frowned. "Jordan said you're a Starlight native. Don't you get used to it?"

Mara and Brynn shared a look. "There are great things about small-town life," Brynn said after a moment. "But even if you grow up in it, having people know your business or thinking that they understand you better than you understand yourself is a challenge sometimes." She rested a hand on Remi's head, and the girl snuggled against her chest. "Plus, people like to judge others or what they don't understand. You have to learn to ignore it."

"I've never been great at ignoring other people's opinions."

"This is your chance to choose who matters to you. You get that choice."

Cory let out a long breath. She hadn't expected to jump right in with a deep, emotional conversation at a dinner party, but being honest and then supported for it did wonders for her confidence.

"I appreciate you connecting me with Ella," she told Mara. "She's been a lifesaver staying with Ben while I work." She glanced at Brynn. "She takes care of Remi during the day, as well, right?"

"I'd be lost without her," Brynn admitted. "Although, I kept waiting for her to tell me she's heading back to her traveling nurse career. I'm not sure anyone expected her to stay in town this long."

Cory got the same impression but didn't mention it.

"But you're here for the long haul," Mara observed, her gaze steady on Cory. "Jordan certainly did a good job of playing his cards close to the vest on the relationship front. No one had any idea about you and Ben."

Including Jordan, Cory wanted to say. Once again, she hated lying to the people in this town. She didn't know much about either of these women, but they didn't strike her as the type who'd think badly of her for how she'd handled her pregnancy and the months after Ben's birth.

"There was so much to deal with after Ben's surgery," she said, because that much wasn't a lie.

"I can't imagine what you went through or how you handled it on your own," Brynn said.

Cory shrugged and offered what she hoped was a reassuring smile. As nice as these women seemed, she didn't want to relive that time again. "He's healthy now, and I'm so grateful. We're focused on the future."

Brynn squeezed her arm. "I respect that. Speaking of the future…" She leaned in to study Cory's earrings. "Mara tells me you're a jewelry designer."

"Hardly," Cory said with a laugh. "I used to make things to wear and I sold a few pieces, but I'm just getting back into it. I took a few art classes in college, but don't have any actual expertise."

"You have talent," Mara said. "That's obvious. I'd totally wear that necklace."

"Thanks." Cory pressed a finger to the beaded chain she wore, a blush rising to her cheeks at the way the two women were studying her.

"Have you heard about the upcoming Maker's Market we're hosting at Dennison Mill?" Brynn asked. "In addition to our regular shop vendors, we're inviting other local artisans to set up booths around the property. We've done the event before, and it's been really popular. There isn't a lot of time, but if you want me to save a space for you, I'm sure our customers would love your designs."

"That's a lovely offer, but…" Cory paused and swallowed back her refusal. In truth, the idea of selling her jewelry appealed to her in a way she couldn't explain. It might be difficult to craft enough items to make it worth it, although she'd fashioned a dozen pair of earrings just the other night while Jordan was at the bar. She'd gotten so caught up in the relaxing rhythm of her work that she hadn't even realized how much she'd done or how late it was until the grandfather clock in his family room chimed midnight.

"Can I think about it and give you a call tomorrow morning?" she asked Brynn. "I'll have to take a look at my supplies and the timing to figure out if it's something I could manage."

"But you'll consider it?" Brynn grinned. "I'm so happy. Yes, call me whenever."

The guys came back into the kitchen at that moment, and the rest of the evening went by in a series of bright and easy moments filled with laughter and conversation. It was becoming clearer with each moment that Starlight was the kind of place Cory would be lucky to call her home. She tried not to think of how much Jordan was coming to mean to her. But after they drove home in companionable silence, they put Ben down for bed together, and to Cory it felt like they'd become a family. It felt like everything she'd secretly dreamed of, so when he drew her into his arms and then his bed, she let herself go without reservation.

"I've missed you, babe."

Cory whirled around at the sound of the familiar voice. The jar of pureed sweet potatoes she'd been taking from the shelf crashed to the floor and shattered. Chunks of orange goop splattered across the white squares of linoleum and onto her jeans.

"Still a klutz," Kade said with a smirk. "One of the things I love about you."

Her brain continued to have trouble with the fact that her ex-boyfriend was standing in a grocery aisle, so close she could reach out and touch him if she wanted. She didn't want to touch him or talk to him or even acknowledge his existence, although Kade was a hard man to ignore. His hair was close cropped, the way he'd always worn it, and he was dressed in a striped button-down, dark jeans and a leather jacket. No one could deny his raw masculinity, but seeing him only made Cory somewhat sick to her stomach.

She tried and mostly failed to calm her breathing as she looked past him to the grocery store clerk who'd appeared at the end of the aisle.

"I'm so sorry," she said to the older man even as she stepped in front of the cart that held her groceries and Ben. For some reason, she felt the need to put herself between her son and Kade. "It slipped from my fingers."

"We'll get it cleaned up in a jiffy," the clerk told her. His eyes widened as he realized who was standing with her. "My son and I loved watching you in the playoffs this year, Mr. Barrington."

Kade flashed his patented thousand-watt smile. "New England was a tough loss."

"You'll get them next year." The man pulled a cell phone from his pocket. "Would you be willing to take a selfie with me?"

"Sure thing," Kade said easily, then glanced at Cory. "Give me a minute."

She didn't answer, but there was no way she was giving her ex even one solitary second. As soon as Kade started toward the clerk, Cory unsnapped Ben's infant seat from the shopping cart and headed in the opposite direction, leaving her groceries deserted in the aisle.

She'd almost made it to her car when she heard the sound of footsteps jogging toward her.

"Babe, come on. Don't be like that. I came all this way."

She didn't break her stride. "For nothing, Kade. I don't want to talk to you like this."

"Then you should have texted me back." He caught up to her as she unlocked her car. "You didn't return my phone calls, either. I needed you after that last game. You're the only person I wanted with me."

"We're over." She opened the car door and bent forward to clip Ben's seat into the base. "We've been over for a while, Kade. Even before I left Atlanta. You know that."

"Is that our boy?"

Anger clawed at her throat, making it difficult to breathe. "He's not yours." She shut the car door and turned. "You know that, too."

"He could be." Kade gave a dismissive shrug, the diamond stud in his left ear glinting in the pale sunlight. It had rained overnight, so the air smelled like pine and forest even more than usual. She tried to let the scent calm her thudding heart.

"I'll give him my name," Kade told her like he was offering to bestow some kind of prize on her baby. "I'll give him everything you and I never had. All the things we wanted. The best schools, the biggest houses."

"That's not what I want for me or for my son." She shook her head. "It never has been."

"What do you want?" His expression tightened with obvious frustration.

"A happy life," she said simply. "What happened to the new girlfriend, Kade? I heard you were engaged."

"I broke it off because she wasn't you. We're still a part of each other, Cory." He reached around her and tapped his open palm to the peeling roof of the Buick. "You think you're going to get some fairy-tale happiness with Jordan Schaeffer?" Kade gave a dismissive sniff. "That guy was washed up before he even left the team. He had potential but no follow-through."

"How do you know about Jordan?" she demanded. "How did you even know where to find me?" She held up a hand before he could answer. "My mom told you." Kade was the only thing in Cory's life her mom approved of.

"At least she would talk to me." The irritation in his tone was clear. Kade had always been one for instant gratification, so Cory could imagine that not being able to immediately reach her had been a real problem.

Too bad his problems were no longer her concern.

"She shouldn't have done that," Cory said tightly, although it didn't surprise her. Even at Gran's funeral, Cory's mom had taken the opportunity to lecture her about how much she'd given up when she and Kade broke up.

"You're not a part of my life anymore," she told him, proud when her voice didn't waver. "You made it clear what it would take for me to stay in yours. I'm making choices for myself now. For my son." She pointed a finger at him. "Not yours, Kade. Mine."

"Give me a break." He shook his head. "I know you, Cory. I understand how you operate. You left me and went running home to your grandma, and when she was gone you decided your next best bet was latching on to Schaeffer. You never do anything for yourself."

The words hit like a series of blows. She knew in her rational mind that they weren't true, but in some ways, he was right. Cory should have never agreed to the pretend relationship with Jordan, but she had because it was easy to go along with what worked for somebody else. Because starting over in a new place totally on her own was terrifying, and relationships were her comfort zone. She knew how to be a daughter, a granddaughter, a girlfriend. What she'd never mastered was taking care of herself.

She'd thought she had a chance for a real change to how she did things in Starlight. At least that was what her plan had been. But her life here was based on a lie. Madison was the only person who knew the truth. Would her other friends stand by her when and if they realized her duplicity?

"Wow, your sweet words are really melting my heart." She glared at Kade. She might not be the best example of independence, but she didn't deserve to be shamed for it. "If I was such a needy, clingy drain on you, then what are you doing here?"

For a moment, there was a flicker of true emotion in his gaze. "Like I said, I miss you. You might be a train wreck, but you're my train wreck."

"I'm not yours," she said through gritted teeth. "And I'm not a train wreck. Not anymore."

"Sorry." He held up his hands. "I meant it as a compliment. I miss taking care of you. I miss having you waiting for me at the end of the night. I miss us."

"There is no us, Kade. I'm sorry you made the trip for—" She broke off, shook her head. "Scratch that. I'm not sorry. You coming here was your choice. I didn't ask for it, and I didn't invite you. Yes, I let you take care of me because it was easy. My mistake. I should have realized I don't need anyone to take care of me. In some ways I owe you, because leaving you taught me a lot about myself. I appreciate the history, but I'm not going to repeat. Not with you or any man."

"Come on, babe." Kade took a step closer but stopped when she held up a hand. "If you want something different, I'll give it to you. Whatever you want. Just say you'll try again."

"No."

He stared at her like he expected something more, but she just returned his gaze without emotion. Why had it taken her so long to realize that "no" was a complete sentence? She didn't owe him an explanation. She owed herself a chance.

He reached into the inside pocket of his leather jacket and pulled out an envelope, shoving it into her hand before she could protest. "I booked us a trip to Fiji. That's where you always wanted to go, remember? I've got time off. My agent wanted me to go right to a deodorant commercial shoot, but I said I've got to reconnect with my best girl first. I even hired a nanny for the kid and rented a separate condo for them. We'll have a real vacation, Cory. Just come with me and then you can decide about the future. Let's enjoy right now."

The scattered fragments of her resolve coalesced inside her until they obscured all of her doubts about her own strength. She wasn't the woman Kade wanted her to be. Maybe she never had been, only now she had the courage to step into the new version of herself. "I am enjoying my life right now," she told him. "I don't need a beach vacation to make me happy. Ben makes me happy. My life makes me happy." *And Jordan*, she wanted to add, but didn't. Because as happy as Jordan made her, Cory knew they had to go forward without anything fake between them if they were really going to have the chance she wanted.

It would be the first time in forever she hadn't taken the easy way out. But he was worth it. She was worth it.

"Good luck, Kade. I wish you the best, but you're not the best for me."

She climbed into her car and drove away. The envelope sat on the passenger seat, unopened. Maybe she should have forced him to take it back, but it didn't matter. She had no intention of using the ticket. Her life was here, and it was time she claimed it.

Chapter Sixteen

Jordan's heart plummeted to his toes as he pulled up to his house later that afternoon to witness Cory loading boxes into the back of her old sedan.

He'd come to love that automotive behemoth in the weeks she'd parked it in his driveway. It represented something about the woman and her quiet independence. At first, he'd offered daily to lease something new for her or to buy her a more reliable used car.

But she'd insisted she liked the Buick just fine, which was difficult to believe, because it drove like a tank. But Cory was proud and determined to do things on her own, and he respected her for it.

So why was she packing up now?

He refused to believe she didn't want to be with him. Not when their time together felt so right. He couldn't be the only one who sensed their bond deepening with every passing day. Yes, they talked about the time when they'd have to come clean about their relationship, but the longer it continued, the more certain he became that didn't have to be the only option.

They could be together for real.

He parked in front of the garage and got out of the truck, doing his best not to appear as alarmed as he felt.

"Cleaning out closets?" he asked with fake cheer.

"I'm leaving," she said as she closed the trunk.

"Leaving." He repeated the word numbly, feeling like he'd just taken a swift kick to the family jewels. His past had taught him not to reveal his emotions because that would give whoever was hurting him the upper hand. Whether with his father or on the line of scrimmage, Jordan never flinched.

He didn't shy away now, although his insides felt like they'd been sent through a meat grinder.

"What does that mean? You taking a girls' trip?"

"The pretend relationship ends now," she answered. "I'm going to stay with Tessa for a few days until I can make arrangements to rent my own place."

"You can't do that." He shook his head, grasping at anything that would keep her there. "We had an arrangement, Cory."

"Which we should have stopped when your mom left, Jordan. We both know it."

I don't know anything of the sort, his heart screamed. "Do we?" was his response.

"I told you from the start that I didn't seek you out because I had expectations. You deserved to know the truth about your son, and I wanted you to have a chance to have a relationship with him."

"How am I going to do that if you take him away?" he demanded, his voice cracking on the last word. He sucked in a breath and tried to muster some semblance of calm. "You can't take him from me, Cory."

"I wouldn't do that. Tessa's cabin is ten minutes away, and I'm not planning to leave Starlight. But I need to know I can make it on my own without having to rely on someone to take care of me."

He wanted to argue, to tell her that he was the one who needed her. That his house would be nothing more than a shell without her in it. That he loved her. But he didn't say any of those things. He'd spent his whole damn life hiding emotion because emotion made him weak, but somehow acting strong didn't make him feel any more in control at this moment.

Ben made a noise from inside the car.

"I have to go," Cory said gently. "I'm not walking away, Jordan."

"It sure looks like that from where I'm standing."

"I'll call you tomorrow," she said. "We can figure out how to start fresh. This isn't the end."

She went up on tiptoe to kiss him, but he turned his head so her mouth brushed his cheek. As angry as he was, he still wanted to kiss her. But he was half-afraid that if he let himself get close to her at this moment, he'd lose it.

He could feel her gaze on him but refused to look. After a few tense seconds, she squeezed his arm and moved away. He felt her absence like an icy wind. She could talk all she wanted about this not being the end, but watching her brake lights flash before she disappeared down his driveway, it sure felt like the end to Jordan.

Birds chirped in the trees overhead, and the afternoon sun warmed his shoulders. It seemed somehow wrong that the world could continue when it felt like his chest was splitting open and his heart would be irrevocably fractured.

After a few minutes, he went into the house. It was so damn quiet. Not the good kind of quiet, either. The kind that reminded him he was once again alone.

Unable to stand it on his own, he left for the bar. He arrived in the middle of happy hour, and the booths and tables were crowded with a mix of locals and out-of-towners. After greeting a few customers by name, Jordan headed for his office but made a detour for the bar when Tanya gestured him over.

"We've got a problem, boss."

He glanced over his shoulder at the groups of boisterous customers. "Tell me."

Before she could answer, a crash sounded from the kitchen, loud enough that people at several tables looked toward the swinging door that separated the two spaces.

"On second thought, don't tell me." He gave a small shake of his head. "I'll deal with it."

He entered the kitchen, which was filled with a tense silence only punctuated by the sizzling of the grill and the bubble from the fryer. In the past few weeks, since Cory's arrival, he'd gotten used to laughter and conversation among his staff as they worked.

Madison stood behind the stainless-steel counter, glaring down at a bowl of steaming pasta. "You'd better get out of my kitchen," she said without glancing up, "before I fillet you open like today's fresh catch."

"What happened to your new leaf and kinder, gentler personality?" Jordan asked, arching a brow.

"I'm kinder and gentler, just not to you." She met his gaze, pointed the tip of her knife in his direction. "You cost me my best employee."

Jordan blinked.

"Cory," she clarified, as if he couldn't tell who she was talking about. "She stopped in earlier and told me she was looking for a new job. The kitchen staff is supposed to be mine, Jordan. You're the boss of the front of the house. I run the back."

"I didn't fire Cory." He ran a hand through his

hair. "Hell, I didn't even know she was planning to quit."

The chef stepped around the prep counter and lowered her voice so that only he would hear her. "Doesn't that seem like something you should know about your own fiancée?" She gave him a hard stare.

"She didn't tell me. You can't blame me for something I didn't do."

"I'm not blaming you because she quit. I'm blaming you for making her want to."

"What does that even mean?"

"I know about your little arrangement," Madison said, leaning closer. "The truth. I'm the only one who knows the truth."

"Then why are you acting surprised this happened? It was bound to fall apart eventually."

She threw up her hands. "Only because you're an idiot. I don't care what Cory told me about the two of you being all for show when she first got to town. Things changed, didn't they?"

He pressed his lips together but gave a tight nod.

"You fell for her, and not just for pretend."

"What does it matter when she left?" He forced a breath when he realized he was starting to raise his voice. "She left me, and it looks like she left you."

"She quit the job in my kitchen." Madison inclined her head, giving him a funny look. "Yeah, it makes me mad because I liked working with her. She knew nothing about cooking, but she tried hard and never complained. Plus, she's a damn fine waitress. She and I will still be friends. The way she explained it to me, she ended the pretend part of your relationship. The part where you were playing house but not really committed. She wanted something real, and you wouldn't give it to her. She quit this job because she thinks it will be too hard to see you every day."

"That's ridiculous." He shook his head. "She knows I want her in my life for real. Hell, I put the toilet seat down after I flush."

Madison made a show of patting the pockets of her white chef's coat. "Too bad I'm fresh out of gold stars. You definitely qualify for one. Cory doesn't know you want to be with her for real."

"She should."

"Why?"

"Because I would never let anyone as close as she's gotten to me if I didn't want them for real."

"But did you tell her?"

"I didn't have to tell her," he insisted, although the argument sounded weak even to his ears. "I showed her."

"The testosterone in here is making it hard to breathe." Madison waved her fingers in front of her nose. "I'm gagging on your male stupidity."

"Not helpful," Jordan muttered.

"About as helpful as allowing a woman who's always considered herself a drain on the people she cares about to believe you were doing her a favor with your affection."

Jordan crossed his arms over his chest like that would protect him from the onslaught of the truth being hurled at him like spikes. "Let's not forget, she's the one who walked away."

Tanya came through the sliding door that led to the front of the bar and quickly approached. "Jordan, there's someone asking to talk to you."

"Can you handle it?" Jordan kept his gaze on Madison. "Comp their tab if you need to. We're in the middle of something important here." He had a feeling this conversation might help him fix the mess of his life.

"Kade Barrington just took a seat at the bar," Tanya said. "I don't think he's going to care that I buy him a drink."

Jordan's gut tightened. What the hell was Kade doing in Starlight? Did Cory know her ex-boyfriend had shown up in town? Something like panic niggled its way along his spine, but he pushed away the doubts. He couldn't allow himself to believe that her walking away earlier had anything to do with Kade.

"We're not finished," he told Madison.

"I've got cheese to fry," she answered and turned away. "But let me just mention I'll make a batch of your favorite cookies if you turn that rat-fink jerk out on his ear."

"No fighting," Tanya told him as they headed out of the kitchen.

"I break up fights," Jordan reminded her. "When have you ever known me to get in one?"

"I've never known you to be in love before Cory," Tanya answered. "Love changes everything."

Jordan muttered a curse. "Is it that obvious?"

"To everyone but the two of you, apparently."

Kade was sitting alone at the end of the bar as Jordan approached. It was the first time Jordan had ever seen the marquee quarterback without his crew of sycophants surrounding him. Somehow it made him look younger and less cocky than Jordan remembered.

No one in the bar paid him much mind, which was also strange, since Kade was a bona fide sports celebrity. Then he lifted his head and fixed his steel-blue gaze on Jordan, and the reason he was being left alone —as well as the reason for Tanya's warning about fighting—became clear. Kade Barrington had murder in his eyes.

"You're a long way from home," Jordan said casually, picking up a beer glass to dry as he moved closer.

"I'm here to collect what's mine," Kade said without preamble. "I'm not going home without her."

Jordan didn't pretend to misunderstand the other man. "Cory doesn't belong to you. She doesn't belong to anyone, and she gets to choose whether she stays or goes."

"You think she's going to choose you?"

"I think she's happy in Starlight."

"I can make her happier." Kade flicked his fingers across the bar. "I can give her way more than a small-time bar in a two-bit town. I can show her the world."

"Maybe she doesn't want to see it on your terms," Jordan suggested tightly. He was doing his best to keep a lid on his temper, but Kade's arrogance didn't make it an easy task.

"You had no right to touch her." Kade downed the remainder of the dark liquor and thumped the empty glass against the bar top. "Not then and not now."

"Again, it's her choice. Cory chooses who she allows close to her." He placed his hands on the edge of the bar and gripped it tight. "She chose me."

"Because I didn't want her at the time. Now I'm back, and she's coming with me. She's meant to be mine." Kade tapped a finger on the rim of his glass. "Another round."

"No." Jordan shook his head. He'd only had to kick a handful of customers out of the bar since he took ownership. Normally he could mitigate a situation before it came to that. He had no desire to defuse anything with Kade. Jordan wanted the cocky son of a gun gone before they both lost their tempers. "Go drink someplace else, Kade. Or better yet, go home to Atlanta. This isn't your place."

"I'll tell you where I'm going." Kade drew out an envelope from the inside of his coat. "I'm heading to the beach, and Cory's coming with me." He slapped a piece of paper that was clearly an itinerary with Cory's and Kade's names typed across the top. "You can't begin to hold a candle to what I can give her, Schaeffer. You're a washed-up former baller who's way past your prime, and your prime wasn't impressive to start."

Jordan couldn't seem to take his eyes from the paper with Cory's name printed alongside of Kade's. Was the timing of her moving out an actual coincidence, or could she be going to some fancy resort with her ex? Would she be swayed by the promise of some grand lifestyle? Jordan's dad had been kicking and screaming mad when Jordan retired and threw away the perks that came with being a professional athlete. He hadn't given a damn that Jordan didn't want to play the game anymore. It was like a knife to the gut to think Cory might feel the same.

"You know what your problem always was?" Kade grabbed the paper and shoved it back into his pocket. "You didn't have enough fight in you. Yeah, the coaches and management thought that was such an asset. They held you up as some sort of example because you're so cool and collected. No one ever figured out the reason. It's because you didn't really care. Not about the game or winning."

The other man laughed without humor. "You were meant for a smaller life," he chided. "But Cory deserves bigger and better. I'm going to give it to her."

"Get out, Kade." Jordan felt a muscle ticking in his jaw. He felt the buildup of pressure in his chest and knew he was close to the point of no return.

Kade climbed off the bar stool with a smirk, like he'd accomplished what he set out to do tonight. Jordan hated that he'd given the other man any satisfaction. "You know what else?" Kade's chest rose and fell with a deep breath. "I'm going to be the man who raises your son. God knows, the kid needs a fighting chance to turn out normal—not a quitter like his daddy."

Suddenly all Jordan could see was a red haze in front of him. The anger came swift and sure and practically knocked him sideways with its force. He didn't hesitate or think for one second before he stepped around the edge of the bar.

Kade immediately swung at him, but Jordan dodged the blow.

He threw a punch that landed with a satisfying crunch against Kade's perfect face. And all hell broke loose.

Cory arrived early for her first shift at Main Street Perk. She was scheduled to begin training at ten, and Tessa had agreed to watch Ben for the day when Jordan didn't return Cory's calls or texts the previous night.

His silence weighed on her and broke her heart even more than his casual indifference at her leaving. She believed him when he told her he wanted to be a big part of their son's life, and she hated to even consider that his feelings might change once she'd ended their fake relationship.

In truth, she'd hoped that her decision to move out would be a new beginning for them. Surely he knew what she felt about him. Surely he understood that the only way for them to truly be together was for him to freely choose her, not because of ease or some arbitrary necessity to put on a show for friends or family.

So why the radio silence?

"Hey, Mara," she said as the coffee shop manager and baker extraordinaire noticed her approaching the front counter.

"You're early." Mara glanced at her watch with a raised brow, then flashed a smile. "I like early."

"Does she ever," the dark-haired barista standing next to Mara said with a laugh. "Sometimes she thinks that because she's up at four in the morning to start baking, the rest of the world should follow suit."

"At least you work in a coffee shop," Cory said, feeling the heavy weight of her thoughts about Jordan start to lift. She'd reached out to Mara after she got settled at Tessa's and had been grateful when she received an immediate answer and job offer. "There's an endless supply of caffeine to get you through the day."

"Oh, she fizzles out right around two." The barista ignored Mara's eye roll and held out a hand to Cory. "I'm Ellen, and I'll be showing you the ropes today."

"Don't get your attitude from this one," Mara said, but she placed an arm around Ellen's shoulder and squeezed.

The small gesture made tears prick the backs of Cory's eyes. One of the things that had been the hardest about tendering her resignation with Madison was the thought of losing the connection between the kitchen staff. When she'd dated Kade, he hadn't wanted her to take a job that would compromise their time together, so she'd worked as a receptionist in the car dealership managed by the younger son of the team's owner. It was fine, but the connection to Kade ended up leaving her feeling like she had nothing that truly belonged to her.

Why had it taken her so long to realize she deserved that?

"You won't have to worry about my attitude," Cory promised, trying for a laugh, which came out more like a sob.

"Okay." Mara grimaced. "Why don't we start with a tour of the kitchen?"

Ellen, who clearly hadn't noticed Cory's upset,

gave her boss a funny look. "Don't you think we should start with the cappuccino machine while we aren't too busy?"

"That's fine," Cory said, and drat if her voice didn't crack again.

"It will just take a few minutes," Mara told the barista, then crooked a finger at Cory. "First rule of Perk. Do what the boss tells you."

That earned a genuine laugh from Cory. "You might have a few things in common with Madison."

"Don't say that again," Mara said at the same time Ellen whispered, "I like this one."

Cory followed Mara into the kitchen. Unlike the back of the house at Trophy Room, this space smelled like sugar and butter. Cory breathed deeply. "This is how I imagine the scent of a perfect childhood. Your daughter must love it here."

"She does." Mara grabbed a snickerdoodle from the cooling rack and shoved it toward Cory. "What's the problem?"

"There's no problem."

"If my baristas are choking back tears in front of customers, that's a problem."

Cory popped a bite of cookie into her mouth. "I have allergies."

"Do they have to do with Jordan beating the crap out of Kade Barrington last night at the bar?"

Cory choked on the cookie. "What are you talking about? Was Jordan hurt?"

Mara gave her a hard pat on the back, then turned to fill up a glass of water. She handed Cory the glass. "The way I heard it, Jordan took care of business. I assumed you knew." She leaned in. "The way I heard it, their beef had something to do with an old grudge from the days they played together back in Atlanta. But I think there's more to the story. You're that more."

Cory took a long drink of water and then wiped a hand across her mouth. All the while, her mind whirled with the idea of Jordan and Kade getting in a fistfight and the fact that it could have anything to do with her.

"I don't…" She wanted to deny it but couldn't bring herself to tell another lie to someone in this town she cared about or might one day consider a friend. "I don't know how to keep pretending like I know what I'm doing."

"You don't have to have all the answers," Mara said gently.

Cory gave a shaky nod and shoved the last piece of cookie into her mouth. "No chance of that," she admitted. "I have no idea what happened at the bar. Kade showed up in town yesterday, but I sent him away. I didn't think he'd seek out Jordan. Who, by the way, doesn't seem to be speaking to me at the moment. My life's a mess."

"Messes can be cleaned up," Mara said. "Trust me."

"Would it be okay if I just got to work? Right now I need a distraction, and I promise no tears."

Mara studied her for a long moment. "Sure," she said finally. "And if you're going to cry, come back here. Free cookies for your first day on the job."

"I might take you up on that. Now I'd like to learn how to make a fancy coffee."

Chapter Seventeen

Jordan parked his car in front of the small cabin tucked away in the trees and wished that a million things were different in his life at the moment. Most of all, he wished that Cory wasn't coming down the front steps holding his baby and an overnight bag to give to him.

The soft pink sweatshirt she wore highlighted her creamy skin, and her hair was pinned back from her face in jeweled barrettes. She offered a tentative smile as she got closer, but the smile faded when she took in the bruise that darkened his left eye. "What happened to you?"

He shrugged and reached out a hand to smooth

it over Ben's head. The boy gave him a wide, tooth-less grin, then curled shyly into his mother's chest, which made Jordan's chest ache. "Things got a little out of hand at the bar. No big deal."

"Did that out of hand involve Kade?" she asked quietly.

Jordan couldn't read her expression. "If you're asking, then I think you know it did. Word travels fast in a small town. And Kade did more than his share of talking last night."

Her mouth thinned, and she glanced away. "I hope you didn't believe him."

"You're still here. If he'd been telling me the truth, you'd be on your way to Fiji by now, along with Ben."

"Things are over between Kade and me," she said. "They have been for a long time."

"Does he know that?"

"He does now."

Jordan nodded slowly and thought about what to say next. The truth was he didn't want to say any-thing. He wanted to pull Cory into his arms and hold her close. He wanted to breathe in the scent of her hair and feel the warmth of her body pressed against his. He hated the distance between them and the way she wouldn't hold his gaze. "I wondered at the tim-ing of you ending things between us and then Kade showing up at Trophy Room. Had you seen him be-fore you left?"

She gave a tight nod. "But Kade isn't the reason I

moved out of your house, Jordan. Although, talking to him did make me realize some things about how I want my life to be."

"And I take it that doesn't involve any football players, ex or current?"

Her brows drew together like she didn't understand the question. "I want to make a good life for my son."

"Our son." Ben decided at that moment that Jordan passed the familiarity test and reached for him. As soon as he took the boy into his arms, emotion clogged his throat. "I missed you, buddy. We're going to hit it hard tonight. Maybe even peas and pears for dinner."

He felt a ridiculously inflated sense of pride when Cory laughed at his corny joke.

She passed him the diaper bag and duffel she'd packed. "If you need anything, call me. This is the first time since he came home after his surgery that I've been away from him for the night." She swiped at her cheeks. "It's going to be strange."

"It doesn't have to be like this," Jordan told her.

She shook her head. "I'm done pretending."

He almost staggered back a step at those three words. Was that all he meant to her, really? A pretend relationship that she no longer wanted or needed?

"Okay, then. That makes it clear." He turned and secured the baby into the car seat, stowing the bags on the floor of the truck. "I'll call you tomorrow about dropping him off. Thanks for letting me keep him for the night, Cory. I guess…" He rubbed a hand over the back of his neck. "We'll have to come up with a more formal custody agreement going forward."

"Yeah," she agreed and swallowed hard. "I'm hoping to get more hours at the coffee shop after I finish training." She looked at the ground. "I ordered some supplies to start making more jewelry. I'm going to try to get enough inventory to participate in the Dennison Mill event, and whatever's left over I'll list online. That should bring in some extra cash, and it's something I can do at night while Ben's sleeping."

"I don't want you to worry about money," Jordan told her. "If you need anything, I can help."

"I want to make it on my own."

"But child support is a thing, right?" He shook his head. "It feels like we're going at this all backward. I want to support you and Ben."

"You don't owe me anything," she reminded him.

"I do," he countered. He wanted to say more. He wanted to disagree and tell her he owed her for bringing him back to life. For making him see that there was so much more happiness available to him if he just was brave enough to reach out and take it.

"Cory, I—"

"I should let you get going." She crossed her arms over her chest when a breeze kicked up.

"How are things going at Main Street Perk?"

"Good." She drew in a breath. "Everyone is really nice."

"Madison is distraught without you. She blames me."

That earned a half smile. "She knows it was my decision. She just likes giving you grief."

"Good to know. I guess I'll talk to you later, then."

"I'm a call away if you need me." She bit down on her lower lip. "If Ben needs anything."

An important distinction, Jordan supposed, because it felt like he needed her more than he needed his next breath. But he didn't know how to say that and not risk having his heart crushed into a million pieces, so he just nodded, got in his truck and drove away.

The panic set in seconds later. Panic at the realization that he was responsible for Ben for the next twenty-four hours. Without hesitating, he picked up his phone and hit the number to call his mom.

She answered on the first ring.

"I messed up bad," he told her and then proceeded to explain the entire situation from the beginning. Cory's arrival in Starlight. His idea for the pretend relationship at the funeral and how that led to an extended ruse when Kathy announced her plans for a visit. His feelings for Cory were real, even if their relationship had started out fake.

His mother listened to his entire story, then immediately lectured him on making a call while behind the wheel and the dangers of distracted driving. For some reason, that small bit of maternal scolding relaxed him more than he would have imagined.

"Okay, I'm home," he told her as he pulled into the garage. "Will you tell me how to fix things now?" He cradled the phone between his cheek and shoulder as he got Ben out of the car and headed into the house.

"Do you love her?" his mother asked like it was the easiest question in the world to answer.

And suddenly it was. "Yes," he told her. "I love her so much it hurts."

"Have you told her?"

"Oh, hell no."

"No cursing, young man. And do you see the problem with that?"

"Not one bit. What if she doesn't feel the same? She told me she was done pretending, Mom. Those exact words. How can I tell her and risk freaking her out? And what if I freak her out so much that she doesn't want to let me be part of Ben's life?"

"Wow," his mom murmured with a soft laugh. "Those are a lot of potential issues."

"Exactly."

"I never took my son for a coward."

He paused, held the phone in front of him, unsure he'd heard her right. "How does being cautious suddenly translate into being a coward?"

"I don't know your Cory well," his mother answered, "but she didn't strike me as the kind of woman who would keep you from having a relationship with your son. Do you really believe that?"

"No," he admitted. "She would never use Ben that way."

"Good. And did it ever occur to you she might be having the same worries as you?"

"She's the one who walked away."

"Did you give her another option?"

"Yes. I told her…" Jordan broke off and thought about what he had and hadn't told Cory over the past few weeks. "She knows how I feel."

"Because she's a mind reader or because she has such a great track record with men in her life doing the right thing?"

"I'm not like Kade or her dad or any other guy who's treated her like she doesn't matter," Jordan insisted.

"Then show her," his mom urged. "Tell her. I saw the two of you together, Jordan. There's something special there. Now you both just have to be willing to go after it. You've always pursued what you want, son. Don't let this be any different."

"Thanks, Mom." He placed Ben on a blanket and sank down next to him on the carpet. "I appreciate the advice. I should go now."

"Maybe you could plan a weekend to drive over to Spokane?" His mom's confident tone had suddenly gone tentative.

"That would be great." Jordan blew out a rush of

air. Never would he have imagined himself in the position to want his mother to be a part of his life, but it felt strangely right now. It felt real and right.

"Don't cry."

Cory met Madison's steely gaze and nodded. "I'm holding it together."

"I swear, I won't let you in my kitchen again if you cry."

Cory and Tessa had arrived at Madison's near downtown Starlight twenty minutes earlier. The house was a charming Craftsman style, with glowing fir floors, lots of built-ins and a brick fireplace in the living room. The kitchen was small but had beautiful butcher-block counters and stainless appliances. Madison's home felt welcoming and cozy, and it was like getting a peek inside the secret soul of the hard-nosed chef.

They hadn't had a club meeting scheduled, but Tessa took one look at Cory's face after Jordan and Ben drove away and called an emergency session.

They were making enchiladas because Madison deemed them the ultimate comfort food.

"She's not going to cry," Ella said and wrapped an arm around Cory's shoulder before glancing at her. "Oh, she's totally going to cry."

"Think about something happy," Tessa advised.

"All of my happy thoughts involve Ben," Cory

said, and then her voice broke. Her throat and eyes burned with the effort of holding back the ears.

"Think about cute puppies and kittens," Tessa advised with a cheery smile. "That always helps me feel better."

"But don't think about those humane-society commercials with the abused animals," Madison added as she whisked the cheese sauce heating over a gas burner on the stove. "Those are a total downer."

Cory let out a laugh that quickly turned into a strangled sob. "You give the worst pep talks in the history of the world."

The other woman shrugged. "Pep talks aren't in my wheelhouse. But these enchiladas are going to blow your mind."

"Shouldn't we be helping?" Tessa asked and then plucked a chip from the bowl on the counter and dunked it into Madison's homemade salsa. "I thought the point of this was for us to learn."

"We're learning by osmosis," Ella said and then took a long pull on her beer. "Besides, I'm not sure there are any men out there even worth learning to cook for. That just supports the patriarchy."

"Jordan appreciated when I tried to make dinner," Cory said with another sniff. "Even though I wasn't good at it. He did plenty of the cooking and always brought me coffee in the morning. He was perfect."

"Jordan Schaeffer is not perfect," Madison said,

then bobbed her eyebrows. "Okay, physically he's perfect, but he has faults."

Ella squeezed Cory's shoulders. "Top of the list is that he let you walk away."

"Exactly," Madison agreed.

To Cory's surprise, Tessa shook her head. "Not so fast. I'm not sure I agree that's a fault. Maybe it's because my mom was a big Sting fan, but I think his sage words of 'if you love someone, set them free' ring true in this case." She threw up her hands when Cory, Ella and Madison just stared at her. "Come on—you know what I'm talking about. 'Free, free, set them free,'" she sang in a ferociously off-key soprano.

"Sting is great for an old guy," Madison agreed.

"Also still hot," Tessa added, tipping her wineglass to drain it.

"Kind of gross, but okay." Madison poured the sauce over the rolled enchiladas and popped the baking dish into the oven. "But Jordan should have fought for our girl."

Tessa wrinkled her nose, clearly disagreeing. "Maybe he thought she wanted him to let her go, and that he was doing the right thing by her."

"Whose side are you on?" Cory asked, feeling miserable.

Tessa frowned. "Yours. Whose side are you on, Cory?" She stepped around the counter and squared her shoulders. "Because I've heard you crying in your bedroom the past few nights when you should be asleep. I've listened to you talk about happiness and making a good life for Ben, but isn't part of that having the cojones to go after what you want?"

"I have cojones," Cory muttered.

"You love Jordan."

Cory drew in a breath, wanting to deny it. As reserved as Tessa could be, she'd picked an interesting time to grow a backbone. "I do."

"But you won't tell him."

"I don't want to give him a chance to hurt me."

"Give the man more credit," Tessa insisted.

"She has a point," Ella said. "Plus, if a man made me coffee every morning, I'd never let him go."

"That's the problem," Cory told them. "I don't want to let him go. Ever. I see a future with Jordan. The kind of future I desperately want. I didn't even know I could want something so badly, that I could love a person other than Ben so much. It scares me, because love makes me weak."

"That's a fact," Ella said.

"Amen, sister," Madison added.

"No." Tessa shook her head. "The right kind of love makes you strong. It makes you brave enough to take on anything, because you know you'll have a soft place to land at the end of the day. Just because all of you have been hurt before, that doesn't make love bad. It means you have to make better choices the next time around."

"I choose Ben and Jerry," Ella said.

"And Henry Cavill in that show where he's got the long hair and leather pants," Madison said with a sigh. "I don't need any other man."

Tessa gave Madison a pointed look. The chef turned to Cory. "I agree Jordan is a good guy. And he obviously cares about you and Ben. I mean, you could do worse."

"High praise," Ella said with a laugh.

"I told him I don't want a pretend relationship," Cory argued. "I can't go crawling back to him now."

"Your feelings aren't pretend, honey." Ella's smile was gentle. "Neither are his. That changes everything."

"Love changes everything." Tessa nodded.

Cory's nerves buzzed with the idea that she could actually go after a second chance—or possibly a third chance—with Jordan. She realized she wanted everything Tessa was talking about, and she wanted it with Jordan.

Now the question was how to make it happen.

Chapter Eighteen

Jordan had planned to talk to Cory when she came to pick up Ben the previous night. He'd had flowers and sweets at the house all ready to go as olive branches or tokens of his affection or…well, he hoped the gifts could communicate what Jordan hadn't figured out a way to say.

He didn't even know her favorite flower, but he'd figured he'd go with the classic staples of roses and a box of chocolates for wooing a woman. In truth, he had no clue how to woo a woman. He'd never cared enough to try.

Cory was worth wooing. She meant everything to him, and he desperately wanted a chance to prove it.

But now it was Saturday morning and the flowers sat wilting on the counter, much like his self-confidence. When she'd come by last night, she'd been tense and stressed about her booth at the Dennison Mill market. He'd also seen a sense of determination in her. It was clear that Cory was different from the uncertain woman she'd been when she arrived in Starlight. She was coming into herself, and he didn't want to take a chance on derailing or distracting her from the life she was building in town.

He wanted her to be happy more than he wanted her for himself.

If it wasn't so pathetic, he'd laugh at his skill at rationalizing his cowardice. He was afraid to give her a chance to reject him outright. His mother would have counseled him that it was worth the risk. Madison and Tanya would probably have told him to pull up his big-boy boxers and stop acting like a wuss.

Cory had texted him late last night, asking if he would pick up Ben from Tessa's house that morning because she had to set up early. He'd agreed but now regretted not saying more.

So many regrets. Jordan hated regrets.

He grabbed his phone from the counter and sent a message wishing her luck and then asked if she would have dinner with him after the market. Baby steps were better than nothing, right? He waited with his breath held as the three little dots flashed on the screen while she typed her reply.

Yes on dinner. Thank you for the luck. I'll need it.

That was a start, he thought, trying not to be disappointed she hadn't messaged him more. It felt ridiculous that he wasn't with her to offer support in person. His mom's words about going after what he wanted echoed through his mind. Jordan wanted a chance at a real future with Cory and Ben.

His phone dinged and he checked it, the message sending a jolt of emotion through his body.

She'd sent him a red heart emoji.

And suddenly that one colorful shape changed everything inside Jordan. He'd been a fool and a coward, just like his mom had gently admonished. He was so busy trying to protect himself from being hurt, he hadn't realized he was only hurting himself.

He hurriedly typed in his reply.

You're going to do amazing today. You are amazing, Cory. I can't wait to see you shine.

He went to hit Send, then added his own heart emoji. God, he felt like a lovesick schoolboy.

As he drove to Tessa's, he came up with and rejected nearly a dozen plans for how to show Cory what she meant to him. What he needed was a night to binge-watch all the rom-com movies ever made for inspiration.

He could borrow an old-school boom box from

someone in town. There might even be one in the bar's storage room.

No, that was stupid.

What about serenading her? Only problem was Jordan couldn't carry a tune to save his life.

Maybe he'd borrow the classic "you complete me" line. She did, as far as he was concerned, but he didn't want to recycle someone else's moment for his.

He'd worked himself into quite the emotional frenzy by the time Tessa answered the door.

"What's wrong with you?" she asked, taking a step back like he was a feral animal. She held Ben a little closer. "Your eyes aren't right."

"What's wrong is that I miss Cory like I've lost a piece of my heart. I'm going to fix things with her," he vowed, his voice sounding panicked even to his own ears. "I have to fix it."

Ben turned at the sound of his daddy's voice and gave an excited squeal. At least the baby wasn't wary of him this morning. Jordan didn't hesitate in reaching for his son, and his heart slowed a bit in its frantic thudding when Ben cuddled against his shoulder. "I need help," he said to Cory's friend.

The pretty redhead nodded. "You don't ask for help easily."

"I never ask anyone for help," he clarified. "But my usual way isn't working. I'm kind of desperate here."

One corner of her mouth curved. "You love her."

"More than I ever could have imagined. She's everything to me."

Tessa's grin widened. "Did you consider telling her that? It's pretty convincing."

He shrugged and looked out to the wild expanse of forest surrounding the cabin. "What if it's not enough?" he asked, then added, "What if I'm not enough? If I can do something huge and flashy to convince her…"

"Jordan, stop." Tessa placed a gentle hand on his arm. "Do you understand how much time she's put into getting ready for today's market?"

He glanced back at her. "A lot."

"A whole lot. And it made her happy. Being with you and Ben as a family made her happy. If Cory wanted flashy, she'd be on a beach in Fiji with that tool ex of hers. I can't guarantee what she'll say if you tell her how you feel, but I think the risk of truly showing her your heart will be worth it in the end. I can tell you have a good heart, Jordan."

He blew out an unsteady breath. "Emotional risk isn't exactly something I excel at, you know?"

"I can appreciate that." She winked. "It also wouldn't hurt to ask Madison to whip up a batch of fried cheese. Cory's kind of a goner when it comes to cheese. It's the little things."

"The little things," he repeated as an idea dawned on him. "Thank you, Tessa." He leaned in for a quick hug. "You eat and drink on the house at Trophy Room for all of eternity if this works out."

Her mouth dropped open, and then she gave a ladylike fist pump. "I like the sound of that."

As Jordan walked to his truck, his mind whirled with everything he needed to do before he headed toward the market. Today he was going to show Cory how much she meant to him in a way that he hoped would mean as much to her.

Cory surveyed the empty table in front of her with a happy heart. The Dennison Mill Maker's Market had been a huge success. Crowds of shoppers had browsed the booths situated around the large court-yard, and Cory had catered to a constant stream of customers. She'd sold every piece of jewelry she brought with her and had orders from almost two dozen women for additional items.

The weather had been perfect, sunny and warm with the scent of spring in the air. She wasn't sure if the beautiful day had brought so many people to the shopping and dining area or if Brynn was truly some kind of small-town marketing genius.

Either way, the pride Cory felt in what she'd ac-complished nearly brought tears to her eyes. She fi-nally was certain she'd found the life she wanted in Starlight.

She'd been too afraid to trust that something good could happen to her, too scared to go after her dreams.

No more excuses and no more letting other people's expectations guide her life.

She was making her own choice on her terms.

As Gran would tell her, Cory had the power to figure it out. And next on the list was determining how to make that happen with Jordan at her side.

She'd found herself in Starlight—true friends and a real community. She'd discovered a home.

But it was incomplete without Jordan.

She was incomplete without him.

For the first time, loving another person didn't make her feel weak or like she was giving up too much of herself. Her love for Jordan—and the way he loved her in return—made her strong. She believed with her whole heart that being with him would give her a foundation from which to build her life into something even better.

Okay, he hadn't exactly told her he loved her.

But he'd shown her in so many ways that meant the world to Cory. He listened to her and supported her, even when he didn't necessarily agree with her choices. He let her make her own choices. She had to trust that his actions counted for something. She knew how hard it was for him to talk about his feelings, just like it was for her.

But they could get through that. She wasn't going to give up on him, and not just because they shared a son. Jordan was her other half.

She shook her head as she started to pack up her

empty display fixtures. No, that wasn't right. She was whole on her own. But he complemented the person she wanted to be. He'd helped her find the strength to be that person. Cory bent over to pick up a piece of ribbon that had dropped on the ground next to her chair.

"Looks like you finished strong."

Lost in thought, she startled at the sound of his deep voice, banging her head on the table. "Ouch." She mustered a smile as she straightened. There were still vendors talking to customers on either side of her booth, but when her eyes met Jordan's, it somehow felt like they were the only two people on the planet. Well, three people, since he was holding their sweet baby.

"Are you okay?" he asked, his gaze searching hers, gentle and almost cautious.

"Just tired," she said, rubbing the back of her head. "My blood sugar could use a boost, as well. I haven't eaten since you brought me the salad for lunch. Thank you, by the way. And for watching Ben." She pushed back from the table. "If you have other things to do…" She broke off. This was not how she wanted things to go between them. Passing the baby back and forth. She wanted to be a family. "I'm glad you were here, Jordan. It meant a lot to me."

He seemed to suck in an unsteady breath before flashing the grin that always made her knees go weak. "There's no place I'd rather be, and I'm happy to spend the day with our son." He glanced over his shoulder, then back at her, and she had trouble reading his expression.

"What's going on?" she asked.

"Could you come with me for a minute?" His smile faltered slightly. "I wanted to talk to you and to show you something."

"I have to get my booth cleaned up, but then—"

"Sure, she can go with you," Tessa said as she and Ella materialized at his side.

Cory frowned. "Were you two hiding behind him to eavesdrop?"

"Of course not." Ella reached for the baby. "But you do look like you need some food. We'll take care of packing the rest of your stuff, and I'm happy to hang out with my favorite little man." She nuzzled Ben's neck, and the baby giggled with delight.

Cory couldn't understand what was happening. She felt the weight of Jordan's gaze, and her body went on full alert. Awareness pulsed through her veins like a double shot of espresso, but she kept her features neutral.

"Okay," she said slowly as she shifted her gaze to her two friends, both of whom looked far too innocent. "But if you're letting him lead me off for some nefarious purposes, I'll tell you right now that paybacks are hell."

"Duly noted," Ella said.

Tessa yanked her around the side of the table. "Get going, you two."

"That didn't go quite as smoothly as I planned," Jordan told her as she fell into step next to him. He led her around the corner of the old mill building.

She cocked a brow and glanced up at him. "You have a plan?"

"It's evolving," he admitted. "But yes."

They got to the back of the building, and her mouth fell open.

The flagstone courtyard that flanked the building had been strewn with fairy lights, and a round wrought-iron table sat in the middle of the patio.

Madison, who was lighting a candle situated in the center of the table, turned as they approached and muttered several colorful curses before grinning at Cory. "Sorry, I'm supposed to be gone by now. Have fun."

Before Cory could respond, her friend darted past and then called over her shoulder, "Always remember, chicks before...well, you know."

Cory turned to Jordan. "Why do I feel like I don't actually know anything right now?"

"Evolving," he said with a grimace. "But stick with me, okay?"

He looked so uncharacteristically discombobulated, Cory couldn't help but smile. "Yeah," she whispered. "I'll stick with you."

Jordan must have heard the unspoken promise in

those words, because he visibly relaxed as he linked his fingers with hers and moved toward the table.

"I have some things I need to say to you," he told her. "And a gift that goes with each one." He squeezed her hand. "It's not flowers or chocolate or anything all that mind-blowing, but…"

"Let me be the judge of what blows my mind," she told him.

He led her to one of the chairs and grabbed a small striped gift bag from the table as she sat. "First I want to tell you I'm sorry." He handed her the bag. "I'm sorry I made you feel like I was giving up on us. I let my fears and doubts get in the way. I won't do that again, Cory. No matter what you decide, I'm not leaving or running away. You can trust me with your heart. I promise that."

She struggled to catch her breath as the magnitude of his words rushed over her. "Jordan, I—"

"Open the first gift," he said.

She dug through the tissue paper and pulled out a garage door opener. "Um, thanks?"

His cheeks bloomed with color. "There's a key chain in there, too. It has two keys on it. One for my house and one for the bar. Everything that's mine is now yours. I want to come home to you. I want to be the man you come home to." He knelt down in front of her. "You are my home in every way that counts. I love you, Cory."

Was it possible for a heart to actually burst from

happiness? Because that was the only explanation for what was happening inside Cory. Her heart pounded so loudly she couldn't even hear herself think.

But she didn't need to think. All she needed was to feel the joy of this moment. She leaned forward and wrapped her arms around Jordan's neck.

"I love you," she said, then kissed him with an intensity that made her forget her own name. After several minutes, she pulled back and stared into his captivating green eyes. The same eyes as their son. "I'm yours, Jordan, and you are mine. Whatever life brings us, we're in it together."

"So the garage door opener was better than flowers?" he asked with a self-satisfied smile. "I can't wait to tell Madison."

"It worked for me," she told him, then kissed him again.

"I have one more gift," he said. "Also not flowers." He reached into his pocket and pulled out a velvet box.

Cory's breath hitched again.

His smile turned tender. "My mom left this with me," he explained. "She noticed that you didn't have a proper engagement ring."

"We weren't properly engaged," Cory couldn't help but point out.

"I want to change that." Jordan opened the box to reveal a pear-shaped diamond set in a delicate band of gold filigree. "This belonged to my great-grandmother. She and my great-grandpa were married fifty-eight years, and family legend goes, he loved her more every day. That's what I want, Cory. That's my vow. I'll be your partner. I'll be the best dad I can to Ben and to any other children who bless our lives. I'll be whatever you need me to be, because you are my everything. Will you marry me?"

Tears streamed down her face as he slipped the ring onto her finger. "Yes. I'll be your wife and your partner and your friend for always, Jordan. I'm all in."

They kissed again, and Cory knew that she was well and truly home.

* * * * *

MILLS & BOON

Coming next month

FROM BRIDAL DESIGNER TO BRIDE
Kandy Shepherd

"I'm thinking of the questions people might ask us at the wedding."

"Where did we meet?"

"Perhaps we met in LA. At a party."

"To which, sadly, I was not invited," he said with a mock mournful expression.

"Shame. There was a party at a waterfront venue in Santa Monica. I went outside for a breath of fresh air. You were outside—"

"Taking a break from a particularly boring business dinner." He paused. "And I saw this dark haired girl leaning against a palm tree. I was struck by her beauty."

Eloise giggled. "I like that. So what happened?

"I opened a conversation with a witty remark."

"I responded with something equally witty."

"We struck up a conversation. You hung onto my every word."

"Huh! How about I made you laugh?"

"You do that in real life, so that could work. Then you said you had to get back to the party."

"No! I'm sure I would have wanted to stay with you."

"Would you?" he said.

"Yes." Her gaze connected again with his in that surprisingly intimate way.

"I got your number. And I called you straight away to check I got it right."

"So when did you call me?"

"I asked you to call me when the party was finished. You did. Then I took you back to your hotel room."

"And...?"

"We talked all night until the sun came up," he said a smile dancing around the corners of his sexy mouth. "I was a gentleman."

"And I was wishing you weren't." She slapped her hand over her mouth. "Scratch that!"

He laughed. "So I wasn't such a gentleman the next night."

"Really," she said trying to sound prim instead of turned on.

It took a real effort not to focus on imagining the exciting details of his fictional ungentlemanly behaviour and her fictional response. Since that first kiss she had spent too much time fantasying over the prospect of making love with Josh. Now he sat so near to her in the privacy of her home, it was impossible not to acknowledge that intense physical pull. "And we spent as much time as we could together before you had to go back to Boston."

"We did. In fact, we hardly left your hotel bedroom." His tone was so exaggerated in its lasciviousness it made her laugh.

"If you say so," she said.

"I wished so," he said with a grin.

She was glad she had decided not to sit next to him on the sofa. It would be only too easy to let this game get out of hand and practice for real.

Continue reading
FROM BRIDAL DESIGNER TO BRIDE
Kandy Shepherd

Available next month
www.millsandboon.co.uk

COMING SOON!

We really hope you enjoyed reading this book.
If you're looking for more romance, be sure to
head to the shops when new books are
available on

Thursday 4th March

LET'S TALK
Romance

For exclusive extracts, competitions
and special offers, find us online:

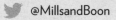

facebook.com/millsandboon

@MillsandBoon

@MillsandBoonUK

Get in touch on 01413 063232

For all the latest titles coming soon, visit
millsandboon.co.uk/nextmonth

MILLS & BOON

THE HEART OF ROMANCE

A ROMANCE FOR EVERY KIND OF READER

MODERN

Prepare to be swept off your feet by sophisticated, sexy and seductive heroes, in some of the world's most glamourous and romantic locations, where power and passion collide.
8 stories per month.

HISTORICAL

Escape with historical heroes from time gone by. Whether your passion is for wicked Regency Rakes, muscled Vikings or rugged Highlanders, awaken the romance of the past.
6 stories per month.

MEDICAL

Set your pulse racing with dedicated, delectable doctors in the high-pressure world of medicine, where emotions run high and passion, comfort and love are the best medicine.
6 stories per month.

True Love

Celebrate true love with tender stories of heartfelt romance, from the rush of falling in love to the joy a new baby can bring, and a focus on the emotional heart of a relationship.
8 stories per month.

Desire

Indulge in secrets and scandal, intense drama and plenty of sizzling hot action with powerful and passionate heroes who have it all: wealth, status, good looks…everything but the right woman.
6 stories per month.

HEROES

Experience all the excitement of a gripping thriller, with an intense romance at its heart. Resourceful, true-to-life women and strong, fearless men face danger and desire - a killer combination!
8 stories per month.

DARE

Sensual love stories featuring smart, sassy heroines you'd want as a best friend, and compelling intense heroes who are worthy of them.
4 stories per month.

To see which titles are coming soon, please visit

millsandboon.co.uk/nextmonth

JOIN US ON SOCIAL MEDIA!

Stay up to date with our latest releases, author news and gossip, special offers and discounts, and all the behind-the-scenes action from Mills & Boon...

 millsandboon

 millsandboonuk

 millsandboon

It might just be true love...

GET YOUR ROMANCE FIX!

MILLS & BOON
— blog —

Get the latest romance news, exclusive author interviews, story extracts and much more!

blog.millsandboon.co.uk

  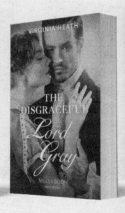

MILLS & BOON
MEDICAL
Pulse-Racing Passion

Set your pulse racing with dedicated, delectable doctors in the high-pressure world of medicine, where emotions run high and passion, comfort and love are the best medicine.